A RELUCTA

Alison Bond worked as an agent for writers and directors in film and television for ten years before stepping to the other side. She has been published in a handful of national newspapers and magazines, and when not busy working on her next novel she has been known to dabble in hopeful screenplays. She lives in London with her family.

A Reluctant Cinderella

ALISON BOND

PENGUIN BOOKS

PENGUIN BOOKS

Published by the Penguin Group
Penguin Books Ltd, 80 Strand, London WC2R ORL, England
Penguin Group (USA) Inc., 375 Hudson Street, New York, New York 10014, USA
Penguin Group (Canada), 90 Eglinton Avenue East, Suite 700, Toronto, Ontario, Canada M4P 2Y3
(a division of Pearson Penguin Canada Inc.)
Penguin Ireland, 25 St Stephen's Green, Dublin 2, Ireland
(a division of Penguin Books Ltd)
Penguin Group (Australia), 250 Camberwell Road, Camberwell, Victoria 3124, Australia
(a division of Pearson Australia Group Pty Ltd)
Penguin Books India Pvt Ltd, 11 Community Centre, Panchsheel Park, New Delhi – 110 017, India
Penguin Group (NZ), 67 Apollo Drive, Rosedale, North Shore 0632, New Zealand
(a division of Pearson New Zealand Ltd)
Penguin Books (South Africa) (Pty) Ltd, 24 Sturdee Avenue,
Rosebank, Johannesburg 2196, South Africa

Penguin Books Ltd, Registered Offices: 80 Strand, London WC2R ORL, England

www.penguin.com

First published 2010
1

Copyright © Alison Bond, 2010

The moral right of the author has been asserted

Except in the United States of America,
this book is sold subject to the condition that it shall not,
by way of trade or otherwise, be lent, re-sold, hired out, or otherwise
circulated without the publisher's prior consent in any form of
binding or cover other than that in which it is published
and without a similar condition including this condition
being imposed on the subsequent purchaser

Typeset by TexTech International
Printed in England by Clays Ltd, St Ives plc

ISBN: 978-0-141-02681-7

www.greenpenguin.co.uk

Penguin Books is committed to a sustainable future
for our business, our readers and our planet.
The book in your hands is made from paper
certified by the Forest Stewardship Council.

I

For as long as she could remember Samantha had nurtured a single dream. To succeed. And her dream was about to come true.

It had been years since she'd first sniffed the heady, sour mixture of industry, exhaust and ambition that lifted her sagging spirits like fine perfume. London. The town where you could be anything.

And she wanted to be a success.

This phone call was the sweetest of her career.

'Thirty million pounds all told,' she said, casually dropping the figure as if this happened every day.

On the other end of the line she thought she heard a rush of breath.

'The second-to-biggest deal in the history of Premiership football,' she added. 'And the tenth biggest in the game. Ever.'

It was late, very late, but she didn't care.

'So what do you say, do we have a deal?' She had the phone on hands-free so that she could pace the floor. Otherwise the nervous tension would sneak into her voice and betray the confidence she needed to project in order to close this thing. She was, still, the only woman in the world making deals at this level.

She walked over to the window. A view like this meant success, didn't it? The streetlamps that studded the South

Bank reflected in the Thames, Westminster floodlit and glowing golden in the night, a city of glass and steel stretching to the sky, a million windows, eight million lives, this town, its infinite possibilities, all at her feet.

She held her breath.

The pause filled the office for an intolerably long moment and she felt nauseous, compelled to plug the silence with promises and persuasion.

'You have to trust me,' she said. 'You know I'll look after your boys. I want the Welstead brothers to go to the right club for their career. And this is the right club. You know me; I'm not just about the money. It's not just pounds and pence to me – I care about the bigger picture.' Compassion, warmth, sensitivity. Being a woman had never been an advantage, not in this old-boys'-club business, but she would call on any feminine trait available if it helped to close a deal.

Monty and Ferris Welstead. Sublimely talented players. Ferris was better looking but Monty was the one with the personality. Together they were an advertiser's dream. The thirty million would be just the beginning. The man she was talking to was their manager, but he was also their father. He was selling their talents, their careers. He was selling their lives.

'Do we?' she repeated. 'Do we have a deal, sir?'

The 'sir' was a nice touch. Respect, humility, charm. He would get a kick out of it, a hard-working dad who seemed perpetually dazed because he'd accidentally raised sons who were two of the most extraordinary football players in a generation.

Trust me, I'm a woman.

He issued a little hesitant cough that chilled her blood. He was all that stood between her and her dream come true.

Then at last, after six months of tense negotiation, he said the magic words.

'We do.'

She punched the air with her fist and her feet lifted off the floor one after another in a muted jig of celebration.

She had lied through her perfect white teeth. Samantha Sharp was all about the money. Always. And thirty million pounds was a hell of a lot.

I made it.

Could people tell just by looking at her how far she'd had to climb, hand over fist, to get here?

It was worth every blistering, painful moment.

Her most vivid childhood memory was of being alone.

'You'll be all right,' their mum had said as she piled more cheap clothes into her cheap weekend bag, already bulging at the seams. 'You take care of each other, okay?'

Samantha looked at Liam, her big brother, and wondered what taking care of him meant.

Their mum had all her make-up on. A face which took so long that if Samantha watched her, lying on the big double bed while Mum sat in front of the mirror, she would fall asleep before the end, hypnotized by the brush strokes and swirling fingertips that went towards Mum's going-out face, drugged by the tang of perfume and hairspray and nail polish.

She would wake up and her mother would have disappeared, only the smell of her remaining to soothe Samantha to sleep. If she slept where she lay, in the big double bed, it would be hours later that she was lifted, with a murmur of protest, back to her own room, awake just long enough to sense the shifting figure of a stranger, always a new man, waiting to take her place.

'There's beans,' said their mum, opening one of the top cupboards and then realizing her mistake and moving sixteen cans of baked beans down to a cupboard they could reach. 'There's beans,' she repeated, 'and bread and apples, and plenty of milk and juice in the fridge. And there's chocolate.'

'Chocolate?' said Samantha hopefully.

'Only if you're a good girl,' said her mum, unearthing a foil-wrapped bar of chocolate and waving it just out of reach. 'Will you be a good girl for Mummy?'

Samantha nodded.

Scared already, but not sure why.

'It's a secret. You understand?' Mum put both hands on Samantha's shoulders and dropped to her knees so that they were level. 'You know what a secret is?'

'Something you don't tell,' said Samantha.

'Good girl.'

The brisk hug was almost an afterthought, but Samantha didn't care – she cherished the feeling of arms around her more than anything, even more than chocolate.

She looked across at Liam. A whole head taller than her and always so serious. He made her feel silly sometimes. Like now. Silly for being scared. So she put on her best brave smile and told her mum to have a nice time.

'Okay then.' A final smile, her hand already on the front door handle, her heart and mind already in Ibiza and a week without her kids. 'I'll be back Tuesday morning. What do you do in an emergency?'

'Dial 999,' said Liam.

'Good boy.'

And she was gone.

They both stood there and watched the door, in case it was just a joke. Then a little while later, when it became clear that she wasn't coming back, Liam reached out his hand until it touched his sister's. Then he held it and told her that everything would be okay.

'It'll be an adventure,' he said. 'We're like castaways.'

'Is that like pirates?'

'A bit,' he said.

That didn't sound too bad. 'Can I have some chocolate?' she asked.

Liam picked up the bar of chocolate and solemnly snapped off two squares each. 'We should make it last,' he said.

Liam was nine years old and Samantha five. They were on their own.

'What'll we do now?' she asked.

Liam looked up at the clock, his lips moving silently as he worked out the time. 'I think we go to bed,' he said.

'But I haven't had my bath.' She chewed her lip doubtfully.

'Some nights we don't though, do we? When I'm in charge. So this is one of those nights. It's not that different.'

But it was. To five-year-old Samantha this night felt very different indeed. Like the first time she'd slept without the light on, or the first day Liam went to school. Everything had changed and her world had gone sort of wobbly. She didn't like it.

He found her favourite pyjamas. The pink ones with pictures of orange cats. They stood together on the step-up to the sink so that they could brush their teeth.

'Do you need to do a wee?' he said.

'I don't think so.'

Her face flushed warm as her eyes filled with tears.

'What's wrong?'

She fought off the scratchy tight feeling in her throat. Mummy didn't like it when she got upset and that meant bed in the dark without any dinner or, if there wasn't really any dinner, or she'd been really naughty, then locked in the

6

bathroom so that she couldn't run crying to her brother the way she always did.

But Mummy wasn't here so she could tell the truth.

'I'm frightened.'

'Pah! What's there to be frightened of, Sammy?' He put his wiry little arm round her and led her across the landing. 'This is still your house, isn't it?'

She nodded.

'And this is your bedroom? And this is your bed?'

He folded back her duvet and patted the bed. She climbed in.

'And that's your pillow? And this is your teddy?'

She held fast to his hand even as she curled herself into the tight knot she made to sleep.

'See? Nothing to be frightened of.'

'Tell me a story,' she said.

'I don't know any stories.'

'Sing me a song.'

So Liam sang the first song he could remember, about a place over the rainbow where happy bluebirds fly, and he stayed by her side until her scrappy breaths became long and smooth. Slowly and carefully he opened out her hand, finger by clinging finger, to free himself from his sister's grip, then he crossed the room to his own bed and slept until morning.

They were discovered of course. A schoolteacher noticed that Samantha was wearing the same clothes three days running and watched to see who collected her from school. Seeing her leave hand in hand with her young brother, she chased after them.

'Does Mummy know you're walking home on your own?' she asked.

'Mummy's in Beefa,' said Samantha. She squealed in pain as Liam pinched the soft flesh on her inner arm. 'But it's a secret. I forgot. So don't tell anyone.'

That night, instead of playing pirates with Liam, which meant an eye-patch and cold baked beans out of a can – *pirate food, Captain* – the children were placed in emergency foster care.

They had been unable to place them together on a few hours' notice.

'Say goodbye to your brother,' said the social worker, and, her head addled from the events of the day, Samantha thought she meant for ever.

No! Not Liam, they couldn't take Liam. She looked wildly around for somebody to help her, but all she saw were two grown-ups that she didn't know, both smiling, which made it worse. In the stories the baddies were always smiling. Where were they taking him? Why wasn't she going? Had she been really naughty? So naughty that even the damp, dark bathroom wasn't bad enough and Liam was going somewhere nice while she went . . . where?

Her breath quickened as she conjured up nasty unformed thoughts one after another. Soon she was gasping for air.

She started to scream. She lashed out at well-meaning hands that tried to calm her.

In the end one of the smiling strangers picked her up and hauled her away so that she didn't get to say goodbye at all.

She screamed so hard that she fell into an exhausted sleep and when she woke up she was in a big house that smelt funny, on a sofa she had never seen before, and a fat woman who was not her mummy was pretending that she was, making sure that she washed her face and cleaned her teeth.

Robotically she brushed up and down with the brand-new toothbrush and toothpaste that tasted of strawberry not mint.

Somehow her cat pyjamas had found their way to a pillow on a bed in a small room upstairs. But it was not her bed.

Even though she asked again and again, this fat not-mummy couldn't tell her if Liam would be here to sing her to her dreams. And so she cried herself to a fitful sleep, horribly confused and clutching her duvet around her to keep out the scary night.

She was five. She loved her errant mummy desperately. She didn't know what a mother was supposed to do. She didn't know she had a bad one. So when the police arrested her mother at the airport and allowed her only a brief visit with her children, Samantha kicked the social worker with her tiny feet and told her mum that they should try to escape.

'We can run away! Let's go, come on, while no one's looking.'

'Not this time, Sammy.'

'I'm sorry I told the teacher about Beefa.'

'Me too,' said her mum.

Liam understood a little more. He refused to kiss his mother, told her that he hated her and so she lavished attention on him, ignoring the smiling Samantha who had more kisses inside her than she knew what to do with.

Then very soon it was time to say goodbye and go back to the foster family.

'What about the chocolate?' she asked, concerned about the six squares left at home that they had diligently denied themselves.

'You should have thought about that before you told on me and spoilt everything,' said her mum. 'This is all your fault. You know that, don't you? Your teachers tell me you're so bloody clever but you're stupid. Stupid.'

'Leave her alone,' said Liam.

'Oh, Liam, I'm sorry. It's such a mess.'

Liam wrapped his arm round his sister. 'We'll take care of each other,' he said. 'We don't need you.'

Soon they found a permanent family to take in both of the Sharp children. Although Samantha painfully learnt the meaning of a big word like permanent. It meant: for a while. A year or two. Maybe even four or five. But not for ever.

One day she would have her own home. A front door to which only she held the key. Then everything would be okay.

By the time she was ten years old she had been to four different primary schools. Then they were placed in Nottingham with a kind-hearted woman and her lorry-driving husband. It was the closest thing either of them had ever had to a family. Except, that is, for each other.

'We'll never live with Mum again, will we?' whispered Samantha one night.

She was lying on the floor of Liam's bedroom, twisting her hair into a plait so that when she woke up it would be wavy. They were too old to share a room, but she found that she couldn't sleep unless she was with him right before she tried. Otherwise bad dreams woke her, sleep-stealing nightmares that she could never remember.

'Why do you say that?' he said.

'When she said that one day she would want us again she lied, didn't she?' Samantha concentrated on winding her hair because she was afraid of his answer.

It was supposed to be just a few months while Mum got herself together enough to prove to the authorities that she could take responsibility for her children. But months became years and though at first they saw her from time to time eventually the supervised visits stopped. Then the letters stopped too.

'I don't think she lied,' said Liam. 'I think she really thought that one day she would be a different person.'

She wanted to grasp what Liam was trying to say. She didn't want her to be a different person.

'That she'd be a mother?' she ventured.

'Exactly.'

One night they were told, calmly and compassionately, by the kind-hearted woman they had grown to love, that Samantha's dreams of being a family again one day were over.

'Liver failure,' she said, her gentle arms reaching out instinctively for the little girl who'd just lost her mummy.

She tensed in the embrace. She wasn't that little any more. She was old enough to know this meant their mother had drunk herself to death.

So that's it then.

She should probably be howling or something, but felt far from tears. The arms round her felt odd, not comforting, just cold. The only word that presented itself in her head was, *pathetic.* That wasn't right. It was disrespectful.

She must be a terrible person.

A quick glance at Liam. His face was cold and hard as stone.

After it got dark they shared two enormous plastic bottles of cider amongst the trees at the bottom of the park across the street. The irony of getting drunk that night was lost on both of them.

She was fourteen.

'Am I supposed to care?' asked Liam repeatedly. 'Cos I don't. I don't give a fuck. She didn't, did she?' He tugged at his thick, dark hair, the exact same colour as her own.

She twisted the cheap earring in her left ear and didn't reply. She could see the pain behind his teenage swagger, could sense that like her he was confused by a crushing feeling of desertion that made very little sense.

'Take care of each other.' That was how Mum always said goodbye.

And Samantha had tried, she really had tried. But perhaps not hard enough.

3

Thirty million pounds.

The haze of dawn was creeping in at the edges of the thick damask curtains and she lay in bed smiling. Not because she had slept well – she had not slept at all. Not because the aftershocks of her last orgasm were still making her twitch between her legs. Not because the Egyptian cotton she lay upon was so crisp and cool, or the duck-down duvet was so soft, or this Westminster penthouse was so in-your-face-so-there flash. She smiled because the deal she had closed a few hours before made her happy.

Thirty.

Three zero.

Jackson Ramsay, her boss and mentor, would make her partner at Legends now for sure. It was the second-biggest deal in the history of his company. He had to. The only deal bigger had of course been one that Jackson had made for his star player Salvatore Salva. She had wanted to match it, and nearly succeeded. She smiled again at the thought. That would have made Jackson mad; the Salva deal was his crowning achievement.

Thirty million for the clients . . .

It was early. She had plenty of time to review some paperwork in her home office before she saw Liam.

So that's six million in commission . . .

She always took Thursday mornings off to hang out with him. Luckily she was far too valuable to the company for this personal arrangement to be an issue. Besides, she worked more than enough hours late and at the weekend to make up the time.

And a million for me.

In a few months, when they handed out the bonuses, she would be a millionaire.

Gently, oh so gently, she eased herself out of the king-size bed.

But he heard her.

'Darling?' He pulled her back down and into the curve of his body. 'Don't go,' he said.

She paused.

His warm flesh against hers made her want to stay. The feel of the coarse hairs on his chest brushing the soft, smooth skin of her back tickled her to a state of drowsy acceptance, his hand lightly stroking her shoulder blade. It would be so easy to fold herself into him and sleep. 'Shh,' she said, swinging her feet onto the floor more quickly, determined to get away.

'Must we go through this every time,' he said wearily. Awake now, and sounding angry. 'I'd like, just once in a while, to wake up with you by my side.'

'Jackson, please, you know why.'

She avoided his accusing steel eyes. Even out of the boardroom her boss was still intimidating. His broad chest and shoulders never failed to make her feel feminine and oh-so-slightly helpless. Of course she wouldn't admit this in a thousand years.

'Because you like waking up alone? Sweetness, I've seen

you without your make-up and I'm not that scared.' He grinned and she was impelled to lean forward and lick the cleft in his chin, but she resisted.

'Don't be sarcastic,' she said. 'It doesn't suit you.'

She stepped into her knickers and wriggled into her pencil skirt, ignoring his groan of desire when she bent forward to put on her bra.

'This is unfair,' he said. 'You're a cocktease, you know that?'

'I'm not sure you can say that after what we just did.'

'So come back to bed and we can do it again.'

She searched the room for her other shoe, knocking over his precious cricket bat, which made him even grumpier than he was before, and when she found her shoe she was ready. She sat down on the bed to kiss him goodbye, wanting to part on good terms and not have another one of the rows that blighted this otherwise perfect relationship.

Great sex. No ties.

She worked so hard she deserved to succeed, and she knew what would be said if people found out that she was sleeping with the boss. She would stop being a force to reckon with and become a sleazy joke. They would say that she'd shagged her way to the top, that it wasn't her brilliant mind, but another piece of her anatomy altogether that had taken her so far.

'I still don't see what difference it makes,' he said. 'Sleeping over, not sleeping over. It doesn't change a thing. Sam, it doesn't change how I feel about you.'

Don't say it.

'I love you, I adore you,' he said. 'Now I'm asking you nicely: please will you stop being a bitch and come back to bed.'

'No,' she said. And then she left.

She had arrived in a cab, but it was shortly after 5 a.m. now and there were none to be seen on the streets in this part of town. It was too early for politicians and the like to be getting to work, and too far off the track for the last of the late-night clubbers. She belted her trench coat tightly against the dawn chill and started to walk towards the tube. She left Jackson's penthouse in the small hours at least twice a week, often more, and so she knew well the time of the first Jubilee-line train.

Logically he was right. What difference would it make to snatch a few hours' sleep together? It shouldn't mean anything. But to Samantha it meant the world. She had to be more than the boss's girl, especially at Legends where being any kind of girl was bad enough. She was so determined that their secret should remain so that she didn't even like to be alone with him in the office for more than five minutes in case someone talked. Jackson said that if they avoided each other so blatantly then that would be even more cause for gossip, but she didn't care. So far, impossible though it seemed, their affair was private, even after four years. And if leaving at dawn helped her to keep her feelings where they belonged, behind the line she drew between her personal life and her professional life, then she would leave at dawn.

Many times she had tried to end things between them.

And failed.

She smiled, thinking about him. Every month that passed she found herself becoming closer to him; he was able to pull her in, so that what was once easy was getting more and more complicated.

Jackson Ramsay understood her. He knew how low she had been one time long ago. He had watched as she pulled herself up with gritty determination, devouring opportunity and never wasting a morsel. They both found naked ambition sexy; they both craved the next deal like an addiction. When they were together the chemistry was explosive.

She couldn't leave him. But she had never told him so.

A power nap and then a few hours' work at home and she was back on the tube again. The underground system swept her beneath eminent London streets in a flash, the white noise slowing her thoughts of work and Jackson and millions and partnership like a meditation.

She waited impatiently for every Thursday to come round, and yet when it did she felt depressed. She forced herself to focus on how much fun it was going to be to tell Liam all about the thirty million.

The tube was dejected and deafening and kept the city and any beauty to be found there obstinately concealed from view. The people in the same carriage that noticed Samantha wondered why she was smiling. Some of them even created a story for her in their heads. None of them would have been close to the truth.

This time the train emerged somewhere past Hammersmith, thrusting her once more into the wintry daylight, where the rooftops were dusted with snow, the gutters clogged with grey slush.

She walked the rest of the way. A kind of gloom settled over her as she neared, as it always settled when she was on her way to see Liam. It was a miserable part of town.

Yet every Thursday, unless she was many miles from home, she made this journey, because he was family.

And this is what family do.

Even if it made her downhearted. He was her brother and she loved him.

No matter what.

A huddle of people still stood outside a set of enormous iron gates, smoking furiously, silently, ignoring each other even though they were all here for the same reason. They were all here on a Thursday morning because someone they knew had landed themselves an extended spell in Her Majesty's Prison.

They were criminals. Just like Liam.

'Hey, Sharpie. Your sister coming today?'

He loved and hated visiting hours with equal measure.

'I think she is, yeah,' he replied. There weren't any international football matches or European ties. So she should be.

There were no surprises in prison, only disappointments. Liam Sharp's visits list only had one name. Sammy. His kid sister. The only person in the world that mattered to him.

In the beginning a few friends made the effort to visit Liam in prison, but fourteen years is a long time and of course they fell away. Now there was only Sammy keeping him sane.

He kept a close eye on the football fixtures to try to predict whether or not she'd show. But really all he could do was wait with the rest of them, try to hide his nerves and hope that his name was called. Inevitably, she failed to arrive from time to time, and he panicked for the rest of the week, worried that he had been forgotten, that she had finally tired of her brother, the convict. Until the next week when she was there, smiling even though he could tell she felt shit. They both did. It wasn't the way they had planned it.

'*Tell her I said hiya.*'

Liam nodded, like he would do that, but of course he wouldn't. Maybe he saw more of this bloke than some wives see of their husbands, but his sister wouldn't be able to pick him out of a line-up. Which, given Moz's propensity for re-offending, was probably a good thing.

'Will do, Moz,' he said.

They loved his sister, the guys in here. He boasted about her, far too much probably, but it was like currency: a sister close to the teams that many of them idolized.

It helped that she was gorgeous, the guys liked that about her too, but he tried not to dwell on this.

Moz, Chalkie, Bazza, Sparks, Sharpie. Nobody used the name their mothers had given them on the inside. It made it easier to pretend you were someone else, that this wasn't happening, not to me, no way. Nicknames didn't imply friendship. These men were not his friends. On release none of them would ever see each other again.

They called out his name. She was here. And again he had those mixed feelings, which made his head ache like a migraine. She was here, but she shouldn't be.

The visiting room reminded him of a classroom. Metal and plastic, everybody on their best behaviour, fearful of being sent from the room if they played up. Liam had been sent out of plenty of classrooms in his time.

His beautiful, sophisticated sister walked across the cheap linoleum floor and dragged the plastic chair out to face him across the chipped wooden table. A sense of deep shame washed over him. He would always be dragging her down, reminding her of a life she might have been able to forget were it not for him.

'You came,' he said.

'Course I did.'

'I wasn't sure.'

'Highlight of my week,' she said.

He looked well, she thought. Pale as usual, as thin as a greyhound, but well. It was always a relief to see him. A few months ago she had found him sporting a black eye, which he was unable to explain.

'I wasn't sure,' he repeated, wondering why he couldn't just say that he was happy to see her. He stood up to hug her briefly, his chair scraping loudly across the burn-scarred floor.

She hugged him back, hoping that he couldn't sense her discomfort. Even after all these years she still felt awkward in this room. Today she thought she noticed more stares than usual.

'They saw you in the newspapers this morning,' said Liam, by way of explanation. 'My sister, the celeb.'

'I wasn't in the newspapers.'

He blushed. 'Yeah, you know, maybe not you, but your deal. Those brothers you sold to Chelsea. I might have told a few people. Word gets around.'

'I thought you hated Chelsea?' she said, and was disproportionately delighted at how quick he was to smile. Liam's smile was one of the small joys of her life.

She knew he thought she hated it here, but he was wrong. As uncomfortable as it was, she looked forward to seeing him and was unhappy when unbreakable work commitments kept her from him. Seeing him reminded her of the life that she had left behind, of the effort she had made to drag herself to where she was now. Without these Thursday mornings, without Liam to keep her real, she might allow herself to be carried away on the glittering London scene. She might lose herself for ever and never return.

She talked to him about the deal, all the little titbits they never put in the newspapers. She told him about her promotion, that she was thinking of getting a new car. She talked of inconsequential things, light aimless chatter that was supposed to distract him for an hour, and he was grateful.

Their time nearly up, he grabbed her hand. 'I have some news,' he said.

Her face lit up.

'It's not good,' he added quickly. 'My parole hearing has been delayed again.' His lips curled in on an uncomfortable smile that was more of a grimace.

'That's not fair,' she said.

Her eyes brimmed with tears and she fought to keep them in check. For years now it had seemed that Liam might be on the brink of release, but after one denial his parole hearing had been subject to an endless string of convoluted postponements. 'Please let me get you a better lawyer, just to look into it. If he thinks there's something to be done, where's the harm?'

'The last guy you found for me was useless,' he said.

She bowed her head. 'I'm sorry.'

'No,' said Liam, 'don't be. I wasn't trying to make you feel bad, I was just joking.'

'Funny,' she said dryly.

'If you can find someone willing to look into it, that'd be great – more than great. Though why anyone would want to bother . . .'

It's called money, Liam, and lots of it. Lawyers like money.

'I'll find someone,' she said. 'Leave it with me.' She usually felt so powerless to help him it was a comfort to have a situation she could throw some cash at.

'How's your boyfriend?'

Liam was the only person she'd ever told about Jackson.

'He's fine,' she said.

'Wedding bells?'

'You know it's not like that.'

Liam winced. 'You're my little sister. I like to think of him as marriage material, okay?'

'Whatever,' she said. 'But he's fine.'

'Tell him I said hello.'

She said she would, but of course she wouldn't. At some point she might have to explain to Liam why Jackson knew nothing about him, or explain to Jackson that she had a secret.

Their time was up. Both siblings felt the usual peculiar combination of regret and relief. They could only dream of one day in the not too distant future when they could be together without time limits, without guards, without the awful sense of shame that filled every inch of this cold room.

'Take care,' he said.

'You too.'

'They say you'll be a millionaire.'

She shrugged. 'Maybe.'

'Lend us a tenner?'

She laughed, glad to end the visit on a high, glad his sense of humour had not deserted him today as it sometimes did.

'Love you,' she said.

'What's not to love?' He winked and waved and then he was gone.

The Legends office throbbed with activity. She liked it; she craved it if she was away for too long. Her idea of hell would be a day under the duvet with a good book or a week on the beach. Time not working was time wasted. There was always another deal to be done, another career to launch or trade.

There was always more money to make.

She was alone in the lift but just as the door was about to close a hand reached in, the doors sprang open again and in came Jackson.

The doors closed on them alone. Immediately he grabbed the nape of her neck and pulled her to him for a hungry kiss. She shoved him away, ignoring the darts of pleasure that fired when he touched her.

'Relax,' he said. 'We have eleven floors.'

She pretended to be angry but she knew he wasn't fooled. They stood like polite acquaintances and she ignored the smile that played across his face.

'How was it?' he asked.

'Not bad,' she said.

Like everyone else at Legends, Jackson assumed that Samantha missed Thursday mornings because she was in therapy.

A brother? No. Samantha Sharp didn't have any family. That's what she said at the beginning and that's the way it stayed. She didn't see it as a lie so much as an omission. It was private, nobody's business but hers.

Was she ashamed of him?

Perhaps.

She compartmentalized her life. In one box her career, in another her relationship and still another for Liam and her past. This ruthless detachment had kept her in control since the day she'd started working here. And now look – she'd made it all the way to the eleventh floor where the biggest offices were. So she must be doing something right.

The lift stopped and the doors opened. Jackson let her out before him, but swiftly kissed the soft skin of her neck as she passed by. She flashed him a warning glance. Okay, so the lobby was empty and the receptionist was facing her computer screen, but he was taking too many risks. There was nothing wrong with having secrets. She had got very, very good at it.

She reached the door of her office, her name etched into the frosted glass. She traced the letters of her name with her fingertips. Something to be proud of.

Something permanent.

Today had been a good visit. When it went like that it was easy to think of him just as Liam, her big brother, a bit soppy, easy to tease. And not think of him as a killer.

But the reality would always get in the way.

4

She was surprised and not particularly pleased when Jackson turned up on her doorstep the following Saturday morning.

'What are you doing here?'

'Charming.' He wandered through to the kitchen and she stood for a few seconds in the open doorway wondering how long he would be staying and whether or not she would still have time to do all the paperwork that she had planned to complete before this afternoon's FA Cup games kicked off.

This isn't working.

The sudden realization stunned her. For years she had thought she had the perfect relationship, perfect for her. Mind-blowing sex, no commitment, someone who understood that work always, *always* took first place. She was in love with him, but her own kind of love. It didn't mean she had to be with him every second; she didn't need to know every thought in his head. She only had time for the basics. Sex, good fun, a few laughs. It was more than enough.

But maybe not for him. Not any more.

He always said that he didn't want to hurt her. But it had never really occurred to either of them that hurt goes the other way too.

In the kitchen he dumped a stack of heavy weekend newspapers on the table and started fussing with the Pavoni coffee machine while he unloaded brown paper bags from the deli on the next street over, full of plump croissants and rounds of French butter and cherry conserve. 'Do you realize,' he said, taking milk out of her fridge in a proprietary manner that set her teeth on edge, 'that you and I have never had a lazy Saturday morning, with the papers, and breakfast in bed?'

'I don't do lazy,' she said.

'Today you do,' he said. 'Are you going to take your clothes off yourself or do I have to do it for you?'

'I have things to do,' she protested, feeling her resistance start to crumble in the face of his good humour.

And it was great. Of course it was. They went to bed, had sex and afterwards it was so comfortable to lie back against the pillows and peruse the newspapers, all of them, not just the sport and business sections. His hand was on her thigh and for a brief while they were just like any other couple. Which was his point.

He reached over to brush a flake of croissant from the corner of her mouth and held her gaze. 'Let's move in together,' he said. 'We could do this every weekend.'

She froze. 'Don't spoil it,' she whispered.

'Damn it, Sam, what is it with you? We can't stagnate. You of all people know that if you're not moving forward then you're not going anywhere. It's been ten years.'

'Four,' she said, quick as a flash. 'Four years.'

'Four since you let me get close, but I've been in love with you for many more than that and you bloody well know it.'

'Where do you expect us to go exactly?'

'I don't know yet, but marriage, kids ... at the very least I think you should allow yourself to stay over every once in a while, maybe go out in public. What about that? Imagine, dinner out.'

'Kids?' she said, genuinely aghast. 'Since when do you want to have kids?'

'Baby steps, Samantha. It'll be okay.'

'I can't.'

'Yes, you can. You've made it, Sam. Don't you get it? The fight's over. You won. You've made it now; you've nothing left to prove.'

Then why did she still feel like she was fighting?

'I think you're trying to save me, Jackson,' she said. 'I don't need saving.'

Jackson got out of bed and started dressing, his mouth set in a firm, angry line. 'I'm going home. I need more. I need more than a woman who is only ever relaxed for about seven minutes after sex and the rest of the time is wound so tight she'll snap if you touch her. I need more.'

She didn't say anything. Nothing lasts for ever. She'd always known it would end one day. Jackson deserved someone who could give him what he wanted. All this time she'd been fooling herself that what was perfect for her was perfect for him. The truth was that he thought he could change her.

She wasn't the changing type.

'This could be so good, Samantha. And I think you know it. You're scared, and that's okay; it's scary stuff. But give us a chance.'

Scared? He didn't know what he was talking about. She wasn't scared of anything. Why must everyone assume that a woman longs to be settled? She didn't need a relationship to feel complete – she was Sam Sharp: Superagent – she was a success; she didn't need a man to validate her.

'I know you, Sam,' he said. 'Don't forget that.'

'There's plenty you don't know about me,' she said. Jackson liked everything to be simple. So she kept things simple for him. What would he say if he knew she had a brother in prison, locked up for being a killer? Liam was a hidden complication that she'd never been able to acknowledge.

'I know you,' he repeated. 'I'm at home all afternoon. When you realize I'm right about us come on over.' But when he bent over to kiss her cheek he couldn't resist adding, 'Come over anyway.'

She waited until she heard the front door close then she dressed quickly, went downstairs and switched on the plasma screen in the living room. She went to fix herself an espresso, gathering some paperwork from her home office as the Pavoni hissed in the background.

Back to business.

With a steaming cup of coffee in her hand and her laptop on the coffee table in front of her, she settled down to give her full attention to the match. Well, most of it. She could catch up on some correspondence at the same time; she was a woman after all – multitasking was what she did best.

She would figure out what to do about Jackson another time. Maybe later she'd convince him to leave things the way they were. Or perhaps it was time to get out before it got too complicated.

But first she had to get her Saturday back on track. She shut out all thoughts of romance and focused on football.

Not unlike, she considered with slight amusement, many thousands of men around the country about now.

FA Cup fourth round. A small non-league team had made it this far and been drawn against Premiership stalwarts Tottenham Hotspur. One of her clients was a star at Spurs. She watched the screen with shredded nerves, hoping that he didn't get injured and wincing at every hard tackle. There was nothing a player feared more than a career-threatening injury. And nothing that an agent feared more than a threatened career.

Compared with losing a player to a shattered kneecap or a broken femur, her boyfriend picking a minor fight was nothing serious.

Nil–nil with thirty minutes played. She wondered if Spurs were getting nervous yet. People imagine that these uneven draws, the nobodies versus one of the giants of the game, end in total annihilation, but the truth was that the teams balanced out much closer on the day. The minnows would be playing as hard as they ever had, reaching for the elusive fifth gear, trying everything, running after every ball and hoping – against all the odds – to get a result. Whereas the millionaire professionals on the other side would have dropped down into third, coasting through the same, more worried about avoiding injury than the goals which they were certain would come eventually. And if they didn't? Well, then they'd turn it up a notch. And if that didn't work, then and only then, they could always start playing properly.

Tottenham had been drawn away, which meant travelling to the suburbs and leaving behind their multi-million-pound stadium and all the luxuries that came with it, like

29

groundsmen, and seats. It was a terrible pitch, bumpy as hell and surely not helped by the wind and the rain that was lashing the players and the overexcited fans that were huddled in the shabby stands cheering lustily for a local team they probably didn't have much faith in until this day.

But now they believed.

You could see it in every face. They truly believed it could be done, that their little David of a team could knock out the Goliath.

She had half an eye on her emails, but a change in the tone of the commentary drew her attention back to the screen a minute or so before half time.

'*And it's Gabe Muswell. Still Muswell. Smartly done. Still Muswell. MUSWELL!!!*'

The minnows were beating the sharks by a goal to nil. Stranger things had happened. After all, this was the FA Cup, the one tournament where anything could occur. If they won it would be an enormous upset. But it was also an enormous 'if'. Nevertheless Samantha pushed her paperwork aside to concentrate on the game. She found herself willing on the underdogs despite loyalty to her client. Samantha liked stories of success against all the odds. She'd lived to tell that kind of tale.

But the Premiership team came out much stronger in the second half, as she had guessed they probably would. It didn't take long before they were two—one up and the glory of the minnows' lead was nothing but a memory. Nice goal though.

She googled Gabe Muswell and found a few items of local press.

Used to be a goalie, then called upon to play up front in an emergency a couple of seasons ago. Never looked back. A good scoring record, nothing unusual in a club of that size where they didn't have a massive squad to rotate. Handsome, in a rough-diamond kind of way.

She noted with a pang somewhere between amusement and pity that he worked in a supermarket by day.

And today you scored against Spurs. Good for you.

Thirty-five. Married to Christine, thirty-four. No kids. See? Samantha wasn't the only one to reach that age and be childless. And she had a career as her excuse – what was Christine's?

Not that you need an excuse.

She drummed her nails on the table top, thoughts of having Jackson's children distracting her. Maybe she should just go for it. She was a partner now, or would be soon, what was the worst they could do? Jackson was hardly in a position to get snippy about maternity leave. Besides, it was only childbirth; she could be back in the office after – what? – three weeks or so? If she timed it right so that she wasn't missing the valuable transfer window, or the run-in, or the start of the season, or the Welstead boys' Chelsea debut, when they'd still need so much support. So not this year then. Maybe next year?

But she could imagine the looks on the other Legends' faces when she announced her pregnancy.

You see, those faces would say, *we always said this was no job for a woman.*

Thirty millions pounds didn't change what really mattered. Asking for maternity leave would be like complaining about period pains. As long as she didn't have a despotic penis and a big set of balls hanging between her legs it would always be her and them, them and her, never just us. If she was the boss's wife it would be even worse.

But for all her thoughts of scheduling and maternity leave and child care she just wasn't sure. It wasn't just about Jackson. She wasn't sure she wanted children. She'd never felt that burning desire she had heard other women speak of, a longing to be a mother. Did that make her a freak of nature? It was one more thing she could blame on her own mother; secretly she was terrified that miserable parenting might be a genetic weakness.

She didn't even know if she wanted a relationship with Jackson any more. Or anyone for that matter. She had lost sight of the point. Sex? Not hard to pick someone up in a club if that's all you wanted. Companionship? Wasn't that just another word for being needy?

More action on the football pitch pulled her back to the FA Cup. There was pandemonium in the home crowd. Unbelievably St Ashton had drawn level. And it was that good-looking Gabe Muswell again.

5

It was the biggest day of his life. No question. Gabe had felt anxious all week long, sick on adrenalin. He wanted to kick out at something, but didn't want to risk breaking a toe. Not this week. Not today.

As a little boy he remembered feeling like this before every match, but as an adult never. Gabe Muswell had been a Tottenham Hotspur fan ever since he saw Ricky Villa score the winning goal in the 1981 FA Cup final replay. It was a Thursday night in the middle of May when his heart went to White Hart Lane for ever.

From that day on he dreamed of playing for Spurs and, even more, he used to worry about how he would perform on his debut. He had long, involved daydreams about missing a penalty or getting injured in the first few minutes of play, his knee getting smashed to pieces, being out for three seasons and returning as a pale pretender to the player he once was.

As it turned out he had no need to worry. These dreams began before his seventh birthday and faded with increasing speed after his twenty-first. He never got to play for Tottenham, and now, at thirty-five, he never would. But today was the next best thing.

Today he was playing against them.

Today he was competing with heroes.

And the boy who had stood in the stands and whooped

for joy at Villa's goal, spinning his black-and-white scarf above his head, would be proud of the way he was playing. What more could he ask?

He was in peak physical condition, the best shape of his life. He'd taken up the running habit when he ditched the Marlboro Lights. If he had stopped smoking and started running a little earlier who could say where he would be? Maybe, instead of playing football for a sorry little non-league team like St Ashton, he would be playing for his country and married to a pop star or a glamour model or an actress.

His wife was not a pop star. Nor a glamour model, nor an actress. Christine worked at a call centre in Aylesbury, a job she never stopped complaining about to Gabe, as if it was his fault, and his alone, that she had to work at all. He'd been a supermarket buyer when they met and he'd never promised her a life of luxury, so why was she so bitter?

It was the biggest day of his life and she wasn't even here to watch.

Before he'd left the house that day he'd asked her for an honest answer. 'Do you think we stand a chance?' he'd said.

'Against Spurs?' Christine had replied. 'Don't be stupid.'

Before kick-off the most that they could hope for seemed to be that they should lose with a shred of dignity intact.

But this was the FA Cup. The one tournament where anything could happen, right? They'd already scraped through to the fourth round thanks to a lucky draw and a couple of even luckier goals. And if anything could happen ... All week long Gabe had been trying to picture running at the Spurs goal, seeing the ball leave his foot with the perfect strike and slamming into the back of the net. Except every time he saw the strong, assured hands of their goalkeeper ruining his fantasy, saving his attempt on goal with ease. So Gabe would start visualizing it all over again.

Then, thirty-four minutes into the most important game of football he would ever play, he scored.

The goalkeeper didn't stop it. The strike left Gabe's right foot hard and true and whipped past him before he could even see it. He watched his own goal as if from above. The way the defenders backed off and backed off until they had nowhere left to go. The gaping abyss that suddenly appeared on the left-hand side of goal, the curl of his foot as he kicked the ball exactly as he wanted to.

Time slowed and was silent. He swore he could even see the moisture on each blade of grass flick off as the ball tore across the turf, and went where he wanted it to go, where he knew it would go the moment he'd felt the clean perfection of his kick.

The back of the net billowed like an explosion and he raised his right fist in the air.

Suddenly blackness as half a dozen players leapt on his back, hugging him with complete and utter joy.

'*Mental!*' Loud in his ear. '*Yeeeees!*'

Someone close by saying, '*Fuck yeah, fuck yeah,*' over and over again.

His eyesight narrowed to a single spotlight of vision. The ball in the goal.

Then he heard the crowd cheering. He saw strangers hug each other, dancing with happiness. Then he saw their goalkeeper disconsolately plucking the ball from the back of the net, wearing a version of the football strip he had idolized since he was a boy. He could have cried then. But he didn't. He would never have lived it down.

To score one goal against the club you had followed your whole life was the stuff of dreams. To score two was unheard of, impossible. Except that's exactly what he'd done. Someone else did all the running up the right wing, and sent over a sexy little sideways pass, which would look great on the telly later, and Gabe was right there to pick it up and tap it in from two yards out. The goalkeeper was utterly foxed by the sudden change of direction. He didn't stand a chance. He had been made to look like a fool. Gabe felt, rather than heard, him hiss something in his ear as he ran into the goal to pick the ball out of the back of his net himself.

Two–two. Perhaps they could score another. This was the FA Cup – anything could happen. So while his team chased him with more congratulations Gabe was thundering back up to the centre spot with the ball.

How much longer did they have? Not long, surely. Not judging by the way his heart felt like it was going to explode and his lungs were screaming for respite. His shirt was clinging to him all over, wet inside and out. In contrast the Tottenham players seemed hardly to be sweating at all. Gabe handed over the ball and wiped his muddy hands across his flat stomach, leaving a wide smear of dirt. He wanted that ball when this match was done. Whatever the result.

The St Ashton players were all struggling now. Making silly tired mistakes, having played too hard and too fast for too long. Surely it was only a matter of time before Tottenham finished them off? Still, they had emerged with far more than a shred of dignity intact. They could walk off the pitch with their heads held high, applaud the fans that had carried them this far. Outplayed perhaps, but not outgunned. If they could just make it through these last few minutes without collapsing from exhaustion, then they could all swap shirts and for ever remember the day they took the game to Tottenham. Just a few more minutes. The fans were screaming for something, anything. Gabe stumbled over his own feet and for a fleeting, shameful moment he wished for a winning goal at the other end. Even if that meant surrender. If the match ended in a draw and they had to face a replay, at White Hart Lane, he knew they would never be able to perform again like this. Tottenham would put out their best team, none of these B-team players, and wipe them off the pitch, making sure that nobody remembered how close they came to losing face.

He could hear his own blood pounding against his skull, thumping like a headache, and he wanted this to be over. He imagined he looked something like a horse at the end of the Grand National, a lumbering beast, foaming with sweat. Somewhere in his hazy peripheral vision he saw the fourth official raise a board declaring injury time. He had no idea how many more minutes were left. He could no sooner read the board than he could fly.

Then the ball was at his feet. He was thirty, maybe

thirty-five, yards out. Two of Tottenham's best defenders, household names almost, were bearing down on him with more speed than he could possibly conceive of right now. How did they still have the energy?

And, because he was tired, and because he was desperate, and because he wasn't really sure if his trembling legs would carry him if he tried to run away with the ball, Gabe pivoted neatly, looked up once, twice and a third time, then audaciously fired the ball towards the goal.

It went high into the air. The goalkeeper was miles off his line and started frantically running backwards as soon as he realized the ball was on target.

Gabe watched the lob soar through the leaden winter sky, incapable of doing anything more. The two defenders zipped past him, but Gabe couldn't move. He watched, and he waited, like the crowd, like every player on the pitch, as the ball reached its zenith then fell in a slow arch towards the goal, went over the scrabbling goalie's head and scraped under the crossbar by a hair's breadth.

Goooooooaaaaaal!

In the stands they started dancing.

St Ashton 3 – Tottenham 2. The final whistle blew before the game really got going again and the hardy crowd were hoarse from screaming their appreciation.

It might not have been the sexiest match they'd ever seen, certainly the setting wasn't very glamorous, and there weren't many big stars out there today, but Gabe Muswell had just scored a hat-trick against Spurs and they wanted him to hear just how much it meant to them.

*

She was already looking up the phone number before the ball went into the back of the net. This kind of thing just never happened. Never. And yet it had.

Please don't let him be ex-directory.

She could imagine some other sports agents across London doing exactly the same thing. She only hoped that they were calling their assistants rather than doing the simple task themselves. A few clicks found just one Muswell in the St Ashton area.

She dialled.

Surely if this was the right number it would be engaged. Not that she expected anyone to be home, but family and friends would be lining up to congratulate the hero, right? But it rang. She would leave a friendly message, offering her services should he require them. She wasn't trying to broker him a new deal with a different club – that would be against the strict FIFA rules that governed the game. If she wanted to do that she'd have to approach the club first, even a small one like St Ashton. When you played football your life was not your own to trade; you belonged to the club just as surely as starlets belonged to their studios in 1950s Hollywood. Besides, it was a lucky hat-trick, beautifully done but too late in his career to have a lasting impact.

She would offer to navigate and negotiate the hundreds of media requests that would be heading his way. Gabe Muswell was the man of the moment and with her help that could be a very lucrative moment indeed.

'Hello, yes?'

Unexpectedly the phone was picked up. 'Hello, have I got the right number for Gabe Muswell?'

'Yes, what is it?'

'Is that –' she flicked back to the article about Gabe and his wife – 'Christine?'

'It is. Who's this?'

His wife was at home? Maybe they'd split up since this article was written or maybe they'd had a baby. Why else would she be missing what was undoubtedly a once-in-a-lifetime event? At least she would have been watching it on television. She was surprised that Christine didn't sound a little happier, more jolly. Her husband was a hero.

'My name's Samantha Sharp,' she said. 'I wanted to get in touch with Gabe, with both of you, and introduce myself.'

'What for?'

'Well, firstly to say well done! I'm an Arsenal fan myself and I can tell you that there's going to be big celebrations in Islington tonight.'

'I'm sorry, what do you want? Are you selling something?'

'I'm a sports agent with Legends. Perhaps you've heard of us?'

'No.'

'Well, that's me, and I wanted to get in contact. Does your husband, does Gabe, currently have any representation?'

'For what?'

'Well, for football, for any media attention, local press, local events, that kind of thing?' Had this woman been drinking in the middle of the day? It felt like Christine Muswell was either dumb or drunk, and her instincts told her that she was not dumb. 'I have to warn you, Christine – may I call you Christine? – that life could get pretty insane over the next few days.'

'Why?'

'Well, because of what your husband just did.'

'Oh no!' The sharp and disinterested tone of Christine's voice changed drastically. 'Has something happened to Gabe? Is he in trouble? Are you a reporter?'

'No, I'm a sports agent,' she said slowly as the truth dawned. 'Have you been watching the match today? The Tottenham match that your husband has been playing in?'

'No. I've been cleaning the bathroom.'

'Christine, Gabe scored a hat-trick. They won.'

'They did?'

'And any minute now I imagine the country's media will be all over him trying to get his side of the story. His and yours.'

'They won?'

'Yes.' She was going to have to spell this out in simple terms. 'That sort of attention can be quite overwhelming if you're not used to it and you might want to think about hiring someone, someone like me, to act as a kind of buffer between you and the tabloid press, who as I'm sure you know are not the most, shall we say, decent types.'

There was a pause at the other end.

'Christine? Are you still there?'

'I've got thirteen missed calls on my mobile.'

'It's been quite a day.'

'I'm sorry but we're not interested,' said Christine abruptly.

'As long as you understand that I'm not trying to sell you anything? I can assure you I'm a legitimate agent. Legends is a global company. You might have read something in the papers about Monty and Ferris Welstead? That was our most recent success.'

She should have said 'my', 'my success'. She was probably the only agent at Legends that didn't like to pretend the entire company would collapse without her. But teamwork was an advantage, and a trait too deeply rooted in her to be brushed aside when it suited her ego.

'The thirty million?' said Christine. 'That was you?'

She recognized something in her voice immediately. A love of money. An avarice that could be exploited. Christine Muswell's greed would be her way in.

Back on familiar footing, Samantha set out her stall.

'My first step would be to sell Gabe's story exclusively to one of the tabloids, the *Mail* or the *Sun* probably. Why tell the same story over and over for free when you can tell it once for money?'

'How much?'

'I'd really have to talk to Gabe before I could put an exact figure on it, but we could possibly be talking several thousand pounds.'

'Really?'

'Absolutely. But it would be essential that he didn't give too much away for nothing, not before we've had a chance to talk.'

And I've found out how much juice we can squeeze from his life story.

'Several thousand?'

'And that would be just the start. There's the glossy magazines, *OK* or something like it, endorsements, television and radio. There's a real window of opportunity here. Once-in-a-lifetime kind of stuff.'

'What's your name?'

'Samantha Sharp – Sam.'

'What do I have to do?'

She took a deep breath. 'There will probably be other agents calling you – they're probably trying to get through right now.'

'But you were first,' said Christine, with a surprisingly simple concept of fair play.

Her eyes flicked up to the clock on the wall. 'I could be in St Ashton in an hour. Perhaps the best thing to do would be to sit for a while and talk about this?'

'I'll expect you in an hour?'

'No problem. And when you speak to Gabe perhaps you could suggest that he doesn't spend too long with the press? Especially not the national press.'

'You don't know Gabe,' sniffed Christine. 'He loves attention.'

'I'll be with you as soon as I can.'

In a daze Christine wandered into the front room and turned on the television. There were scenes of jubilation at the St Ashton ground, and then suddenly there was Gabe, there was her husband, looking knackered and dishevelled but irresistibly sexy.

She had to sit down. That was her man, the man she chose, talking to that nice Garth Crooks from the BBC. He looked happy, so happy.

Several thousand pounds.

She went into the kitchen, determined to find him something special for his dinner, more inclined to be his loving wife than she had been for years.

There was a bottle of champagne she'd been saving since Christmas. She looked at it. Then she opened it. Then Christine poured herself a glass and she drank it.

Samantha stepped out of her house and locked the door behind her, reminding herself yet again to get someone in to see about how it jammed in damp weather. The house was one of a short row of panelled 1970s townhouses, ugly as sin when she bought it nine years ago but with a certain kind of retro chic these days. The front garden was bare except for an enormous magnolia tree which ensured that at least for a few weeks in spring she had the best-looking house on the block.

She climbed into her steel-grey Mini Cooper and started north towards the M1.

Gabe Muswell wasn't going to be a massive earner, but he was a nice little high-profile cherry to top off her month. It wouldn't be complex work. Leanne could handle most of it. Her mind was already processing the best opportunities for him as she crawled through the Saturday-afternoon traffic around Brent Cross, a mental manifesto for all things Muswell.

Not for a moment did she think of Jackson in his Westminster penthouse, waiting for her.

6

Aleksandr Lubin would inherit everything when his father died.

Billions.

So was it any wonder that he was looking forward to it?

He liked drugs, women and football in that order. He was currently flying high on cocaine while he screwed a fabulous-looking woman with the sports news on, muted, in the background, showing the English football highlights. Life was good.

Anya struggled underneath him, playacting, knowing that he liked to feel powerful as much as she liked to feel over-powered. That was why they made such a good couple. That and the fact that such a classic Slavic beauty could only be temporarily tamed by an enormous fortune such as his.

She wrenched herself free of him and rolled them both over with her strong lean limbs, raising herself on her elbows and letting her long dark hair trail over his chest. Aleksandr grabbed her arse and pulled her down onto him. She smiled and tossed back her head so that her perfect breasts jutted out for him to admire. It was only fair, seeing as he had been the one to pay for them.

He reached for her greedily.

There was something about the feel of fake tits that drove him wild. He had tried to work it out once and decided that there was nothing better than a woman who was willing to endure that much pain to make herself more attractive to men. Like high heels and corsets, fake tits meant a woman was willing to suffer for sex.

He pinched her left nipple between his thumb and forefinger, hard enough to make her cry out, and she squeezed him between her thighs.

Anya wasn't his girlfriend, but she didn't know that.

He was born in the Ukraine twenty-four years ago, at his father's holiday home on the Crimean Peninsula. Before she died his mother used to sing him lullabies from that region, songs full of sailors and sea nymphs and pagan gods. He was named for his maternal grandfather, a penniless farmer, who left nothing but his flaming auburn locks to the daughter he adored. She'd married his father for love. She'd stayed with him for money.

Goran Lubin, Aleksandr's father, had seized the chance to make money as Russia emerged from its communist restraints, using his black market expertise to exploit Mikhail Gorbachev's liberalism, sinking every dirty penny he had made into the country's enormous reserves of oil and aluminium, so that by the time the market readjusted Lubin was one of a handful of new Russian billionaires whose dirty money had been washed spotlessly clean by glorious capitalism. After his wife died he sank all his emotions into his only son and so Aleksandr grew up in a sanctuary of privilege and adoration, cared for by a team of nannies as his father protected his business interests around the world.

And every time he came home he brought more extravagant gifts and dismissed the nannies for the remainder of his stay so that he, and he alone, could be with his son.

'You are my boy prince,' he would say. 'You are worth the world to me.'

And that's exactly how Aleksandr felt.

Every time he fucked a beautiful woman he knew that his father would be proud. His father would like Anya. If she was still on the scene when he next visited. He would be a fool to settle down so young. That might have been how they did things in the old country, but times had changed. Thankfully.

On his eighteenth birthday his father gave him the apartment where he was currently banging the gorgeous Anya. A five thousand square foot penthouse on the south side of the Vistula River in Krakow, overlooking the Wawel Castle. Krakow would be the hub of the emerging technologies in the region. It suited Goran to have a base there.

And as the city was renowned for having some of the best-looking women in the world walking its cobbled streets it suited Aleksandr too.

He sat up, pushing his chest against Anya's, gripping her close, and biting her shoulder as he looked over it to see what was happening with the football, just in time to see Gabe Muswell's first goal.

For his twenty-first birthday Aleksandr's father had given him a football team.

Not just any football team, but the White Stars of Krakow, the most successful team in the city's history, and the most reviled of the three teams which played their home games there. Most of their supporters came from the rural areas, attracted by the team's reputation for glamour and violence. The locals, most of whom supported

47

rivals Cracovia or Wisła, feared them. As twenty-first birth-day gifts went, it was impressive.

'Something for you to do,' said his father. 'I know you like football.'

The truth was that investment in a football club was a monetary rather than sentimental decision, and Poland, on the up and up, was as good a place as any to put his money.

For the first few months he had done little more than swan around the executive box at home games and give interviews to the press from his penthouse, boasting of his plans for the team. As their lead at the top of the national league began to look precarious he was forced to take a more active interest. When they slipped from the top and languished outside the top three the fans started to turn on him. One afternoon, after the team's third consecutive loss, he was booed as he left the stadium in his German sports car. He was humiliated in front of the Polish princess he was desperately trying to get into bed. He never saw her again.

Both of his top forwards were out through injury and they currently had a seventeen-year-old kid playing as a lone striker up front. They were holding their position in the table, just, but it wasn't enough. They needed a new striker on loan. They needed him yesterday.

On the screen behind the frantically bucking Anya, Gabe Muswell scored his second goal.

Aleksandr flipped her over so that she was on all fours and stabbed into her from behind. That was much better. He could see the television perfectly. Better still, his security cameras, with tape permanently recording, had a magnificent view of Anya's ecstatic face as he pounded her.

Something to watch later.

He reached over to the bedside table where his little vial of coke was balanced carefully on its end. He sprinkled some of it onto her shoulder blade and then grabbed a handful of her thick hair and tugged her forcefully towards him so that he could lick the cocaine off her arched back.

As the narcotics entered his bloodstream with a potent rush he watched Gabe Muswell score his third wonder goal.

'Fuck me,' cried Anya, as he drove deeper into her. 'That's perfect.'

He couldn't have agreed more.

Later, when he found out that Gabe Muswell had signed with Samantha Sharp, he knew that it was meant to be. It was destiny.

7

A woman who was not his wife was caressing his face. It felt great.

'Try to relax, Gabe,' she said.

He was relaxed. But if this cute blonde make-up artist stroked his face for much longer he might get too aroused. Which could be embarrassing. He imagined her hands straying from his face, stroking more interesting places.

'Your skin's pretty dry,' she said. 'Don't you moisturize?'

'Never,' he said. Okay, so once or twice he had swiped a bit of Christine's stuff, but only in an emergency, like when his nose peeled after a day in the sun, that sort of thing. Gabe was a man, not a pretty boy.

'I think you're the first professional football player I've met who doesn't.'

He didn't bother to correct her. So he wasn't quite a professional, so what? This week he felt more like a football star than ever before and he hadn't touched a ball since Saturday. Whatever happened he would never tell anyone that as far as he was concerned all three goals were lucky. The three luckiest goals of his life. All in the same match. Against Tottenham.

Somebody up there liked him.

Samantha Sharp had been at his house as soon as he got home. A fantastic-looking woman who clearly had a fantastic brain to match. He was surprised that Christine wasn't apoplectic with jealousy. But the two women seemed to be the best of friends and Gabe was happy to let them take over his life. Particularly when that life meant getting rich by talking about yourself to newspapers, being driven around London to various daytime television chat shows, and now, to top it all, appearing on a comedy quiz show he had watched on television every Sunday night since it started.

He looked in the mirror.

The same old face stared back at him. Baggy around the eyelids, his shock of dirty blond hair scattered with grey, his face drawn with the thin lines of slight disappointment. The knowing glint in his jade-green eyes was probably his best feature. His wife once told him he looked like a man with an ace up his sleeve, and he had never felt more like she was right all along. This was his ace. This moment was the glint in his eye.

'Isn't it ridiculous that I'm getting paid for all this?' he'd said the night before. 'I'm having such a good time.'

'Yeah, well, you'll be glad of the money when there's a new flavour of the month,' said Christine, 'so don't go offering to do anything for free.'

'Don't worry. I wouldn't go that far.'

She was out in the audience. This week had been like a second honeymoon for them. She was in love with him all over again, and it was that, as much as the public recognition and the money, that made him feel like such a star.

Last night she had made love to him with the kind of enthusiasm he hadn't seen since their twenties. Under her clothes she wore something black and see-through and utterly impractical that stayed on all night. She twisted and turned her body towards him wherever he wanted, groaning with desire, letting her hands roam over his body and her own so that he could see her playing with herself in the shadows, could see the curve of her waist under his hand as she lifted her hips to his, and he could feel her breath as she whispered, begging him with sweet little sighs to do it harder, to do it slower, to do it just like that.

'I adore you, Gabe,' she'd said afterwards.

And in that moment he adored her too.

'Gabe?' The show's exuberant comic host poked his head round the door of the make-up room. 'I'm Seamus.'

As if he didn't know.

He was still getting star struck despite spending much of his week with some very familiar faces, and he stuttered his hellos to the popular television presenter, wishing that he sounded cooler than he did.

'Wanted to say hiya before we start. Thanks for coming on, we're all very excited to have you here, aren't we, Kelly?'

'Sure are,' said the make-up artist.

'So I'll see you out there. Try not to be nervous.'

'See you out there,' echoed Gabe as the host left followed by a hassled-looking assistant with a clipboard and a stopwatch.

'Do I look really nervous or something?' he asked the cute blonde make-up artist.

'A bit, yeah. But don't worry about it.'

'And I thought your name was Kerry not Kelly?' he said as she whisked thick powder over his face.

She shrugged. 'It is.'

*

It was hot in the studio under the lights. Gabe was embarrassed that Kerry had to come over during a break and pat more powder on his face, but then he saw her doing it to Seamus too and he didn't feel so bad.

He was on a team of three with an England rugby international and a glamour model called Cassandra who kept resting her chin in her hands so that her lovely boobs looked even more lovely on television.

'Funny, ain't he?' she said during the break, nodding towards Seamus.

'Yeah,' said Gabe. 'I've always thought so.'

'I've never seen this show before,' said Cassandra. 'I think I'm a last-minute replacement. Someone must have dropped out. I'm not doing very well.'

She hadn't answered a single question, but he suspected that Cassandra wasn't on the show to act clever. She was the butt of most of the host's jokes, which she took in good spirit, her sexy little giggle softening the otherwise all-male show. Their team was losing dismally.

'You're doing great,' he said.

'You think? Thanks. You too.'

'Nah,' said Gabe, 'I think I'm being too quiet.'

Cassandra shook her head vehemently so that her platinum hair extensions flicked across her face. 'No way,' she said. 'You look all broody and handsome. The strong, silent type.' She reached out under the desk at which they were sitting and put her hand in his lap. 'I like that. Very manly.'

His eyes widened and he looked out past the lights at the studio audience, wondering if he could see his wife, knowing that she could see him. There she was, and though her lips were set in a thin line she cracked a smile when she saw him looking and gave him a wave.

In his lap Cassandra's hand started to roam.

'What you doing after?' she said.

'Do you know who I am?' he asked.

'You're a footballer, ain't ya? I like footballers.'

'I don't think you mean footballers like me,' he said, knowing that Cassandra's hand wouldn't be quite so inquisitive if she knew that he earned less in a year at the supermarket than the kind of footballers she was talking about earned in a week. Still, the attention was good for his ego.

'Back in fifteen seconds, people,' someone shouted.

Cassandra removed her hand and used it to hoick her boobs into a more obvious cleavage.

'If I get nervous,' she whispered, 'will you hold my hand?'

'And five . . . four . . . three . . .'

Gabe wondered when this greatest week of his life would ever end.

Afterwards there were drinks in the bar. The moment that Christine appeared Cassandra went off to try her luck with the rugby player instead. Gabe watched her go. What might this week have been like if he had been single?

'You look really sexy on television,' said Christine.

'Thanks, babe,' he said, dropping a kiss onto her forehead. They had their struggles yet they were still married after eleven years. She might complain, but she was still there. It was only right that she should be enjoying this flush of fame with him. Gabe had been splashed over the centre pages of the *Sun* on Monday in his exclusive interview. She'd run out before it was even light to get a copy, to get a dozen copies, and together they'd had breakfast in bed and laughed at the pictures.

The photographer had posed him with his shirt off, his boots swung casually over his shoulder.

Christine said he looked like a conquering hero.

Gabe thought he looked like a prat.

His wife could be delightful when she wanted to be.

There was also the not insignificant fact that what he was paid for that single interview would pay a big chunk off their mortgage.

The boy done good.

He had sensed for a long time that he was a growing disappointment to her, that their marriage, though never less than he'd promised, was less than she'd hoped. To see her now, gazing at him with proprietary pride, made him feel like a champion.

'Gabe! Brilliant! Great show, one of the best. And who's this?'

'Seamus, this is my wife, Christine. Christine, Seamus McDonnell.'

'Nice to –' started Christine, but Seamus talked over her.

'You should let me fix you up with my agent, Gabe. You've got a real down-to-earth quality, works great on camera.'

'I have an agent,' said Gabe.

'Not this kind of agent you don't. He could do something with you, get you in the jungle or the Big Brother house, you know?'

'I'm a footballer,' said Gabe, 'not a celebrity.'

'Right, sure, whatever. So fuck, Saturday, what was that like, man?' said Seamus. 'I mean, that's real boy's-own adventure stuff, right? Did you think you were going to lose it? I mean, come in your pants right there on the pitch?'

And so for the umpteenth time Gabe told the story of the football match that had changed his life. By now he'd done it so many times that he knew exactly when to pause for maximum drama, which lines would get a laugh, which descriptions would make jaws drop. And he didn't think he could ever get tired of telling it.

Nobody had to know it was pure luck.

Later, when Seamus was off chasing Cassandra, Gabe noticed that Christine was checking her watch. 'Going somewhere?' he said.

'No,' she said, smiling.

'Good, because how often do you and me get to be in a place with a free bar?'

'More often than we used to,' she said as Gabe ordered two more bottles of Becks for them both. 'No, it's just that Sam called earlier, said she'd try to pop down.'

The lovely Samantha, fragrant and friendly, would be a very welcome addition to his evening.

'Look,' said Christine a few minutes later, 'there she is now,' and true enough Samantha was at the other side of the room, making her way towards them. She saw them looking and waved, stopping off to talk to the rugby player for a few seconds before finally joining them at the bar.

She was wearing jeans and a tight black vest top that showed off her perfectly toned figure, yet she still managed to look like a businesswoman. Maybe it was the heels.

'Hi, you two,' she said. 'Having fun? I hear it was a great show.'

'So they keep telling me,' said Gabe.

The women kissed each other's cheeks hello, which surprised Gabe. He couldn't remember the last time he'd seen Christine kiss anyone's cheek but her mother's. They didn't go in for that sort of thing.

'So what brings you here?' he asked.

'I had a very interesting phone call today,' said Samantha.

'More publicity?'

'Not exactly,' she said. 'You remember what I told you on Saturday, about how there wasn't going to be much I could do for your career from a playing point of view?'

'Because he's too old,' said Christine. 'Sorry, babe, it's true.'

It was. He knew thirty-five was no time to be starting a footballing career. If only last Saturday had been fifteen years ago. Perhaps he could have had the world.

'How would you feel about playing football professionally?'

'What?'

'In Europe,' added Samantha.

'Europe!' Christine's eyes fired with imagination as she pictured herself in various plazas and piazzas on the continent sipping espresso or shopping. They could live in town and get a summer place by the beach. They could start trying for a family again and bring up little suntanned, bilingual children who thrived on olive oil and oranges. She could get a convertible. She could get a maid.

'Which club?' asked Gabe. 'Where in Europe?'

'Krakow,' said Samantha.

Both Gabe and Christine looked blank.

'It's in Poland.'

'Poland?' Christine's dreams of sangria evaporated. Poland was cabbage and potatoes and snow, wasn't it? And vodka.

'I didn't even know they played football in Poland,' said Gabe, scratching his chin, which was thick with late-night stubble.

'They do,' said Samantha. 'And, by the sound of it, they'd rather like you to play football there too.'

8

Her assistant took the call. Outside of the United Kingdom Samantha dealt largely with the monster Italian clubs, the French and the Spanish giants. Central Europe was hardly on her radar. Beyond the vaguest trace of name recognition, Samantha knew nothing about Aleksandr Lubin.

But all that was about to change.

If she had known this was to be her last day in the office she would have taken the time to drink in the view she had worked so hard for, but instead she hardly noticed it as she squeezed this bizarre enquiry about her newest client into her busy day.

The message from Lubin was one of many that her assistant Leanne greeted her with after lunch. 'It's been non-stop,' she said.

'Tell me,' said Samantha.

'Are the Welstead boys getting external press agents or are we it?' asked Leanne.

'Who wants to know?'

'We've had calls from the red tops, the *Independent*, the *Guardian*, *Arena*, *Wallpaper*, *GQ*, *Vanity Fair*, all the lads' mags, BBC, Channel 4 and Sky News, plus a bunch of internet sites.'

'We're it,' said Samantha, shrugging off her coat with one hand and taking the bunch of messages from Leanne with the other. 'Get the requests in writing and talk the boys through a strategy.'

'Already on it,' said Leanne. 'What a morning. Plus, I've got a blinding hangover. It was the launch of that new club in Mayfair last night. You know, the one where Daisy-Daisy used to be? The one with the roof garden?'

Samantha didn't know. She hadn't been to the club when it was Daisy-Daisy and she was very unlikely to go now that it was called something else.

Same shit, different drinks.

'I got carried away on the Black Label tequila and didn't get home until 4 a.m.,' continued Leanne, grinning. 'There was so much blow flying around it was like a blizzard hit the bathrooms. Every man I spoke to was grinding his teeth in my face while boring me senseless. Is coke ever going to go out of fashion? Nobody just gets good and drunk in this town. Nobody except me.' She tipped her head to one side, a sign that she was giving something serious thought. 'Do you think it's a West Country thing?'

It would never occur to Leanne that these were not the sort of stories one should be sharing with one's boss. Not that it mattered. As long as her assistant was punctual and efficient then what she did with her free time was up to her. It just so happened that what she chose to do was exploit her position at Legends and get on the guest list for as many events as she could squeeze into her riotous social life. The bouncing blonde from Devon was popular with players and hangers-on alike and knew every doorman west of the City by name.

Leanne wanted to marry a footballer. She probably would too, as soon as she could settle for just one. She was having so much fun as a social butterfly it was inconceivable that she should metamorphose just yet.

It was enough to make Samantha wish she was twenty-two again, except that when she was twenty-two she was clawing her way into the company by working every single waking hour.

What happened with Liam had turned her off partying for good.

She was leafing through the messages and stopped when she got to the Russian's. 'What's this?' she said.

'Oh that,' said Leanne. 'Yeah, that's a whole other thing.'

And she filled her in.

There was something ridiculous about the approach. Who ever heard of a thirty-five-year-old part-timer being offered a professional contract? And that the enquiry should come from a foreign club? It was absurd. But the owner, this young guy Aleksandr Lubin, he sounded serious.

'He can't approach me directly,' said Samantha. 'He's a professional; he should know that. He has to channel enquiries through the club.'

'He knows,' said Leanne. 'This is a general meeting.' She made air quotes with her fingers. 'Not specifically about Gabe.'

'Except that it's all about Gabe?'

'Yeah.'

She sighed.

It wasn't unusual to bend the rules, but she never enjoyed it. Still, so long as she didn't take any money, sign anything or even shake hands with this Russian billionaire's son, she should be clear of any wrong-doing.

There was so much scandal surrounding football agents and illegal transfers these days you could never be too careful, even with what would surely be a relatively cheap deal like Gabe's.

'He said he's sending his jet this afternoon,' said her assistant, clearly impressed.

'His *jet*?'

'What should I tell him?'

'Tell him I'll meet him tonight,' she said. 'Then find out everything you can about him. He's obviously loaded – find out how come.'

'You want me to do you a highlights package?' asked Leanne, referring to the kind of file she often put together for new players or managers.

Samantha nodded. If she was about to enter negotiations with an unknown entity she'd better become an expert, and fast.

She instant-messaged Jackson to tell him of the last-minute trip.

He called her immediately. 'When will we have a chance to talk?'

'Come with me,' she said impulsively. 'There'll be room on the jet. Why don't you come? My meeting won't take long. We can get a hotel.'

It was a good idea. Instead of being lost in a city she didn't know it would be an opportunity to spend some quality time together. Hotel rooms were always sexy, even the bad ones, especially the bad ones. They could order sex food from room service; they could mess up the sheets and make some noise.

'We get to wake up together,' she said.

'No thanks,' he said. 'Unless you can tell me right now that you won't want us to take separate cars to the airport, false names on the flight manifest, sneaking around so that nobody guesses we're together.'

'It's the best I can do right now,' she said.

'I know. That's the problem. I've had it with the cloak-and-dagger routine, Sam. Perhaps I didn't make that clear?'

'I'm sorry.'

'Me too.' He seemed wistful, but then he was back in business mode. 'You're around later? I might need to talk to you.'

Partnership?

'I'm around,' she said. 'Until six.'

'Good.'

And the conversation was over.

A few hours passed busily. Leanne prepped her for the trip. There were a handful of essential telephone calls 'but you can make them from the road', a fresh draft of the Welstead contract to read, 'but you can go through it on the plane', and a pile of requests by fax and email to answer, 'but nothing that can't wait until tomorrow'.

'Nothing to do then,' said Samantha. 'I could have taken the day off.'

'It wouldn't hurt to do so from time to time,' grumbled Leanne.

Yes it would. If she took a day off she'd go mad wondering what she was missing.

'What do you want me to do if Kwame's wife calls about the nanny?'

Samantha sighed. 'You could handle it. Do you know why she insists on speaking to me?' A ridiculous situation had arisen with one of her players, his wife and a nanny. It was really very tedious.

'She wants to know his pre-season fixtures. I've told her, but for some reason she needs to hear it direct from you.'

'Do me,' said Samantha.

'What?'

'Do me. Fake my voice. Oh, don't look so surprised – I've heard you do it before.'

Leanne dropped her West Country burr and said, 'Me? Never. The very idea!' in a perfect imitation of her boss.

'You're really rather good,' said Samantha. 'Maybe I should put you on the phone more often.'

Leanne grinned. 'I did you an itinerary.' She put a neatly printed piece of paper in her hand. 'You arrive just after eight and they're sending a car to collect you. I've told them you'll want to keep the car on standby all night and they don't seem to think that's a problem. However, I'm not entirely sure they know what standby means. Your phone is set up for roaming and these here are all the numbers you could possibly need. Including these two – here and here – cab companies, in case of an emergency. They speak English, I checked.'

'And the car's taking me directly to him? To . . . Aleksandr?' Her tongue curled around the name, igniting thoughts of exotic cold-war thrills.

'At some restaurant. Here's the address in case – well . . . just in case.'

'Perfect. Okay, let's try to get through as many calls as possible before I leave.'

She slammed the door behind her and then jumped with shock when she realized she wasn't alone.

In her office a ginger-haired and slightly overweight rascal was stretched out on her couch.

Richard Tavistock had been at the company since he was seventeen. He came to Legends for six weeks of unpaid work experience and he'd never left. By the time she'd started there as an assistant he was already taking home six-figure bonuses as well as the most beautiful woman in any bar. He could have any woman he wanted.

Any woman except for her.

He was thoroughly charming to her for several months until he realized that she wasn't going to sleep with him and then stopped bothering to hide his brutal competitive streak.

They were born on the same day, exactly the same age. For both of them, success was gauged by watching the other.

'Extraordinary night last night,' he said, smiling lazily, as if he was still slightly drunk.

'Yeah?'

'Ran into your boys down at Mahiki. Those kids know how to party. The women were crawling over them like maggots on meat. Shame you couldn't come.'

She didn't recall being invited. 'Which boys?' She had thirty-four clients, but there would only be two that Richard would try to goad her about this month.

'Monty and Ferris,' he said. Of course.

'Ferris is only seventeen. What was he doing in a night-club?'

'Drinking Perrier?' Richard rolled his eyes. 'Okay, Mum, should I let him know you disapprove?'

'They're just a couple of kids, Richard. They're new to all this.'

'Good job they've got an old hand like me keeping an eye on them then, isn't it?'

'Make sure that you do,' she said. 'If they don't perform right out of the gate for Chelsea they'll have a hard time winning over the fans.'

'Thanks for that pearl of wisdom – I'm new to this football lark myself.'

'Just watch out for them,' she said. 'And that doesn't mean force-feeding them shots of tequila.' The thought of those boys wasting their talents and being led astray by the likes of Richard Tavistock made her nervous. She had seen too many players fail to fulfil their potential, lured by the intoxications of women and drink.

'Don't worry about it. They're sensible lads. They're coming down to Wales next month. Boys' weekend, quad bikes and stuff, maybe some shooting, bit of snooker.'

Richard had a massive house in Wales that he had converted into his own private playground. Samantha had never been invited, not once.

'I hear you're off to Prague or somewhere?' he said.

'Poland,' she said. 'Just for the night. There's an interesting offer for Gabe Muswell floating about.'

'Really? They must be desperate.'

'I'm leaving soon and I have a bunch of calls to get through,' she said pointedly.

'Sure, sure. You want me to take the call if the Welstead boys call in? I could tell Leanne I'll handle it, pick up the slack.'

She wasn't threatened by Richard socializing with her

clients out of work, but letting him into their professional lives would be setting a dangerous precedent. 'There's no slack. Leanne will reach me if it's important.'

'Only trying to help.'

He was such a liar. He would poach Monty and Ferris within the time it took for his Italian sports car to go from nought to sixty if he thought they would leave her.

'Thanks,' she said, 'but I'm on it.'

Leanne came into her office with a small pile of clothes.

'What's this?' said Samantha.

'Hat, scarf, gloves, socks, vest and long underwear,' said Leanne.

'Seriously?'

'I checked. It's pretty cold.'

Samantha grimaced. She was wearing a pewter-grey Prada suit over a red silk shirt and black Gucci boots, an outfit at the high end of her power dressing wardrobe, an outfit that would be thoroughly ruined by a woolly hat and scarf. And long underwear? Forget it.

'I'm going from a plane to a car to a restaurant. How cold is it going to be?'

'Minus two,' said Leanne. 'Better to have them and not need them than need them and not have them.'

Just before she left there was a knock at the door.

'Jackson would like to see you.'

She nodded casually at his assistant, not wanting anyone to know how fast her heart started racing. This was it. Partnership. Her reward for years of hard work.

'I'll be five minutes,' she said. And forced herself to wait for four.

But Jackson did not look happy.

Something was not right. He refused to meet her eye and alarm bells started to ring at the back of her head. She silenced them. Perhaps he was merely adding gravitas. Being made partner was a serious business.

Inside Jackson's office a man was waiting whom she did not immediately recognize. She smiled cautiously at him, his face slightly familiar, and tried to place him. Adrenalin started coursing through her veins. Her body knew before she did that this was not going to end well.

'You remember Carl Higham?' said Jackson. 'From Higham and Colvert?'

A lawyer. Jackson Ramsay's lawyer. She remembered him now. Senior partner at the firm they used ten times a day, every day, whose number was as familiar to her as her own. But they hardly ever saw Carl Higham, instead speaking at length to any of the dozens of top-end lawyers who worked for him. Higham only came out for the big stuff. Having him just sitting in Jackson's office waiting for half an hour would cost them hundreds of pounds. A foreboding shiver travelled down her spine all the way to her toes.

'Am I in trouble?' she said.

'Why do you ask that?' said Jackson.

'You have your lawyer in the room. Should I have mine?' Her palms were sweating now and she fought the visceral urge to hightail it out of the building. She talked herself down inside her head. She had done nothing wrong and if they thought that she had then it was a mistake, and mistakes could be corrected.

'Let me tell you what we know so far and then you can decide. You don't have to say anything.'

'And anything I do say will be taken in evidence and used against me?' Kidding, trying to lighten what felt like a seriously heavy situation.

'I wouldn't make light of this, Sam,' said Jackson. 'You might wish you hadn't.'

This was Jackson. This was the man who had given her a break, who had given her a life. She owed him everything; perhaps she loved him more than she would admit, because he was looking at her like a disappointed father and that's when she realized that the blood pumping around her veins was laced with raw fear. What did they know?

I shouldn't have secrets.

Samantha was the poster girl for Legends. The face they wheeled out when they wanted to look respectable, the proof that not all sports agents were testosterone-fuelled swine chasing after the money. If someone found out about her nefarious past, her criminal brother, one of the newspapers that had long been fascinated by this glamorous, intelligent woman making tidal waves in a man's world, if they found out they would make something of it, they would make headlines, but not in a good way. And if Carl was here to embark on a libel suit, to force the newspaper to admit their lies, she would have to tell them it was true.

Yes, I have a brother in jail. Yes, people are dead because of him. Yes, because of drugs.

Drugs.

The word alone was like cancer to a sporting career. But Jackson would stand by her, right? He knew that she wasn't the same person, not nearly the same. The lost lamb he had found in a hotel room was as good as dead. Too much time had passed. She wasn't that girl any more.

You will always be that girl.

'Would you like to sit down?' Jackson kept glancing at Carl, whether for reassurance or guidance she couldn't tell.

'I'd rather stand,' she said.

He took a deep breath. 'As you know,' he started, 'from time to time we audit our employees to safeguard against illegal business practices and when necessary begin further investigations.'

What?

Of course she knew, with such enormous sums of money floating around full financial disclosure was the only way to be sure that it was all going in the right direction. The scope for corruption was massive. It wasn't exactly unheard of for agents to take bribes and bungs, to 'tap up' clubs on behalf of their clients, to divert money from the usual channels either to avoid the taxman or the transfer fee. Every month it seemed there was a new disgrace in the headlines, bringing the game into disrepute. Legends was one of the few firms that had managed to avoid being dragged into a messy scandal. The firm had a reputation for honesty, which is probably why they snared all the best clients.

What has this got to do with Liam?

'What you won't know,' Jackson continued, 'is that last month after a routine audit we began further investigations into you.'

'Into me?'

'Yes, Sam, you.'

'Why?' Had they found out about the house she purchased and transferred into her brother's name? It was a legitimate transaction – she had paid tax on the money – but they would know she had a brother.

At this point Carl Higham pulled a sheaf of papers from his briefcase. 'Because of this,' he said.

She scanned the paperwork. It was her name, her address, but beyond that nothing was familiar. There was no mention of Liam and slowly it dawned on her that this had nothing to do with him. Nothing at all. In front of her were details of a bank account located with a firm called CoralBanc in Grand Cayman. An account that had received three substantial deposits over the last six months, and no withdrawals, so that the balance stood at an extremely healthy sum somewhere a little over three hundred thousand American dollars.

In her name.

'Is this a joke?'

'What?'

'Is it a joke? It's a pretty good one, I like it much better than that time someone left a bull's penis on my desk, or that Portaloo on the roof that said "Ladies".'

'It's not a joke, Sam.'

She looked down at the piece of paper. 'It isn't mine,' she said automatically, because it wasn't, and she knew nothing about Grand Cayman or CoralBanc, because she understood immediately that she was in deep trouble and all she could think to do was tell the truth.

'You were aware that you had to disclose all personal bank accounts?' said Carl.

Jackson shot him a warning look. 'You don't have to answer that, Sam.'

'Why wouldn't I?' she said. 'Of course I was aware. You might just as well wallpaper my office with the FIFA transfer regulations – nobody knows the rules better than I do.'

'You understand we have a serious problem?' said Jackson.

'We? *We* have a serious problem? I'm the one who's looking at my name on a bank account I've never heard of. You'd think if someone wanted to give me that kind of money the least they could do is let me know.'

'Sam, please, you can't smart-talk yourself out of this.'

'I'm not trying to,' she said, exasperated. 'Check my phone records; check my passport. I've never been anywhere near Grand Cayman, much less opened a bank account.'

'I think this could all be done remotely,' said Carl.

She spun round to face him, her eyes on fire. 'There's a big difference between what you think and what I think, Carl,' she said. 'You clearly think I'm guilty of something, but I *know* I'm innocent.'

'There's no need to be defensive,' he sniffed.

'There's every need,' she said.

What a ludicrous thing for him to say. Why shouldn't she be defensive when clearly she was being attacked?

'This is all a big mistake.'

'We don't think so,' said Carl.

Another explanation occurred to her and the words ran out of her mouth as they chased her thoughts.

'Then somebody is framing me,' she said. 'Somebody who is willing to spend three hundred thousand dollars to discredit me.'

Shop online at whsmith.co.uk

Thank you. Please retain your receipt as proof of purchase.

Customer Relations @whsmith.co.uk
WH Smith High Street Limited Company no. 4504139
Registered in England and Wales
Registered Office: Greenbridge Road, Swindon.

Shop online at whsmith.co.uk

customer.relations@whsmith.co.uk
WH Smith High Street Limited Company no. 6560339
Registered in England and Wales
Registered Office: Greenbridge Road, Swindon,
Wiltshire SN3 3RX
VAT Reg no. 238 5548 36

every year, you
pick up 40 million
unputdownable
books from us

Love books Think
WHSmith
Shop online at whsmith.co.uk

customer.relations@whsmith.co.uk
WH Smith High Street Limited Company no. 6560339
Registered in England and Wales
Registered Office: Greenbridge Road, Swindon,

A snort from Carl. It made her temper flare like a fire-work.

'What?' she snapped.

'Frame you? Do you really expect us to believe that?'

She turned on him, livid. 'How dare you?' she said. 'Do I have to remind you of the amount of business Legends brings your company? Me personally, not to mention my clients? I'd appreciate it if you kept your snap judgements quiet until I have had a proper chance to refute them. You can be sure I'll remember where your loyalties lie when we come to review our legal services.'

'Sam,' said Jackson softly. 'There's going to be an investigation.'

'Good,' she said. 'I would bloody well hope so.'

'And, until we have resolved this, I don't see how we can allow you to remain on the premises.'

'I don't understand.'

'Sam, you're going to have to take a leave of absence.'

Until he said this all she had seen was a massive irritating muddle, the resolution of which would eat into her precious working days. Fucking annoying, but nothing she couldn't handle. At his words she clutched the back of the chair she had previously refused and felt suddenly dizzy.

'What do you mean?' she said faintly.

'Please try to stay calm,' said Carl. 'This is merely a suspension. As and when the facts of the case present themselves more fully you will be informed of our decision regarding your future.'

'Jackson?'

'I'm sorry, Sam,' he said.

She slumped down into the chair. *Suspended?*

'My clients,' she said. 'What will happen to my clients?'

'We'll babysit them – myself, Richard, everyone will help . . .'

No, no, no. But she knew there was nothing she could say.

'What do you think? Do you think I'm guilty?'

'Sam . . .' he implored.

'Don't.'

She stood, without really knowing if she would be able to stand, and relieved when she could. She stepped towards Jackson until she was close enough to smell the intoxicating flavour of his skin, which instantly transported her back to his bed and the last time they'd made love. 'Swear to me,' she whispered. 'Swear right now this isn't personal.'

An odd look from Higham, but she didn't care.

'I swear,' said Jackson.

They locked eyes at last. But she saw pity there and so she had to tear her eyes away because she thought that she might cry. This was happening. It wasn't the latest *hilarious* joke concocted to make life tough, to remind her that she didn't fit in, that her breasts and the space between her legs where a dick should be were a handicap they would never allow her to forget. It was real.

'So what happens next?' She addressed Higham; it was easier. It was too confusing to think about Jackson, much less look at him.

'You should take the rest of the day to wrap up whatever you're working on, leave handover notes where necessary, but you are formally suspended from Legends pending an investigation into your financial practices. Do you understand?'

'Yes,' she said.

Although she didn't understand at all.

She was clean. Part of the reason she loved working at Legends was because she believed in the same things that Jackson did. She believed that a company could be trustworthy and profitable, that corruption was not a necessary by-product of success. She held herself to these standards. Jackson knew that.

Carl Higham didn't respect her. He never had. There was something about her that he just didn't like. Her gender. He would delight to see her fail, because she was a woman and he had never cared for that.

But Jackson had, and he respected her a great deal. He loved her, or at least he was forever telling her that he did. He would be on her side. These erroneous accusations would fall apart under proper scrutiny and she would be back behind her desk in a heartbeat, making heroes out of schoolboys, making millions out of heroes.

She would be back.

Soon.

The alternative was unthinkable.

9

The bank account wasn't hers. The money wasn't hers. The disgrace wasn't hers.

Three hundred thousand US dollars with her name on it.

Why me? Why now?

An ugly stain threatened to spread across her blemish-free professional record. She had no idea what to do to make it better. But she was innocent. She must have faith that soon she would be proven so. Carl had instructed her to take the rest of the day to wrap up whatever she was working on. Which meant keeping her appointment with Aleksandr Lubin in Krakow. What was the alternative? Cancel everything so that she could sit at home and wait for Jackson to call and tell her she could go back to work? She would go mad. No, it was far better to carry on without missing a beat.

But what if . . . ?

She forced down the negative thoughts that bubbled to the surface.

Besides, there was something about leaving the country that always made her feel liberated and optimistic. The moment the wheels lifted clear of the tarmac she would sense a lightening of her spirit, sniff the possibility of adventure on the recycled air. She needed that feeling now more than ever.

She left without saying goodbye.

There was no passport control at Farnborough, no security, no queues for X-ray machines amid chaotic scenes and screaming infants; instead checking in at Farnborough airfield was a simple matter of presenting herself to the immaculately dressed woman on the reception desk, a little like checking into a five-star hotel. Then a car took her right up to the bottom step of the stairway and she climbed aboard Aleksandr Lubin's lavish jet.

Yummy.

There was rich, and there was Russian-billions rich. The jet was the kind of thing that drew the line between them.

Generous padded seats were upholstered in the softest buff leather, the carpet beneath her feet was a hugely impractical cream pile, every surface gleamed with silver or tortoiseshell. Even the seatbelts were something special, a wide strap of resilient material she didn't recognize, some kind of microfibre, like the Japanese football boots some of her clients had fallen in love with, the buckles glinting with platinum plate.

She inhaled deeply, smelling the money. Men like Lubin in the world were a reminder that there was always plenty more out there to be had. Money kept you safe. With money you need never feel quite so afraid.

Growing up she had craved the kind of security that money could buy. Her own home, something permanent in her ever-shifting life, a certain future. And just when it looked possible, on the brink of partnership, things were plunged back into doubt. It didn't seem fair.

It'll be okay.

The first time Liam stole something, the first time she knew of, she made him take it back.

77

'Are you stupid or something?' he had said, facing his little sister with undisguised annoyance. 'What if I get caught?'

'Didn't you think about that when you were taking them?'

It was only a pair of jeans. Levis. Fifty pounds or so, new. But more than either of them could afford. He had tucked them under his parka and dashed out of the store. By the time the security guard made it to the shrieking alarm Liam was long gone.

'Of course I thought about it,' he said. 'But I didn't get caught, did I?' He tugged at the security tag and looked around for a tool to take it off without damaging the denim. 'I can get thirty pounds for them easy.'

'You're not keeping them? You went to all the trouble of shoplifting and you don't even want them?' She had long lusted after a pair of Levis. They were just the thing to show off her fourteen-year-old body, all legs and subtle curves.

'Not as much as I want thirty quid,' said Liam.

'If you want money so much then get a job,' she said. She had started with a paper round, then a shop and then she'd been working behind a bar for three months, lying about her age and flirting like crazy to try to make tips. Every time a customer told her to 'have one for herself' she put ice and lemon into a glass of tap water and one pound fifty into the glass at the side of the till. Liam was eighteen and unemployed. He wasn't even looking.

'Take them back,' she repeated. 'For me.'

He said that he would, but she was pretty sure he never did. Why would he? Thirty quid was a lot to them back then.

Look how far she had come.

A long way down.

A pretty blonde stewardess dressed all in white offered her a glass of champagne before take-off, but she asked for a bottle of water instead, and when it came it came perfectly chilled on a tray next to a glass of ice balls and a twist of lemon.

Her mobile phone rang. Leanne.

'I've got Mr Welstead on the line,' she said. 'Shall I put him through?'

'Of course,' she said, and waited until they were connected.

'How's it going?' she asked.

The Welstead boys had moved into a flat she had found them in Fulham, the perfect pad for two newly minted millionaires, and headed north, home for a visit, with diamonds for their mother.

'Fine, fine,' he said. 'The boys are on their way back down.'

'What can I do for you?'

'Well, I need . . . I suppose you could call it reassurance.'

A nervous father. Perhaps the diamonds were too much; perhaps he was afraid that the boys would change. He'd be right, they would change, but she was happy to tell him whatever it was he wanted to hear.

'What's wrong?' she said.

'I heard a nasty rumour,' he said.

'About the boys?'

'About you.'

It had only been a few hours since Jackson shook her world. Yet somehow, and he refused to say how, two hundred miles away, the Welstead boys' father had already heard that she was in trouble.

'I would hate my boys to be caught up in anything untoward,' he said.

'They're not,' she said. 'I'm not.'

'It's not true?'

'It's a misunderstanding.'

He paused. 'Isn't that . . . I'm sorry, but isn't that what they say in the films right before they disappear with the money?'

'I'm not going anywhere.'

'Your assistant said you were just about to get on a plane.'

'A short trip. I'll be back tomorrow morning.' She looked at the paperwork in her hand, the Welstead contract not yet signed, and a hard ball of fear bounced in her stomach, making her feel sick. Part of her couldn't believe that this was happening and was in a dizzying state of shock, while the other part, the efficient businesswoman, was working damage control.

'Mr Welstead,' she said, 'sir, please, you have to tell me how you heard about this. I promise you everything I've done has been one hundred per cent legitimate, my whole career. These allegations won't stay around, but rumours like this can be very damaging to everyone concerned. Someone told you? Who was it?'

He paused. 'He didn't tell me his name.'

'An anonymous tip-off?'

'He said he was press. I felt stupid even calling you, but now it turns out there's some truth in it . . . well, I just don't know any more.'

'There's no truth in it,' she insisted.

'You're in trouble,' he said. 'He was right about that.'

Yes, he was right. She was in trouble. More trouble than she had realized. There was a potential press leak at Legends and they had gone to where it would hurt her most. She should expect a story about herself sometime soon. Great. Jackson would love that. If she was still in the heart of the company Jackson would do whatever he could to protect her reputation, call in a few favours, place a call to a sports editor and promise him an exclusive something somewhere down the line. But now? She couldn't be certain.

Surely there would come a point where she was more trouble than she was worth.

Insecurity began to chew into her calm exterior. Was she so valuable to Jackson, personally and professionally, that he would never walk away?

She reassured Mr Welstead and was reasonably confident that she had allayed his fears. For now. He was so new to this world that he wanted to believe in her. Someone else might not be so trusting.

It'll be fine.

The engine gathered momentum and they started down the runway.

She sipped her water and started reading the fine print of the thick contract in front of her, checking things she didn't like with spiked grey pencil marks.

It was still a work day.

10

If you ever want to feel like the heroine from a cold-war thriller, then travel to central Europe at the onset of winter. Two weather systems collide there, the Arctic blast from the north and the Siberian winds from the east, and when they meet they are so happy to see each other they sit still for months, sucking every last drop of warmth from the air. The chill is unmistakably foreign, but not at all like the scented Alpine winters or the damp wet days of Milan or Paris. It is the kind of cold that nobody should survive; it is dangerous and romantic, and it only takes a moment to understand something of the people who live in a place like this, how hard their lives must be, how desperate you could easily become in a place this cold.

And inevitably the mind will turn to thinking of things that men and women might do to keep warm.

When she stepped out of the plane the cold hit her smack in the face, through the wool of her coat, through the soles of her Gucci boots and up the ankles of her sleek grey trousers. All over her body hairs stood up in protest.

The landscape was white with snow for as far as she could see and it seemed impossible that planes could come and go in icy conditions that snatched every warm breath from your mouth like some evil spectre.

She rushed across the tarmac to arrivals. Every time she took a breath it was cold enough to be mildly painful.

The men in immigration carried guns, a common sight in foreign places, but one which always caused her a shiver of illicit excitement. She was bewildered by the indecipherable language on the signposts, a language where vowels did not seem to exist. It all seemed far too exotic to be such a short flight away from the familiar.

She was whisked past a small queue to a private office where a swarthy Pole waited for her.

He didn't say a word as he studied her passport. He was young and handsome and she committed his face to memory in case she wanted to use it in a fantasy later.

She suspected that she might.

He nodded her through without a flicker of expression, and even though she tried to break his brooding silence with one of her very best smiles he didn't crack. His short cropped hair was trimmed with military precision so that she thought it might feel like suede under her fingers.

Then she was thrust back into the real world again, away from the privilege of private aviation and into the general melee of a small international airport.

The arrivals hall was tiny and crammed with glamorous-looking women in thick coats and fur-trimmed hats; all the men seemed to be hanging back and smoking heavily. Many people were holding bunches of flowers, waiting for loved ones. She pushed through them all.

The immediate need to deal with a new place and the sensations that come with it was a comfort to her. Anything to block out the thoughts of what was happening back at Legends.

She saw a card with her name on – Mr Sam Sharp. Obviously Lubin hadn't done his homework like she had.

Immediately she felt that if there was an upper hand to be had here, then she had it.

The driver didn't say anything, just flicked his cigarette aside and led her to his car. He was easily over six foot tall, heavyset, with a scar above his left eyebrow.

'Is it always this cold?' she said.

Scarface said nothing.

She was driven swiftly through the snowy landscape in a silver Mercedes. They left the airport traffic behind and the roads were almost empty. In these gloomy deserted streets perhaps she should be worried. She watched the white world outside through her misted window and hoped that being worried wasn't necessary.

She called the office.

'I'm here,' she said.

'What's it like?' said Leanne.

'Odd.' She glanced at the driver in the rear-view mirror. 'I feel like I'm being driven by the baddie in a James Bond film.'

'Cool,' said Leanne.

'What if he tries to abduct me?' she said, only half joking.

'Think of it as an adventure,' said Leanne.

'That's easy for you to say – you're not the one in the back of his car driving to God knows where.'

'Calm down,' said Leanne. 'I'm sure he's lovely once you get to know him.'

'Anything happening there I should know about?'

'Something funny is going on,' said Leanne. 'Jackson's been holed up in his office all day with the lawyers. I think maybe someone's in trouble. Did he say anything to you?'

She would have to tell Leanne the situation before she found out for herself. She had no idea if Jackson would make a comment in her absence, send out a memo telling the entire company that she was under suspicion. It wouldn't be fair on Leanne to find out that way. But not now. Saying it out loud would be just too hard.

'I have to go,' she lied. 'The James Bond baddie is trying to ask me something.'

'Good luck.'

What would happen to Leanne? She'd been Sam's assistant since she was nineteen years old, bringing the same enthusiasm to her job as she did to her social life. Was her job security now precarious too? She would be devastated to leave Legends. How would she ever meet and marry a footballer then?

Despite everything the thought of Leanne hanging around Mahiki trying to score with the top scorers made her smile and forget her troubles long enough to appreciate her surroundings.

It didn't take long before the traffic started to build and she saw the occasional sign in English directing them towards the centre.

It was a pretty place, especially in the snow. They crossed a wide river and on the other side was a magnificent castle, floodlit and frosted, that looked like something designed by Disney, had Disney been going through a particularly gothic period. The roads became cobbled, and grumbled beneath the tyres. Spires towered on every corner. A tram zipped past them. The pavements filled up with people, everyone wrapped up as warm as they could be and walking fast, even faster than they did in London, anonymous in varying shades of brown and grey, blending into the pavement, into the sky itself.

She would freeze to death out there in her Prada. She searched in her bag for Leanne's woollens, but before she had a chance to find them the car stopped in front of a hotel.

'Here?' she said.

'Mr Lubin is waiting for you inside,' said the driver in perfect English. 'And I'll be waiting to take you wherever you wish to go when your business is concluded.'

He gently hummed the James Bond theme tune as he opened her door.

Inside the lobby of the hotel she immediately forgot the bitter cold. An open fire blazed in one corner, smelling faintly of rosemary and thyme, a red velvet chair beside it invited guests to sit and watch the scented flames. It was warm and pleasant, ornate without being dated.

The boots of her heels tapped sharply across an exquisitely tiled floor and the chic receptionist welcomed her with a smile that didn't quite reach her perfectly made-up eyes.

'My name's Samantha Sharp. I'm meeting Aleksandr Lubin?'

'We have been waiting for you,' she said. 'Please follow me.'

She led her through to a softly lit restaurant with tables tucked into hidden corners, the occasional clink of cutlery on china the only sound. They went downstairs into the cellar of the building, which was darker still, lit only by candles, three flames on each table sitting in low candelabra on black lace tablecloths.

It was so quiet that she could hear the echo of every footfall on the stone floor.

There was only one customer. Sitting at a table for two, sipping from a glass of icy beer, was one of the most handsome boys she had ever seen.

She knew this was Aleksandr Lubin, but in the flesh he was far more attractive than the blurry photograph she had seen. The idea of having to negotiate a deal with someone so beautiful was preposterous; she would roll over and give him anything he wanted. He should be on a magazine cover somewhere, not sitting and watching her draw close.

He was unquestionably a boy. His face was as smooth as a baby's, unmarked by times or troubles. He was pale, as pale as a vampire was what she thought, and his thin lips were so red against that pale skin that had he not oozed testosterone from every pore she would have suspected a little cosmetic enhancement. His hair was jet black and cut very short, so that his stark bone structure stood out and his hooded inky eyes flashed in the reflected light of the candles. She knew women who would gladly kill for his eyelashes.

She could tell he was arrogant just by looking at him. But that must be forgiven. It would surely be impossible to look like he did and be humble.

He held her gaze as she approached. She was ashamed of the way her heart quickened. This was a business meeting; he was practically a child.

And yet he had the eyes of a Russian philosopher, suggestive of unfathomable depth. So, an old soul? In such a smoking-hot young body?

Get a grip.

'Mr Lubin? I'm Samantha Sharp.'

Those eyes locked on to hers like magnets. 'You're far more beautiful than I expected,' he said.

'You were expecting a man.'

'And I am delighted to be wrong. Believe me, it doesn't happen often.'

'That you are delighted? Or that you are wrong?' she quipped.

He didn't laugh. Instead he studied her curiously for several seconds until she felt the blush rise on her cheeks. She waited for him to invite her to sit down, but he did not. She stood and felt absurd, and then annoyed. She remembered back some years ago, sharing a house with two men. She would often ask them for their opinion of what she was wearing and they would stare at her just like this, judging her appearance.

Abruptly she sat in the chair opposite him and summoned the hovering waiter with a flick of her wrist.

'A glass of water please,' she said.

'And perhaps a small beer? They are known for it here. I thought because you are English . . .' He shrugged. 'But then perhaps I was also wrong about the English and their beer?'

'I don't drink,' she said.

He said something rapidly in Polish to the waiter and he disappeared.

'Tell me about Gabe Muswell.' The Russian accent made his blunt words sound virtually menacing. And, she noted with a degree of shame, sexy.

Straight to business.

It was probably for the best. Between Jackson's accusations and this manchild's body, practically trembling with sheer sex appeal, she was glad of something to force her to focus.

She rattled off Gabe's playing history, trying desperately to make more of it than there was. Perhaps this man wouldn't know enough about English football to know that she was faking it. After all, she had read in the highlights package that Leanne prepared for her that White Stars was little more than an expensive toy to him. With a bit of luck, she thought, he was a star fucker. It was the only thing that made sense. Lubin could have approached a hundred strikers so he must either be a fan of English football or want the attention a gimmicky deal like this would bring him. She suspected it was a little of both.

'Gabe is a celebrity right now,' she effused. 'The most talked-about man in England.'

'But for how long?' said Lubin. 'Soon he will be back to his pissy little team, no? He will be a nobody once more.'

So he knew that much at least. This was all true. And it would be a waste of time to pretend that big-name clubs were beating a path to her office door. This was Gabe's moment, but it wouldn't last for ever.

'I know enough about the player, what little there is to know,' he said. 'I want you to tell me about Gabe the man. It is just as important to me, to the game I think. The true strength of a player, Samantha, is in his heart.'

The waiter came back with her water. She sipped. Her throat was unusually dry, and the cold water felt as soothing as honey. She fancied he could see the heat rising off her like steam. He made her burn.

Stop it.

She wasn't a fool. She knew that the searing attraction she felt must be in part some kind of revenge thing. After all, the man she was sleeping with had just slapped her in the face. Metaphorically, that is. Suspending her from work was the worst punishment she could imagine. And this from a man who said he loved her. He could have stood by her and to hell with Carl Higham and his judgemental snorts. It was a betrayal. Was it any wonder she was looking for retribution? As revenge fucks went, Lubin would be an excellent choice.

Stop it. Right now.

She was here to do a job, to make a deal.

'I like Gabe a lot,' she said, deciding to be honest. 'He has a brain, which you can see in the decisions that he makes in front of goal. He may not be young, but surely that means he would bring a measure of maturity to any team. He's a responsible player. And if he glimpses goal then he will do his best. I believe in him.'

'Does he have passion?'

'Yes.'

'Are you sleeping with him?'

She couldn't hide her shock. 'What? No!'

'Would he thank me?' he said, moving smoothly to his next question as if his last hadn't been at all provocative. 'Would he be grateful?'

'Yes,' she said. 'He would be loyal to the team, to you.'

It was the right answer.

'Then perhaps we can come to an accord.'

Mmm, maybe we can. But she dragged her mind back to the kind of accord he meant.

'He's under contract at St Ashton,' she said, ever cautious of the regulations safeguarding the transfer market. The very regulations she was being accused of flouting.

'They will let him go on loan. Then during the transfer window they will sell him. I saw their stadium on the television. They will be glad of the money. Perhaps they could afford seats, no? Or a roof to keep the rain off the fans? Some of the fans at least.'

He was a snob. But, these days, who wasn't? The people that lived where she lived would vote for the right people and say all the right things about socialized medicine and education, until they got ill or their child went off to school, then values would be thrown out with the recycling and forgotten. She was exactly the same. Aleksandr Lubin would be too, only more so. One day he would inherit billions. She found this hugely attractive.

She used to think she was attracted to money because money equalled success and drive, but here was a boy who had done nothing to be rich except be born. So it would seem that she was just attracted to money, full stop. Perhaps she should have been ashamed of that, but she wasn't.

They ordered dinner and talked for a while longer about English football in general, about Polish football.

'They have no hunger here,' he said. 'At the World Cup the national coach called his own team average. Can you imagine any England manager saying such a thing and not being killed for it?'

She laughed. 'Gabe has hunger,' she said.

'Then he is just what I need.'

The food was delicious. Perfectly cooked steak and pommes dauphinoise, not a shred of cabbage in sight.

Her face felt flushed and she couldn't stop playing with her hair. She momentarily loathed herself for this.

She could easily imagine the scene if Richard Tavistock were here wooing the Russian heir in her place. He would be competing, trying to out-drink him, asking about Polish women's sexual preferences and bringing out the cigars. Richard would swan back into Legends boasting about his hangover and his conquests, and telling anyone who would listen about his new pal Alek. He would have probably tempted him with a couple more players he thought would benefit from some first-team action or a European sojourn, and he would have sealed the Muswell deal with a wink.

Richard was no better than her, even though he might think that he was. She was a grown woman; she could deal with a boy like Aleksandr Lubin. Animal attraction or no animal attraction.

'Do you have to rush back?' he asked.

'No,' she said recklessly.

'Excellent. Do you mind if I complete my meal with vodka? It is traditional.'

'I wouldn't want to stand in the way of tradition.'

Warning bells were clanging in her head, but she resolutely ignored them.

'In this part of the world we drink shots,' he said. 'You are sure you won't join me? This bar serves over three hundred kinds.'

She giggled. And she was not, as a rule, a giggler. 'How do you choose?'

'It must be Polish,' he said.

'Not Stolichnaya then?'

'She speaks Russian.'

'Sure,' she said. 'Stoli, Smirnoff, um, glasnost.'

'You know what it means, "*glasnost*"?'

She shook her head. He smiled. It was the first time she had seen his smile. She liked it.

'It means openness,' he said. 'Shall we drink to that?'

From nowhere a bottle appeared between them, with two straight-edged shot glasses. He filled them both to the brim.

'To openness,' he said.

'*Glasnost*,' she said.

Then he reached across and he drank hers too.

It was an hour later. He was telling her about his apartment. The wonderful views, he said; she should see them.

'I have to leave soon,' she said. Her voice seemed to come from far away and she shook her head to pull herself back into the here and now instead of thinking about the things he might do to her if they were in this wonderful apartment of his.

'A shame,' he said, and poured himself another shot. 'You are married, Samantha?'

'Everyone calls me Sam.'

'It is a boy's name,' he said, dismissing her nickname of thirty-four years with a wave of his hand. 'You are married?'

'No.'

'Ever been married?'

'No.'

'But you have a boyfriend waiting for you at home?'

'I do,' she said. *Do I?* If she was suspended from Legends what did that mean for her and Jackson?

93

'And he is a nice man?'

'A very nice man.'

'And does being with your very nice man make you long for nasty sex?'

That snapped her back into the here and now all right. 'Excuse me?'

He shrugged. 'Some of the women I sleep with, they have boyfriends, husbands, but they are not happy. You are a very sexy woman, Samantha. We are told that women want to be made love to on a bed of rose petals by candle-light, but I find many of them just want to be fucked.'

'I'm very happy, thank you,' she said, dimly aware that she sounded like a prim school mistress.

'I have offended you?' he said.

'Not at all.' Unbidden, her mind was suddenly full of sexual images, the best sex of her life, some with Jackson, but some not, filthy and erotically charged, without a rose petal in sight. A ball of fire took hold between her legs and slowly suffused the rest of her body with the warm flush of desire. The memories in her mind were replaced in an instant with an image of this man, the Russian boy, forcing her against some cold brick cellar wall and having her roughly and without any grace or forethought. Her skin prickled with excitement.

'I have embarrassed you,' he said. 'Forgive me.'

'I'm not embarrassed,' she said. Though she might be if she left a damp patch on her chair when she stood up.

She couldn't look him in the eye, and yet she couldn't seem to avoid his stare. Her thoughts were twirling frantically between real life and this crazy snowy place where she was propositioned and called sexy. Where she *felt* sexy. The blood was pounding in her temples and she felt dizzy, she felt drunk, but she liked the feeling; it was like a hug from an old friend.

Should she sleep with him? For there was no doubt in her mind that was what he was asking. Should she go back to see these magnificent views with the impossibly handsome young gun? Should she have one wild night of delicious nasty sex and to hell with the guilt, the shame, the consequences? Perhaps it could help her forget the mess that was waiting for her back home. Jackson would never know. And, if he did, then so what? He had let her down. He had hurt her far more than she would have thought possible. For all her self-preservation he held her career in his hands, her most precious thing. To doubt her in business was far worse than to doubt her personally, yet for Jackson she knew the reverse was true and that infidelity would be a greater betrayal.

'I have to go,' she said, and she stumbled up the stairs and through the first door she saw, out into the fresh air, hoping that it would blast away the devilment playing inside her.

She was in a courtyard that looked like something out of a Shakespeare play. In the centre was a fountain, its water frozen into an impromptu ice sculpture. Lubin was beside her.

'It's so beautiful,' she said, without really thinking.

'Krakow is the most beautiful city in the world,' he said.

'More than any in Russia?'

'Russia is a hole in the ground where people shit,' he said. 'You've been?'

'Never.'

'Don't bother.'

95

There was much bitterness in his voice. She wondered why he hated the country that had made his family a fortune.

He gently touched her elbow, guiding her forward. 'Your car will be waiting at the front, this way.'

She allowed herself to be led.

'I'll be in touch,' he said.

'So,' said Liam, leaning in close enough to whisper, 'did you do it?'

'Of course not,' she said.

'Three hundred thousand dollars is a lot of money.'

She couldn't say it, not here, not in this place, but it really wasn't. The truth was that it was a small sum in the context of the game. Just half of one per cent of the Welstead deal, hardly enough to buy a one-bedroom flat in London, the kind of money Salvatore Salva would spend on a car, and hardly the sort of sum you would risk your career for. But enough to jeopardize everything she had struggled to achieve. But how could she say that to Liam without sounding ridiculous?

'Could you go to prison? Wouldn't it be funny,' said Liam, 'if you went down just as I got out?'

On Thursday mornings the only thing that kept her feet moving towards the miserable, soulless visiting room was knowing with absolute certainty that no matter how intimidating and depressing it was for her to be here it was a thousand times worse on the other side of the bars. So, no, she didn't think it would be funny at all.

'You know I'd stand by you, right?' he said with a smile.

Her eyes filled with sudden tears and Liam immediately regretted trying to make light of his sister's dilemma.

'I'm sorry,' he said. 'I'm an idiot.'

She pressed her lips together and tipped her head upwards to make the tears retreat. 'Tell me something I don't know,' she said.

He reached across the table and held her hand in both of his. She tried not to grimace when she saw the home-made prison tattoo on the web between his thumb and forefinger. It wasn't offensive, just two simple shapes that were supposed to be birds flying, like a child would draw in a sky, but every time she saw it she wished he hadn't done it. It was like a brand.

'Even when we were kids you wouldn't take a bribe,' said Liam. 'Do you remember the time that me and Steven Whittaker stole those yo-yos and we offered you fifty pence to keep your mouth shut?'

'I got you up to two pounds.'

'Each.'

'But I still told.'

'Grass.'

'They weren't yours,' she said. 'They were Sharon Mander's and she was crying about it all day. She was one snotty tissue away from telling the teacher. Meanwhile you and Steven Whittaker are having yo-yo wars out the back of the music hut thinking nobody would notice. I didn't grass you up, I saved you.'

'Yeah,' he said. 'I'd hate to think what would have happened to my life if you hadn't saved me from a life of crime.' He smiled grimly. 'I should have listened to you more often.'

They were quiet for a while, thinking of when they were kids. The lives they had imagined for themselves kept them close on the same track. Now they were irreconcilable.

'What about Jackson?' said Liam. 'Can he help you?'

Liam was the only person who knew how deeply her feelings for Jackson ran. If she started to tell him the truth about how things were between them now she knew that she would start to cry for real.

Jackson had called. She hadn't called him back. He wouldn't call again. That was his way.

'Have you heard of Aleksandr Lubin?' she said, to change the subject.

She told him about the peculiar Russian and their meeting, without revealing the simmering attraction there had been between them. It stopped her having to think of her insecure future. It wasn't until later that Liam referred back to that.

'You'll be okay though?' he said. 'It will all get sorted out?'

'Sure,' she said, with far more confidence than she felt. 'It'll all be fine.'

'Good.'

Around them people started to hug and cry and say goodbye as the morning session drew to a close.

'As long as you can still get me tickets if I'm out in time for the FA Cup final,' said Liam. 'That's the main thing.'

'Oh yes,' she said, with equal dryness. 'That's the main thing.'

Secreted in her basement office she could still hear the hammering at her front door above. She was lost in paperwork, the detritus of a glittering career. She was spending her first week off work in almost three years tending to the piles of A4 that had gathered in her home office, reading all the articles she had clipped but never found the time to read, filing all the notes she had never had time to file.

Buried in paper and numbers, with her phones turned obstinately to silent, she felt temporarily in control. If only she had been able to turn the front door to silent too.

Go away.

By the end of yesterday she had successfully convinced herself that this was one of the most valuable weeks she had ever had. Once the investigation into her finances had concluded that this mess was one enormous mistake, once Jackson had reinstated her, she should take a week off annually to do exactly the same thing. She was feeling organized and informed, and confident that when she returned to work her game would be sharper than ever.

In the corner of her desk was the gold-plated champagne bottle that she had been awarded a couple of years back by a prestigious champagne company as their Businesswoman of the Year. She kept it on her desk to remind her how marvellous she was. It might sound ridiculous, but sometimes, stuck on a deal point, arguing with a lawyer, or doubting words said in haste to a client, she needed to be reminded. This week she had looked at that gold-plated champagne bottle a great many times.

The insistent knocking at her front door continued.

It couldn't possibly be anyone she wanted to see. There was nobody. She willed her visitor to give up, but they kept on knocking, on and on, and eventually she caved. She climbed the stairs wearily and opened the creaking basement door, telling herself once again to oil the hinge. She glimpsed herself in the hall mirror and winced at the figure she saw there, dishevelled in shades of grey – skin, clothes and the shadows under her eyes.

She opened the front door reluctantly.

Leanne stood on her doorstep, obscured by a beautiful bouquet of pale silvery-lilac tea roses. 'You took your time,' she said. 'They're not from me. They came to the office, and they're playing havoc with my hay fever. Take them, will you? Can I come in?'

Samantha took the flowers and Leanne followed her inside. She had a feeling that she would have been unable to stop her even if she'd wanted to.

'Nice place,' she said. 'What's it worth?'

'I have no idea.'

'Course you do; you're just being discreet. I'd say a million two, that about right? I've been calling your mobile all morning.'

'It doesn't work in the basement. No signal.'

'Have you done your basement? Good one. That'll add a few grand.'

Leanne lingered in the kitchen while her boss read the card accompanying the flowers. 'Are they from the billionaire?' she asked.

Samantha handed her the card while she inhaled the sweet heady scent of them, a smell that turned her stomach and unsettled her mind.

'It's his father's money. He's not a billionaire,' she said.

'Not yet.'

To thank you, glasnost, *Alek.*

'I don't get it,' said Leanne.

'It's a private joke.'

'Roses *and* private jokes,' said Leanne. 'Is there something going on between you two? Something sexy? A little Eastern promise perhaps?'

'Alek's your age, not mine.'

'Then you should introduce me. Soon.' She nodded towards the flowers. 'They're gorgeous.'

'Coffee?' said Samantha, reaching for the canister of Madagascan beans.

'Much as I'd love to sit here and let my boss make me coffee – which would be a first by the way – I'd rather you told me what's going on. You've been fired?'

'What?' She dropped the canister to the floor and coffee beans rattled across the polished floorboards of the kitchen, falling into the cracks between them, and rolling into corners from which they would never be salvaged. *Fired?* 'Who told you that?' she demanded.

'Everybody. I just nod like a dickhead and say that I know and that I'm weighing up my options. Jackson has told me that there is a job for me if I want to stay.'

Jackson. She missed him.

'I haven't been fired.'

'Well, you know, "let go", whatever.' She made the quotes in the air with her fingers.

'I've been suspended, that's all.'

'Sounds bad.'

'Well, it isn't. I'll be back soon so Richard can just keep on walking by. Prick.' How dare he? 'I'll be back,' she said firmly.

Leanne shrugged.

'Is that really what people believe?' Samantha was crushed. 'What about the clients? Have any of the clients been told? Do they think I've been –' she pressed her eyes closed – 'fired?'

'No, I don't think so. Only a handful have called in. I put those calls through to Jackson.'

'Okay, on whose instructions?'

'Jackson's.'

'What about the Welstead boys?'

'Richard's taking care of them.'

'Okay.' This was bad. Suspension was appalling enough, but rumours about being fired? They would spread like honey around the busy bees of her profession. For all their bullish bravado, sports agents were terrible gossips; a juicy morsel could spread from Newcastle to Portsmouth before you could blow a whistle. So far there had been nothing in the newspapers, but perhaps they were biding their time. If Richard got his perfectly man-manicured fingernails into the Welstead brothers she would have a fight on her hands to get them back.

Think.

Damage control.

It was good of Leanne to come. 'I'm sorry,' said Samantha, 'this must have put you in a very awkward position.'

'I've been in worse positions,' said Leanne. 'Actually I haven't told you yet about the position I got into with that new Nigerian guy playing up front for Charlton Athletic. Talk about athletic . . .'

'Do you want to?'

'No, maybe later.' She leant over the roses and inhaled them, then promptly sneezed. 'What is it, Sam?' she said. 'What's happening?'

So she told her.

Her assistant sat and listened with disbelief as Samantha explained how Jackson and Carl had confronted her with the facts as they understood them.

'I can't work again until I'm in the clear, at least not

officially. I've closed the deal for Gabe Muswell' – she pointed at the flowers – 'but I don't really think anyone will care. It's such a small deal.'

Surely only in this beautiful game could a five-thousand-euro-a-week deal be considered small. But Gabe was happy, Christine ecstatic and Samantha content that she had wrung every drop of potential from Gabe's moment in the sun. To be frank, she was grateful for the distraction.

'I'm in pretty serious trouble,' she said.

'But it's ridiculous. You're so boring it's untrue,' said Leanne.

'Thanks.'

'Yeah, but you know what I mean. You're straight, square, ethical and stuff. Either you're a fantastic liar or you're the last person on earth who would be involved in something corrupt. I'm a good judge of character, ask anyone. Actually don't, I try to play it a little dumb some-times. Don't want you to blow my cover.'

'I'll put you down as a reference for court.'

Leanne paled. 'Court? Surely it won't go that far?'

'I hope not.'

'Maybe you'd better make me that coffee.'

Her assistant (ex-assistant?) went off to snoop around the living room while Samantha swept the coffee beans from the kitchen floor and started grinding some more. She glanced at the roses. She should call him, just to say thank you. The brief negotiations had been handled by a lawyer at his end and they hadn't spoken since the night they met. Sometimes, her thoughts drifted to him and she found herself remembering all sorts of odd things. His eyebrows almost met in the middle in a way that would normally have her reaching for the wax strips, but on him she found it alluring, the way he struggled to pronounce 'th' so 'that' became '*zat*' and her name was '*Samanza*' which made her sound like a different person.

The coffee machine steamed and hissed and she forgot about the Russian and his roses while she fixed their drinks.

Leanne knew absolutely nothing about Samantha outside work. She looked around the tasteful house, all minimalist and modern, giving away nothing about the person who lived here. She thought of her own small flat a few tube stops north in Tufnell Park, scattered with DVDs and half-read novels, the walls coated with art that shouted about her taste in music and her fondness for 1950s glamour. There was no personality in Sam's home.

'I thought you'd moved?' she said.

'Why?' said Samantha.

'A year or so ago,' she said. 'Didn't I spend a whole week ordering furniture and stuff for a house in Kentish Town? Sullivan Street, wasn't it?'

'That wasn't for me,' said Samantha. 'It was a sort of investment.'

'You've been renting it out?'

'Something like that, yeah.' Samantha waved the subject away with her hand. 'So what do you think?' she said. 'How long before I get my job back?'

'You reckon you've been set up?' said Leanne, while she toyed with the touch-screen remote that controlled the entertainment system.

'It seems unlikely. No, I think it's a mistake, a bureaucratic blunder, a sequence of coincidences,' said Samantha. 'Why? What do you think?'

'I think a high-profile woman like you might have made a few people angry over the years, I wouldn't rule anything out.'

'I suppose it's possible, though I can't imagine anyone who would want to discredit me.'

'You need to think about who stands to gain from your disgrace,' said Leanne. 'You need to think about your enemies.'

'I don't have any enemies.'

'Don't be naive, Sam. Everyone has enemies.'

'Do you?'

'There's a bunch of guys scattered around town who probably don't think too highly of me, plus there's a girl down at Chinawhite on a Thursday who despises me. She says I stole the love of her life,' said Leanne. 'I didn't steal him.' She laughed, a dirty throaty laugh that seemed out of place in Samantha's despair. 'I may have borrowed him for a short while, but I didn't steal him.'

They sipped their coffees.

'It's a mistake,' said Samantha firmly. They would find the S. Sharp who had 300K in CoralBanc and the mistake would be corrected. Then she could have her life back again.

'Thanks for coming over, Leanne,' she said, standing up and lifting her chin, fixing Leanne with a defiant stare that she didn't deserve.

She'd made it all the way to the top on her own. She didn't need anyone. Not even now.

12

At seventeen Samantha Sharp left her old life behind and moved to London, intent on making her fortune.

She packed everything she cared about into a small backpack, her fingers trembling with excitement. This was it – this was what she had been waiting for.

The face in the mirror was more beautiful than she realized. She saw unruly wavy hair that cost too much to control, boring brown eyes, and a thin face that needed sunshine and a square meal to look attractive. The beholder saw perfect pale skin, high cheekbones and romantic hair like a gypsy, dark eyes flashing with self-contained intelligence.

Life starts now.

'I'll be back in a few days,' she told her foster parents, a couple in their fifties who hadn't the slightest idea how to relate to this smart and independent young woman living in their box room.

'Call us when you get to your brother's,' they said.

And she did. She called them and told them that she would not be coming back.

'Liam thinks he can get me a job,' she told them, 'in the hotel where he works. I'm going to stay for the summer.' By the end of the summer she would be eighteen and she wouldn't have to tell anyone a thing.

She could hear the anxiety in her foster mother's voice and wondered how nervous she'd sound if she knew she was saying goodbye for the last time. They were probably less concerned about her welfare than they were about getting into trouble with social services for letting her go. But how hard would anyone search for a girl that nobody wanted? Nobody wanted, that is, except Liam.

'Liam will take care of me,' she said. 'We take care of each other.'

She'd done it. She'd really done it. She was free. She felt like dancing.

'You told them?' he said, waiting for her in the pub across the road from the phone box with two bottles of beer and a bag of peanuts. He lifted his glass to his little sister.

'To Samantha Sharp,' he said. 'May all her dreams come true.'

She was with Liam, in the greatest city in the world, and they had nobody to answer to but each other. She was already halfway there.

She fell for London quickly and passionately, a teenager with a crush, ignoring all the faults in the object of her desire and seeing only the good and the long, happy life they could have together.

One night, early in the relationship, she found herself in Soho as it was getting dark. She bought a bunch of grapes from a market stall at end-of-the-day prices and stood in the shadows on Berwick Street watching the traders pack up their fruit and veg, popping the sweet crimson grapes into her mouth one at a time. A man with a fluorescent orange jacket washed the street clean with a hose and the neon lights of Rupert Street reflected in the wet surface. Shops pulled down their shutters with a determined rattle and their staff locked up and said their goodbyes. The offices nearby spewed out their workforce relentlessly and the streets were crammed with thirsty media types, heading into bars in packs, picking up take-out as they headed for home, jabbering into mobile phones and generally not letting the pace of their lives slip even for a moment.

After a while it grew quiet, the last market trader pulled away in a white van, the last shop flicked out its lights and the last worker found a place to wind down for the evening. There was no traffic and a peaceful hush fell over this lively little corner of her new home town.

London. At last.

The kind of place where you could become whatever you wanted without anyone around to tell you no, to tell you to be realistic, to think smaller. And though she had no idea exactly what it was that she wanted to be, she sensed that here she would discover herself.

'I love you,' she whispered.

An unshaven man carrying his worldly goods in a pink holdall he had found dumped at Victoria Station heard her as he made himself comfortable in a shop doorway. 'Thanks, darling, I love you too. Spare any change?'

She found her way with nothing more than her small backpack and a copy of the Carnegie book, *How to Win Friends and Influence People.*

His rule number one: don't criticize, condemn or complain.

For the first time in her life she had nothing to complain about. She was in London, with Liam, and the rest of her life stretched tantalizingly ahead. She would get a job, she would save her money, she would buy her own house and then she would be happy.

She knew everything there was to know – she was seventeen, an adult – and foremost among these things she knew was the value of money. She was sick of being a 'have not' surrounded by irritating 'haves' who never missed an opportunity to rub her face in their good fortune. Whether it was the girls at school with their expensive haircuts and active social lives, or the woman at the pub where she worked who always complained about ridiculous things, like her husband not having enough annual leave to go on all the holidays they wanted to take. She didn't know how she was going to do it, but she was determined to have enough money to feel comfortable, to get a professional haircut without worrying that the same amount of money could feed a family for a week, to take a holiday somewhere other than a Haven holiday park, to live a little, to live a *lot*.

Liam worked at a busy hotel popular with middle management and the middle classes, the Royal Victoria, a seething mass of cheap labour with a constant turnover of personnel. Until he found her a job there she stayed on his sofa in his tiny flat in Camberwell and cleaned and cooked for him in lieu of rent.

'Anything?' she asked, eating vegetable curry for the third time that week, the end-of-the-day vegetables from East Street market and the spices from a little shop she had found off the Walworth Road. A full belly for barely more than the cost of a first-class stamp. They spent more on the beer to wash it down. And if there ever came a day when it was a choice between food and drink they would both take drink. When you had enough to drink you could forget that you were hungry.

You could forget everything.

'Not yet,' he said, reaching for second helpings because he'd skipped lunch. 'But there's a rumour that one of the chambermaids is about to be fired for offering "special services". Something will turn up.'

Everything was so expensive here. They stretched the little they had as far as it would go. Liam scavenged what food he could from the hotel kitchens and they would get a buzz on at home before taking the bus into the West End around chucking-out time so they could laugh at people piling out bleary eyed onto the street, diving onto tables of half-finished drinks and polishing them off. They drank a lot. But they were young; they could get away with it. They still thought that they would live for ever.

Sometimes, before he clocked off for the night, Liam would take her for a spin around Chelsea in one of the hotel cars.

He was in the driving pool, which meant a lot of waiting around for not much money. But, as a special treat sometimes, instead of driving impatient hotel guests to appointments he would drive his giggling little sister up and down the King's Road until one or both of them had had enough. Usually him. She could never have enough of these streets, of this city.

She liked to watch Sloane Rangers striding into Oriel in their beautiful clothes, their high heels tapping past a tramp and his dog without even glancing down. She laughed at the Japanese tourists who liked to stop dead in the middle of the pavement gazing forlornly at a fold-out street map while men in grey suits swerved around them with sour faces as if the fraction of a second this curve added to their commute was a fraction of a second too long. She liked it best when their late-night drives coincided with the end of a play, either at the Royal Court Theatre or sometimes the Palace, and the way the empty road suddenly filled up with smartly dressed culture vultures picking over every black cab, or tourists trailing around the corner like sheep to take the coaches back to middle England, back to the kind of place she had left behind for good.

By her eighteenth birthday she had a steady job as a chambermaid at the Royal Victoria. She learnt how to clean a room in five minutes flat so that she could spend the rest of the allocated fifteen minutes lying on the bed reading the guests' magazines, browsing through their wardrobes, or testing the lotions and potions left in the bathroom. She liked to pretend, even if just for ten minutes, that she was someone else, someone better.

She learnt how to steal food from the room-service tray before it got to the room rather than waiting for the leftovers. What to steal from which mini-bars that would go onto a guest's bill unnoticed. Always the corporate clients, never the holidaymakers. Holidaymakers checked their bills meticulously; businessmen generally didn't give a shit. She learnt how to increase her chances of a big tip from any long-term male guest by making sure that she met them, preferably when they were only partially clothed so that she could blush and avert her eyes and make sure they developed a little crush on her.

And of course she called them 'sir' whenever she could. Little things, but they all added up.

Gradually she became more dishonest. She learnt when to take a fiver here, a few coins there, a twenty if she thought there was little risk. If someone had had too big a night to remember. She could always tell if a guest had been drunk the night before, an opened blister pack of painkillers by the sink, the tell-tale disarray of a frantic over-sleeper. If there was a used condom in the bin or lipstick on the rim of a glass she knew there was someone else who could be blamed if a twenty-pound note was missed.

She got so drunk on her eighteenth birthday that she split her lip falling down the stairs at Leicester Square tube station. At the time she thought it was hilarious. Even as her mouth puffed up she was laughing.

'It's all your fault,' she said.

Liam assumed a look of mock outrage. 'My fault? Why?'

'If you hadn't scored that speed I'd have stopped drinking hours ago.'

'No you wouldn't,' he said. 'But you might be unconscious by now. Here, try rubbing some speed into that cut.'

'Why?'

'Just to see what happens.'

She laughed some more and dipped her finger into the little bag of white powder, yellowing and damp in places, which made her think it had been cut with some kind of bathroom cleaner. She touched her powdery finger onto her sore lip. 'It'll make it go numb,' she said.

'That's a good thing, right?'

The first pub they tried wouldn't even let them through the door.

'But 'smy birthday,' she pleaded with the tuxedo on the door. 'My eighteenth.'

'Maybe you should think about taking your girlfriend home, eh?' he said to Liam, not unkindly.

'She's not my girlfriend, she's my little sister,' said Liam.

'We take care of each other,' said Samantha, still hoping they might get past the bouncers.

'Not very well by the looks of it.'

'What's that supposed to mean?' said Liam, the alcohol and the speed making him belligerent, totally unaware that he was slurring his words and swaying from side to side.

'She's had a skinful, mate,' said the bouncer. 'If you weren't holding on to each other you'd be crawling on the floor by now.'

'I'm not your mate,' said Liam.

'Please?' said Samantha, smiling in a way that she thought was sexy but looked grotesque, her lip bleeding and make-up smeared across her face.

She wanted to get into the pub and up to the bar. They could have another drink if only they could get inside. They still had some money left and even then she could tell people it was her eighteenth birthday, which had worked wonders in the last place.

Where was that again?

'Not a chance, sweetheart,' said the bouncer, nodding through the people behind them.

'She's not your sweetheart,' said Liam. 'You fucking people are all the same, bunch of power-crazy Nazis. What happened? Fail the police entrance exam, did you? Get chucked out the army for being a lardarse? Well?'

Suddenly the pavement dropped away from under his feet and he found himself moving backwards into the wall. The bouncer had picked him up by both shoulders. His back slammed into the damp brick and he struggled to get loose.

'One more word, *mate*, and you and little sis here will be singing happy birthday down the police station. All right? You got that? It's time to go home.'

In the end they walked to Primrose Hill.

'Should have had champagne,' said Liam. 'How's your lip?'

'It's okay,' she said.

London stretched in front of them as far as she could see. The Post Office Tower, Centre Point and in the distance the floodlit dome of St Paul's Cathedral, and the blazing lights of the Square Mile office buildings, and everywhere the rooftops of eight million people that called this city home. The light atop the brand-new Canary Wharf development winked at her.

'I love you, Sammy,' said her brother.

'I love you too.'

Neither of them noticed that it was cold, and that the bench where they sat was covered with the lightest dusting of frost. They were too wasted to feel much of anything.

'I used to dream of living in London,' she said.

'Nothing to it,' said her brother.

Somewhere beneath the long night she could feel a trace of disappointment. If this was her dream come true then why were tears always close to the surface? Not just today, but practically all the time.

Perhaps she was just born to be unhappy. Some people were lucky and some were not.

He reached for her hand. 'Have you had a good birthday?'

'The best,' she said. And she meant it. Not that she had much to compare it to. Past birthdays had involved curfews and, except for that handful of happy years in Nottingham, the company of strangers.

'Let's get a tattoo,' she said impulsively.

'Excellent idea,' said Liam. 'What'll we get?'

They went back into Camden where they found a late-night tattoo parlour doing reasonable business and while they waited they browsed designs. She thought she was looking for a heart and dagger, something raw and dramatic, at the very least a Chinese character meaning strength or fighter or something tough. Liam pointed out a jet black Celtic symbol meaning 'fraternity' and suggested that they both have the same. She loved the sentiment and agreed, but her eye kept getting drawn back to a small pretty picture of a bluebird and no matter how hard she tried to like the stark Celtic symbol she felt the bluebird was singing to her.

'I'm getting that,' she said, pointing.

He looked at it in surprise. 'Really? But I thought we'd get the same.'

She shrugged. 'So get a bluebird.'

'Okay.'

She went first in the tattooist's chair. It looked like an old dentist's chair and was stained with all the colours as if a rainbow had exploded there. The ink was drilled into the yielding patch of soft flesh on her back just inside the shoulder. A clear cerulean blue, the colour of a sunny sky. The punching motion of the needle wasn't unbearable, but it made her wince. Liam was quick to notice.

'Bite down on this,' he said, offering her an empty cigarette packet. She put the cardboard between her teeth and tasted fresh tobacco, bitter and bracing. Lyrics from *The Wizard of Oz* played in an endless loop in her head, Judy Garland's distinctive voice keeping her company as the grinding pain of the needle went on and on.

When they walked out again the sun was rising. A greasy-spoon café nearby was crammed with late-night people filling up on alcohol-absorbing carbs before going to bed with the dawn. They bought two fried egg sandwiches to take away and munched contentedly as they waited for the tube trains to start running.

'Are you happy, Liam?' she said.

'Yeah, I think it looks cool.'

'I didn't mean the tattoo. I meant everything.'

'Everything?'

'You know, life.'

'Oh, that. Yeah, I suppose. What more do you want?'

The cool air and the dull pain from her shoulder had sobered her completely and she knew that if she was to be happy, a truly happy little bluebird, she would need to do more than merely change strangers' sheets and steal petty amounts of cash from their wallets. She was eighteen now. She was a grown-up.

It was time to change.

The bluebird on her shoulder would sing to her for the rest of her life.

13

One of the many things Gabe Muswell had always liked about his wife was that she coped well with change. She packed away her dreams of Milan or Madrid just as easily as she had buried the dreams they'd had long ago of a family. She had shelved her continental fantasies and replaced them with visions of edgy Eastern Europe cool. After all, Krakow was the new Prague – that's what everyone was saying.

Thanks to Samantha's latest killer deal, Gabe would now be earning in a week a sum equal to their annual mortgage repayments. Not bad for a baker's son.

He knew his wife thought he was obsessed with football, and that she'd previously blamed this obsession for holding them back. She thought that devoting two evenings a week and every single Saturday to something which in her eyes amounted to little more than a hobby was too much, and it was time and energy that could be better spent elsewhere.

Now he didn't know what she thought at all.

This was a new start for them. They needed it. Badly.

Walking into their temporary new home at Hotel Copernicus made him feel like a rock star.

'Do you like it?' he asked.

She paused, and for one frightening moment he thought she would complain. Then she gave a little jump of delight.

'I love it!' she squealed. She sounded more like a twenty-year-old disco chick than a thirty-four-year-old wife.

Then as well as sounding like an overexcited twenty-something she started acting like one too.

She pushed her husband back onto the bed, straddled his waist and began popping open the buttons on his shirt.

'Hotel rooms make me feel sexy,' she said.

They had shared countless hotel rooms over their fourteen years together. As far as he could remember there had never been one that made her act like this. But he wasn't about to contradict her.

So far he liked being a professional footballer.

A lot.

After they had christened the room he lay back on the bed and watched his wife walk naked around the room admiring everything she saw. The old-fashioned decor was offset with every modern convenience, a giant plasma in the bedroom, a tiny one in the deluxe bathroom. The antique bed was piled high with heavy white cotton and delicately patterned silk. The view from the window, of a gothic church and adjoining convent garden, was like something from a classic fairytale. He liked to see her happy. She still had a cracking figure, a bum she moaned about but he loved and tits she liked as much as he did.

'Come here,' he said, and she flopped onto the bed beside him. 'I've got an idea.'

'What?' Something shone in her eyes. Love? He hadn't seen that for a while.

'We're pretty good at that, aren't we?' He raised his eyebrows. Sex with his wife was still horny, but infrequent. 'I think, in Krakow, every day.'

'Every day?'

'Every day,' he confirmed.

'What if we do it twice?'

He rolled on top of her and started trailing kisses over her collarbone the way he knew she liked him to. 'Let's call that extra time.' For an instant he regretted using the football metaphor, but then she started to respond beneath him and he realized that football references were one more thing his wife wouldn't complain about any more.

Thank you, Samantha Sharp.

The next day he was due at the White Stars training ground at 10 a.m. He decided to walk even though fresh snow had fallen overnight and the chill in the air was not so much bracing as numbing. Within fifteen minutes he could no longer feel his toes and his unsuitable canvas trainers were damp and cold. He picked up his walking pace to a jog, fearful of turning up to his first day's training with ice blocks for feet. He ran through the snowy park, hardly noticing the quaint street lights or the impressive statues that dotted the path here and there. He was alarmed by a pull in his chest after only a few hundred yards.

He wasn't out of shape, surely?

Okay, the last month or so had seen less in the way of sport and more in the way of stardom, but still he had been out running whenever he'd had a chance, and training with St Ashton regularly.

A few more yards and he realized it was the cold, biting down into his lungs, a dry kind of cold, wholly different to the soggy winters of England. Far more disturbing though was the way the cold was nipping at parts of his body he had never even considered. His bum was going numb beneath his short jacket, and the chill was creeping down the open neck and up the sleeves. Only when a third person stopped and stared at him did he realize that this morning he was the only bare-headed, barehanded, bare-necked person on the street. Everybody else was trussed up like they were going skiing.

And didn't they look nice and warm too.

Eventually he made it to the stadium on the eastern side of the city, found the correct entrance and walked into his first day on the job as a pro.

The dressing room was practically empty. A handful of players looked up briefly when he arrived but didn't bother to give him a second glance. He noticed that they were wearing long sweat pants and undershirts, most of them had fingerless gloves.

He admitted to himself that he had been expecting more of a welcome. He didn't need 'Welcome to Poland' banners exactly, but a little acknowledgement would have been nice. He was Gabe Muswell – last week in England he had been a hero, and last night his wife had screwed him like they were on their honeymoon all over again, but now he felt quite unsure of himself, not unlike being the new kid at school.

He stripped to his shorts and training top, prepared to show them how they did things in England. So it was brisk out there. So what? A few laps, a kick-about, he'd soon work up a sweat. One of the other players said something in Polish and made the rest of the room laugh. He tried to fight the paranoid feeling that they were laughing at him.

He packed his outdoor clothes away quickly, not wanting to be last out onto the pitch. The truth was he wasn't quite sure which way he was supposed to go.

Standing by the goal the rest of the squad watched him walk out.

His eyes took in his new team mates and it took him a moment to realize what was wrong with the picture. Apart from the two young lads that were loaded down with nets full of footballs, every last man was smoking a cigarette. Now there's something you didn't see in England. He felt a pang, his first in months, for a puff. So he could fit in. Instinctively he did as he had always done during the early days of being a non-smoker: he filled his lungs with fresh air and thought of them working for him. He was a professional sportsman, an athlete, a champion. He wasn't the new boy at school. He had scored a hat-trick in the FA Cup – that was impressive enough; he didn't need a cigarette to feel like he belonged here.

In the end he moved away from the group and started some warm-up stretches on his own. He wasn't here to make friends; he was here to play football.

The training session was hell on his unpolluted lungs. Annoyingly the others seemed to take it in their powerful stride. It was the cold. It would take some getting used to. The pace of the training was no tougher than at his little club back home, but the searing air was merciless. There were forty minutes of drills and then a kick-about. He wanted to impress, but he would have to be satisfied with not embarrassing himself.

The ground underneath his feet was frozen solid. Obviously they had yet to install under-surface heating. He was terrified of falling over on the unforgiving earth and hurting himself, breaking a leg or something – his professional career over at the very first training session. But he didn't fall. He didn't score either, but he felt that despite the conditions he had performed pretty well for his first run out. At least he hadn't made any howling errors.

Afterwards he hit the showers. He listened to the indecipherable snatches of Polish and wondered if he'd ever get to grips with the language. Samantha had made it pretty clear that he should try. He wasn't looking forward to it, but as he looked at the training schedule he could only hope that he was translating it correctly and a few lessons would make sense. After all, when he scored three goals on his debut he should know how to count them. The thought cheered him and he was just about to leave and make his way back to the hotel when the door of the changing room flew open and the imposing presence of Aleksandr Lubin walked in.

'Where is the new boy?' he shouted, and with a few deferential grunts the men between Gabe and his new boss fell away.

He felt suddenly, inexplicably, that he should bow.

It was a ridiculous compulsion. The kid might be his boss, but he was still unquestionably a kid. Gabe had Saturday staff working for him at the supermarket with more maturity. *Used to*, he reminded himself. That wasn't his life any more. This was his life, fresh from the shower after his first pro training session, his bare torso still drip-ping with water, meeting his new boss for the first time. Aleksandr had a powerful presence, sure, but Gabe was determined not to bow to it.

'Gabe Muswell!' Aleksandr declared, clasping Gabe's hand in a double-handed shake, then clapping an arm round his shoulder. 'We meet at last. Come, finish dressing, I want us to have lunch. Everything has been okay today? Some-body was here to greet you and to show you around?'

'Actually, no, but I managed.'

Lubin's face clouded over and he rattled off a harsh burst of Polish to one of his staff. '*Peshka*,' he growled, and the unfortunate subject of his wrath cowered under the attack.

He turned back to Gabe. 'That is regrettable,' he said. 'I apologize. I intended to meet you myself, but circum-stances were against me. Ice on the runway, you know? However, I did send someone in my place.'

Gabe started to say that it was no problem but was cut off.

More brisk Polish followed as Lubin conducted two conversations at once. One with Gabe, friendly and cas-ual, and one with the unfortunate Pole whom he realized was in the process of being fired. He tried to intervene.

'Perhaps I went to the wrong entrance – forget about it. I didn't expect special treatment.'

But the lambasting continued until with a final grandiose sweep of his hand Lubin turned sharply back to Gabe.

'So, lunch?' he asked as the man he had just fired slunk off with his bag over his shoulder, his shoelaces still undone.

Several of the team glared at them as they walked out. He held his firm jaw high and reminded himself yet again that he wasn't here to make friends. He was here to play football. He had been given one last chance at something he had wanted for as long as he could remember, a dream that he had resigned himself to never achieving.

If he wanted to be best mates with the man that was making it happen then sod the dirty looks.

Lunch was served in the executive box with a commanding view of the stadium. In contrast to the awkward wooden seats and bare concrete stands in obvious need of an overhaul the executive box was a no-expense-spared slice of luxury, complete with cushioned leather seating and ornate fixtures perhaps better suited to a box at the opera than a sporting arena.

'So, you must have been very happy to secure a professional contract,' said Lubin as they ate perfectly cooked pasta washed down with chilled white wine. Apart from the unbelievably small wine glasses the food and drink were faultless, as good as any he'd ever had in England, or for that matter on his honeymoon in Italy.

'But perhaps a little confused?' Lubin smiled thinly. Not a good smile. 'It is unusual, a player of your age?'

The truth was that he hadn't actually given it much thought. Obviously White Stars had signed him because he had scored a hat-trick in the FA Cup, one of which was a world-class goal. Wasn't that so? Saying any of this would make him seem arrogant, and though he suspected that arrogance might be a trait the Russian admired, he instead murmured something about being grateful for the opportunity and then despised himself for being a pussy.

'I think English football is the best in the world,' said Lubin.

You and everyone else, mate. It had long been said that despite the inflated salaries of the Italian game, the inflated egos of the Spanish and the flair of the French, the English game was something special.

'And you are here as their ambassador. I would like you to counsel me on why my team do not have passion. You will play with them for a while; you will be able to tell me, no?'

'I, uh . . .' He could hardly refuse. But it was surely a psychological question? A cultural difference, nothing that could be easily defined, let alone taught. He was neither a psychologist nor a coach, and no expert. He kicked balls at goals – that's what he did. But he thought it prudent to assure Mr Lubin, his new boss, that he would do whatever he could to bring a little English spirit to the Polish game.

'Good,' said Lubin. 'And what are your first impressions? Is it very different from what you are used to?'

Apparently his counsel would start immediately.

He searched for anything worthwhile he could say. 'Smoking before training wouldn't fly well with any English manager, I'll tell you that much.'

'Interesting,' said Lubin.

'I used to smoke twenty a day,' he said, largely to distract his host from asking anything further. 'I was stuck in goal for fifteen years, then I quit, got fit. The coach tried me up front more for a laugh than anything else, and suddenly I'm a striker. Scored my first match goal at the age of thirty-two. Makes you wonder what I might have done if I'd found that form at twenty-one, doesn't it?'

'Then perhaps you would not be here, Gabe,' said Lubin, 'and we are very glad to have you.'

Lubin changed the subject and started talking about Krakow, Gabe's new home, recommending places with complicated names that he would never remember. He told him where he could eat and drink, where his wife could shop, where he could buy a car. 'You like cars?' he said.

'Well enough.' He was hardly about to tell a man who had a football club as a hobby that he drove a Ford Mondeo. 'I like motorbikes,' he said. 'When I was a kid I loved my Triumph Bonneville.'

'I have a bike,' said Lubin. 'Come, I will show you it, my cars too.'

Cars plural?

Underneath the stadium there was parking space for a dozen cars. Four of the spaces were occupied with the kind of luxury vehicles that Gabe lusted over on television. The rest of the spaces were empty. The cars gleamed like treasure in the dimly lit garage. A silver Bentley Continental GT, a Ferrari 550 Maranello and, almost as an afterthought, a TVR Cerbera. There was also a Ducati Testastretta superbike with tyres that looked as pristine as the sole of an unworn shoe. Those tyres must have been gagging for the open road.

Gabe's shoulders twitched to ride that bike, to feel the powerful engine between his legs, to control a machine of such force, to feel the ground zipping past his knees on tight bends, to feel free.

There and then he decided to get another bike. Christine wouldn't like it, but maybe given her newfound adoration he was willing to bet that she wouldn't complain.

A wiry-looking kid was polishing up the bonnet on the Bentley. One of his team mates, a nippy little striker who, if he remembered rightly, was called Josef.

Lubin said something to him in Polish and the kid finished up quickly and disappeared.

He couldn't be much more than sixteen. What kind of wages must that kid be on if he cleaned the boss's car for extras?

Cars, plural.

Lubin seemed to be waiting for Gabe to comment, but he had no idea what to say. How do you comment on what must be a million pounds' worth of machinery?

'Impressive,' he said eventually, in the fraction of a second before the silence became uncomfortable. Why was Lubin trying to impress him? 'Do you have a favourite?'

Lubin laughed and clapped his arm round Gabe's shoulders. 'That's like asking if I have a favourite child,' he said.

It really isn't.

He laughed anyway and let his new boss talk him through some of the features on the Ferrari, the custom-designed interior of the Bentley and about the Porsche he had back home in Russia.

'Talk to me about Samantha Sharp,' said Lubin.

'About Sam? Why? What do you want to know?'

'She is very highly regarded?' said Lubin. 'For a woman, I mean.'

'For anyone,' he said, because Gabe had been brought up by a strong mother who would never forgive him for

128

letting such a statement pass uncorrected. 'But I really don't know her very well.'

'Extremely fuckable,' said the Russian, flicking a tiny speck of dust off the bonnet of his TVR.

'I, er, I suppose so, yes.'

'There is no suppose,' said Lubin. 'That mouth, those legs.' He laughed. 'And everything in between. You and her, you have never . . . ?'

'I'm married,' said Gabe. What was he meant to say? Of course Sam was fuckable, she was bloody gorgeous, but she was also a class act, not some trollop barfly out on the pull.

'That's not an answer,' said Lubin. 'Maybe you have something to hide?'

Gabe stuttered. He wasn't sure he liked where this conversation was heading. Then the Russian laughed abruptly and patted Gabe's shoulder.

'I am joking,' he said.

'Right,' said Gabe, forcing out a sour chuckle. 'Good one.'

'A woman like Samantha Sharp would need more of a man than you.'

Gabe waited for Lubin to say that he was joking again, but he did not. Rankled, Gabe looked for a way to tie up the meeting, eventually using the excuse that he was meeting his wife. *Like a good husband.* He wished that he had been able to come up with something that sounded a little tougher, but it was too late.

He relaxed the moment they said goodbye.

He left the stadium with his cold hands tucked deep in his pockets. Would he ever make enough money to be able to afford cars like that, and, even if he did, is that what he would spend it on? After the bike, what next? He couldn't imagine going home to Christine and telling her that he'd just bought a car worth more than their house. Perhaps if he said it was a gift for her? No, then she'd probably guess what he was trying to pull and punish him by never letting him drive it.

But it was good to dream.

Nothing that ostentatious then, but still a luxury, a Merc maybe, a BMW even. They weren't far from Germany – maybe he was well placed to get a bargain.

So lost was he in thoughts of the car he would buy if his wife would allow him to that he didn't notice the two young men that had approached him in the deserted street.

One of them started talking to him in Polish, at least he thought it was Polish – it could have been anything as far as he was able to tell – while a second one pushed a map at him, quite forcibly.

'I don't understand, mate,' he said. 'English? I'm English.'

It didn't make any difference. The two men continued to jabber at him, stabbing their fingers into the map.

'No *comprenez*,' he said, starting to get irritated. 'No savvy, you get me?'

Then he tried to walk away and felt his first flash of fear when one of the men, his face cold and unsmiling, grabbed his wrist and stopped him.

'Hey, watch it,' said Gabe.

Suddenly the atmosphere turned dark. He sensed he was in danger, and assessed the threat. Two of them, one of him, but because of the way they were positioned he couldn't make a run for it.

Shit. This could be trouble. My legs, don't go for my legs. Wouldn't that just be too unlucky? The chance of a lifetime, a professional football contract, wasted because of a smashed fibula.

Then out of the blue stormed Josef, the little car valet, brandishing what looked like a – could it be? – a baseball bat, and hollering in Polish, a thundering voice coming out of his small frame, his sleeves pushed up to reveal surprisingly powerful biceps, blue eyes flashing an icy warning.

Josef grabbed the arm of the one holding Gabe's wrist, twisting it so that Gabe was immediately released.

Josef shouted first at one assailant and then the other.

Gabe, who knew perfectly well that this kid was on his side, was scared, so could only imagine what the two little scam artists thought of the sudden ambush by this angry young man. They shrunk under his wrath, exchanged glances and scarpered, running off round the corner at speed, shouting insults as they left, but leaving all the same.

Gabe tried to thank his rescuer in awkward English.

'Thank you,' he said. 'They surprised me. They appeared from nowhere, whoosh!' His heart was racing. 'It's Josef, isn't it? I'm Gabe.' He patted his chest. 'Gabe.'

'I know who you are, mate,' said his junior saviour. 'Loving those goals against Spurs, nice one. Josef Wandrowszcki. But you can call me Joe, yeah?'

'You're English?'

Joe flashed an open and easy smile. 'And they say all footballers are thick.'

14

Samantha stiffened when the knock on her front door came again in the middle of the day.

One thirty, bang on time.

She could ignore it. She wanted to ignore it, but from experience she knew that ignoring it wouldn't make it go away. Last week it had shouted through the letterbox until she opened the door. She dropped the sample contract she had been only half reading, ostensibly brushing up on the finer points of licensing image copyright and loyalty bonuses, and walked resignedly to the door to let in Leanne.

Without these daily visits the only person she would see was the guy who sold her daily coffee and her reflection in the mirror. It occurred to her that this was quite unhealthy, but until she was allowed to return to work she had no intention of doing anything other than waiting.

For how long?

As long as it takes.

Her bare feet tingled on the cold wooden floor in the hallway. One good thing about this enforced leave of absence: it gave her a break from heels. And that was really the only good thing. If she stopped to think about it she even missed the heels. Mostly though – to her dismay – she missed Jackson.

She would forgive him. All she wanted was her job

back, and until that happened she wouldn't be speaking to him again. Mistakes were made, she knew that better than anyone, made and corrected. She wouldn't hold a grudge. But she must be absolved. And when this mess was cleared up she would be back at her desk within an hour working as hard as she ever had.

I miss my life.

Her current occupations were a poor substitute. Keeping the boredom at bay by reviewing old paperwork, and having a lunchtime conference with her assistant, who would probably get into trouble if anyone at Legends knew she was there. Surely there must be rules about consorting with the recently disgraced.

She opened the door without even saying hello.

Leanne was happy to get into the habit of dropping in on Samantha during her lunch hour. It meant that she didn't get back to the office until gone three o'clock but nobody noticed. Lately she spent most of her days bidding for vintage clothes on eBay. Nobody noticed that either. To her horror she found that she was a teeny bit bored.

'Any idea when you'll be back?' she asked casually, passing over the same Marks & Spencer sandwich she had brought Samantha for years. Everything was in a state of flux, but the lunch order remained the same.

'Soon,' said Samantha. 'Surely it'll have to be soon.' She picked the bacon out of her BLT, and nibbled at the edges. Being away from work was like an illness, sapping her strength, killing her appetite. Every day that went by she felt herself being cast further adrift. It was as if she was walking around with an enormous question mark over her head, one that would remain over her trustworthiness until she was cleared. And even then a trace of the question mark might haunt her for years to come.

But the next day everything changed. Instead of lunch, Leanne came bearing a newspaper, a yellow Post-it note marking a story. 'I have to show you something,' she said.

Samantha lifted her head, only mildly interested, expecting a bit of gossip about some WAG or another. But when she saw Leanne's ashen expression and the way her hand trembled when she passed the newspaper over her stomach lunged with a dreadful sense of foreboding.

Leanne hung back, afraid that Samantha might kill the messenger. But Samantha was too busy staring at her own picture in the newspaper and seeing her career flash before her eyes, as life does in moments near death.

She scanned the article frantically and with each damning word her hopes for a simple conclusion to her current circumstances plummeted. Next to her picture ran an overstated self-righteous piece about the latest scandal to sour the flamboyant world of high-end football transfers. It detailed Samantha Sharp's career, from her improbable rise to her latest coup, the multi-million-pound deal for the two Welstead boys. The article practically made her a poster girl for everything that was wrong with the game. Money ruined football, that was the common consensus, and Samantha Sharp was all about the money.

Leanne watched anxiously, knowing the adage about all publicity being good publicity was just plain wrong.

Samantha closed her eyes. But when she opened them again the offending article was still there. 'Has Jackson seen it?'

'I assume so,' said Leanne. 'I thought you'd want to know.'

'I do,' she said. 'Thank you.' How ridiculous, thanking someone for bringing this small time-bomb into the Belsize Park living room, all done up in calming beige and mushroom tones, high-maintenance white upholstery, low-maintenance bamboo floors. Now splattered with scandal.

'How did they find out?' she murmured. The media destroyed people every day. They could destroy her too.

'I couldn't say,' said Leanne. 'But you don't know how three hundred thousand dollars found its way into your life either.'

'It's all the same person,' said Samantha faintly. It had to be. It would seem she had enemies after all.

The last vestiges of denial were blown away. This was no mistake. Somebody had leaked this story to the press. Somebody had planted the vicious sum of money in CoralBanc that threatened to dismantle the life she had so painstakingly constructed.

She had tried to be good. To play fair. Other agents would ride roughshod over anyone in pursuit of their goals, but not Samantha. She went out of her way to ensure that she didn't antagonize people as she climbed to the top. So she was well liked in her business, but evidently not by all. By someone, she was hated. And if it wasn't someone in the business, then who? Something personal? Impossible, she had no personal life. There was no skeleton of a significant ex or a betrayed spouse lurking at the back of her closet. Liam was the only family she had. Leanne her only friend. But she knew in her gut that somebody had her in their sights. She felt hunted. She felt like checking her doors and windows even though rationally she knew that they were already locked.

She closed her lips and eyes tight. It looked as if she was trying not to cry, but really she was trying not to scream.

She had been so stupid believing that her innocence would be enough to save her. She should have known better than that. It wasn't enough to be blameless. The world just didn't balance so fairly, and especially not when someone was tipping the game wildly against her.

Who was doing this? How do you fight an enemy you cannot see? How do you make them stop?

'They called the office,' said Leanne gently. 'A journalist asking lots of questions about your past, about your family.'

Her head snapped up. 'What did you tell them?'

'Nothing. I didn't tell them anything; I don't know anything about your family.'

'I don't have a family,' said Samantha.

She swallowed down the bitter bile that rose in her throat. The tabloids would go into a feeding frenzy if they found out about her brother. She told herself that she was protecting Liam, admitted to herself that she was protecting them both, but knew deep down she was keeping him secret for the sake of her reputation. What little reputation she had left to salvage.

An unstoppable wave of nausea overcame her and Samantha darted to the bathroom to unload her anger and her guilt.

After she had thrown up she stared at her own pasty reflection in the bevelled-edge mirror and watched the tears well in her bewildered eyes. Her neck and shoulders were taut with anxiety and she rubbed them with her fingers, trying hard to think of how she could pull this back from the edge.

Is this the end of me? It wasn't fair. Hadn't she had enough to fight against? A shitty childhood, a brother in jail, a tangled love life, chauvinist pigs in every meeting she took looking at her like she had no right to be in the same room. Yet, despite this, and sometimes she thought because of it, she had made a name for herself. She had never done anything to deserve such malice. No, it wasn't fair. She was a stranger to self-pity, but now its insidious ache clawed at her and shook her strong foundations.

Beneath her fingertips her bluebird tattoo reminded her of those hopeful days when all she wanted was success. She had been so close. She wasn't ready for it to be over. Her career meant everything to her. Instead of being the success she had always dreamt of she would be nothing.

Once more.

She pulled down a long cool breath and held it there, closing her eyes, determined not to open them again until they were dry. It was her mother's voice she heard. Telling her that crying was for babies, threatening to lock her in the bathroom. Laughing and calling her stupid.

Leanne smiled hopefully when Samantha walked back into the room. 'You okay?'

She nodded hesitantly, hating herself for feeling unsure.

'Look, the way I see it,' Leanne ventured, 'you play at the top, don't you? You, Jackson, Richard, a couple of others, you're like the Premiership of sports agents. When you play at that level then the setbacks are more extreme; it comes with the territory.'

'So I should expect to get screwed?'

'When I have a big drama at work you know what I ask myself?' said Leanne.

'No, what?'

'What would Samantha do?'

That was funny. Trust Leanne to make her see the chink of light at the end of this particular tunnel.

'So?' said Leanne. 'What would you do?'

'I'd stop acting like a woman and start thinking like a man.' Instead of crying she should be working. Instead of cogitating about who was firing the bullets, she should be stemming the flow of blood.

Damage control.

'Come on,' she said to Leanne briskly, hustling her out of the living room and downstairs to the basement office. 'Pretend you're my assistant. I know it's a stretch, but try it.'

There was a familiar fire in her eye, the kind of look she got whenever they were frantic, whenever there was a deal to be done It was a spark of her killer instinct once more.

'Get the Welsteads on the phone for me. I have to give them the impression that it's business as usual.'

Monty and Ferris were the jewels on her client list, the one relationship she must protect before all others.

Leanne called the Welstead boys, but there was no reply.

'Mobiles?' said Samantha.

'I've tried both of them, and the Fulham apartment too.'

Pinpricks of fear travelled up and down her spine. 'Try Yorkshire,' said Samantha, 'try their home.'

At last they made contact. Not with the boys, but with their father.

'Mr Welstead? Hi, it's Leanne at Legends. I have Samantha for you. I'll put you through.'

Leanne maintained the charade of business as usual by holding the phone for a few seconds before passing it to Samantha, like they were both in the office and not crammed into this windowless room pretending everything was fine.

Samantha's sense of dread grew sharper still as she listened to what he had to say.

He told her perfectly nicely that, yes, he had seen the piece in the paper, but Richard Tavistock had explained the situation to him some time ago, so it wasn't a shock and he hoped that everything would be sorted out soon. Until then he was happy to let Jackson and Richard pick up any slack (that was the word he used, 'slack') and, no, as far as he was aware the boys didn't have any concerns they needed to discuss with her.

'Because you understand I'm here for you one hundred per cent, don't you?' said Samantha.

It was like she was scrabbling at the cliff edge, trying to grab on to roots and rocks to stop her from tumbling down. It was a horrible feeling.

'You've been very good to us, to the lads,' said Mr Welstead. 'We appreciate everything you've done, we really do.'

It sounded like goodbye.

Leanne could tell that the call had not gone well.

'Call in sick for the rest of the afternoon,' demanded Samantha. 'I need you.'

Her mind raced, bouncing from one futile idea to another as she tried to work out what she could do to help herself. She had to know who was behind all this. Perhaps some player who felt mismanaged, some wife who felt let down. It was possible, she supposed, that she had made an enemy without even noticing.

She knew that the journalist would never reveal his source so she instructed Leanne to follow the money instead. How hard could it be to call a bank in the Cayman Islands and find out some pertinent details? Like where the money came from in the first place. After all, the account was ostensibly in her name. She could give them all the security information they needed, date of birth, previous address, the works. All except her mother's maiden name. She had never known that.

When Leanne hit a brick wall Samantha took over with the bank, redirecting Leanne to review all the email correspondence from the last twelve months to see if there was something she had overlooked, some pissed-off agent or manager that might have the means and motive to launch a vendetta against her.

'Twelve months?' said Leanne, aghast. It was a mammoth task.

'The sooner you start the sooner you will be finished,' said Samantha, picking up the phone to get back on to the bank.

It was useless. She gained nothing from a day on the phone to CoralBanc but an expensive phone bill. The account had been frozen pending money laundering investigations and other than that nobody could tell her a thing. Worse than useless, because there would now be a record of her making this call, which could be construed as suspicious. Damn it. She would have to disclose it.

'Email Higham and Colville,' she said to Leanne. 'Explain that I asked you to call the bank.'

'You're sure?' said Leanne.

'Just do it.'

'Where are you going?'

'To see an old friend.'

Why were the streets of London so crowded in the middle of a weekday afternoon? Surely they couldn't all be tourists? Hadn't they got jobs to go to? Was the blonde with the purple Liberty bag a trophy wife or a high-class call girl? Was the mop-haired youth a student or the bass player in a hot new band she hadn't had the time to hear of? Had they always been here, all these people packing out the pavements of Oxford Street, and she just hadn't noticed? Had she once been so busy that she simply didn't see them?

She was a part of them now. The aimless. A stupefying dullness had blanketed her days until she could hardly muster the effort to turn on the radio, never mind read a newspaper or apply herself to saving her career. But now she knew that the only way to blow everything out in the open was to find out who was behind all this. And defeat them.

She was on her way to a dingy office above a haberdashery on Berwick Street. As she twisted through the streets of Soho on her way there she became certain that she was being followed.

The man behind her looked both familiar and out of place.

Was it possible that he was someone she knew?

Or perhaps he recognized her. Perhaps he was a football fan.

Except that wasn't it. Fans looked for a way in – when she caught his eye this man looked for a way out, dropping his gaze immediately and crossing the street.

It could be that she was paranoid.

But it could be that she was being watched.

'Remember me?' she said, in the Soho office of Eric Royston, a private detective she had employed on a client's behalf a few years ago.

'Miss Sharp,' he said warmly, as her previous business had been both straightforward and lucrative, his favourite kind. 'One of your players got himself into a spot of bother again?'

Last time he had helped her find some information on a girl that was blackmailing her client so that they could persuade her to stop. Or, as he had succinctly put it at the time, counter-blackmail. It had worked.

'Not this time,' she said. 'This time it's personal.'

She didn't get an enormous sense of assurance from him, but he bit down on her case with the hunger of a starved dog. She knew the look in his eyes. He could smell money. She knew the look because she saw it in the mirror every morning.

Was it any wonder that Carl Higham thought she was corrupt? She had worked at Legends a long time and in that time had never given the impression that there might be a limit to what she was willing to do for money.

'We have an excellent track record in tracing offshore

funds,' he said. 'Excellent. Asset location is the cornerstone of our company.'

'Really?' she said.

'Oh yes. We have a particular method of identifying the beneficial owners of offshore trusts, as well as the source.'

'So you've done this kind of thing before?'

'Not this exactly,' he said. 'Divorces, isn't it? Rich husbands trying to hide their true net worth from estranged partners in an effort to pervert the course of justice.'

'And rich wives, I presume?'

Eric Royston laughed jovially as if she'd made an excellent joke.

She read the banner headline advertising the *Evening Standard* as she passed a newsagent, but she didn't really take it in until she was half a dozen steps past it, so she walked back. And she read it again.

Superagent in New Drugs Shame.

Couldn't be her. She didn't take drugs. So it couldn't be her.

Yet even as she bought her copy she knew her past had found her.

The photograph had been taken very recently, she could tell from her unhappy expression and her casual clothing. She looked drawn and haggard.

This woman, said the article, this evil woman, started her career as a millionaire sports agent by supplying drugs to some of the Premiership's top stars.

This woman was a one-stop shop for class-A drugs, an agent who lured young players into her den of iniquity, a seedy drug dealer.

Samantha Sharp sold drugs to young impressionable boys who just wanted to play football.

Lock up your children.

She found a bench, damp with cold, in the shadow of St Margaret's church, and read the article twice, feeling the last remnants of spirit leave her. New sensations that taunted her. Shame. Shame and regret.

The article was inflammatory and salacious, the sort of writing that could ruin lives.

And it was true. However much you stretch the truth it's still not a lie.

Once. It had happened once.

She hadn't been at Legends very long, a few weeks. There was a party. An extraordinary party that made her feel like she had been kidding herself before, thinking she was living in London when really she'd been on the outside, and not just geographically, looking in. To think, all those nights she had been watching television with Liam there would have been parties like this one going on behind closed doors. Parties where beautiful people chatted and chatted up, parties with waitresses and goodie bags, themes and dress codes, hundreds of people having a thoroughly sybaritic time. And she was a part of it.

And so when a footballer, a client, cornered her on the dance floor and casually put his mouth close to her ear to ask if she knew where he could get any cocaine she had nodded with assurance and used the number she had on her phone for a pal of Liam's that she knew dabbled with dealing.

She wasn't trying to corrupt anyone. She even thought that perhaps procuring drugs was all part of the service. Jackson sometimes procured women, escorts, for his stars.

God, she had even felt *proud* back then that she was able to help him out. Like she was streetwise, connected. She was little Miss Fix-It – ask and she could get an old friend to deliver.

She had talked about it indiscreetly. Naming names. She told the dealer who it was for. She told a couple of colleagues later. It had been a bit of gossip, something to say for a girl trying to make new friends.

And someone had remembered, the player himself perhaps, because he never amounted to very much, and now she was a drug dealer. It said so in the newspaper so it must be true.

In the cold shadow of St Margaret's church Samantha turned the page of the newspaper. Another photograph, this one better. She looked drop-dead glamorous, a designer dress and plenty of red lipstick. She looked like a gangster.

The sort of high-class sleaze that would have a dealer on speed dial.

Outside her front door a handful of reporters was waiting. She wasn't sure what was going on until she was close enough for them to see her. Camera bulbs flared and she was so stunned by their presence that for a moment she just stood there, slack-jawed and speechless.

In all the newspapers the next day she looked vacant and exhausted. As if she'd been taking too many drugs.

'Samantha,' they called. 'Sam, this way. Any comment on the allegations in the paper today? Any comment on the darker side of sport?'

Flash, flash.

'Excuse me,' she said. But they didn't move.

'Sam, what sort of impression does it make if an ambassador of the game supplies drugs? Sam, Sam, over here.'

What was she supposed to do?

No comment, no comment, no comment.

She had to use her elbows to get past them, head down, their questions and accusations raining down on her like hailstones.

'Please, fellas, can I get to my door, huh?' She tried to appeal to their better natures, after all, surely many of them had been on the phone to her office in the past wanting information or quotes for stories and she had always been nice to the press, always.

Unless someone was being a pain in the arse.

Was this how they felt? Those clients of hers who were caught in flagrante delicto, or pursued by rumours that may or may not be true. Did they wonder if they would ever be able to leave their homes again? She advised them to ignore it, always to ignore it, but now she saw just how useless that advice had been.

How could you ignore something when it was waiting on your doorstep?

Slowly she beat a path to her door and closed it shut behind her, hearing their plaintive pleas as she did so.

Whoever it was that was out to get her must be laughing now. They must be tasting triumph and finding it sweet. The thought enraged her. It pumped her with anger and indignation, but all the vitriol had nowhere to go and so it simply churned around in her head until she was exhausted by her own thoughts.

One day she would find out who was responsible, if only to stop herself from going crazy with bitterness.

Next came the call from Legends.

'At your convenience,' said Jackson's assistant.

She resisted the urge to tell her that her convenience wasn't hard to come by.

She dressed for business. A striking suit in oxblood red with a pencil skirt and a tightly fitted jacket. A suit that said, don't fuck with me, I'm a woman.

Her hand shook as she did up the zip at the back of the skirt.

You're innocent.

She kept reminding herself of this fundamental truth.

She pushed her feet into her highest, sharpest, blackest heels.

Leanne was hovering in the main reception. 'You'll let me know what goes on?'

'They'll find something for you whatever happens, Leanne,' she said. 'You're a good assistant.'

'I know I am,' she said. 'That's not why I care.'

Jackson didn't smile when she walked into his office. He didn't ask how she'd been or what she'd been doing to keep herself busy. She despised the way her heart bounced with a jolt of desire when she saw him. She'd thought she was stronger than that.

Carl Higham sat next to him once more. This, and the fact that there wasn't an ice bucket cradling a bottle of champagne to toast her unconditional return to the fold, made her sense that the news would not be good. The constant feeling of dread that she had been keeping at bay for weeks settled onto her shoulders, pushing her down. She had a terrible feeling she might be fucked.

She was right.

'We have been unable to make any satisfactory link to the source of the money,' said Jackson, his voice cool. 'In fact, aside from the address details and so on, we have as yet been unable to connect S. Sharp of the Cayman Islands account with Samantha Sharp of Legends, with you.'

'You won't be able to,' said Samantha. 'I told you that.'

Jackson ignored her. 'However,' he said. 'There have been a couple of other developments, which impact on the situation.'

She waited for him to continue. She didn't like the sideways look the two men shared. She didn't like the way Jackson looked down at the table rather than straight in her eyes. She thought about their past, about everything he had done for her and stupidly trusted a tiny flutter in her gut that said he wouldn't let her down. Not after everything.

'Monty and Ferris Welstead have asked to have alternative representation in this agency,' he said.

She took a step back as if she had been hit in the face. The Welstead boys had *fired* her? Her number-one clients, the ones she had discovered in the backwoods of the North East and signed to the richest club in the best league in the world. They had asked for a substitute?

'When?' she asked, her mouth dry as sand.

'Yesterday,' said Jackson. 'Their father called, said he had to think about their future.'

'Thinking about their future is my job,' said Samantha. Or was.

'I tried to talk him down,' said Jackson. 'But he was adamant.'

She knew damn well that it was better for Legends to keep them as clients in whichever way they could. The boys had irreplaceable talent; she was just an agent. And if she was lined up against a wall with a couple of thirty-million-pound players like Monty and Ferris Welstead then she could expect to be shot. She knew because she would do the same thing herself – that was the true shame of it. She could choose to feel betrayed, she could choose to feel hurt, but ultimately those boys weren't her friends, they were her business, so what right did she have to expect their undying loyalty? Still, it burnt.

'Don't patronize me, Jackson, please. I know how these things work.'

'You're right,' he said. 'I'm sorry.'

'What else?' She was hiding her distress as best she could, but inside she was screaming. 'You said there'd been a couple of other developments. So what else?'

Jackson sighed. 'It's the press, Sam.'

'What about them?'

'You know this agency has always maintained a cordial relationship with the media. That relationship is an integral part of what we do.'

'Of course I know that.' She spent half her working hours at Legends telling reporters very sweetly to piss off one day and asking for a favour the next. The appetite for football stories had not waned over the years, only the tone had changed. Where once footballers had been idolized for their skills, now they were vilified for their scandals. The agency's relationship with the press was more important than ever. 'But good God, Jackson, you know I'm not a drug dealer.'

Carl interrupted. 'So you're saying there's no truth in these allegations?'

'They are wildly exaggerating something that happened years ago.'

Carl sat back with a thin little smile. He had his answer.

'I can handle a bit of bad press. Don't worry about me.'

'I'm *not* worried about you,' said Jackson, raising his voice for the first time. 'I'm worried about my company, and so is the board of directors.'

Carl Higham shot him an odd little look, something like a warning.

'What I mean to say is,' he said in measured tones, 'the reputation of this agency can withstand scrutiny, but I don't want it to.'

'What do vicious irresponsible rumours have to do with being a good agent?'

'Nothing at all,' said Jackson. He paused. His voice became gentle, something more like that after-hours Jackson she was scared to realize she had been horrendously in love with. 'There's a rumour about a brother?' he said. 'You told me you didn't have any family.'

'I don't have to answer that,' she said, looking instinctively towards the lawyer who avoided her eyes. He wasn't here to help her.

Nobody in this room was on her side.

'I apologize,' said Jackson, 'of course you don't.' He looked hurt for a moment, but then toughened and continued.

'The facts remain, there is the matter of hundreds of thousands of dollars and now with this press attention . . .'

'So, what? You're firing me? You can't do that, not without proof about the money. And you can't fire me for PR reasons.'

'No,' said Carl. 'We can't.'

She sensed the way this meeting was going to end. 'I have a contract,' she whispered.

Jackson lifted remorseful eyes to meet her bewildered ones and they stayed there like that for what seemed like an age, Sam and her mentor, closer to equal than they had ever been but still with a generation of experience and knowledge between them.

Jackson had a flash of Samantha Sharp as a young girl, a lost and lonely girl who wept herself into her first job and then clung to it with a tenacity and talent that had surprised them all. She could have had the world at her feet. With his heart he wanted to believe in her innocence, but she wouldn't be the first great agent to take a bribe, and his head knew it.

Samantha Sharp was far from innocent. She was a player and sometimes, just sometimes, all players were tempted to cheat.

The seconds dragged by until light dawned in her eyes.

'You're waiting for me to resign,' she said.

'I am,' said Jackson. 'I don't see another way forward. I don't see how this situation can be resolved to the satisfaction of both parties. If you resign we can make a clean break. There will be no FIFA investigation. You won't even lose your licence.'

He said it like he was doing her a favour. Like she should

be thankful. Like because she once made a mistake, and somebody called S. Sharp had a bank account with dirty fingerprints on it, that she should be grateful.

To hell with that.

'Stop talking like a bloody lawyer, Jackson,' she snapped. 'Everyone in this room understands perfectly well that the only reason you're not firing me is because I'd sue you for unfair dismissal and you can't afford the hassle. So you're ending this to the satisfaction of one party: yours. I resign or what? You stick me in a third-floor office and pick off my clients one by one? If you say I'm over at Legends then I'm over. We both know it. So you can call this my resignation if you like, and protect your precious company, but we both know what's really going on. Don't insult me by pretending otherwise.'

'I would never want to insult you, Samantha.'

'You just did.'

She needed Jackson now. If there was any love there then she had to believe that he would help her.

'Someone is framing me,' she said. 'This is too much all at once; it must be a coordinated vendetta against me. It has to be. Someone set up that bank account and led you to it, then they made damn sure that everybody knew about it by calling Toby Welstead, by calling the press. Don't you see? Someone is setting me up.'

'Who?' said Carl.

There was a long pause, because that was the big question, wasn't it? And she had done everything she could think of, but was nowhere near an answer. 'I don't know,' she said.

'Then I'm very sorry,' said Carl. But he wasn't sorry to see the back of her. She looked like trouble from the minute she'd arrived at the firm. He was only grateful she'd never tried to pin them with a sexual-harassment suit over the jokes and general misogyny she'd had to put up with.

She looked at Jackson, but he pressed his lips together and said nothing. Nothing at all.

She had lost. There was nothing left to do but walk away.

'What do I do now?' she whispered, thinking aloud. Jackson had shaped the last decade of her life – perhaps he could tell her what to do next. This was all she knew.

'What about . . .' She wished that Carl wasn't here. She didn't want to talk to Jackson, her boss, any longer; she wanted to talk to Jackson, her lover. 'You would do this to me?' she said.

Jackson straightened up behind his desk, fixed her with his intense stare, the one she found so sexy, just about the only thing in this world that could make her feel weak. She remembered the time he had pinned her down on that very desk and made furious love to her until she was dizzy. 'Yes,' he said. 'I would. It's over, Sam.'

'Bastard.'

She hadn't been prepared for this. Perhaps she should have, because only a fool expected innocence to triumph these days. Her career, the glittering prize at the end of her onerous journey, had been snatched from under her. All that was left was leaving with dignity. Suddenly it mattered.

She spun on the point of her black high heels and walked away.

15

'You're the most selfish person I've ever met. Typical fucking woman.'

'But I'm your sister,' she simpered, 'so you have to love me.'

By the time she was nineteen Samantha was working at a much better hotel than the poxy Royal Victoria and making, in those relative teenage terms, far more money, but to Liam's annoyance she insisted on keeping her outgoings tiny and saving the difference. The Camberwell sofa had been good enough for months so it would be good enough for a few more too.

'I want to buy a house eventually,' she said. 'You can live there as well.'

'I want to buy some blow,' he countered. 'Today.'

They still got drunk together, but he got drunker. She didn't like turning up at work with a hangover. She refused to spend any of her money on cocaine, his drug of choice. Or at least it was his drug of choice up until the first time he experimented with crack.

'You have to try it,' he said, meticulously preparing the little pipe with his precious crystals. 'It makes coke look like ProPlus.'

Outside police sirens wailed, red buses rumbled by and they could hear voices raised in argument. Liam called the neighbourhood 'lively'.

'Try this, Sam, it'll blow your head off, I swear.'

It was eleven o'clock in the morning.

'I have to go to work,' she said.

The hotel was called Seven Dials, after the area where it stood and she had been a chambermaid there for a just a few months. She loved it. Unlike the Royal Victoria the Seven Dials hotel was a home from home for celebrities and captains of industry, not tourists and salesmen, a younger crowd, with money to burn. Their breakfast was à la carte and featured kedgeree and soda bread, not a soggy buffet. The bar served champagne and cocktails, not cheap house white and Carling Black Label. The staff all looked like they might be taking time off between modelling gigs, staff like Samantha with her long legs and her enigmatic smile that made you wonder what she was thinking.

When she walked in, with a red net petticoat peeking out from under her full black skirt, the job was already hers; the interview was just a formality.

She broke her habit of petty theft. If she saw a pile of twenties carelessly left on a bedside table, she would straighten them and weigh them down with an ashtray. Sometimes she still spritzed herself with the guest's perfume, but that was it. She wanted to be promoted to housekeeper. She was young for the position, but she knew there would be an opening soon. She took evening classes in Japanese because she thought that would help her chances.

Liam was forever nagging her to get him a job at Seven Dials too.

Whenever she refused he looked for a second like he hated her, but swiftly returned to his usual cajoling tactics. 'But it's only fair,' he said. 'I got you one.'

There was no arguing with his logic, but lately she was worried about his drinking and even more worried about the drugs.

'You're sure you have it under control?' she asked him.

'Don't you worry about me, little sis. I'm not stupid.'

'Maybe you should quit for a while?'

Liam missed shifts all the time. She couldn't stand the thought of getting him a job at Seven Dials only for him to blow the opportunity, for him and perhaps for her also. So she told him that there weren't any openings for drivers.

Nobody at work knew she had a brother.

Liam knew she was lying, and he could guess why. She was well out of order, getting a bit too up herself. It was his responsibility, as the older brother, to knock her back down to size. But how? She looked so fucking happy these days, and why not? With her cushy job in swankyland and her growing stash in the bank. Meanwhile he owed his dealer a hundred and hadn't scored any overtime for weeks.

He hated where he worked. He didn't like the guests or the other staff, and every single shift felt like too much effort.

He would hang out in the dismal staffroom behind the kitchen and wait to be summoned to work. Sometimes he played cards with the off-duty busboys or flirted with the waitresses but often he walked out back, ostensibly for a cigarette, but he'd smoke a little rock if he had one or sprinkle some charlie into a cigarette to try to get the same hit.

He shouldn't get high on the job, but really what else was there to do?

One of the Aussie chambermaids dealt a little cocaine on the side, bad shit, tiny twenty-pound bags that everyone knew she filched from the hotel high-rollers and then cut with something dumb, maybe aspartame, to make it go a little further. You were lucky to get a decent high but right now, with his dealer after him for what he owed, he didn't have much of a choice.

That night, the worst night of his life that would change everything, he had two hours to wait around for a pre-booked job, so he stood out back in the freezing cold and carefully, oh so carefully, placed his last rock, nothing more than a sliver, into his foil-covered pipe.

Even as he sparked the lighter he was already worrying about where he'd buy his next hit and with what. Then the flame melted the precious rock and his worries took flight.

The high was unbelievable. He thought maybe his feet would lift off the ground and he could soar over the hotel and away. He fancied that he could feel every vein in his body dilate so that he could soak up the feeling as it coursed through his bloodstream.

Yeah, just like that.

He sank down onto the cold stone step and relished the sensation.

'Liam? Yo, Liam, you out here, man?'

It was later, maybe as much as an hour. Time flies when you're having fun. His boss, a twitchy little Ecuadorean guy was calling his name. Instinctively he palmed the pipe he still clutched in his hand and tucked it into his pocket. He would be fired if he was caught. He knew it.

'Got a job for you. Be out front in forty minutes, okay?'

Drive? Now? Gingerly he got to his feet. He felt okay. How long had it been? He felt more than okay; he felt like he could do with a line of something to stay on top of this buzz. Forty minutes. He knew a guy in Vauxhall, just a little south, not far. He could make it, though it would be tight. It had been a while, but hopefully he'd answer his door. A buy tonight would wipe out the last of his money. If only he could persuade his little sister to part with some of her cash. He knew she had loads stashed away, she must do, and for what? Some stupid dream of a house? What was the point? Everyone knew the London property market was on the brink of collapse. Perhaps if he told her that they needed the money for something she'd consider legit . . . perhaps he could take a part out of the fridge or the telly and say it needed fixing.

He made it to Vauxhall and back in under half an hour. He felt so good by then he was whistling as he waited kerbside, holding the back door to the car open and ready. He had enough rocks to last him for the next week or so, plus a neat little bag of blow on tick. The dealer liked Liam because he had a job, not like most of these crack-head losers who couldn't stay on top of their addiction. Good one, he'd be a return customer there for sure.

He always paid special attention to his passengers. He liked to make up stories about them in his head. It was also the best way to get tips. He opened the door for the ladies and gents alike and made polite conversation if he felt they wanted it.

Tonight's ride was for a gorgeous redhead and her much older man.

Husband? Boyfriend? Who could tell?

But from the way they were going at it in the back seat he suspected boyfriend. Married couples didn't go at it like that in the back seat.

They were heading for a quiet piano bar in Pimlico, a little-known place that the hotel recommended to guests all the time in exchange for a similar referral. He wondered where these two had come from. He sounded English, she definitely didn't. She really was beautiful. Her accent reminded him of James Bond villains.

He played with a little fantasy whereby he was James Bond, undercover, pretending to be a lowly chauffeur so that he could kill the bad guy in the back seat, and when he had revealed his true identity and dispatched the baddie he and Redhead would drive off into the sunset. Nice.

She had her head on her lover's shoulder now, her eyes closed, laughing softly at something he'd said, and he was absent-mindedly pulling his fingers through her long flaming hair. The gesture pulled at Liam's hardened heart. They were in love.

This job was getting boring. Maybe he should aim higher.

Maybe not.

He had driven this route a hundred times or more. The roads were blissfully empty. But he didn't see the traffic light on red until it was too late and he was already committed to the right-hand turn. He was over the speed limit too, just over but enough to ensure that when the white transit van ploughed into the passenger side both vehicles went spinning across the road in a mess of burning rubber and splintering glass, into the path of oncoming traffic.

There was a rush of unbearable noise, screams and crunching metal, and then nothing – as if the world had stopped and was still.

Only the rhythmic clicking of his indicator. *Tick, tick, tick, tick. Look out, car turning.*

He could feel wetness on his face, his hands came back covered in gore and behind him there was silence. The woman had been thrown forward over the passenger seat on impact and her head had smashed the windshield; strands of her hair mingled with the blood there. The seat where the man had been sitting was simply gone, obliterated into a twisted heap of metal.

On the streets the late-night traffic stopped to stare in horror.

Tick, tick, tick, tick.

Liam was the only one in the car who was still alive.

Nobody thought to tell her that her brother had been in an accident. The sad and simple truth was that there was nobody who cared about them enough to alert her, nobody who even knew her phone number. When he didn't come home that night she went to bed as usual. It wasn't the first time he hadn't returned. The following evening she went to meet him from work.

'Hey,' she said, recognizing the Australian chambermaid but forgetting her name. Had they ever been properly introduced or had she simply handed her money in exchange for drugs now and again? 'Is Liam around?'

The girl's hand went to her mouth. 'Honey, you didn't hear?'

'Hear what?'

'There was a car crash.'

She thought he was dead. She truly thought that he was dead.

Take care of each other, their mother had said, and she had failed.

The Australian girl was saying something she struggled to hear through the black fog that had descended. *Just a few cuts and bruises.*

'Say that again?'

'Liam was really lucky, he could have . . . I mean, people *died*, Sam.'

'But Liam's okay?'

'Just a few cuts and bruises they said.'

'Is he in the hospital?'

The girl laid a comforting hand on Samantha's trembling shoulder. 'Honey, he's at the police station.'

Liam was refused bail. Night after hollow night she felt like she was losing her mind. Too often she would sit in the empty flat in Camberwell, staring at the television without really seeing it. This was the part of the story when she was supposed to give up on her dreams and go home, except she had no home to go to, neither of them did.

Home for Liam was a twelve-foot cell. He would remain there until his trial.

She felt most at home in the quiet moments shortly after waking. Then she would remember who she was and feel utterly lost.

'Is there something we should know about?' asked her manager, genuinely concerned. They were optimistic for this once vibrant and ambitious young woman, but over the last few weeks she had been reprimanded several times for lateness and a general slide in attitude. It was sad to see.

'I'm sorry,' she said. 'There was a death in the family.'

'Do you need time off?'

If she took time off then how would she pay the rent? How would she keep things together so that when Liam came back they could start over? He would clean up now, he would have to. It was also likely that he would have to pay an enormous fine as well as undertake a considerable amount of community service. The court-appointed lawyer said there was a very slim chance that in the absence of a criminal record and a hitherto unblemished reputation he could avoid a custodial sentence. She had to pin her hopes on that. If only they hadn't found so many drugs on him.

'It's okay,' she said to her boss. 'Actually, if there's any overtime?'

She was working for both of them now. When he was released he might not find work immediately. Besides, what else was she to do but work? If she sat any longer in the empty flat without him she thought that she might drown.

Then came the trial.

She took a few days off. She had no idea how long it was supposed to last. Liam had been charged with vehicular manslaughter and possession of drugs. There had been several attempts to cut a deal and plead guilty to a lesser charge, but nothing ever came to the table without a jail term. His lawyer felt they would stand a better chance at trial and though a guilty verdict looked likely it was not assured. Also the character references and Liam's good behaviour on remand would count in his favour when it came to the sentence. It would all depend on the judge in session.

Samantha dressed carefully for court. A sensible brown skirt and a cream blouse, low heels, her wild hair pulled back from her face. Restrained and respectable. She would be asked for a character reference at the end of the trial, though she was not a witness and so she was able to watch from the public gallery.

She had visited Liam regularly, but it was still a shock to see him looking so pale and thin. Hearing him referred to as the 'accused' made her skin crawl. The suit she had bought for him to wear was too large for him, hanging off his gaunt frame and making him look far younger than he was, younger even than her.

If he was scared he was hiding it well.

To begin with there was legal jargon she could not follow. But as the first day progressed his lawyer stressed the accidental nature of the alleged crime. The way he spoke it was as if Liam had merely run a red light. He talked about the long hours that hotel drivers worked, the poorly maintained cars, the lack of training, and produced witnesses to validate his stance that Liam was not a criminal, merely terribly unfortunate. He didn't mention the drugs. He didn't mention the victims. Not once.

Liam was careful not to smile when he saw her. A smile, his lawyer had said, could be construed as callous, as showing a lack of remorse. But he held her gaze long enough so that she knew he was smiling inside.

She went to bed that night feeling optimistic and allowed herself to imagine that one day soon he might be home and they might start over together.

She washed his sheets but would not allow herself to make up his bed until she knew for sure. Sitting on his bare mattress she wondered if she had left it too late in life to start praying.

The next day the prosecution tore into Liam's working record, calling supervisors to attest to his bad habits, and despite several objections an entirely different picture was painted. One of a man with a drug problem.

The first policeman on the scene was called. He described Liam's erratic behaviour following the accident. Yes, the blood alcohol level had been nil, but he was carrying, and in his opinion . . .

Liam's lawyer objected and the objection was sustained, but the jury knew where his testimony had been heading.

It only took two days.

By the time he stood in the dock Liam had prepared himself for the worst. Which was just as well.

Guilty.

Before sentencing she gave her character reference, she told the court how Liam had found her a job and a place to live and that she would now repay the favour. In fact, she lied, there was a good chance a position would be found for him with her current employers.

The judge was old and ornery. He had never suggested rehabilitation for any drug-related crime and he wasn't about to start with Liam Sharp.

Sixteen years. Death by dangerous driving and possession of a controlled substance.

Absurdly she waited for him to say that he was joking.

But he was done.

She had known this was possible. So why was she shocked? Why did it feel like a baseball bat to the side of her head?

Samantha started to cry. Loud ugly sobs that drew the attention of the court and made at least one jury member feel guilty that night when he got home.

'Don't cry, Sammy,' yelled Liam. 'It'll be okay.'

Okay? How could it possibly be okay?

They were supposed to take care of each other and she had failed him completely.

The guilt crashed down on her. She stared at him, the tears rolling freely down her cheeks, and couldn't think of anything to say, no last words to comfort him.

She gazed blankly at the doorway long after he had been taken through it to begin his stretch. It was too awful to contemplate.

It was a mistake, just a stupid mistake. He didn't mean to kill anyone.

But he had, and this was the price he had to pay.

The courtroom session ended and the mundane business of preparing it for the afternoon seemed intentionally callous. If she wanted to believe for a few minutes that there was anything special about Liam's case then the sight of court clerks binning paperwork and replacing water glasses, sharpening pencils and rearranging chairs ensured that she would not.

He was just another junkie. Another drain on the tax-payer. Another jailbird who was where he belonged.

She staggered from the court and out into the street with a buzzing in her ears and a haze of disbelief across her eyes. It was the first time in her life that she didn't notice London even though it was all around her. The spires of the central court, the press pack waiting outside for other, more news-worthy, cases. There would be no headlines wasted on Liam. She wandered aimlessly down Ludgate Hill, through the shadow of St Paul's without looking up.

Sixteen years. By the time he was free they would both be old.

She limped through the next few weeks. Without Liam, and without the prospect or hope of his return, her ambition and motivation deserted her. Why should she care?

She missed him.

He took advice and immediately launched an appeal against the sentence, but even his lawyer thought he had little chance.

She did whatever she could to avoid going back to the flat, to avoid the meaningless hours between finishing work and going to bed. She started going to the cinema alone, but could never concentrate for long enough and after wasting her money twice she never went back. It was easier just to find a bar and talk to strangers; a pretty girl could always find company.

One Saturday night she was invited to a party. One of the waiters either had a crush on her or felt sorry for her or both, but regardless she fell on the invitation hungrily. The weekends were the worst.

But she was nervous when she arrived and couldn't find anyone to talk to. She ended up weeping behind a bedroom door, eyeing up the pile of coats on a big double bed and feeling a wave of exhaustion consume her. In the middle of a crowded party, surrounded by the sound of people having a good time, Samantha slept more peacefully than she did in her own bed.

She was thinking of quitting her job. She didn't know what else to do. She just knew that she couldn't go on like this. Perhaps if she left her job the adrenalin would send her off in another, more bearable, direction.

She struggled to understand how it had come to this. That first day she arrived she'd thought it was the beginning, now it seemed that it was just the beginning of the end. She found herself clawing through Liam's room. She upended his shoes and cleared out his pockets. She looked in every corner and every fold. She was looking for drugs. Maybe if she took something, maybe then she could understand how he had fucked up everything. His life. Her life. Everything.

But there was nothing.

'Hey, gorgeous, where you going?'

There were two guys in the bar as she was about to leave work. They were already drunk.

'I'm going home,' she said.

'It's early. Won't you have a drink with my friend and me? I'm Paul,' he said, 'and this is Andy.'

She craved conversation. It would block out the miserable thoughts that were her constant companions.

If I pretend to be your friend will you pretend to be mine?

They said they were just in town for two nights, for work. And even though it was a Saturday and they only looked about twenty years old she didn't push them for details; she just sat with them and drank fast and played dumb as they spent a small fortune on vintage champagne and asked her juvenile questions like what bra size she wore and where she lost her virginity.

'Paul's still a virgin, ain't that right, mate?' said the one called Andy.

'Piss off,' said Paul, topping up Samantha's glass as well as his own.

I lost my virginity when I was fourteen years old, a few weeks after my mother died, because I wanted to feel something and it was either that or scrape beautiful shiny razor blades over my perfect thighs.

'I'm still a virgin too,' said Samantha.

'Really?'

'What do you think?'

One of them decided it would be fun to do some tequila shots, and by now Samantha was drunk enough to think that was a *really* good idea and after one round suggested they did it again. The empty champagne bottles were mounting. She had stopped caring long ago that this was where she worked. So she might get fired – it didn't matter. She needed a change. Just look at her life, getting drunk with total strangers, anything to avoid going home.

Let me tell you a sad story, the story of my life. First my mother left me, then my brother. Let me tell you how lonely I am. Let me tell you.

Her thoughts were growing unwieldy and somewhere in the back of her mind she knew she wasn't far away from passing out.

I think I used to want something more than this. I think. Maybe.

She saw one of the bar managers staring at her reproachfully, but ignored him. He was management, but not her boss. Not directly. If he wanted to report her to one of the housekeepers then let him. Right now the next round of drinks was more important than her job.

She couldn't remember what she had been so upset about. No wonder her mum loved a drink. What's not to love?

Another bottle of champagne appeared, and three more shot glasses. She licked salt from the crevice between Paul's thumb and forefinger, threw back the burning liquor, and bit down on a wedge of lime.

And another.

The next thing she could clearly remember was lying beneath the two of them on an enormous hotel king-size. Andy was naked, kneeling over her, and pulling down her knickers. Paul's bare torso blocked most of her view and he was fumbling at the waistband of his jeans. Her skirt was bunched up round her hips and somewhere along the way she had lost her top. Her bra was practically off, tangled around one arm.

Had she agreed to this? When did they leave the bar? How did they get here? She took an inordinate amount of pleasure from recognizing the Seven Dials bedroom. At least she would know her way home after . . . after what? Her head swam and she struggled to maintain consciousness.

They wouldn't hurt her. They were good boys.

Paul shucked his jeans and started toying with her breasts, pinching her nipples painfully so that the sensation awoke what little of her mind was still functioning. He tugged off her bra.

'Lovely tits,' he said.

'Turn her over,' said Andy.

Wait. No. Wrong. All wrong.

She opened her mouth to speak but no words came out. She felt her heavy eyes start to close and summoned that little part of her that was still able to protest. If she told them not to then they wouldn't. She said something, but still nothing came out.

Paul rolled her onto her stomach and she felt Andy pressing himself into her exposed curves, lifting her hips, delving deep into her first with his fingers and then briefly, she was sure, with his cock.

'Great tatt,' said one of them. He stroked the bluebird tattoo on her shoulder.

She struggled to her knees but this only meant she was pressed tighter to him and he loved it.

'Yeah, sweetheart,' he said. 'That's sexy, there's a good girl.'

Paul was playing with himself, inches from her face, and laughing.

'Stop.' The word came out thin and hoarse. She licked her lips. 'Please stop.'

But nothing stopped.

She started to cry silently, burrowing her face in the pillow, listening to them discuss who should go first, as if she was a toy they had to share nicely. She wanted to get off the bed and run from the room but she had no energy, no drive, nowhere to go. Why shouldn't they get what they wanted? They had bought her all that champagne, lonely little Sammy Sharp, who didn't deserve anything.

Wasn't this, even this, better than being alone?

Paul's face was suddenly close to hers.

'Are you okay?' he said. 'Andy, hold on, stop it, will ya?'

She turned her face and looked at him, leaving her tough face of red lipstick and black kohl on the pillow. He smiled at her and, because it had been so long since anyone had smiled at her, she smiled back.

Suddenly the door of the hotel room was flung open and a big, booming voice bounced around the room.

'What the *fuck*, guys? I said no girls and not too much booze. Christ, look at this place, just look at it.'

There was much activity on the bed as Andy and Paul frantically retrieved their clothes and dressed themselves.

She looked at the newcomer through a curtain of her thick dark hair. Tall bloke, older, needed a shave. Was he their dad? No, not quite old enough.

She dragged herself deliberately up the bed until she was sitting, holding a pillow over her exposed chest. She saw her bra peeking out from under the sheet and grabbed it, missing on her first attempt but managing to focus by squeezing one eye shut.

'God, what have you done to her?' said the man that could be their father, but probably wasn't. 'She's completely messed up.'

'She's just a bit drunk,' said Paul.

'A bit? You all right, sweetheart?'

She nodded.

And then she burst into tears.

*

171

The man's name was Jackson Ramsay. Paul and Andy were footballers, his clients. He sent them off to get coffee for her and he stood with his back to her while she dressed.

'They don't mean to hurt anyone,' he said, savouring the glimpse of her naked back that he could see in the bathroom mirror and then looking away hastily. 'They're too rich for their own good, which is probably my fault.'

He asked for her story and she told him, instinctively leaving out the part about Liam being on a manslaughter charge, but gushing out her heart to this kind stranger simply because it had been so long since someone was kind to her at all.

'Here,' he said, offering her a box of tissues when it got snotty.

'What if I get fired?' she said. 'After tonight.'

'Do you like your job?'

'I used to.'

'And now? What do you want to be?'

'A success,' she said, her watery eyes still as naive as they were the day she got off the train. 'Like you. You're a success, right? I can tell.'

'I earn a lot of money if that's what you mean. I have my own business, a house, a car – does that make me a success?'

'Yes.' What else could there be?

'It wasn't easy.'

'I don't expect it was.'

She gathered her things and tried to tidy up her hair and make-up. As she stood in the doorway Jackson pushed something into her hands.

'Wait a minute,' she said, looking down at three crumpled fifty-pound notes. 'What is this?'

'Just take it,' he said. 'You've been through an ordeal here tonight. Treat yourself to a cab home.'

'I don't want your money. I'm not a prostitute.'

'Don't moralize yourself out of a hundred and fifty quid,' he said. 'That would just be foolish, and despite what happened here I don't think you're a fool.'

'I'm not,' she said. 'Not at all.'

She folded the notes into a tight square and stuffed them into her pocket. Her fingers were on the door handle, but something made her turn back. The scent of opportunity. 'Give me a job,' she said.

'What?'

'Why not? I'm a quick learner, I can type, fetch coffee, anything. Please? You said yourself I'm no fool. It's your fault if I get fired.'

'And how do you work that out?'

'You were supposed to be keeping them out of trouble, right?' she said. 'Well, I'm trouble.'

She didn't feel embarrassed around him. He exuded confidence and security and this made her brave. He was the kind of man she wanted to marry one day.

'I'm serious,' she said.

'You have absolutely no experience.'

'Please. Be a hero. Won't you give a girl a chance?'

Goddamn her. Did she have any idea how sexy she was? No wonder his boys had been dumb enough to get her drunk. She was trouble all right, a walking talking sexual-harassment suit waiting to happen.

He should push another fifty on her to stop her running

to the newspapers and get the hell out of there as fast as he could.

'The pay would be shit and the hours would be dreadful,' he said. 'I doubt you'd last a month.'

She took that as a yes.

'Thank you,' she said. 'Thank you so much. You won't regret it.' She held out her hand for him to shake.

Bemused, Jackson shook it.

And Samantha was on her way.

16

Fired.

Without her career who was she?

She was a sister. Not a very good one. Once a week on Thursday mornings she was a sister. The rest of the time she denied his very existence.

She wasn't a mother or a daughter or a wife.

The closest thing she had to a friend was Leanne, a girl who wasn't even her assistant any more.

She didn't have any hobbies. So she couldn't call herself a painter or a writer or a musician. She wasn't a film fan and she hadn't read a book for years.

She was a career girl without a career, a working woman without a job to do. Washed up at the age of thirty-four. Over.

The thought of getting a life was crippling.

She had never belonged, not really. She was reminded every single day. She saw the shock on people's faces when they discovered she was a woman, heard surprise in their voices on the telephone. That's why she liked to do so much by email. Sam Sharp – androgynous enough to garner the respect that came automatically to others. There were twenty Richards at Legends and she had caught each and every one of them looking at her on occasion with contempt, lust or a condescending smile. But never respect. Never fear.

She had been waiting for this for years, to get kicked out of the boys' club all the way back to the girl she had never truly buried, just hidden for a while and not too well. Not well enough.

What were you thinking?

She was a joke that went too far. A lie she was stupid to believe.

The one colleague who valued her contribution was Jackson and just look at how much good that had done in the end. She used to think that he was on her side. Now she realized she had been naive. If it came down to it the only side he would ever really be on was his own. Jackson was a fighter just like her. Like she used to be.

Who was she now?

He came to see her at home the night he fired her. He was holding a bottle of whisky. 'Not for you,' he said. 'For me.'

'You don't normally drink when we're together, Jackson.'

'This isn't a normal day.'

'And as of six hours ago we're not together,' she said.

He wanted to explain. Not apologize, explain. When he was done she suspected she was supposed to throw open her arms or her legs and tell him everything was going to be okay.

She settled for throwing him out of her house instead.

'Sam, please try to be mature about this. You were the one who never stopped going on about how we had to keep business and pleasure separate. What happened today was business. Given that advice, in those circumstances, you would have done exactly the same.'

'Did you honestly expect things between us to remain as they were?'

'Great,' he said. 'Now they can change. If I'm not your boss then you're free to be with me, really be with me. We're fucking amazing together – can't you let yourself imagine where we could go from here?'

'Get out of my house.'

He raked his fingers through his thick brown hair in exasperation. She saw the deep furrows in his forehead and the circles beneath his eyes, the signs of his stress, and thought – *good.*

'I can't lose you,' he said.

'You didn't lose me, Jackson. You threw me away.'

'Legends is a clean company, Samantha, spotless. I started with nothing and I have spent my entire life building an honest brand, and yes sometimes that means letting people go when they have question marks over their reputation.'

She gasped with indignation and started to speak. 'I don't –'

'No, Sam,' he said, cutting her off, 'the press, the bad press; shit sticks and that's just the way it goes. I read it in the paper so it must be true.'

'That's not honesty,' she said. 'That's just bullshit.'

His steel eyes blazed with sudden anger. 'You of all people should understand. What would you have had me do? Huh?'

'Stood up for me. Issued a press release giving me your full support. Refused to accept the premise of the accusations. Told Carl there was no way I would take a bribe, that I don't have it in me to be dishonest.' Her skin prickled with anger.

'But you do,' he said. 'You lie every day, about you and me.'

'I don't want to deal with their snide remarks,' she snapped.

'I wasn't talking about them,' he said. He moved closer to her and stroked his fingertips round her tense shoulders and down her back. Then she could feel his massive hand on the small of her back and some of her fury dissolved. 'You lie to yourself,' he said. 'We both know damn well you're in love with me.'

She calmed herself a little and considered what he was saying. 'Maybe I was,' she admitted. 'And that's why it hurts so much.' Their lips were so close she could feel his warm breath tickling her mouth. She closed her eyes and surrendered to the inevitable. Then opened them again when she felt him sigh and pull away.

'Grow up, will you?' he said. 'Either you love me or you don't. It's not a there-one-minute-gone-the-next thing.'

She bristled with humiliation. 'Then I never could have loved you,' she said, closing the door on that chapter of her life.

So she lost him, or they lost each other. He was mad if he thought she could feel anything for him now but the raw wound of his treachery. He was insane. She could forgive many things. She was an open-minded woman. But not this. Not her career. That grip on the ladder where she had clung and climbed so determinedly. He *knew*. More than anyone else, he knew. Because he had been there for every struggle. And now, even though he was not the architect of her disgrace, she held him responsible, because he didn't trust her enough to save her. He didn't love her enough to be true.

Leanne turned up the following day at half-past one just like she had every day for the last few weeks.

'What are you doing here?' said Samantha. Irritation simmered, scarcely off the boil. She just wanted to be left alone to grieve for everything she had lost.

'You look like crap,' said Leanne.

She hadn't slept all night, hadn't eaten a thing and her face bore the remnants of long ago make-up. Losing the only worthwhile thing in your life takes its toll on your appearance. She pulled the towelling bathrobe she'd been wearing all morning tight around her body, defending herself from the world.

Leanne sailed past Samantha and into the house, plonking a sheaf of paperwork on the kitchen counter. 'I wrote letters on your behalf to the clients,' she said. 'Here's a pen, sign them.' She flicked on the coffee machine with practised ease.

Samantha picked up the letter. For a few seconds it might as well have been written in Japanese (and her Japanese was rusty) for all the sense it made. It stated that she had parted company with Legends without going into detail, maintained a warm and respectful tone and wished the client every success in the future. She turned it over in her hand, confused. 'Why?' she said. 'What's the point?'

'You were going to leave without saying goodbye?'

'Leanne, all the clients will have been picked up by someone else at Legends. If you don't think Richard and all of them were on the phone within an hour of my leaving the building then you must be unbelievably naive.'

'Which I'm not,' said Leanne, twisting the steam valve with asbestos hands so that it hissed and then roared. 'Don't kid yourself; Richard would have been on the phone before you were even out of the lift.'

'So why bother?'

'You're not *dead*, Sam. You haven't even lost your FIFA licence. Isn't it possible that you might want a career in, gee, I don't know, sports management? Here, drink.'

Samantha knocked back the blistering espresso in one gulp and sucked in sharply as her gullet screamed in fiery protest. She slammed the little cup back down. 'Don't you get it? People remember a scandal.' All that hard work, all those hours, the sacrifice and for nothing. 'There's no way back for me,' she said. 'Not after this.'

'Yeah,' said Leanne, 'that's the attitude.' She sipped her espresso and rolled her eyes. 'Fine, I'll forge your signature, okay?'

'I don't care. Do what you like.'

'And what will you do?'

'I might go away,' she said impulsively. 'Maybe I'll bum around the world for as long as I like. There's other things I want to do besides work, you know, like learning how to sail or cook – I used to make a really good curry – or, like, seeing the pyramids and the Taj Mahal.'

'Yeah, right,' said Leanne, 'but what are you really going to do?'

'Give me those damn letters.'

'Here's a pen.'

'Whatever, just pass them over. I'll do them later.'

Leanne stayed for a little while and then before she left she told Samantha she wouldn't be coming back. 'Until you need me. I'll stay at Legends – they've found me a desk with the commercial department. But when you do decide how you're next going to take on the world and win, will you let me know? I enjoy working for you; I'd like to do it again someday.'

'I didn't win,' she said. 'I was beaten.'

'Maybe,' said Leanne. 'But somewhere along the way somebody cheated.'

'I think you're right. But who?'

'I don't know.'

'You don't think . . .'

'What?'

'Nothing,' said Samantha. 'It's just what you said, a while ago, about who stands to gain from my disgrace. I was wondering how Richard was doing. Has he picked up all the clients?'

'A few,' said Leanne. 'The Welsteads, of course. But, to be honest, most of the good ones have gone to Jackson.'

Both women fell silent. 'He wouldn't bring shame on his own company,' said Samantha eventually. 'That would make no sense.'

'You're right,' said Leanne. 'Besides, Jackson's crazy about you. I mean, not like that, not that way, but you know what I mean.'

Once, a long time ago, she had read that the sign of a great businessman (or woman, presumably) was not making the first million, but losing the first million and then making it again. At the time she remembered thinking – who would be stupid enough to lose a million?

She had been so sure that she would grasp whatever she managed to make of herself and never let it go. What she hadn't realized, until now, was that anything can be wrenched from your hands – your money, your career, your reputation. There isn't a grip in the world tight enough to hold on no matter what.

So now what?

Perhaps thirty-four wasn't too late to start over after all. *Give it time.*

The injury of Jackson's betrayal, of her fall, was still raw. It was several days before she saw a way back up.

Late one night, as she was having a hot bubble bath that was supposed to make her relax but really just made her edgy, the telephone rang. She picked up the cordless phone by the bath automatically.

'Hey, it's Gabe.'

He was calling her from a bar she guessed, the buzz of background conversation was discernible even though he was shouting to compensate for it. The pause dragged on. 'Gabe Muswell,' he prompted.

She felt a pang of guilt. Her most recent signing. At least she'd had the chance to make one last dream come true.

'How's it going?' she asked politely.

'Great,' he said. 'I'm loving Krakow. Bit of a party town. First home match on Sunday. Any chance you might come and watch?'

'Did you get my letter?' she said.

'Nope.'

She took a deep breath, inhaling the warm fragrant steam. 'I've resigned,' she said.

'Come again?'

'We wrote you a letter, special delivery. I've resigned from Legends.'

'What does that mean?'

'I'm afraid I'm no longer your agent.'

'Was it something I said?' He laughed. He was definitely in a bar. She could hear the clink of glasses, practically smell the beer on his breath.

'You really didn't get my letter? Nobody from Legends has called you? Richard Tavistock?'

'Nah, thankfully. Wasn't he that arse who left the price tag on his shoes that time? What kind of dickhead spends three hundred quid on a pair of shoes? They weren't even trainers.'

She smiled. Her first smile for days it seemed. Poor Gabe. He was the client that nobody wanted. Yet she had a soft spot for him.

'I'm sorry, Gabe.' She swished the hot bathwater around with her fingertips, creating miniature whirlpools and eddies. 'The situation was out of my hands.'

'You were fired?'

She hadn't gone into details with anyone else. Perhaps the bath was relaxing her after all. 'Not technically,' she said, and was surprised to hear her dry little laugh. Progress indeed. A few days ago the thought of being all but technically fired was enough to reduce her to tears.

'So what are you going to do now?' he said.

'Honestly? I have no idea.'

'Then there's nothing to stop you coming out here on Sunday. You still like football, right?'

The truth was she wasn't sure if she'd ever liked football. She appreciated talent, she worked hard to get very rich in a very rich world, but ultimately it was twenty grown men kicking a ball around a field and she watched games with her head and not her heart. Of course, she had never told anyone this. They would have blamed her ambivalence on her gender. As a woman it was often assumed she 'didn't get it'.

She answered Gabe with a noncommittal 'hmmm' but her head was opening up to the possibility.

Why not take a short trip out to Krakow? She got on well with Gabe and Christine. It would be like a holiday. She could watch a football match; it wouldn't kill her. And perhaps she could catch up with Aleksandr Lubin again.

That final thought made her feel hot between her legs.

And she was single now, wasn't she? She could never forgive Jackson for what he had done to her.

Could she really go through with it if she saw Lubin again? He was so young. She was so old. Unconsciously her hand smoothed over her full slippery breast and dipped under the water where she felt her wet skin slide beneath her fingers.

'So you'll come?' Gabe said.

Abruptly she stayed her straying hand. She couldn't go running off to Poland just to hook up with the last male to pay her any attention. She wasn't that needy. And, besides, now that she was no longer Sam Sharp: Superagent, he probably wouldn't find her attractive in the slightest.

'Maybe,' she said.

17

The moment she saw Josef Wandrowszcki kick a football Samantha was determined to introduce him to the world.

It was bitterly cold. The air nipped at her gloved finger-tips and she applauded every tackle just to keep them warm.

You could take the girl out of the agency, but you couldn't take the agent out of the girl. She tried to be cautious, but she couldn't take her eyes off the skinny kid up front wearing the number-eleven shirt.

Wow. It was the only word that came to mind. *Wow.*

Everybody always thinks they've found the new Pelé, or the new Wayne Rooney, the next Gary Lineker, and it rarely proves to be the case. But this kid, he really was that good.

And the dying embers of ambition in Samantha's belly bloomed into flame once more, burning bright.

He was everywhere, swarming across the pitch like he had more energy than all of them, but always where he should be, just behind the forward line ready to pick up every hopeful pass and run at goal with a fearless pace that gave her that hot little feeling in her gut.

He's a hero waiting to happen.

It didn't matter that she wasn't with Legends any longer; it didn't matter that she wasn't even an agent any more. She had a duty to discover him. She owed that much to football fans everywhere. It wasn't right that he was stuck out here with nobody to watch him but a small domestic audience. He needed a bigger stage.

She had never felt this way before – the instant attraction – like a young girl in love, the certainty that he was The One. She didn't want him, of course not, not in that way; he was a child – it wasn't like that at all. When she saw Joe she didn't see a man, or even a boy. She saw a player.

Who one day would play in front of the entire world.

Another dash at goal, another lucky save from the over-worked goalkeeper.

The old guy on her right, his voice muffled by collar, coat and scarf, shouted something excitable and thumped her on the shoulder.

Of course she didn't understand, but number eleven had the home crowd all fired up.

The inspired way he played football reminded her of England striker Wayne Rooney at his very best, but with a grace more usual in a South American or perhaps African player. The ball seemed to stick to his feet and no matter where he picked it up he would turn and run hell-bent at goal, pulled towards it on an invisible thread. Defenders might try to stop him, but he would sidestep them as if he was merely dancing, keeping the ball close to him, twisting first one way and then the other.

He couldn't see the opponents. He only had eyes for goal.

During the second half she saw him flick the ball high over the head of a bullish defender, almost mocking his attempts to steal possession. And when he casually controlled the ball so that it fell back to earth precisely where he wanted it she could have sworn she saw Josef flash a cheeky grin.

Wow.

For the first time in weeks she stopped mulling over the three hundred thousand, she stopped obsessing over the enemy that had orchestrated her demise. She lost herself in the beautiful game.

He was the kind of player that made you love football, even if you never thought you would.

Gabe was waiting for her in the players' lounge afterwards. What had once been a grim, depressing place reminiscent of a staff canteen could now, thanks to Lubin's revamp, compare with the hippest bars in Central Europe. For a bar in Poland owned by a Russian, this place did a mean coffee. This country where she felt utterly foreign was starting to get under her skin in a way she couldn't quite fathom.

'So what did you think?' he said.

She could hardly tell Gabe that she hadn't been watching him, that her eyes had been glued to another man. A boy. And, as every agent knew, the younger the better. So she nodded and said something encouraging, while keeping a keen watch on the door, waiting for the kid. Gabe noticed.

'Looking for someone?'

'I, er . . .'

'Are you and Lubin having a fling?'

'What? No. Where did you hear that?'

'He was asking about you.'

She was flattered, but decided to tell Gabe the truth. 'I was looking for number eleven. The striker.'

'Josef Wandrowszcki?'

'That's right.' She'd read his name in the flimsy match programme.

'Little Joe. Good, isn't he?' said Gabe. 'Special.'

'He can't pass,' said Samantha, trying to be pragmatic, trying to contain the feeling of utter infatuation, like a girl with an inappropriate crush, 'and his finishing could be sharper. Plus, he didn't score, did he? And for a striker I'd say that's imperative.'

'But he's the best young player you've seen for years, right?' Gabe motioned to one of the passing waitresses who looked like a supermodel. A moment later he had a beer in his hand.

'I think,' she said, willing to concede, 'that he's the best young player I've ever seen.'

Gabe's spirits sank. She saw them go and she knew why. Joe was better than Gabe, a lot better, and they were essentially chasing the same spot on the first team. His first professional contract, and probably his last, and he was outplayed by a kid young enough to be his son.

'He's a smashing kid,' said Gabe grudgingly. He cheered himself up a bit by watching the supermodel waitress from behind.

Samantha saw the line of his sight and frowned. She was used to having to keep a close watch on her young players, to make sure they didn't misbehave, not too much, but she had hoped Gabe would be mature enough to realize he didn't have to change just because his pay packet had. But then she hadn't really known him before. Maybe he'd always had a roving eye and, as she watched him make short work of his beer, a sizeable thirst. But she had an instinct for these things and it was telling her that Gabe Muswell might be one to watch. And not in a good way. She pulled the conversation back to the boy wonder.

'He's a friend of yours? Josef?' she asked. 'How's his English?'

Gabe paused, his glass halfway to his mouth. 'What? He *is* English. Didn't you know?'

That's when she suspected that Joe might just be a megastar.

Joe gave himself a pep talk in the empty changing room.

So you didn't score, so what?

It must have been his nerves. Gabe had told him that Sam Sharp was in town and knowing that the powerful agent lady was out there somewhere watching him, the kind of person who could take him out of this poxy team, out of this poxy bloody country and into the beautiful game for real, had put him off.

England. Where players earned millions and got all the pretty girls.

Where every young boy dreamed of being a footballer, where he would be a hero to thousands every Saturday afternoon and on telly every Saturday night.

Where his dad would be able to see him on the back page of the papers and say, that's my boy.

So he didn't score. He had still played well. He thought he'd shown off some pretty silky skills, especially in the second half when he could tell some of the more experienced players were tiring while he still felt like he could go for hours. He'd run up the left wing at top speed, clocking a sixty-metre time that must have been right up there with the very best athletes; he'd weaved and dodged tackles like a rugby pro. But he hadn't scored. And football was about balls in the back of the net. That was the only score that counted.

Idiot.

It was Joe's dream to play football in England. He wanted to move in with his nan, play for Arsenal and marry Layla Petherick.

Dickhead.

Sometimes when he was drunk he amused himself by trying to decide which he wanted to do more, play for Arsenal or marry Layla Petherick. He never could come down on either side. He couldn't play for Arsenal for ever, whereas wedded bliss with Layla would last a lifetime. On the other hand, he didn't stand a chance with Layla unless he did something, was something, incomparably impressive. So where did that leave him?

It was simple. He'd have to do both.

How often did a top football agent come all the way over to this European outpost? Never. Hardly ever. Except today one had. And he hadn't scored. And his dad wouldn't be able to say, 'that's my boy' at all.

Shit.

She saw pound signs flashing in front of her eyes when she saw Joe walking towards them. The kid was gorgeous, talented and above all English. He was a rough diamond, but his potential was unmatched on the English football stage. He was the kind of player the country had been waiting for, hoping for, praying for. The kind of player you'd take out to a tournament as a wildcard, a playmaker, somebody to bring on in the last fifteen minutes when you needed a flash of creativity, when you needed a miracle.

Her head was spinning. What could she do? How could she play this? Nobody influential would have seen this kid yet, otherwise he would have been snapped up. She had him exclusively in the palm of her hand, but for how long? White Stars had made it through to the last thirty-two of the UEFA Cup. If they made it to the last sixteen then it was only a matter of weeks before his talent was exposed to a wider audience and then surely others would come calling.

Think, Sam, think.

What could she offer him? Her brain felt stiff from lack of use. It wasn't fair to be given this opportunity if there was nothing she could make from it, yet her options were few. She could introduce him to an old friend, someone at Legends whom she liked, except there was nobody there she felt inclined to do a favour for, not even Jackson. Especially not Jackson.

A club manager then. She could make one last deal. A blistering, headline-grabbing deal that would sweep the bad press away and remind anyone who cared that she was Sam Sharp: Superagent, not some drug dealer running out of luck.

Think.

She could set up on her own. Her stiff brain flexed in response to the good idea.

That's exactly what she should do. There was nothing to stop her. She still had her FIFA licence. But who would trust her? Perhaps if she was to set up out here she could put enough distance between a new venture and her soiled reputation in England. She would have Gabe still, and maybe Joe too, unless he knew how good he was, because if he knew how good he was then why on earth would he want to sign with a disgraced and fallen agent like her when he could wait and see what other offers he might get?

'Good game,' she said.

'I didn't score,' said Joe woefully, rubbing his nose as if he was embarrassed.

'I did,' said Gabe.

But she hardly heard him. Was her idea to relocate really feasible? It would be like starting over, but with all the skills and contacts she had taken half a lifetime to accumulate. She could keep her ear to the ground, employ some Slavic assistants who spoke the languages and tap a market that so far had produced few stars, save for a couple of Czechs and Croatians. Who else was looking out for the new players? A few scouts spread thinly across the region – that would be her only competition. They were all EU now, weren't they? One big happy European family. So there wouldn't even be work-visa issues (it was surprising how much red tape could hamper a deal for months).

She could bide her time and wait for the important transfer window. From the first day of January players could be bought and sold for one month and one month only. She could launch back into the business on a flurry of lucrative deals. She would have to fund herself until January. If she missed the transfer window she would have to wait until summer to transfer players and that would put too much strain on her finances. She could lose everything.

So until January. Two months, a little less. It was no time at all. Then one day if her name was cleared she could go home. What better way to win a war against some unknown adversary than refuse to be cowed? To come home a bigger success than ever? It would be two fingers up to everyone who had doubted her.

Sam Sharp: International Superagent.

Could she? Could she really?

The important agent lady was hardly even looking at him. She looked like something was funny. Him probably. Joe cursed himself for getting all worked up about an opportunity that was probably all in his head.

What did he expect? That she would swoop in, be dazzled by his talent and fly him off in a helicopter to Arsenal HQ where he would have a one-to-one with the manager, sign a contract on the spot and drink champagne to celebrate? Yeah, maybe in Poland he was a pro footballer, when both the first-team strikers were out through injury, but that didn't mean anything. Look at Gabe, for heaven's sake: a non-league player who was as old as his *dad* had made the team. That should surely tell him something about standards.

He immediately felt bad. Gabe was a decent enough player, and running him down wouldn't make Joe feel any better.

But he had been unable to sleep the night before with a sense of anticipation that within a few short hours he might be that inch closer to his dream. 'My agent is coming to see me play,' Gabe had said, and since he'd said it Joe had thought of little else. Without someone else's intervention he wouldn't have the first idea how to get a trial for an English club, how to even make sure that the right people knew he existed.

In his imagination Samantha Sharp had become a kind of fairy godmother who made dreams come true.

And he hadn't even scored. But he really wanted her to like him.

She asked Joe small-talk questions about his background. He was the product of a passionate fling between his Polish mother, Ana, and his father, Simon. Seventeen years ago Joe's father was watching the fall of communism on the news and knew with a true hedonist's instinct that one of the greatest parties the world had ever seen would be kicking off all summer long in Eastern Europe.

'The way he tells it,' said Joe, 'you'd think he knocked the Berlin wall down on his way. Mum says he was five days too late and everyone was already hungover by the time he got here.'

Great story. Samantha was already thinking of the glossy magazine that might pay for such a tale.

Joe had been around White Stars first as a dogsbody, then as a junior, now finally as a player. Every spare moment of his life for as long as he could remember had been spent with a ball at his talented feet. 'I've always spent summers with my dad,' he said. 'I love England, but I was lucky to be born Polish. I'm not good enough to play for Man United. I know that. But out here, I make the team. Now we're in the UEFA Cup. Dad'll be able to tell all his mates.'

This wasn't the time to tell Joe that she thought he was wrong. He *was* good enough to play in England, and the fact that he didn't know it yet was part of his charm. Seventeen years old and oozing enough raw talent to ensure that some-where soon they would be chanting his name. He could be hers, but she had to play it just right. If the kid knew how good he was he could be running off to Legends in an instant.

'Listen, Joe,' she said, 'I'd really like to see you again.'

Gabe sighed. 'Will you two cut it out? You're acting like a couple on a first date.' Impatiently he poked Joe in the back to make him move closer. Then he reached out for Samantha's shoulders, turning her so she faced Joe dead on. 'That's better,' he said with satisfaction, reminding her of a photographer arranging a shot.

'Now, Joe,' he said, 'just before you came out Sam said she thought you were the best young player she'd ever seen. Sam, Joe was so worked up about you being here today he put his boots on the wrong feet.'

They both said, 'Really?' at the same time.

Joe had a really sweet grin, and she had a prescient flash of all the prepubescent girls (and boys too) who would have his poster on their walls when he was a big star.

'Thanks, Gabe,' she said. 'I was trying to play it cool.'

'Me too,' said Joe.

'Just get it on, will you? You're making me feel like a right gooseberry.'

'So let's talk,' she said to Joe. 'Who looks after you?'

'My mum,' he said, and she thought he had misunder-stood and rephrased her question.

'Your career, I mean. Who looks after your career?'

'Still Mum.'

'Bring her then. Tomorrow? Say twelve noon? I'm stay-ing at the Sheraton.'

'She has to work,' he said. 'Wednesday's her day off.'

'Wednesday then,' said Samantha. In England, a player of Joe's calibre could ensure that his mother would never have to work again.

There was a buzz at the far end of the bar. The boss had arrived.

Aleksandr.

Without thinking about it, her hands smoothed her clingy black top down over her waist and hips and she stood a little taller in her black spike-heeled boots, both items chosen with care. Just like the stockings and suspenders she was wearing underneath. She had been waiting for him. Even as she watched the match and talked to Gabe and then to Joe she had been waiting.

She took two steps towards him and then stopped.

He had an exquisitely formed blonde draped over his arm. Of course he did. He was a beautiful, extraordinarily rich young playboy, the same person he was last time, but she wasn't Sam Sharp: Superagent any more. Three hundred thousand dollars had seen to that.

She turned back to Gabe and Joe and tried to ignore the Russian.

Yet she could sense him getting closer. The sound of his name on others' lips drew nearer, the hum of his presence pulled all eyes to him and it was impossible not to turn and watch him come.

Slowly (or perhaps that was just her perception of his achingly measured movement) he made his way across the crowded bar towards them.

'Another great goal, Gabe,' he said. 'And, Josef, what's that? Two games lacking your name on the score sheet now?'

Joe ducked his head, suddenly fascinated by the tops of his shoes.

She felt a defensive stab of outrage. He was being unfair. The ball wouldn't even have been there for Gabe if it hadn't been for Joe's lightning run up the wing and deft lob into the area. Besides, Gabe's goal really wasn't that great, a scrappy effort a few feet off the goal line. It was as much luck as judgement that put the ball in the back of the net.

'Is comparing two performances really the best way to motivate your young players?' she said.

He looked at her, momentarily taken aback. She had a humiliating sense that he had forgotten who she was.

Oh shit. She'd meant it light-heartedly, but it hadn't come out that way. Her rush of jealousy had tinged the comment with bitterness.

Then he lifted her hand and pressed it to his mouth. 'A pleasure to see you again, Samantha,' he said. 'Why don't we ask him? Joe, do you feel motivated to score goals?'

'I . . . er . . .' He looked from Samantha to Lubin, his eyes wide, torn between two people he needed to impress.

'Every player does,' she said smoothly, saving him. 'Every player worth knowing about.'

'And you know all there is to know, isn't that right?'

'I like to think so.'

He dropped his voice to murmur into her ear. 'I have been thinking of you.' He hooked her in with those dark and dangerous eyes and she hoped he was picking up the scent of Dior on her throat. She arched her back slightly as the shockwaves from his breath on her earlobe travelled south.

'Not too hard I hope,' she said.

'Hard enough.' He turned her gently away from the two players to make their conversation more private. Gabe latched on to Lubin's blonde without a hope.

'I read these terrible things in the newspapers,' said Lubin, 'and I wonder how you are coping.'

'I can handle it,' she said.

'I'm sure.' He nodded thoughtfully. 'You have your nice boyfriend to help you to handle it? He is with you on this trip?'

She smiled thinly at the way he made a nice boyfriend sound like a bad rash. 'We aren't together any more,' she said.

'I see.'

Gabe glanced in her direction and said something to Joe and the blonde, who both laughed. Were they laughing at her? She turned firmly back to Lubin and tried not to feel so paranoid. Most paranoid people, someone wiser than her once said, are merely self-obsessed. Just because you're constantly thinking of yourself doesn't mean anyone else is.

'Unfortunately I am with someone tonight,' said Lubin, as if to suggest that otherwise he wouldn't leave her side until morning. 'But tomorrow I would very much like to take you to dinner if you are free. You are free?'

'I am free,' she said, unsure whether they were both talking about her plans or her romantic status. But either way the answer was the same.

18

The restaurant he had chosen was high above the Rynek Glowny, the medieval square dominated by the elaborate Cloth Hall. Late at night, now that the stall holders had gone home and taken their touristy wares with them, it was easier to imagine the city as it would once have been, a wealthy trading centre, rich in art and beauty.

She threw some coins at a violinist on the street, the eerie melody capturing her mood perfectly. Just being here made her feel more European, less like a typical English person treading carefully through life, fearful of embarrassing situations. What better place to start over than somewhere new? London was full of her past. A place like this could be her future.

She climbed the stone stairs to the restaurant. So deep in thought was she, thinking of offices somewhere on this very square, of swarthy Eastern European defenders and cunning deals, that she was in front of Lubin's table for a few seconds before she looked up and saw him.

His eyes narrowed and the meanness of his expression snapped her back into the evening ahead.

'Sorry,' she said, slipping into the seat opposite him. 'I was miles away.'

He looked confused and she wondered if the idiom had been lost in translation.

'I was thinking about something else,' she said. But that

sounded even worse. She smiled and took a deep breath. 'How are you?'

'I am not used to waiting,' he said.

She was only ten minutes late.

She couldn't think of anything to say so she looked down at the menu instead. It was all in Polish.

Lubin suggested that he order for both of them, and from his tone she suspected that it was not so much a suggestion as an instruction. He didn't ask her for any likes or dislikes, just rattled off a stream of indecipherable Polish to the supplicating waiter and then dismissed him with a wave of his hand.

Too young, too moody. I shouldn't be here.

And yet she squirmed in her seat, imagining what he would be like when he was truly angry. For so long it had been Jackson, only Jackson. The idea of a new lover, this one, young and vital, awakened fresh desire that made her burn.

He looked out of the window and took a deep breath and whatever was irking him lifted from his features. He wasn't smiling exactly, but he was no longer looking at her with something close to hate.

'I especially don't like waiting for you,' he said. 'The thought of a beautiful woman is too tormenting.'

'Um, thank you?'

'You're most welcome.'

This fling, if that's what it was to be, couldn't possibly go anywhere. But then didn't that make it the perfect relationship for her?

'You didn't grow up in Poland?' she asked. 'How long have you been here?'

He didn't take much prompting to talk about himself. He told her about his humble childhood in the Ukraine. He brushed sharply aside the tragic death of his mother and she wondered whether that was because it was too painful to talk about or perhaps not painful enough. For it was startlingly clear that Aleksandr was his father's son, and the conversation was thick with mentions of Goran Lubin's name.

'My father can defend every acquisition that he made,' he said, over an appetizer of faultless caviar. 'There are no ethical question marks above his interests. This is rare in modern Russia.'

Rare? She thought it was unheard of. To hear others tell it you could almost believe that induction to the Russian Mafiya came free with every first million. All that money made directly after the fall of communism was made in a lawless land. Only the most determined and ruthless emerged grasping such enormous wealth. Either his father was the last honest billionaire in Russia or his son was so blinded with hero worship that he saw only that which he wanted to see.

He had ordered duck for both of them, which wouldn't have been her first choice even though she could tell it was perfectly cooked and served. Having never been the subservient type she wondered if this was what it would be like to be in a relationship playing that role. Constantly bending your appetite to another's will. After a lifetime of making decisions there was something liberating about relinquishing responsibility for a while, even if that meant you did end up with duck. Jackson never dominated her. Unless she wanted him to.

'You are staying at the Sheraton?' he asked, clearly disgusted.

She cocked her head to one side, curious. 'You don't like the Sheraton?'

'The British are like the Americans – they are drawn to names they know; they trust the familiar.'

'And you?'

'I enjoy the unknown. And I trust no one.'

He drank a bottle of champagne without her help. 'Your trouble, in England,' he said, 'it is over?'

'Not really. I've hired a private investigator.'

'Why?'

'What do you mean? So that I can clear my name.'

'You want your old job back?'

'I don't like being under suspicion,' she said. 'I think somebody is trying to ruin me. I want to know who. I want to know why.'

'And you think that knowing this will make everything okay again?'

'You don't?'

'The Lubin family name has been dragged into scandal numerous times. I do not worry. Enemies are a by-product of success. I think scandal makes headlines. The truth does not. Even if you find out exactly how this happened to you, and you tell a hundred reporters, you think they will print anything? You think anyone will care?'

'I care,' she said.

'But you already know you are innocent.'

There was an undeniable truth to what he said. The old uptight thoroughly British Samantha might battle on purely for truth and principle, but perhaps this new European version of herself could be more relaxed. About everything. In time the scandal that made her leave behind her old life might be the best thing that could have happened.

All her dreams of success had been so fixated on London she had forgotten that there was an entire world out there to conquer.

She could just let it go.

She snapped out of her thoughts to find him staring at her again. When he looked at her like that she felt like an item on a menu, like he wanted to *eat* her, and she was stirred in his presence.

'So tonight you will see my apartment,' he said.

She wanted the adventure of him. And yet, damn it, she knew that it would be a reckless escapade, full of risk, promising nothing. Was that really the best way to start over in a new town? 'I'm not sure, Alek. It's late and I have a full day tomorrow.'

'It wasn't a question,' he said. 'Tonight you will see my apartment. If this was about business I would have invited you to lunch.' He assumed they had both known that dinner in the finest restaurant in Krakow was just a polite preamble to the real reason they were here.

She could still say no.

She pictured herself going home to her empty hotel room. If she went with him she knew that she might regret it, she might not. If she went back to the hotel alone she thought there was a good chance she could end up ordering porn and feeling lonely as hell. She would regret that for sure.

The building where he lived looked unspectacular from the outside; a slash of graffiti on the messy brick wall was half hidden by an enormous mountain of snow that had been piled up by a snowplough and left to get dirty and grey. She had to tread carefully in her heels. Not very romantic. She wanted to keep her buzz, so concentrated on how beautiful he was, and rich, and young. Like a footballer only better. Footballers rarely wanted to tolerate powerful women. And they all wanted kids. Their taste vacillated from mother to whore with very little in between, and she was neither. Lubin wasn't threatened by her strength. And she found that attractive.

In the shadows behind them she saw a dark figure and flinched. Was someone following them?

'Don't worry,' he said. 'I'll protect you.'

She laughed, because the idea of Samantha Sharp needing to be protected was absurd. 'I've been taking care of myself for . . . years,' she said. She'd almost said exactly how many years, but had stopped herself just in time. But she looked behind them again all the same. 'Do you ever feel like you're being watched?' she said.

'Why?' he asked. 'Is that the kind of thing that gets you hot? You're very safe with me, Samantha. I stand to inherit over seven billion dollars. I have the most secure apartment in Krakow.'

He pushed through thick wooden doors and they walked across a cobbled courtyard, unprepossessing even in the dim light. But at the far end, through another set of doors, they entered a beautiful atrium, the soaring glass ceiling above the perfect modern contrast to the cobbles underfoot. A liveried doorman nodded at them, but was ignored.

In the elevator Lubin took a key from his pocket and

inserted it into a discreet niche by the panel of numbered floors.

She wondered if he would grab her in the elevator, but he didn't and the sexual tension ratcheted up another notch or two until she was so turned on she thought perhaps he could feel the heat radiating from her. They moved smoothly upward until the doors opened straight into his truly glorious penthouse apartment.

He knew she would be impressed. Women always were. He enjoyed seeing her expression as she took in five thousand feet of spectacular city living, the floor to ceiling windows across the width of the room showing off the city, the lights of the bridges over the Vistula River, the floodlit Wawel Castle in the foreground and the terracotta rooftops of churches and convents caught by street lights stretching towards the main square.

In London, she thought, if such a place existed, it would cost millions. In London such an enormous space would surely have been converted into ten regular-sized apartments and sold for a million each.

The apartment itself was austere, the walls a uniform slate grey, pieces of sculpted art sparsely displayed where they could cast the most dramatic shadows, an enormous stone fireplace cut into the wall. Modern touches came in the form of a plasma screen and a stainless-steel kitchen. The whole place was cold and masculine, the only warmth was the aged oak parquet beneath her feet.

'Wow,' she said. She knew a response of some kind was expected.

'Of course I cannot be sure,' he said. 'But I think I have the finest view in the city.'

It was spectacular. She was unable to stop staring out at the fairytale concoction of castles and spires. He came up behind her and his arms looped around her waist. He swept her hair away from one shoulder and dipped his head to kiss her neck. It was the first time he had touched her and she felt herself turn liquid, melting.

She twisted towards him, offering up her lips and he pushed her against the cold glass as he pressed a kiss upon them, clutching a handful of hair at the base of her neck so that she couldn't move. She was hungry for him, probing deeper, feeling the kiss all the way down to her high heels. After a moment he drew back.

'Is something wrong?' she asked, her legs trembling, longing to sit down, to lie down, longing to be kissed again.

'Perhaps this is a mistake. We do business together.'

'Don't you think,' she said, snaking her hand round his waist and feeling the mean muscles on his back, 'that you should always mix business with pleasure?' Her voice was husky with desire, her lips still moist from his kiss.

Lubin walked over to the kitchen. She watched with some dismay as he took a small wrap from his pocket and started to cut two lines of cocaine on his stainless-steel work surface. She winced as he spilt some and brushed it carelessly onto the floor.

Once Liam would have worked a whole week to afford what you just spilt.

He took a small silver straw from his inside pocket and snorted up one of the lines before offering the straw to her.

She shook her head. 'Not now,' she said, 'maybe later.' She meant 'never' but it seemed too judgemental to say so.

Jackson hated drugs.

Jackson. She knocked back the thought of him.

He shrugged and had the second line himself. 'Later we'll be busy,' he said. He sniffed loudly and patted the edge of his nose with his fingertips. 'Take off your clothes now.'

'Just like that?'

'Just like that.'

God, the thrill of being ordered around. It was shameful. She shrugged off her jacket and twisted out of her skirt, stepping from it carefully. Then she slipped off her shirt so that she stood in front of him in just her heels and her black satin underwear.

She stared at him provocatively, running a lazy hand over her own curves. She knew she had a beautiful body. Funny how being half naked made her feel more powerful.

He came to her again and kissed her, biting at her lips, his hands moving across her body, his breath coming throaty and warm. It seemed like she was drowning, her body lost to the exciting sensations of an unfamiliar touch. Between kisses he kept telling her she was gorgeous, fucking gorgeous, and she told him he was turning her on and making her burn. He stopped, eyes hungry, hard-on unmistakable, mouth wet from her kiss.

'Now what?' she teased.

'The window,' he said thickly, dragging off his shirt and fumbling with his flies, 'get up against the window.'

She pressed her palms against the freezing glass.

He placed his hands on either side of her hips, pulling her back into him. She shuddered with responsiveness. His fingertips played across her bare belly and the tops of her thighs, tantalizing her. She stared down at the city far below and felt dizzy. She bit down on her lip as he grabbed at her breast with one hand while reaching into her with the other. She pushed up against his hand, grinding disgracefully, desperate to feel him inside her.

Then abruptly he pulled back. His head whipped round the far side of the room and she noticed the faint whirring sound of the elevator.

He sprang away from the window and cursed in Russian: '*Yob tvoyu mat!*'

It was like a bucket of cold water. She was confused, watching as he bolted to the kitchen and hastily pocketed the cocaine wrap and the straw, frantically wiping down the surface to ensure no tell-tale trace of white powder remained.

'Dress yourself,' he said, throwing her suit and shirt at her feet. She did as she was told, the abrupt change of mood like a dream rudely interrupted.

'What is it?' she said, but was ignored.

Mere seconds later the door to the elevator opened and his father stepped into the room. She recognized him from the cover of *Fortune* magazine, and, besides, his son's cowering reaction would surely have tipped her off.

He was unhappy. He barked something in Russian, flicking his hand towards her.

'Father, this is Samantha Sharp. She's an agent from London. This is a business meeting.'

Goran Lubin switched seamlessly to English. 'Then I suggest you do up your shirt.'

She tried not to smile. Aleksandr diminished as she watched, no longer a billionaire playboy, just a boy, and one clearly terrified of Daddy. He fumbled with the buttons on his shirt, his eyes darting around the apartment, no doubt checking for more contraband.

'My son and I have personal business to discuss,' he said, fixing her with an uncompromising gaze, his eyes solid like blocks of onyx. 'I'm afraid you'll have to leave.'

She didn't need to be told twice. She gathered her things and said a brief goodbye to Aleksandr who looked as if he'd push her from the window if it meant she'd leave sooner. As the doors to the lift closed behind her she thought she heard his father shouting in Russian.

She leant against the wall and started to laugh. Behind every rich playboy is a father that must be obeyed. Suddenly she saw all Aleksandr's posturing as a poor imitation of his father's power. *He's really far too young for me.*

But she couldn't help thinking about what would have happened if they hadn't been interrupted. And she enjoyed thinking about it too much to say never again.

19

Layla Petherick lived next door to his grandmother and Joe had been in love with Layla since he was seven years old.

One day he would tell her and they would live happily ever after.

Even at seven Joe was rarely to be found without a football at his feet, except when annoying things like eating or school got in the way. His father encouraged his son's football craziness; without it he wouldn't really know what to do with him.

Until he was about thirteen Joe thought that his dad lived here with Nan, in her West Sussex semi-detached a short drive from the sea, not realizing that Simon lived in a small one-bedroom flat in east London in a neighbourhood full of flats just like it, swarming with traffic and trouble, and not much else.

No place for a child, so when he visited England to see his dad they went to Nan's, which was ace, because he got to play football in the garden and watch Brighton and Hove Albion play at home, and he got to meet Layla.

Seven-year-old Joe was thwacking his football, a new Adidas one, up against a brick wall in the back garden, trying hard to find some pattern between the way he kicked the ball and the way it came back at him, already aware that it was supposed to make a difference. He'd heard a man called Des Lynam talking about 'side' and 'spin' on a football programme called *Match of the Day* and if that's what Dennis Bergkamp did then Joe wanted to learn how.

Over and over again he would kick the ball – first on the left, then on the right – until he could safely predict which way he had to move to connect with the rebound. His little seven-year-old face creased in concentration while he practised, with annoyance when he made a mistake, and sheer delight when the ball went just the way he wanted it to.

Left, right, left, right.

It was starting to get dark and he knew that soon his nan would call him in for dinner and then his dad would get back from work and his precious football time would be over. Dad liked to have a kick-about in the garden, but that was always the same: he stood in goal and let Joe score. It was fun, and he particularly liked making his dad laugh with elaborate scoring celebrations, but it wasn't making him a better player. If he wanted to play for Arsenal one day then he needed serious practice, not silly games.

And Dad never took anything seriously.

Thwack went the ball against the brick wall. Thwack. Thwack.

He heard the back gate of the house next door open and heard footsteps in their garden. Then a little blonde girl that looked pretty enough to be on the telly sprang through a hole in the hedge, surprising him and making him miss, kicking out at nothing and almost falling over.

She walked to the stray ball, picked it up and walked away with it under her arm without saying a word.

'Hey!' said Joe. 'Hey, that's my ball.' It was a recent gift from his dad, the exact same style of ball that was being used in the World Cup qualifiers, a ball too big and too expensive for any regular seven-year-old, and Joe loved it dearly. 'Hey!'

But the little girl didn't even turn round. So Joe did what any seven-year-old would do. He ran inside and told his nan.

His lip quivered as he told the tale of the terrible thief next door and the loss of his beloved ball, so she marched next door with her grandson and rang the front doorbell.

The little blonde girl answered, her nose high in the air. 'May I help you?' she said.

'That's her,' said Joe, nudging his nan with his elbow and glaring at the girl. 'That's the robber.'

'Hello, Layla,' said his nan, who had known the little girl since the day she came home from the hospital as a pink newborn. 'What's all this about you stealing my grandson's football?'

'I didn't steal it,' said Layla. 'I confiscated it.'

'What does "confiscate" mean?' said Joe.

'Who are you and why do you talk funny?' said Layla.

'This is my grandson, Josef,' said his nan. 'He lives in Poland. Joe, "confiscate" is just a big word that means taking something away. So why did you confiscate his football, Layla?'

The little girl took his nan's hand and led her through the house to the back garden. Joe followed, convinced that this girl was evil incarnate.

'See there?' said Layla, pointing at the big brick wall he had been practising against, the perfect wall, big and flat with a smooth, even lawn in front of it. 'That's where he was kicking.'

'That's my wall,' said Joe.

'No,' said Layla, 'it's mine.'

She took them back inside and Joe realized that actually she was right; his wall belonged to her house and he had been aiming the ball roughly at the place where the television was. 'Bang, bang, bang,' she said. 'It was too noisy.'

'Oh,' said Joe. He could see how it might be.

'You can have your ball back when *Grange Hill* has finished and the news is on,' she said. 'Okay?'

'What's *Grange Hill*?'

Layla's eyes widened in alarm. How could anyone not know what *Grange Hill* was?

'You can watch it with me if you like,' she said generously. 'I've got Quavers.'

He didn't know what Quavers were either. He looked at his nan, who nodded and smiled. 'Would you like that, Joe?'

How was he supposed to know?

By the end of the short children's television programme Joe had decided that he loved English television, he loved English crisps, but mostly he loved the girl called Layla who lived next door to his grandmother.

The courage to tell her had eluded him for the last ten years.

His nan still lived in the same place, and though he had by now seen and stayed at his dad's place in Leyton (and his dad had by now moved to a two-bedroom place, which he had briefly and disastrously tried to share with a raunchy black woman called Maureen), Joe much preferred spending his English weekends in West Sussex. Simon came down as soon as he finished work on Friday and they spent the next two days as a relatively happy family.

Joe was sharing a cup of tea and a biscuit with his nan while they watched one of her favourite daytime quiz shows when he heard the tell-tale crunch of the gravel in next door's driveway. He looked up immediately, like a deer hearing a twig snap in the woods and his nan smiled affectionately. 'Go on,' she said.

It had been almost a month since he'd last seen Layla. Weekend fixtures had kept him away. He wondered whether she had thought about him in that time. It was stupid to think that she might have thought about him as much as he thought about her, but it might be nice if he had entered her head once or twice.

Joe thought about Layla pretty much all the time.

He wondered what she was doing, who she was spending her time with, what she thought about things that were in the news, whether she liked records he heard or was interested in the English books he started to read just in case she might read them too. He thought about the shape of her face, the angles of her smile, the sweet curves of her body. Mostly he thought about what she would say when he told her that he loved her, and how he would ever find the courage to say it at all. Because Joe truly loved Layla intensely, like the lyrics of a love song, but he was convinced that she could never love him back, so he kept silent.

One day he thought the perfect moment would arise. In his most frequent daydreams about that moment he didn't have to say anything at all; she realized that he was her soulmate, and they just sort of fell into each other naturally and made plans for the rest of their lives.

He watched her now as she parked her new Fiat Uno in the driveway and spent a few moments gathering her things before getting out of the car. He stayed hidden in the alleyway, finding intimacy in the simple act of observing her and knowing that she was being entirely herself, unaware that she was being watched. The way she lifted her thick blonde fringe from her eyes almost killed him.

Maybe the perfect moment would be tonight.

She climbed out of her car, one shapely denim-clad leg at a time, wearing boots he hadn't seen before, but carrying the same handbag she'd had last time, and he stepped out so that she would see him.

'Joe!'

Her grey-green eyes flared with an easy smile and he felt his heart lurch sideways as it always did when Layla smiled.

'Nobody told me you were coming,' she said. 'It feels like ages.' She threw her arm round his shoulder in half a hug.

'Four weeks,' he said, and then immediately wondered if that sounded weird, like he'd been counting.

She released her grip on him then and his soul gave a little sigh of disappointment, already wondering when next he might touch her.

'Come inside,' she said. 'Shall we have a drink? Do you have time before your dinner? I've so much to tell you.'

'Me too,' he said. He wanted to tell her about signing with Samantha Sharp, about playing in the UEFA Cup, about edging one step closer to his dreams. He wanted her to be proud.

Joe had been looking forward to telling his dad about the UEFA Cup almost as much as telling Layla. Telling Dad lasted less than thirty seconds, then he sat on his own and watched telly while his dad told everyone else. He knew that he should have been pleased by the way his dad leapt up to phone all his mates, but he felt a bit hollow. It was clear that his dad was proud, but Joe would have liked some of that pride to be reflected onto him instead of immediately thrown out to the wider world. Instead of 'well done, son,' it was more a case of 'hasn't my son done well?'

When he told Layla she reacted exactly the way he would have wanted her to.

'Ohmigod! That's amazing!' she said, and she flung her arms around him again, pressing her chest up against his so that he was scared she would ask him why his heart was racing, thereby presenting him with the perfect moment to tell her that for years now she had been the measure of his dreams. He wanted to tell her how he felt about her, but nothing terrified him more.

'I was wondering,' he said nervously – for what he wanted to say now was not a declaration of love, but it was still scary – 'I was wondering if maybe you fancied coming over for the match?'

'To Krakow?'

She'd never been, and he thought this was an opportunity. He would play the best game of his life, score a hat-trick, be named man of the match. She couldn't fail to be impressed. His mind had played out a thousand times what it would be like to show her his home town, where he could take her to the hidden romantic spots where one thing might lead to another and kissing her on the lips would be as easy and natural as breathing. Or maybe if that didn't work then getting her drunk on Polish vodka instead.

She liked drinking, Layla, and the last time they were drunk together, New Year's Day, she'd been totally blotto on Nan's lethal punch and he had thought at one point that if he'd snogged her she would have been up for it. She might not have *remembered* it, but she would have snogged him back all the same. But his nerve had failed him that night. In Krakow, fresh from a triumphant football match, on his turf, maybe (surely?) things would be different.

'When is it exactly?' she said, and he gave her the date, trying not to sound like her answer meant everything to him.

'Oh shit,' she said, 'I think we have plans. I can see if I can get out of it.'

He felt dizzy and saw spots in front of his eyes. *We? We? Who the fuck was 'we'?*

'We?' he said faintly.

'Me and Daniel. Ohmigod! I haven't told you about Daniel?'

And so Joe sat there for twenty minutes, without question the longest, most painful twenty minutes of his life, feeling like someone was scraping out his heart with an old teaspoon while Layla, his soulmate, the only girl he had ever loved, described exactly when and how she had fallen in love with someone else.

20

Samantha felt like crying. 'No, no, you're not listening to me! We've been through this already. Why don't you *listen*? There has to be a way we can make this work.' The will to live drained out of her and her voice dropped to a whisper. 'There has to be.'

'I'm sorry Ms Sharp, but there are no direct flights between Georgia and Croatia. The only way you can be back in Krakow for the seventeenth is to drop one of the destinations on your itinerary, or leave a day earlier and take a connecting flight to Frankfurt.'

Her mobile phone started to ring, the shrill sound making it even harder to concentrate. How could it be so difficult to book a few flights?

'Just forget it,' she said. 'Forget the whole thing.' She slammed down the phone and picked up her mobile. 'Hello?'

'Samantha? This is Natalya. I wait for you in the square but you do not come?'

Shit. She checked the time. She was over an hour late for her second Russian lesson. How could she have forgotten about it? 'I'll come now,' she said. 'I'll come right now.'

'I'm sorry. But I have another student. I will see you next week?'

'Next week I'm away, two weeks, okay? I'm so sorry, Natalya.'

At this rate it would take her for ever to learn a few words of Russian. She thought back to learning languages at evening classes and from tapes a decade ago, how quickly her callow brain had picked up the new skills. It seemed harder these days.

When she told Liam that she was moving abroad for a while she admired the way he had been able to pretend that it didn't bother him.

'It's a good idea,' he said. 'Running away works, I don't care what they say.'

'Is that what you think I'm doing?'

'Aren't you? I'm serious. It works. You can't get out of trouble by sticking around. You think I wouldn't have run if I'd had the chance? I lie in bed sometimes thinking about exactly how I would have pulled it off if only I'd had the forethought.'

'What do you mean?'

'I'd have run away from that accident as fast as I could have. My legs were still working, weren't they? I'd have gone to Uruguay I think. Today it's Uruguay, last week it was New Zealand and for a long time it was Tahiti. Imagine what kind of adventures I might have had, eh?'

Samantha couldn't tell if he was joking or not. She experienced a stab of something that felt suspiciously like indignation. She knew it was silly and selfish but . . . he'd have run away, would he? What about her?

'Just daydreams,' he said, 'just killing time. I have plenty of that. No adventures, just time. Tell me about Poland.'

'Not just Poland,' she said. 'Most of Central Europe, and certainly Eastern Europe is currently underexploited.

There's a few big clubs getting the scouts' attention, but there are plenty of smaller leagues too and I'm convinced they'll have some kids worth knowing about. It'll be hard, but . . .'

'If anyone can do it,' he said, 'you can.'

She twisted a piece of paper between her fingers, a flyer she hadn't even looked at yet. 'I'll try to get back whenever I can,' she said. 'I just don't know if it will be every week.'

Liam shrugged. 'When was it ever every week?'

'I'm sorry. You know I look forward to seeing you so much.'

'It's all right, Sammy, really. My next parole hearing is just round the corner. It's almost over.'

Hope leapt in her belly, but she had been disappointed in the past and allowed herself just a modest amount of cautious optimism. 'Great,' she said. 'That's great news.'

'Maybe. Let's wait and see.'

'I'll miss you.'

He didn't say that he'd miss her too. She was sure that he would; she was the only person in his life, after all. But, still, it might have been nice to hear. She was secretly nervous as hell about her new project. It was brave and bold and ambitious, all the things that she saw as her greatest assets. But perhaps, just perhaps, she might be aiming for something impossible. Each day that passed in Krakow presented a new challenge. Nothing had been easy.

The phone beeped with a call waiting. It was a representative of the football club in Georgia she had hoped to visit, wanting to know if she would need a hotel.

'I'll have to call you back.'

Hang on. If she was an hour late for her lesson with Natalya then that meant that any minute now . . .

There was a knock at the door. 'Miss Sharp? We were unable to reach you on the phone. There is a gentleman waiting for you in reception?'

'Thank you. If you tell him I'll just be a minute?' She had to find her shoes and her jacket; her day had started before she was quite ready. 'Five minutes!' she added, remembering the Polish tendency towards literalism.

She finished getting dressed and located the paperwork for this meeting under a bunch of unpaid invoices she'd had from the freelance translators she'd hired to set up initial introductions to the top clubs. Through them she had been able to speak to coaches and garner invitations to training sessions. Now they all needed to be paid. She was happy enough to use her own money to set up. She would pay herself back after the transfer window, but the time necessary to open a Polish current account and write some cheques was eluding her.

Much as she hated to admit it, things were getting on top of her. And, thinking again of Aleksandr, unfortunately not the right things.

She made it downstairs just a few minutes late, in time to meet and greet the coach of the top club in Warsaw, in town with his squad for a match with one of Krakow's other teams. He had said that he spoke English, but once they got talking it was clear he'd had somebody else write the emails they'd exchanged. The language barrier was insurmountable and the entire meeting was a waste of time.

She was disappointed with his lack of English.

He was disgusted that she was a woman.

Breakfast, she decided. Maybe with some food inside her she would feel more positive, and it would stop looking as though she had taken on too big a challenge. Why had she decided to set up here where she knew no one and the damn language was a constant frustration? Why not England?

You know why. In England she was tainted with scandal, had resigned in mysterious circumstances, was fired by her biggest clients. And she'd immediately left the country so she *must* be guilty. Perhaps she had played this all wrong. Perhaps her tactics were fatally flawed. If she didn't get it together out here then what?

Would she have to admit that she was a failure?

The restaurant had stopped serving so she went to the sports bar on the ground floor where she'd be able to get some eggs.

At least in the Sheraton you never had to worry about the language barrier. It was well known that they paid the highest wages in town, but you had to have at least three languages, one of them English, to even be seen for a job. And be beautiful. But beauty came as standard in this part of the world.

'Orange juice and coffee, please,' she said while she perused the menu.

Maybe if everything fell apart she would get a job here. And who could say that she wouldn't be happy as a waitress? Noticing the little things instead of her manic focus on the bigger picture. Where had being this career woman taken her exactly, except all alone?

A familiar voice was the perfect salve for her crisis of confidence. 'Mixing your drinks, Sam? At this hour?'

Leanne was perched on a bar stool slurping a mint-chocolate milkshake.

Samantha jumped up and hugged her former assistant.

Leanne pulled back in disgust. 'A hug?' she said. 'You've never done that before. Things must be worse than I thought.'

'How did you know I was here?'

'Everyone knows. It's quite the buzzy topic. Sam Sharp's off in some Eastern European backwater trying to find the next Davor Šuker.'

Good. Her activities still caused ripples back home. It would help when she unveiled her slate of players for sale. A slate that currently stood at one inexperienced seventeen-year-old. She needed to get it together, and fast, if she wanted to make her splash in the transfer window. 'You're here to visit?'

Leanne shrugged, offering the lifeline with about as much ceremony as a stick of chewing gum. 'I thought you might need my help,' she said.

'They fired you too, didn't they?' said Samantha.

'Of course not!' said Leanne indignantly. 'I'm shit hot at what I do. Though evidently that's not enough to save your job in a place like Legends.'

'No,' said Samantha. 'It isn't.'

'Don't worry. I left of my own accord. If I wanted to work for a dickhead like Richard I'd go and work in the City for a lot more money. I realized that what they did to you was bullshit. And, besides, I've always fancied Eastern European men. That Luka Kovač off *ER*? Hot. Viggo Mortensen? Hot.'

'I think he's Danish.'

'Oh.' Leanne looked disappointed. 'Well, never mind. There's bound to be somebody that catches my eye.'

She didn't doubt it. 'I can't pay very much,' she said. 'Not to begin with.'

'You didn't pay me very much before.'

Within a week she realized that Leanne was the missing element in her grand plan. She didn't know how she had managed without her.

'You didn't,' said Leanne. 'Simple.'

Leanne made her operate more efficiently, kept her diary, opened bank accounts, found a new travel agent who worked miracles and soon Samantha went off on her mission to discover the best unknown talent that there was.

'I didn't expect it to be easy,' she said to Leanne during one of their nightly telephone catch-ups, 'but some of these guys are locking into seven-year contracts; they've already got agents. I met a Hungarian kid yesterday who signed with an agent when he was thirteen. *Thirteen!* Am I supposed to do a tour of schools?'

'You did plenty of school visits in England,' said Leanne.

'True, but . . .'

'This isn't some unknown mountain village,' said Leanne. 'It's Europe. They have broadband internet and everything. They're clued up.'

One dismal hotel room blended into the next and she thought about giving up. There was no way this was going to work. How had Jackson done it all those years ago? Building something out of nothing was hard. And she was no Jackson Ramsay – who was she trying to kid?

Somewhere in deepest Slovenia she found her confidence again.

She was standing in the rain, a puddle of muddy water collecting around her wellington boots as she waited with infinite patience for the manager of the team out there training. He was late for his appointment with her. Her feet were as sensitive as bricks on the end of her legs and her face was raw from the lashing downpour. She had her hat pulled low and her scarf pulled high but apart from that the only thing she had to shelter herself was a newspaper, which she had held above her head for so long that it was falling apart.

Still, she didn't mind too much. She was watching her quarry, a twenty-one-year-old midfielder she had never heard of until six days ago when she'd picked him out of a highlights package that Leanne had put together from this small, and so far terribly damp, country. He was good. Good enough to warrant waiting in the rain for his manager, an Italian gentleman she had been exchanging emails with for the last few days. She wasn't prepared to miss this appointment for the sake of a bit of weather.

Eventually she saw a portly man dashing over to her, the rain bouncing off his bare, bald head.

'Sam Sharp?' he shouted. 'Inside, please, it is raining.'

I noticed.

She followed him gratefully to a warm anteroom outside what she presumed was the dressing room, where she unwrapped her wet scarf and took off her hat, her hair tumbling down her back.

He looked at her with amazement.

'I'm sorry,' he said. 'I thought you were someone else.'

'I'm Sam Sharp.'

'You can't be.'

'I'm pretty sure I am.'

'You are a woman.'

'I'm pretty sure of that too.'

'Sam Sharp?'

'Samantha,' she said, shrugging, confident that was explanation enough.

'But this is ridiculous! I cut my lunch short to talk to a top agent about my star player, not meet with a woman about . . . about what exactly?'

'About your star player.'

'But you are a woman.'

'So we have established.' She sighed. Hadn't she spent enough years already trying to break down barriers? Was she really expected to do it all over again? She jerked her head towards what she presumed was his office. 'You have a computer in there?'

He nodded.

'Take five minutes,' she said. 'Google me if it will put your mind at rest. I'll be out here checking my lipstick and, well, you know, women's things.'

He studied her, curious and then amused. 'You are not wearing lipstick.'

'No,' she said. 'Neither are you. Perhaps we have more in common than you realize. Such as recognizing Marco Vesna as a potential star and a goldmine for your club.'

'A goldmine? I'm sorry,' he said, 'my English . . .'

Smoothly she switched into Italian and he was grateful and perhaps a little bit impressed. Certainly he was impressed enough to take her to meet Marco Vesna, whom he intended to sell as soon as the price was right.

'You should tell people you are a woman,' he suggested as they said goodbye.

'Why? Do you tell people you're a man?'

'But is rare, no, for a woman to be in this business?'

'It's unique,' she said. And for the first time in her career she speculated that might be a blessing and not a curse.

She stopped questioning why any decent player would want her, a woman on her own, when they could sign with a major agency, an agency like Legends. As a woman she had gifts to draw upon that men might not have. Intuition, sensitivity, tact and a special kind of charm. She had to believe that Samantha Sharp was a force unto herself, the best in the world, not just the best they could get.

And if she had to stretch the truth a little, then so be it.

'One of the big London clubs,' she told an Estonian goalkeeper who didn't stand a chance with Arsenal or Chelsea, but might land a high six-figure sum with Millwall.

'Manchester United,' she told the mother of a talented nineteen-year-old Georgian who could possibly be seen by Manchester City if she called in a favour.

And slowly she began to build her roster.

I can do this.

Of course you can.

21

She didn't realize everyone at Legends thought she was sleeping with Jackson Ramsay until she had been working there for almost six months. Up until that point she just thought that everyone hated her because she was useless.

The night before she started work she was too nervous to get much sleep. She lay in bed, Liam's bed, and thought of him locked up in prison.

Was it wrong to be following her dreams?

From now on I'll dream for both of us.

She looked across at the second-hand suit she had bought from the Red Cross shop on Albany Road hanging on the back of the bedroom door. It had cost more to dry-clean it than to buy it. She imagined herself inhabiting that suit, inhabiting the personality of success, walking through corridors of power and making something of herself. This was the first step on the path. Her best chance.

Now all she had to do was not mess it up.

Jennie, Jackson's assistant back then, watched her trying to use a fax machine on day one and snatched the papers off her, slapping her hand away with a sigh, then fed the pages to the machine face down as they should have been and rolled her eyes. 'What kind of admin assistant doesn't know how to use a fax?'

Samantha bit back her response – *an admin assistant on her very first day* – because she badly wanted to do well and be popular.

Soon she realized that one was not entirely dependent on the other.

She stopped taking public transport after three days of commuting. She'd never tackled rush hour before, fighting her way onto the overcrowded bus to get to Kennington tube just so she could feel strangers' thighs pressed against hers for the fifteen-minute journey to Embankment. By the third day she was exhausted and strung out before the working day had even begun.

That evening the air was warm with the bud of spring. When she reached the tube station she stared forlornly at the masses tumbling into the underground cans and she just kept on walking.

She thought that perhaps she would pick up a bus somewhere along the way, but her legs kept placing her feet one in front of the other and soon she was wrapping herself against the cold chill off the Thames, walking past Lambeth Palace and a Southwark library, and then soon enough she was in Camberwell, her cheeks flushed from the walk, her heart glad with the exercise.

From that day forth she walked every day, immediately immune to the delays and the tube strikes and the rush-hour doldrums that blighted everybody else's day.

On day six, the beginning of her second week, she watched Jennie struggle with an Argentinian player on the telephone, trying to communicate simple instructions over the language barrier, and stopped off at the library on the way home.

It was quiet and calm inside and she felt soothed just by being within the hushed cool of the enormous Victorian building. You never would have known that outside four lanes of traffic went thundering past. Two forms of ID and she could borrow what she liked. It was like having an obliging friend with a fabulous old house and a massive collection of books and microfiche.

In the stacks, crammed in between out-of-date road atlases of Europe, she found a set of dusty Berlitz teach-yourself-Spanish cassettes, their cardboard cases falling apart, held together with brittle elastic bands. She popped the first one in her newly acquired Sony Walkman as she walked out.

It took her almost an hour to walk to work every day, and an hour to walk back, and though she got some funny looks at pedestrian crossings when she repeated the Spanish phrases aloud, it didn't take long for the basics to sink in.

'Let me,' she said to Jennie when she felt confident enough to try. She enjoyed watching the other girl's incredulous expression as she spoke to the Argentinian client with her newly learnt Spanish, making herself indispensable in the process. She learnt Italian next, then Portuguese. She had a bit of Japanese from evening classes that she hardly ever used and a smattering of French from school. But then everyone had a bit of French.

'If you're after my job,' said Jennie primly, 'it won't work.'

'I don't want your job,' she said truthfully. She had her eye on a bigger prize than that.

With Liam gone it was too expensive to stay in the Camberwell flat. She took a room in a house-share in Elephant and Castle. An ugly squat house of orange brick with no redeeming features in a nervous neighbourhood. The box room had space for a single bed and a narrow clothes rail. She took it unquestioningly, which surprised the twitchy art student showing her around. Samantha was the perfect flatmate: clean, tidy and never around.

'What about when I'm back?' said Liam. He was currently in the midst of his appeal. 'My new lawyer seems a bit more clued up.'

By the time he came out it wouldn't matter that he no longer had a poky flat to go home to on Camberwell New Road. By then she'd be a success.

'I'm going to earn so much money,' she said, 'you'll be able to employ the best lawyer in London.'

She followed a comforting routine. Walk to work with her language tapes for company, work hard, a baked potato in the microwave for lunch, work hard, walk home. She sat in her room at night eating baked beans on toast or sometimes pasta and always an apple for pudding. She liked reading books she borrowed from the library. Even though Jackson was paying her a pittance she was able to open a savings account. When she felt miserable she looked at her paying-in book and watched the figures in the right-hand column steadily grow.

'Neville Potterton's office, can I help you?'

Soon she was promoted from general assistant to Neville's assistant. Only problem was she thought Neville was a dickhead. Working in his office was a dead-end – you could see it from the top of the road.

'Oh, hi, Mickey,' she said. Mickey was typical of the clients in this office. Old, past it, retired and earning nothing.

Neville Potterton needed to draw some young blood and quick, but instead of looking out for new talent he spent most of his time catering to the whims of his doddering clients.

'Remember,' Neville told her once when he (wrongly) accused her of being disrespectful, 'these men were heroes. Ask your father – he'll tell you.'

'I'd have to find him first,' said Samantha.

Neville spluttered an apology and seeing him squirm like that was the highlight of her day. She wasn't mean spirited – it was just that she was bored with making restaurant reservations for grown men who really could be making their own.

Today Mickey wanted to get upgraded on his flight to Florida. 'Taking the kids to Disneyland,' he said, misjudging the depth of her interest.

'Let me speak to our travel agent,' she said.

'We're taking the mother-in-law, so she can sit in economy with the kids if that helps.'

Charming.

Neville poked his head out of his office. 'Is that Mickey? Why didn't you say?' he reprimanded. 'Let me speak to him.' Then he snapped his fingers at her even though she had asked him very politely not to do that any more.

She united Neville and Mickey and tuned out the sycophantic noises that were soon emanating from his office. If that was how her boss wanted to spend his time then it was little wonder that he was the least profitable agent in the company. But she hated that it made her look bad.

Jackson's company was going places. Nobody was quite sure where exactly; a few eyebrows had been raised when he had audaciously called his firm Legends, but it was starting to seem prophetic as he siphoned clients from more established agencies, wooed agents with promises of perks, agents who brought their lists across with them, while men with more gumption than her boss scoured the country to find newcomers who became sensations. Soon Legends was a powerful player in a very rich man's game. Samantha had joined the right company at the right time.

But she was stuck in the wrong office.

Early in the new year Jackson decided to throw a party to show off.

Maybe she was just an assistant, maybe she was at the party as window dressing or logistical back-up, maybe she looked impossibly gauche as she watched sports stars pile into the east London warehouse where this glittering event was taking place, but she didn't care about any of that.

Wow.

This party was dynamite.

She didn't even mind that she had spent her whole week explaining to Neville's dreary clients why, no, they couldn't bring two dozen friends with them; they were lucky to be here at all.

The air was thick with the sound of laughter and the thump of the bass from the sound system in the marquee outside. Man-sized canapés were circulating, slices of rare roast beef rolled around caramelized onions, salty roast potatoes and individual chicken pies. There was a cocktail bar where drinks were flamboyantly mixed, a champagne bar with prominent branding and trays of drinks somewhere nearby whenever you needed one. At the far side of the warehouse people were queuing up to take a ride on one of the NASA flight simulators that had been hired for the party.

She'd already spotted Gary Lineker and Paul Gascoigne, the only two footballers she was confident of recognizing, but soon she realized that it really didn't matter if she didn't know the faces yet. You could tell a world-class football player as soon as he walked in the room.

It wasn't the expensive suit or the perfect body and clear skin – it was the glow of sheer Alpha-ness that surrounded each of them, like a ring round the moon. It was magical, like a force field of testosterone that would crackle when you touched it.

Next to men like that men such as Mickey-bloody-Jenkins looked decrepit.

Across the room she saw Jackson. He was holding his own amid all this man candy – as well he might, being the munificent host. She thought he looked very handsome in his deep purple suit; not many men could carry off such a colour. She decided, perhaps unwisely, that this was a perfect opportunity to push for some career advancement.

'Jackson!' she said. 'Great party, thanks for inviting me.'

He looked at her blankly for a second and then remembered exactly who she was. He hadn't recognized her out of that dreary business suit she wore every day.

'Great dress,' he said.

She fingered the deep rose silk that showed off her long legs. 'It's second-hand,' she admitted.

'Vintage,' he said. 'Nobody says second-hand any more.'

'Can I talk to you?' She stumbled over her words and

took a deep breath to steady herself. She felt unexpectedly shy. It must be the excitement.

'People aren't dancing,' said Jackson. 'Do you think we misjudged the music? Should it be more poppy, less house?'

'I think it's still early,' she said. 'Give them time; they'll dance.'

'Maybe it was a mistake to set up the marquee outside, too separate.'

'It's pretty warm in here now,' she said. 'Why don't you open both those sets of doors over there and roll up the long side of the marquee? Then it'll be more integrated.'

He saw that she was right and swiftly organized things as she had suggested. She watched while he supervised a team.

'You're nervous,' she said, surprised.

'This is a very expensive party.'

'Relax,' she said. 'You might as well try to enjoy what you're paying for.'

He smiled at her logic. 'I'm sorry,' he said, 'you wanted to ask me something?'

She did? Oh yeah. 'Yeah,' she said. 'What the hell were you thinking when you employed Neville Potterton?'

'Excuse me?'

'Neville.' She grinned, to show that she wasn't being a bitch necessarily, just cheeky. 'He spends all day on the phone with his useless clients, thinks it's his job to play social secretary for a bunch of has-beens, using company money, *your money*, to wine and dine them then falling over himself with excitement if one of them gets a job opening a poxy supermarket. And then –' she broke off as Jackson took her arm and manoeuvred her away from the crowds, but she quickly picked up again. 'And then you show him an approach for a French kid who is just going to *blister* he's so hot right now and Neville's all, like, no, sorry, not enough hours in the day, when it's totally obvious if he spent a little more time hustling and a lot less time licking *arse*, then . . .' She tailed off, forgetting her point and feeling a little ashamed of her outburst.

'Finished?' said Jackson. 'Because if you're going to start again then can you keep your voice down? There's a lot of those has-beens here tonight.'

She looked around and realized they were all alone, set back from the party in a little nook just past the kitchen. 'Sorry.'

'Neville was with me the day I started,' he said. 'I couldn't have done any of this without his name on the letterhead. He was a giant in the eighties.'

'But . . .'

'But nothing. I made a deal with him. He knew he wasn't going to have to graft any more with me. I wanted his name, and his clients' names too. We deal with the dads, don't we? Makes Dad feel secure if you've got a name like Mickey Jenkins on the books. Neville can take it a little easier. He doesn't have to try to keep up with the aggressive little sods like me.'

'But me. My job. I hate it. I feel like I'm being wasted.'

'You've been here, what? Four months? Listen to Neville. You could learn a lot from him. I did.'

'He's a dickhead,' she said stubbornly.

'I'm going to ignore you just this once because you're new. But I hear you call one of my senior partners a dickhead again and I'll fire you. I don't care how good you look in that dress.'

She blushed. 'You think I look good?'

He stared at her so intensely that she thought he was about to kiss her. Then a veil of indifference dropped across his face. 'Excuse me,' he said. 'I have three hundred other guests to talk to.'

He left her standing on her own. So rude. And to think that once she even thought she might fancy him a little bit.

For the rest of the evening she made sure that she sparkled. She wanted him to see her having a fabulous time. She danced with every good-looking young man she could snare, she made witty conversation with colleagues and clients and she always knew where Jackson was at any given time. Often, when she looked across, she caught him watching her. No doubt he was thinking what an asset she was to the company, a spirited, pretty young girl wearing pink to make the boys wink.

Later, when a wannabe she didn't know asked if she knew where to get cocaine she hooked him up with her old dealer with absolutely no regard for any future consequences. *So helpful.*

By midnight the party was thinning out. She scanned the room for any of the man-sized canapés to nab for the night bus home.

'Looking for someone?'

Jackson was at her side. Emboldened by the success of the party she told him the truth. He smiled. He had a lovely smile, and he rarely used it. 'Follow me,' he said.

'Where are we going?'

He went through the double doors and into the kitchen,

where he opened one of the fridges and started to make her a roast-beef sandwich.

'Are we allowed to be in here?' she said.

'I'm paying for all this, remember?' he said.

'Must have cost a bomb.'

'A fair bit, I suppose. Do you think people had a good time?'

'Everyone I spoke to said it was the best party this year,' she said.

He nodded, pleased.

'So far,' she teased.

He watched her devour the sandwich, as if she hadn't seen a proper meal in weeks. He would never tell her so, but he couldn't help but admire her nerve approaching him earlier. Most of the assistants were too scared to talk to him, and mostly he liked it that way. He was a fair boss, but firm, and a little bit of fear got results. But with Samantha it was different. Was it that he felt a protective instinct because of the state he had found her in? He wanted to think so. Life could get far too problematic if it was more than that. But in that dress, with those legs. A man would have to be a saint, and Jackson Ramsay was many things, but no saint. 'Do you need a lift home?' he asked.

'I'm fine,' she said quickly, tossing her hair back from her face and looking him straight in the eye.

Could she tell what he was thinking? He sincerely hoped not.

'But thanks for the offer,' she added. No way was she giving him the opportunity to see the dive she lived in. Besides, she knew for a fact that he was Primrose Hill, in a completely different direction.

Maybe he was coming on to her.

And that would be too complicated.

She fell asleep on the night bus and woke up halfway to Brixton, so she walked back through some of the most dubious areas in London, fearless.

She tried to do as she was told, but all she was able to learn from Neville was that footballers were like gods and must be treated as such. Never leave them on hold, never cut them off; he was never on another call, just unavailable. Once he turned an alarming shade of puce when two of his top clients called at exactly the same time. And she learnt that he now took three sugars in his coffee instead of two and that he liked enough milk in there to turn it lukewarm.

She saw Jackson around the office. She could sometimes hear him on the phone and once a week at the company meeting he described glamorous deals worth millions and foreign trips and tax-efficient investments that sounded like dirty talk to her ambitious ears. She wanted more.

Liam's appeal approached. She visited him on Thursday mornings, regularly begging the time off work by lying and saying she was in college studying part-time for her law degree. It occurred to her that she should study law for real if she wanted to be negotiating her own million-pound deals one day. She started investigating evening classes at the place where she had once learnt Japanese.

'Why do you want to do that?' asked Liam. 'I thought you liked your job.'

'I like the company,' she clarified. 'My job is just entry level.'

'So now you're going to be a lawyer.'

'No,' she said. 'An agent. A sports agent.'

'Shame,' he said. 'I could use a better lawyer.'

He was right. The appeal was thrown out of court within an hour. The verdict and the sentence would remain unchanged. He looked across at her and mouthed words which broke her spirit.

I'm sorry.

This time when they took him away they took all of Samantha's remaining faith with him. A searing bolt of resentment hardened her heart. He could have been anything. But now his hope would have to wait. What were the chances of dreams outlasting that kind of incarceration? He had screwed up his life and in so doing he had left her completely alone. They were supposed to take care of each other. Bullshit. The only person you could rely on was yourself.

That night she went to bed shortly after midnight, but remained far from sleep. She lay awake and wondered what Liam was thinking. She felt angry at him, and guilty for being angry, then angry at herself for feeling guilty. Nasty thoughts circled in endless rotation, each bumping into the next, like dodgem cars in a brash fairground. The knowledge that being deserted felt familiar crept under her skin and unwelcome memories of their mother brought tears to her eyes.

Even after all these years she still wanted Mummy? No, she was stronger than that.

She yanked the bedcovers away and ran from the room. She had to get out. She thought of the ordered piles of paper on her desk at work, each one needing a direct course of action, a black-and-white solution, no grey. She gathered up her bag and her keys, left the house and started walking north.

The Legends offices were different at night, peaceful, resting after the dramatics of a typical day. She found it calming.

She sat down behind her desk, smoothing her hands over the cold, flat surface. She picked up the first piece of paper that her hand fell upon and began to work.

Later, when her systematic approach had lulled her racing mind to a quiet hum, she took a break.

It was nice to wander the calm corridors. She liked going into the empty offices and looking closely at people's desks. Trying to guess whose baby that was in the photograph on Richard's desk or if the diet pills in superslim Karen's drawer meant she was anorexic. An entire drawer in Jennie's desk was packed like an overnight bag with spare underwear, deodorant, toothbrush. Was prim little Jennie a secret dirty stop-out?

She hesitated outside Jackson's office but pushed open the door, idly considering the probability that this might have been her destination all along. His desk was unexciting. A neatly stacked outbox, an empty inbox, pens and pencils stored in a stainless-steel tankard commemorating Coventry City's 1987 FA Cup victory. She sat in his leather swivel chair. She turned away from the desk and put her feet up on his windowsill.

Jackson had a knockout view. Below her London glittered.

So no more Liam. Except on Thursdays. Maybe . . . just maybe . . . was it too awful to think that her life might take shape more easily in his absence? Wasn't it true that even before these catastrophic events they had been growing apart? That they no longer found their thrills in the same places? She dreamed of a career, a house, her own front door. Of success. To Liam success had become possessing the name and number of a failsafe dealer who delivered. She must truly be a terrible person for having such disloyal thoughts.

'Who's there?'

She spun round at the sound of his voice. 'Jackson? What are you doing here?'

'In my own office?'

'I mean, it's so late.'

'It's six a.m. Most people would call that early.'

Six? Already?

'Why are you here so early?' she said.

'I always start work at six. But I can't start work until you get out of my chair.'

'One day,' she said, 'I'm going to have a view like that.'

'You like it, huh?' He smiled, even though he was trying his hardest to be authoritative and angry.

'I like everything about this company.'

This company was his baby and he liked it when his baby was complimented. 'Last time we spoke you told me you hated it here.'

'I hate my job,' she said. 'But I think your company is pretty incredible.'

'Then why do you hate your job?'

'Because it's boring. I could do it in my sleep.'

'Is that what you've been doing all night?'

'No, I had, well, I had a bad day yesterday,' she said. 'A real shit. I needed . . .' She paused. Then she was crying. *Again*. Was she set to cry for sixteen years? Was that possible?

'You want to talk about it?' asked Jackson softly.

'It's a family thing,' she said. 'You ever have those? No, I thought not. Let's see, only child, mum and dad still together? Proud of their son? See them three weekends a year and home for a week at Christmas?'

'St Kitts,' said Jackson. 'Last Christmas I took them to St Kitts. My dad and me played some cricket.'

'Nice.'

He nodded. 'It really was. What about you?'

'What?'

'Your family?'

'I don't have any family,' she said. For a moment she allowed herself to believe that was true, that there was no Liam to feel dismal about, no dumb brother to drag her down. The lie gave her a thrill.

'Oh? But I thought you just said . . .'

She waved his confusion away. 'It's complicated.'

'Family shouldn't be complicated,' he said. 'Mine is pretty much the only undemanding thing in my life.'

'Well, you're lucky,' she said. 'You think that's what made you a success?'

If so then she had no chance.

'Success always seems to me to be the logical result of hard work and application,' said Jackson. 'It's not a lottery. You make your own breaks.'

'It doesn't feel like that to me,' she said. 'I'm doing

243

everything I can think of to move forward in this company. I'm learning languages, I've signed up for evening classes in law, but I'm stuck out there with Neville so nobody will ever even notice. So you have to ask yourself, what's the point?'

'Be patient. You'll find a way,' he said. 'You're a special girl. I could tell the first moment we spoke.'

'You're right,' she said slowly. 'So why am I working so hard when I'm obviously going nowhere? You only gave me this job because you felt sorry for me. I'm your good deed, not your protégée. I want to be more than that.'

Clarity. A moment of clarity. She only had one life.

'I quit.'

'What the hell?'

'I've seen people, people close to me, who have wasted their lives, totally wasted them, and I don't want that to be me.'

In Jackson's experience, people that came to work at Legends would slave for months doing whatever they were told just to have the chance to work here. His assistant had a file of CVs as thick as the phone directory of excellent people willing to work for free merely to get a foot in the door. Yet this girl, on salary, was walking out on him. She thought she could do better. She was – what? – twenty-one and she thought he was holding her back. And maybe he was.

'I wouldn't want you to feel like you're wasting your life.'

'Which is why I should go.'

'I think . . .' he said, '. . . that you should stay.'

'I really don't want to work for Neville any more.'

'I think we can probably fix that.'

She smiled. 'Can I get that in writing?'

'You have my word. We'll sort something out by the end of the week. Now will you get out of my office before I have to call security?'

She walked past him and was almost at the door when something made him hold out his hand to stop her. Perhaps it was the curve of her hip as she shimmied past him, or the sheer audacity of her promotion-grabbing dramatics, but he couldn't let her go without telling her something.

'I didn't give you a job because I felt sorry for you,' he said.

'No?'

'I gave you a job because I admired you.'

She frowned.

'What?' he said. 'Oh relax, I mean after you'd put your clothes on. Your little speech about me being a hero? Clever.'

'I'm not going to sleep with you just to get promoted,' she said seriously.

'Good,' he said. 'But who knows? Maybe one day you'll sleep with me just for the hell of it.'

'Don't count on it,' she said.

'Sam, I don't count on anything until the deal is done. But, like I always say, anything is possible.'

Neville found himself a new assistant, a mature woman called Yvonne who made his coffee just the way he liked it, and Samantha was shifted sideways to work for Graham, a young agent who needed a right-hand man.

'Right-hand woman,' she corrected.

'Not too many of those in this business,' he said, clearly not counting the accounts department, secretaries and assistants that made it difficult to get mirror space in the Ladies' on a Friday night.

'Why do you think that is?' she asked, genuinely curious. If she was going to blaze a trail then it would be useful to know the pitfalls.

'Too competitive,' said Graham. 'Women don't have the . . .' He paused, searching for the right word, then laughed. 'The balls,' he said. 'Women don't have the balls.'

'Then I'd better get me some of those,' she said.

'The Russian called again,' said Leanne. 'Sexy accent. Asked where you were.'

Every day Leanne called her on the road and gave her a rundown of what was happening back in the new Krakow office. Most days it was the only time she spoke to another woman. Which was fine.

'If you're not interested,' said Leanne, 'can I have a go?'

'Who says I'm not interested?'

'I thought he was, like, young?'

'Whereas I am . . . ?'

'Old,' said Leanne bluntly.

Was she really that old? She wasn't confident enough to be old. She wasn't rich enough. Or wise enough. 'I'm back tomorrow,' she said. 'I'll deal with him then.' She looked out of her window. The Croatian town of Zadar was bound to have some pretty parts, but she couldn't see them from where she was standing. She only saw the cranes and forklifts of the busy port. And yet she couldn't even see the water.

'Deal with him?'

'Speak to him, call him, you know what I mean. Anyone else?'

'Eric Royston?' said Leanne. 'Do you know him?'

'I'll deal with that,' said Samantha. 'Give me the number.' It had been weeks since she had heard from the private detective.

She rang him immediately. 'You have news?' she asked eagerly.

'Yes,' said Eric, 'but I'm not sure you'll like it. It wasn't easy, but I managed to trace one of the deposits to a bonds and securities firm working behind what I assume is a mail-forwarding company.'

'What does that mean?'

'It means that at least one of these deposits was made with loaned money.'

'So whoever did this might have been borrowing the money to do so?'

'Possibly. Or possibly they are just using the company as cover.'

'And the other deposits?'

'I don't know,' he admitted. 'Maybe from the same place, but I just don't know.' She could hear the finality in his voice and it alarmed her.

'So this loans company,' she said, 'we can go after them? Find out who they are fronting?'

'We can try,' he said, 'but it'll likely prove fruitless. After all, hiding people is what these companies are paid to do.'

She gritted her teeth to stop her anger and disappointment becoming tears. 'And you, Mr Royston,' she said. 'What are you paid to do?'

She slammed down the phone. She knew an impasse when she heard one. But she would still get a bill for his services, even though the information he had provided her with was utterly useless. She felt like throwing something across the room. The frustration of being denounced for a crime you didn't commit was maddening. At least when Liam was jailed he *knew* he was guilty . . .

Stop. It was an ugly comparison. She was ashamed.

Perhaps it was time to admit that she couldn't find the answers that she craved on her own. She needed help. Until a few weeks ago she would have asked Jackson. Jackson would have known what to do next. Frighteningly, she was running out of options.

She unpacked and took a shower, trying to wash away the disappointment of a dead end. Afterwards she flicked through the television channels looking for English, finding none. She glanced at herself in the mirror. These weeks on the road had wrecked her appearance. Standing on too many terraces in freezing temperatures had made her lips chap and her skin protest by breaking out in small red patches across her forehead and cheeks. She had hardly worn the power suits she had carefully packed in tissue paper and instead buried herself beneath winter layers, conducting much of her business standing on muddy training pitches, grateful for her rubber-soled sheepskin-lined boots.

Beneath her clothes her skin was pale and dry. It was all she could do to shower when she got to each depressingly similar hotel, never mind exfoliate and depilate and moisturize.

No wonder she felt like crap.

'Does this hotel have a spa?'

Leanne didn't bother to wonder why she was asking an assistant hundreds of miles away instead of sticking her head into reception to find out. 'You're kidding! This is a budget tour. Cheap hotels, you said. "All I need is a bed and shower," remember?'

'A girl can hope,' said Samantha.

'There's not much, a stack of four-star hotels west of the old town. You want me to switch you?'

'No, this is fine.' Funny how modest your tastes became when you were footing the bill yourself. She tried to imagine Jackson being comfortable in a tourist-class hotel like this. He'd be in a courtesy car to five-star luxury before he'd even put down his suitcase. Having to carry his own suitcase would be enough to send him scuttling towards the nearest power shower. But he'd earned his luxuries. She was just starting out. He'd told her stories of the early days, running Legends from a quarter-share of a hot-desk in Soho Square. So, no matter how fat her various savings accounts and investments were, she must cut back on indulgences. Perhaps being brought up in a succession of frugal households had lasting benefits. She congratulated herself on her humble tastes.

'You want me to book you a one-day pass into the fanciest, most luxurious spa in Zadar?' said Leanne.

'Hell, yeah.' If she could only relax, then surely the next step would become more clear.

Her skin was being worn down to the bone. She was scrubbed and buffed and rubbed by a briskly efficient mute who looked as if her last post was with the Croatian shot-putting team. The friction between the sea salt and her damp, oily skin was creating so much warmth that she felt like a fillet of hot smoked beef smothered in Maldon flakes.

Which was appropriate because this room looked like a place for preparing meat. The stone floor and cold plastic surfaces were clean and bare.

Her tormentor grasped her arms roughly and forced her onto her side so that she could better attack the small of her back with persistent little punches that felt like a drum roll. After a few minutes of that she washed her down with a showerhead, the cold water like pinpricks on her raw skin, the grease and salt swishing down the plughole in the concave tiled floor beneath her down-turned face. Then she slathered her in foul-smelling mud and a layer of clingfilm and, as a final indignity, set a kitchen timer for twenty minutes before she left the room.

Her skin tingled.

She wondered idly if Leanne had sent her here as a joke, but grudgingly acknowledged that the sprawling hotel above this basement torture room would suggest that luxury lay beneath. And admittedly her fiery body was invigorated and alive. The same could not be said for her mind and spirit, still tired from so much use, and so in the warm fug of mud-scented steam she drifted off to sleep.

The shrill bell of the kitchen timer woke her and she was hustled under a power shower to wash away the mud. Her skin felt like cashmere. Then she was led to a room that belonged in the kind of spa she'd had in mind, all soft colours and mood lighting. She lay on her front and swapped her towel for a small white sheet, which covered her now peachy bum and not much else.

A slight, blond-haired man entered the room and folded back the sheet right to the curve of her bum.

'Are you comfortable?' she was asked, and she grunted assent.

Her nose filled with the sultry scent of sandalwood and jojoba as slick hands massaged her back and shoulders with essential oils. She murmured with pleasure, her mind playing back the last couple of weeks, thinking not of its labours but of its rewards. She'd found a kid in the Ukraine who could be the next Andriy Shevchenko, she'd wooed a Romanian international unhappy with his current representation and here in Croatia she had signed up a rock-solid goalkeeper that had never left the country and never played against a team that might test how good he really was.

These, and several more, would form a slate of players that would stand up under the most severe scrutiny. The transfer window was fast approaching. At Legends this window saw tempers flare as millions changed hands. She adored the inevitable mayhem that came from trying to do so much business in a few short weeks. She thrived on the cut and thrust of chaos. It was her favourite time of year.

And right now the transfer window was more important than ever.

She could hardly wait.

Oily hands smoothed over her legs, pushing out the tension that had gathered there, working down to her toes and pulling at each one in turn, then her arms and her fingers.

She must remember to thank Leanne for this idea. She would add it to the list of things for which she had to thank her indispensable assistant. It would be a great shame if Leanne's dream of being a footballer's wife and doing nothing all day came true. She was organized and enthusiastic, two traits which would carry her far if she wanted a career. But times change. Women were seeking out traditional roles once more, wanting to be wives with rich husbands. All the hard work done by feminism had been undone by an eternal passion for shopping.

Luckily she had never been one for shopping.

The hands on her body were firmer now. She could sense that she was finally nearing the end of what had turned out to be one of the more satisfying beauty treatments of her life. She savoured the feel of human contact, the thumbs that teased the last little bit of resistance from her muscles until she felt like she couldn't move if she tried. She hovered somewhere between liquid and solid, between wakefulness and catatonia.

Then the hands stopped. It was over. And she sighed one all-conquering sigh, breathing in again with refreshed body and soul.

'Hello, Samantha.'

Samanza. She recognized the voice. Russian. But she wasn't in Russia, she was in Croatia. So she must be dreaming.

'Don't fall asleep here,' said the familiar voice. 'I have a far more comfortable bed upstairs.'

She clutched at the sheet as she lifted her head to see. 'Alek?'

Instead of the slight Croatian she had seen when she last opened her eyes, Aleksandr Lubin stood behind her with a slight smirk, his hands glistening with massage oil.

She no longer felt relaxed.

'What . . . ?'

'What am I doing here?' he said, looking intolerably pleased with himself. 'I would have thought it was obvious. I wanted to see you.'

'Get out!' she said, horribly aware of her nakedness, shocked at seeing him. Realizing that his hands had been on her body without her knowledge or consent made her feel frightened. 'Get out,' she said again, 'before I scream.'

'There is no need to be dramatic.' He picked up one of the spotless white towels and wiped his hands. 'It wasn't easy to find you.'

'No?'

'No, I'm lying, it was ridiculously simple. You should be careful. One day it might be someone else, someone who wants to harm you.'

She was utterly vulnerable, lying there unable to move an inch lest the tiny sheet that stood between her and a modicum of modesty should fall.

'You can't do this to someone, Alek,' she said. 'You can't just walk in and hijack a massage. It's over the line, way over. You scared me. Please, just get out.'

He rolled his eyes. 'I was trying to be romantic. You felt wonderful, you know, under my hands. Should I carry on? I have been told I am a skilled masseur. Perhaps a little more *intimate*?'

'Leave!' she said. She picked up the plastic bottle of jojoba oil and threw it in his direction. It was a fabulous shot considering her prone position, and hit him square in the chest, leaving an oily mark in the centre of his perfect dark-blue shirt.

He looked down with displeasure. 'Now look. I will have to change.'

'Good. Piss off and change.'

'You are a very rude woman.'

'And you're a very rude man.'

He lifted one eyebrow. 'Then we should be rude together, do you not think?'

She picked up the closest thing to her, another bottle, and made as if to throw it.

He raised his palms. 'I'm going, I'm going. Don't be angry. Meet me in fifteen minutes. I came all this way.'

He left. What an unbelievable nerve. She started pulling on her clothes quickly as she punched out Leanne's number on her mobile phone.

'How dare you tell Aleksandr Lubin where I was?' she demanded. 'What were you *thinking*? Have you completely lost your mind? Were you trying to be funny?'

'Whoa, hold on there, tiger. Slow down. Lubin? I told him you were away on business, that's all.'

'You didn't tell him I was in this hotel? In Zadar?'

'I didn't even tell him you were in Croatia.'

'Oh.'

'Say sorry,' said Leanne.

'I'm sorry,' said Samantha automatically. 'But he's here.'

'Lubin? Wow, what a coincidence.'

'I don't know what he's doing here, but it's no coincidence, I'll tell you that right now.'

She shivered, despite the warm room. She hadn't told anyone but Leanne where she was going or where she was staying. Yet Lubin was outside waiting for her. It made her skin prickle with paranoia. She wasn't sure if she could ever cope with being with a man so well connected that it would be impossible to hide.

'What do you think he wants?'

Leanne laughed, that dirty laugh that drove the boys

wild. 'My mum once told me that men are only after one thing.'

Samantha held the phone under her chin while she pulled on her jeans and boots. 'Come on, seriously,' she said.

'Why not?'

'He goes for these emaciated little model types.'

'Stop fishing for compliments,' said Leanne. 'It doesn't suit you.'

'I wasn't –'

'Other line's ringing, gotta go.'

And Leanne hung up.

He was waiting for her in the lobby and, from somewhere, had managed to procure six of the same gorgeous silver roses that he had sent her months ago to celebrate Gabe's deal.

'I'm sorry I scared you,' he said. 'It was not my intention. Forgive me?'

It didn't win her over, but she did allow him to take the lead.

He didn't try to dazzle her with opulence. If he had it might have been easier for her to resist. Instead they went for a walk by the water. Finally she saw the charms of this city, the pastel-coloured houses that climbed the hillside, the ancient rough-stone wall that had safeguarded Zadar for thousands of years and the constant lap of a sea that thrashed with fish, fish being pulled out as quick as the fishermen could cast their lines.

With each step she thought about how good his hands had felt on her skin.

The stone promenade was crowded with tourists taking

in the sunset for which the town was famous. Above them the clouds flushed candyfloss pink, blushing before their big performance. Every few yards the soundtrack to their evening changed as a new street musician came within earshot. They seemed to be spaced just so, so that their tunes never overlapped and competed.

They stopped by a man selling fragrant pizza and walked together, eating a slice contentedly along the marina. It occurred to her that maybe he, or more realistically his father, could afford to buy any one of the boats moored there, including one of half a dozen mega yachts at the southern end.

She pointed. 'Is one of them yours?'

'Ours is in Spain,' he said nonchalantly. 'I think. Or maybe Dubai. Why? Would you like to visit her?'

She imagined the Lubin yacht to be like the jet but on a bigger scale. Would she like to swan around the Med on a floating palace? Sure, why not? 'Is that an invitation?' she asked.

'I could make a few calls,' he said. 'We could be there tonight.'

What it must be like to live life without having to consider practicalities. No work to miss, no money to stress over, no responsibilities. A normal life was the sort where you daydreamed and said without any expectation, 'Wouldn't it be nice to jet off to Paris for lunch?' Lubin's was the sort where you'd be ordering your *pommes frites* for real a heartbeat after the whim took you. He was inviting her to live that kind of life with him, temporarily of course, and who knew for how long? But nothing was permanent, so what did it matter?

'Is that how you found me?' she asked. 'You made a few calls.'

He shrugged a half apology. 'What can I say? The Lubins are well connected.'

The implications of this bounced around inside her head for a while as they strolled along the promenade, looking like any other couple. Did he have the where-withal to track her flights? Her credit card? Her mobile phone? Perhaps his people had called all the hotels in Zadar or all the football clubs in Croatia to find her. What else might he know?

'How well connected?' she asked.

'Why? Is there something you want?'

Yes. There was something she wanted dreadfully. So much that she lay awake at night worrying that she might never have the chance. 'I want to clear my name,' she said.

He crushed his napkin into a ball with his fist and aimed it squarely at a wastebasket, making the shot. 'Your reputation is important to you.'

'Of course.'

'Why?'

'Money comes and goes,' she said. 'A reputation is for ever. If you – *when* you die it's the only thing that lives on.'

They reached a set of wide steps cut away from the promenade leading to the water. People were sitting here and there, mostly in pairs, watching the sky as it turned from pink to purple. He found a quiet spot and lay down his jacket for her. She heard a ghostly sound, like a pod of whales singing, that seemed to echo all around her.

'What is it?' she asked, spooked by the mysterious harmony.

He pointed to the regular gaps cut out of the steps. 'A wave organ,' he said. 'Beneath us the sea pushes air through her pipes to make music.'

They listened silently to the rise and fall of the bizarre melody.

She found herself thinking of a day in her childhood, a weekend visit with her mother when they were still seeing her regularly, and they had piled into the car in the middle of the night and driven to the coast to watch a thunderstorm. She had gazed at the angry sea, holding Liam's hand in the back seat as the waves battered the coastline in the grey morning. She wasn't scared until they clambered out, unable to resist getting closer, and the wind had been so strong it had pushed them back, blowing hair and sea spray into her face so that she was choking. She wanted to go home then but their mum had insisted that they sleep in the car for a few hours before the drive back. She listened to the gentle music of the Zadar wave organ and thought about the many guises of the sea.

Aleksandr stared at the two tufted islands out to sea and spoke gently, almost to himself. 'I was ten years old when my mother died,' he said.

There was a long pause. 'How did she die?' asked Samantha. Were those real tears in his eyes, or was it just the salty sea air making them water?

'They said it was an accident, but I know she was killed. She had been seeing another man; she was with him when she died. That is the reputation she left behind. My father told me the truth about her. He wanted me to know who she really was.'

What kind of father would taint the remembrance of his ten-year-old boy? She would have said so, but she knew enough about their relationship to sense that he wouldn't stand for any criticism of his beloved father.

'But how was I to do that?' he continued. 'I will never know who she really was, only who she was not. She was not a devoted wife and mother. If she had been, then she would still be alive. My father would have protected her. But he was never the same. To him, her betrayal was as painful as her death.'

The last golden sliver of sun slipped into the Adriatic and he reached for her hand. 'So I do understand about reputations. If you want me to help you I will. Tell me what I can do.'

She shivered. The night had encroached and she was suddenly chilled, but the thought of getting some answers insulated her.

'Do you have contacts in the Cayman Islands?' she said. 'Financial connections?'

'Of course,' he said, as if the Lubin family had money stashed everywhere across the world, and who was she to say that they didn't.

'I tried to find out about the money, but it was impossible,' she confided. 'Maybe someone who was a valued customer somewhere, maybe someone like that would have more success?'

'I will do what I can,' he said. 'Leave it with me.'

The wave organ wailed beneath their feet, putting sound to the constant swell of the water. She thought about it crooning to itself late at night, when it was empty here and there were no tourists to hear the melancholy song of the sea. 'It's beautiful,' she said.

'As are you,' he said swiftly, a little too swiftly. She'd

cued up the line. Would he think she was fishing for compliments too?

'Why are you here?' she asked. 'It's a long way to come for a slice of pizza.'

'I was looking for you,' he said. 'We are not children. I think you know what I want.'

He pulled her to him and kissed her deeply. They sat on the stone steps beneath a sky speckled with stars now.

She thought of her crummy hotel room, the last of a long line of empty nights and empty beds. He was young, too young. There was something sleazy about his insistent pursuit of her, but something undeniably attractive too.

Her nerves danced as he pushed his body against hers.

He was just a boy, a boy in the shadow of his powerful father.

She thought about Jackson and for the first time in months she felt nothing, just an empty space where her feelings used to be, a space longing to be filled.

Lubin was right there asking her to be with him. Even if it was just one night.

What harm could it do?

23

Gabe was looking for a place to live. Christine wanted a big townhouse on the eastern edge of town, near the botanical gardens and the posh part of the university district. Something with 'character'. Gabe wanted a flash apartment in the centre. If there was a compromise of some kind then they had yet to reach it.

Years of marriage had taught him how to read her unspoken signals easily, a dozen every day, and he knew she wouldn't be happy until she got her own way.

'Can we get a move on?' he said. 'I said I'd meet Joe later.'

'Again?'

She said it like he was out every night. Which he wasn't. He liked a few beers every now and again – where was the harm in that? It felt to him that living away from home brought out a needy side of Christine he hadn't noticed before, and didn't much care for. What was he supposed to do? Stay in the hotel with her every night and watch *EastEnders* on cable? But he didn't want to fight about it. He was saving his battles for the more important things in life. Like an apartment he had his eye on in the spanking new development two minutes' walk from the centre. The middle of town, that's where he needed to be, in the heart of the action. If he'd wanted suburbia they could have stayed in England. There would be plenty of time for that when they were old.

'Why do we need all this space?' he said as they walked around a beautiful brownstone, the sort of thing that would cost millions in London or New York but here they could buy for the same price as their modest St Ashton semi.

'You never know,' she said.

'You never know what?'

She shrugged. 'Maybe we try IVF again,' she said quietly. 'Now we've a bit more money.'

He didn't want to say no, but his sperm count didn't exactly leap at the prospect.

'You don't have to be sure,' she said. 'It's just something I was thinking about.' She smiled in a hopeful way that made a lump come into his throat. Because he knew that when Christine thought of IVF treatment she thought ahead to a plump little baby, the image of them both, and the family they would become. But when Gabe thought of IVF he looked back and all he could see was the look on her face when they failed for the third time. Part of her was dying a slow and agonizing death. He couldn't take it and was ashamed of himself. They stopped trying because their marriage could not survive another attempt. Now they were in a different city, in a different life, so of course she thought it might be time to try again.

His reluctance was clear. She could read his unspoken signals too.

'Just keep an open mind, okay?' she whispered sharply, and he wasn't sure if she was talking about the house or the treatment. 'You think you can manage that?'

When had it started to fade? he wondered. Once upon a time he would have done anything for her, anything she asked. The day that she agreed to marry him was the happiest day he had ever known. Until he scored three goals against Spurs. Once all he wanted was a big house filled with Christine and their children. Now the thought of rattling around this empty house with her made him panic. And hidden somewhere at the back, behind the nice guy that he tried to be, was a deeper fear that having a child was a dream that belonged in the past not the future.

Gabe seized upon a friendship with Joe in the way that countrymen tend to do when abroad. But Joe was glad to have him so everyone was happy.

At first they talked mostly of football of course. Gabe told Joe the story of *that* match, the story he would never grow tired of. They talked about the English Premier League, who was playing well, who was disappointing, which teams could hope to finish where. They gossiped about players much in the way that women do about the wives and girlfriends, the WAGS: who's doing what, who had the best style, who's the most likely to go far.

Joe and Gabe would have been annoyed by the comparison.

After a few weeks, when both men had had the chance to size each other up and decide that the other was sound, the conversation drifted into the personal. So Gabe knew about Layla, and now he knew about Layla and *Daniel*.

'So go on,' he pressed Joe, 'then what did you say when Layla told you about this new bloke?' Joe led them through the cobbled streets of the old town, glad that he had a friend at last to keep his misery company.

'What was I supposed to say? I said I was really happy for her.'

'In other words you lied.'

Joe nodded glumly. He had lied. But then hadn't he spent the last ten years lying by omission?

He turned into a narrow alleyway before ducking through the doorway of an imposing tenement building where he bounded up three flights of stairs and pushed through an unmarked metal door. It opened, somewhat surprisingly, onto a bar with battered old sofas and a fantastic view of the main market square.

'Nice place,' said Gabe.

Joe looked around as if he was seeing it for the first time, even though the pretty waitress greeted him by name. 'I suppose,' he said. 'But there's about a hundred places just like it. Trouble is most of them are too easy to find.'

Joe ordered the drinks. Gabe still had trouble when pronouncing the ubiquitous Zywiec beer, something Joe said would immediately mark him as a tourist, so as they waited for their beers he spent a minute coaching Gabe until he sounded like a native. At least he now knew one useful word of Polish.

Gabe exchanged loaded looks with the dusky waitress and wondered what time she might finish. The mixed blessing of Polish licensing laws meant that you could get a beer practically any time you might want one, but meeting one of the universally sexy waitresses after work would mean staying up until dawn. He wasn't even sure if he had the guts to cheat on his wife, but the idea excited him far more than house-hunting. He finished his first drink quickly just to have an excuse to talk to her. Meanwhile Joe lingered over his first, despite Gabe's urgings to drown his sorrows the old-fashioned way.

'Last night on the piss, isn't it?' said Gabe. 'Going booze-free next week in preparation for Saturday.'

'That's a good idea,' said Joe. Gabe drank quite a lot, Joe realized, and it felt like every time they went out Gabe managed to drink one more than the time before.

'It's a bloody necessity. I don't know how these Polish boys do it. I've seen them out downing the vodkas, but they're always pretty sharp at training the next day.'

Should Joe bother to explain that vodka was just a part of life for some of them? Especially those from rural Silesia. Back home their fathers probably still regularly drank a glass of vodka with breakfast in winter, but would frown upon excessive beer drinking as a boorish sin against God. No, it wasn't worth trying to bridge the cultural divide. Joe had been trying to keep a foot in both camps for most of his life, and knew better than most how hard it was. Instead he asked Gabe's advice: what should he do about Layla?

'Sorry to say this, mate,' said Gabe. 'But I think you've got to move on.'

'Where?'

'I mean move on from this Layla girl. She's with someone now. You had your chance; you blew it.'

'What if she comes next Saturday?'

Gabe paused for thought. 'You mean if she blows off this Daniel geezer to come and watch you play football?'

'Yeah. Surely that means something?'

'Do you think she will?'

'No,' said Joe. His chin sank down into his chest. He swigged at his pint, trying hard not to picture Layla, his Layla, wrapping those slender arms round someone else.

266

'Cheer up,' said Gabe. 'You're going to be a massive football star; you'll have more women than you can handle. What do you want to tie yourself down for anyway?'

Joe tried not to think of tying Layla down, but it was impossible. For the first time he thought that perhaps he wanted her more than football.

In the summer the sunlight started to gently burn away the night around four in the morning, sometimes even earlier, but in the middle of winter four o'clock in the morning was black as midnight. Gabe and Joe had drunk enough, but they were still thirsty. Joe because he was trying to dull the ache of a broken heart and Gabe because he was living the dream, and a big part of that dream was being in a place where some of the finest beer he had ever tasted could slip down your throat at less than a pound a throw.

They grinned at each other.

Joe thought Gabe was fantastic. They got on brilliantly. He didn't even realize that he was drawn to Gabe in an effort to create the kind of closeness he had never felt with his father. And for Gabe, who had never had the son he had once wanted so much, Joe was a safe substitute, although Joe, simply by virtue of having his entire life ahead of him and the freedom that comes with that, made Gabe feel old.

'Let's go to a club,' slurred Gabe.

'Okay,' said Joe. 'What kind of club?'

'There must be a kick-arse lap-dancing club somewhere?'

Joe wasn't sure. And unfortunately the few friends he had that might be able to tell him wouldn't appreciate being woken at 4 a.m. But there must be. In the summer this city was overrun with British stag parties.

They would find a taxi. Polish taxi drivers knew everything.

After speaking English all night and drinking far more than he ever usually would, Joe found that the word for 'stripper' had fallen out of his head and he wasn't sure if he had ever known the word for 'lap-dancing' to begin with. Instead he asked the taxi driver to take them to a bar with girls and he was relieved when he seemed to understand what they wanted, even if he did start the meter at twenty złoty, which seemed more than strictly necessary.

'Don't worry about it,' said Gabe. 'That's like – what? Four quid? It's nothing.'

They crossed south over the river into the no-man's land of Podgórze, but this didn't overly concern Joe. He could well imagine that this lesser-known area, far from the tourist trail, was where things started to get interesting. He hoped Gabe would be impressed.

Gabe was currently trying to engage the taxi driver in conversation, impossible given that they only spoke three words of the other's language, but still there was laughter and good spirits. Joe was happy.

So this is what men do . . .

It had been just him and his mum for all this time, and his devotion to football was what he had in his life instead of friendship. Until now. Until Gabe.

Between Gabe Muswell and Samantha Sharp his prospects for the kind of life he might want for himself given the choice were much improved. Samantha had been amazing, talking his mum through all the pros and cons about playing in the Premiership and assuaging all her fears, which Sam seemed to intuitively know were more about Joe spending too much time with his father. His dad would *love* Gabe. Next time his dad was over they could all go out. The three of them. Men around town. Yeah, sod Layla Petherick.

The taxi pulled off the main street, did a couple of turns and drew up in front of an ugly post-war block, the ubiquitous grey of communist Poland. The meter had somehow climbed to the lofty heights of one hundred and seventy złoty, a large amount in any currency, but clearly nothing to Gabe who threw two hundred at the driver and told him to keep the change.

Joe felt a flicker of apprehension pierce his beer buzz as he looked at where they were, a building with nothing to distinguish it from its neighbours save for one small red lightbulb in the first-floor window, but before he could voice his concern Gabe had waved the driver off and they were stranded. He figured they might as well go in.

The bell was answered by a large man with close-cropped hair and a suspicious expression. Gabe started making a noise in English and almost got the door shut in his face until Joe stepped in with his native tongue.

'*It's okay,*' he said. '*He's cool, I swear, he's cool.*'

'*What do you want?*'

'*Wine and women,*' said Joe, and flashed his most persuasive smile. The one he used on his mum when he wanted to get his own way.

It worked. The doorman's steely demeanour almost cracked, but not quite, and he moved aside to let them

269

through. They climbed dark narrow stairs to the first floor.

The place reminded Gabe of the working-men's clubs that his dad had taken him to as a kid, long ago. The kind of bar where he would curl up in a chair and fall asleep under a coat while his dad rolled fags and swapped fruitless racing tips with the locals.

The walls were yellowed by years of smoke, and the cheap tables and chairs were decrepit, the wood splitting into splinters waiting to happen. There was a small bar and he sincerely hoped that the barmaid wasn't part of the entertainment. She was caked in thick make-up that failed to mask her terrible skin, with dyed black hair that hung in ratty clumps around her plump face. He wondered if she was told to wear those clothes or if she actually thought she looked good. Tight jeans and lacy camisole tops should really be left for the girls and this woman hadn't been a girl for years. But the beer she served was cold and lively, particularly sweet after the dry taxi ride.

Only two of the tables were occupied. At one sat three men in their fifties, none of them speaking, and at another a couple, him older, speaking in heated whispers.

At the far end of the room was a small platform perhaps a foot high, not enough to call a stage, and not a pole or a hot Polish girl in sight.

'Where are the girls?' hissed Gabe.

'Dunno,' said Joe. 'Give it a few minutes and then I'll ask.'

The minutes ticked by and no entertainment appeared. The brutish doorman came up to the bar and engaged the middle-aged barmaid in conversation. Gabe nudged Joe who had to pretend to have more courage than he did to ask the doorman, '*Where are the girls?*'

'*Making themselves pretty for you,*' was the reply that Joe translated for Gabe, who seemed happy.

They ordered more beers, yet more beers. Joe's head was starting to swim, and just as they started drinking them half a dozen women filed out onto the stage.

There was no music, no spotlight, they were not dancing. They walked out slowly and stood like they were in a police line-up.

'Come, come,' said the doorman in English, and then to Joe, '*They will do anything, all of them. Pick one.*'

'Oh, mate,' said Gabe, showing a sudden burst of perception. 'I don't think this is a strip club – it's a brothel.'

Joe started to explain to the doorman that there had been a mistake, but it was hard. Gabe was talking over him, ignoring the language barrier. 'We were misinformed,' he said. At the same time he was looking at the girls. One of them, at the end, was quite beautiful. She saw him looking and smiled. It was a coy smile, but loaded with sexual possibilities. Gabe glanced at Joe who was getting into a heated debate with the doorman. He wandered over to the girl at the end of the line.

'You speak English?' he said. '*Angielsku?*'

She turned down her lower lip. 'Little bit,' she said, holding perfectly manicured talons an inch or so apart.

She had wide cheekbones and pale-green eyes, and was very young. If he had seen her in England he might have thought she was a schoolgirl, but in any country in the world he would still have noticed her endless legs. In her heels she was taller than him. There wasn't a scrap of fat on her. She was squeezed into a pair of cheap nylon hot pants and a little white top through which he could faintly see the outline of her tiny nipples.

'How old are you?' he said.

'Twenty.'

Old enough, unless she was lying. His cock stirred as he thought of nailing her.

'Joe,' he said. 'Hey, Joe, wait a minute.'

Was it cheating on his wife to sleep with a prostitute? Okay, yeah, course it was, technically, but it wasn't as bad as picking up a girl in a bar, was it? It wasn't like he wanted to flirt with this little minx and have some kind of clandestine affair. They wouldn't be swapping mobile phone numbers and making up some kind of code for when she called. This wasn't a thing. It was just sex. How could Christine be threatened by that? How could Christine even *find out* about that?

The amount of beer he had consumed was enough to make him think he could do anything.

The girl ran her hand casually across her body to land on her skinny hip and her gaze dipped blatantly to the bulge in Gabe's trousers.

He looked at Joe again, but he hadn't noticed, and was still arguing with the doorman.

Then he pointed at the girl and she took his arm. Together they walked out of a side door and disappeared.

She had lovely little tits. The most exciting thing about them was that they weren't Christine's full fleshy handfuls, but little pointy ones that jumped to his touch, tiny nipples the colour of bubblegum. He was excited. It had been years, *years*, since he'd enjoyed the feel of a different boob. He'd looked of course, and he'd fantasized plenty, but he hadn't touched. She was quite happy for him to rub her with one hand and himself with the other. Her skin was pale, nothing like Christine's faintly Mediterranean looks that no genealogy could explain. This girl had skin the colour of mashed potato.

He willed himself to stop thinking of mashed potato.

And to stop thinking about his wife.

She lay back on the bed and peeled off her tight jeans, looking like the kind of girl he'd had crushes on at school. The cool ones that would never look at him, let alone talk to him or peel off their jeans for him. He thought of a girl called Jenny Lewis, the last girl he'd had a crush on before he met Christine.

Damn it, Christine again.

The young Polish prostitute smiled up at him and touched herself through her skimpy white knickers. Schoolgirl knickers. Knickers like Jenny Lewis probably wore beneath her too-short school skirt.

He felt himself growing harder.

What was the Polish for blowjob?

He couldn't quite believe that Gabe had deserted him. He was stuck in an argument with this doorman, who by now he had learnt was the owner, about money. He was insisting that they would have to pay for the privilege of being in his club regardless of whether or not they took advantage of what was on offer, and Joe was trying to explain that there had been a mistake. When he turned to Gabe for moral support all he saw was Gabe's back exiting stage left, his arm linked with that of one of the girls.

'*Your friend has the right idea,*' said the owner. '*If you don't like ladies try another club.*' He sneered and Joe's face burned with confusion.

Gabe was going to have sex with her? Just like that? Was he happy that they were here? Was this what he wanted all along? But he was married; Joe had met his wife. He'd thought, as much as his limited experience of such things allowed, that Gabe and Christine were a normal happy couple. Joe had never been to a lap-dancing club or a strip bar; perhaps this was a standard night out for Gabe? For English men?

No, he'd watched enough English soap operas to know that sleeping with hookers was not something married men did without getting into trouble.

He was waiting for Gabe to come back. To say that the girl had just been showing him to the bathroom or something. But this wasn't going to happen. Gabe was out the back somewhere having *sex*. Just like that.

'*Is that right?*' The owner was goading him. '*You don't like women?*'

'*I like women.*'

'*Then pick one. We don't have all night.*'

Joe looked at the girls on stage. None of them seemed troubled that they were being so obviously appraised, but none of them seemed particularly bothered about attracting his attention either. Except one on the end, slightly older, who smiled at him gently.

'We can talk,' she said in English. 'But I will tell your friend we did more.' She took his arm, firmly but kindly. He looked back at the owner who immediately seemed less confrontational, and allowed himself to be led.

Did this mean Gabe and Christine were on the rocks? Was this the first time? As he, Joe, had brought Gabe here, was it his fault? Had he, even inadvertently, destroyed the very state that he idolized – that of happy marriage? Did this make Gabe a bad person? Could they still be friends?

He knew it was stupid, but he felt like crying.

The woman holding his arm led him through a dark corridor to an unmarked door. It opened into a tiny room with a mattress on the floor covered in a flowered sheet, a sink in one corner and an open window up far too high to offer any kind of view. The only light came from a small lamp on the floor with a tatty fringed lampshade.

He walked around the room wishing that there was more to look at, smiling at her occasionally and feeling very awkward and impossibly sober.

'Don't worry,' she said after a while. 'This will be easy.' She sat on the edge of the mattress and patted the space next to her. 'Sit,' she said. 'We wait for a few minutes then we leave. I tell them whatever you want. You were great, you were . . . um . . . large?'

She had bright blue eyes that gazed at him with warmth and humour. Her curly brown hair reminded him of a dog his next-door neighbours once had, but he thought better of mentioning that.

'*Why are you being so nice to me?*' he said in Polish.

'*The other girls are younger and prettier. You picked me, so you are being nice, not me.*'

'*You're not Polish?*'

'*Lithuanian.*'

'*I don't speak Lithuanian.*'

'*Nobody does,*' she said sadly.

275

She played with the sheet on the mattress, smoothing it out and tucking it into the corner near her. Joe slipped his mobile phone out of his pocket and checked the time. It was almost five. His mum wouldn't be too worried; she knew he was with Gabe and she would have called him if she wanted him back. It wasn't unusual to stay up all night. He suspected that she would be pleased he had found a friend at last. But he wondered what she would say if she knew what kind of man he was. There was so much he didn't know about Gabe. He looked towards the door, wondering where Gabe was, trying not to think about what he was doing, but wondering how long he would be.

'*You are thinking of your friend?*'

Joe nodded. There was something very sweet about this woman. He felt as if he could tell her anything. '*He's married,*' he said.

'*Lots are,*' she said. '*I was once.*'

He lifted his head in surprise. He never would have thought of a prostitute having a husband. '*While you were . . . working?*' he said.

'*We needed the money. I have children. Four.*' She slipped a book out from under the mattress and a photograph from between its pages, as any proud mother would. He looked at four blue-eyed children, smiling for the camera, nothing to distinguish this family from a million others.

'*They're nice,*' he said, because he didn't know what to say.

'*Don't worry about your friend,*' she said. '*He is not a bad person. Not for this.*'

She put one hand on his shoulder and the other on his cheek, turning him to face her. '*You are a sweet boy,*' she said. '*You are sure there is nothing you want to do together?*'

'*I'm a virgin*,' he said.

'*I would be your first?*'

He nodded.

'*You want me?*'

Joe looked at her and thought about what it would be like to lose his virginity here in this room, on these cheap sheets. To walk out in a little while and be a proper man, divesting himself of his virginity at last. Something he had imagined doing countless times, but never like this. He looked into her kind blue eyes and considered the possibility, but then he shook his head. '*Thanks*,' he said, '*but I think I'll wait.*'

'*Wait for what?*'

'*For love*,' he said.

They stayed in the room for a few more minutes and then they left.

Back in the bar Gabe was sitting on his own at a small round table looking into an empty glass. He lifted his head and Joe noted that while he didn't look the least bit guilty or ashamed, something of his trademark swagger was lacking. If anything he just looked tired. What had Joe expected? A contrite and cowed Gabe who couldn't meet his eye? Once more Joe berated himself for being naive. Just because Joe hadn't done anything didn't mean Gabe hadn't either. Then he remembered that the only people who knew what had happened to Joe in the back room were Joe and the woman concerned, whose name he hadn't even bothered to find out. Why on earth should Gabe be repentant when he thought that Joe had been off doing exactly the same thing? Joe knew he would never tell Gabe the truth.

'All right?' said Gabe.

'Let's go.'

The doorman dropped a folded bill on the table in front of them and Gabe opened it, fishing for his wallet at the same time. Then he stopped. 'What the – ?'

He passed the bill to Joe. Over ten thousand złoty. Something close to two thousand pounds.

The doorman hovered, his face impassive, his bulk clearly situated between them and the exit.

'Listen, mate, is this right?'

The doorman remained blank. Gabe looked to Joe for help.

'*This bill is too much,*' said Joe. '*There is a mistake.*'

'*That is the price.*' His shrug was comprehensible in any language.

'You're having a laugh,' said Gabe. He was tired, sobriety was fast approaching with a killer hangover on its heels, and he was feeling the emotional fallout of having cheated on his wife for the very first time. All those years of fidelity, of making the effort to stay in love, ruined for a pair of irresistible tits. He felt awful and he wasn't in the mood to have some bruising bouncer yank him around by his dick. 'We're not paying this much. Sorry, mate, but that's the way it is. Understand?' He looked at Joe again. 'Tell him,' he said.

'*We will not pay this much,*' said Joe.

'*I think you will.*'

Joe felt Gabe stiffen beside him and followed his eyes to the bar, where two men who could have been the bruising bouncer's big brothers had suddenly appeared.

'Shit,' muttered Gabe. 'Deep shit.'

Joe felt scared then for the first time. His fear was three-fold. One, what would he tell his mum if he got a black eye? Two, what if they broke his arm or did something else that would keep him out of next Saturday's match? And, three, what if they killed them both?

'*We know who you are,*' said the doorman. '*You think we never watch sports on television? We have White Stars fans here. We know you have money.*'

'They're fans,' relayed Joe. 'Football fans.'

'Fucking funny way of showing it,' said Gabe. He sized up the situation and realized that he was two grand down for the night. It was a lot of money, but perhaps they deserved to be ripped off. After all they'd been stupid enough to come here in the first place, to partake of beer and birds without asking the price. He tried not to think of two grand in terms of Old Gabe – supermarket man – but New Gabe, international footballer. It made their idiocy a little easier to bear. 'Ask him if he'll take a cheque,' he said to Joe.

They wouldn't, but they did offer to drive them to an ATM so that they could retrieve the cash, an offer which they made begrudgingly, like it was an inconvenience to them.

Gabe and Joe were quiet in the car. Gabe withdrew the money and though he felt like stuffing it into the throat of the nearest bad guy he handed it over with little rancour, and tried not to be too surprised when they drove off and left them in the middle of the dark and deserted street.

'Do you know where we are?' said Gabe.

'More or less,' said Joe. He started walking north, knowing that sooner or later they would hit the river and he could get his bearings.

'What a night, eh?' said Gabe.

'What a night,' said Joe.

'One best kept between ourselves.'

'What happens south of the river stays south of the river?' suggested Joe.

'Good call.'

Joe climbed into his bed as the birds were singing, having slyly dodged the spots in their apartment where the floor creaked so as not to wake his mum. Of course she had been awake from the moment she heard his key in the door, and hardly really asleep before then. She listened intently to her only son as he crept around trying not to wake her and wondered if she should be worried. He was her boy, and without a father to guide him he would be pulled in all sorts of directions. Once upon a time she was grateful for football, something to focus him and keep him out of trouble. She was only just starting to realize that football would bring trouble of its own.

Gabe climbed into his bed and couldn't bring himself to touch his wife. He thought of the leggy teenager who called herself Aska and had given him one of the greatest blowjobs of his life.

He stared at the familiar elegant lines of his wife's shoulder blades as she lay with her back to him, peaceful and trusting as a child.

Guilt gnawed down on his conscience.

He felt like a total bastard.

24

The city of Krakow had gone football crazy. Utterly, beautifully, tits-up crazy. For one weekend the Polish were as fanatical about their football as the English. Flags fluttered in the most unlikely windows, from grand old villas and concrete tower blocks alike. She was proud to be a part of it.

The UEFA Cup was regarded by many football fans as the poor relation of the Champions League. A snivelling cousin trailing after a richer, sexier, more dynamic elder and taking its cast-offs. Teams that were dumped out of the Champions League qualified automatically for the Cup, which did nothing to help its lesser stature. It was not worth as much in terms of prestige or cold, hard television rights. By the truly snobbish it was sneered at.

Until your team made it to the final stages. And then suddenly the UEFA Cup became a very big deal indeed.

But for Samantha it was the start of her new life.

'You want me to come with you?' Leanne had asked at the end of the day before.

'I'll be okay,' she'd said, as if she was playing, not just watching.

She arrived at the stadium early, her nerves propelling her out of the soulless hotel room and into the streets. She wandered slowly through the tourists in the main square, no longer feeling quite like one of them, and to amuse herself on the way to the stadium she counted every White Stars flag or banner that she saw. Near the beautiful old university a rank of taxis stood idle, their drivers gathered by a statue of Copernicus, the most famous alumnus, and every taxi had a White Stars scarf across the back or tied to the door handle.

Her stomach somersaulted. There was too much at stake. She wanted them to win, but more than that she wanted them, her boys as she thought of them, to play well, for in the box watching with her would be her two invited guests: Dave Withington, second in command for the England Under-21 squad, and Alan Bull, an important backroom staffer for the senior team.

She'd invited the managers of both England squads, not expecting them to attend but knowing that the invitation would trickle down, in much the same way that Leanne picked up all the invites that fell beneath her remit. Dave and Alan were quite near the top of the pile considering that she was asking them over to see two players that weren't even on their radar, in a country hardly renowned for producing footballing genius. Two relatively important voices made it this far solely because of her reputation as an agent and spotter of talent. Samantha Sharp didn't waste people's time. If she said there was something worth seeing in Krakow then the people came to Krakow. It was as simple as that.

The stadium was already starting to fill up, with hours yet to go. But she was the only person in the executive box. Later it would be filled with chatter and the chink of glassware but now she had it all to herself for a few moments.

She walked to the expansive window and looked out on the ailing pitch, its brown patches shamefully outnumbering the green. How very wrong of Lubin to spend more on the players' lounge and this executive box than he had on the playing surface. She looked at the hardcore fans, dotted here and there, draping their homemade banners over the terraces, preparing for the long wait until kick-off and she felt, as she often did, that it must be nice to have something that you felt so passionate about. She only felt that way about money and success, and she was wise enough to know that wasn't the same as following a team, sharing a common purpose with a stadium full of like-minded fans, a collective ideal that victory would be theirs.

Today she wanted it so badly that she felt close to them, the fans, closer than ever.

If nothing came of today's match, if Dave and Alan from the FA went home disappointed, then she would be off to a terrible start. They would go home and report that Samantha Sharp was building castles in the air out here in the middle of nowhere, chasing an unlikely dream, merely consolidating her failure. Whatever eye she had once had she had lost. Legends had been right to let her go.

No pressure.

She had underplayed the significance of the game to Joe in particular, not wanting him to be nervous.

'Do it,' she whispered, pushing lightly on the glass with her fingertips. 'Do it for me. Please.'

'And if they lose?'

She spun round. She wasn't alone. Lubin was sitting quietly in a chair in the far corner of the room. Watching her.

She blushed. The last time he'd seen her she had been naked.

'Please,' he said, waving his hand in the air. 'Please, go on.'

He really should have made his presence known. It was impolite. And now she had been caught talking to herself, praying almost.

His father is one of the richest men in the world. Do you honestly think he cares about being polite?

'I didn't see you,' she said.

'Evidently.'

She had left him sleeping in his hotel room in Zadar, creeping out at dawn to catch her flight back to Krakow after a night of ferocious sex that left her breathlessly satisfied but emotionally numb. He had sex like he was in a competition. And whatever he was competing for it was clear he thought he had won. Afterwards he had hardly looked at her before he fell asleep. She tried to sleep too, only because she wasn't confident of finding her way back to her own hotel. She couldn't even remember the name of it. She had to wake Leanne at 6 a.m. just so she could collect her bags on the way to the airport. Since then he had contacted her twice, but she hadn't returned either call.

'I owe you a call,' she said.

'You don't owe me anything.'

The sex had been hot, but they could teach each other all there was to know about playing it cool and they both knew it. She thought of taking him off to a quiet corner and screwing his brains out.

Just to relieve some of her stress.

The door to the executive box flew open and a party of six came noisily in. He greeted them warmly in Russian and left her by the window, but as he walked away he brushed his hand down her arm from her elbow to her wrist, his fingertips touching the bare skin where her sleeve ended, sending an involuntary shiver down to her toes.

Maybe after.

Joe slumped to his knees in front of the toilet and voided his tumultuous stomach, wiping away the choking strands of vomit from his lips and waiting for more. When he was satisfied that this violent attack of nerves was over he pushed himself to shaky feet and closed his eyes in silent prayer.

Let me play well, he said to his personal God, the one who was able to put the speed of the wind in his legs and the deft touch of inspiration in his feet.

Let me make her proud. 'Her' was his mother sitting out there in the stadium already, his biggest fan. 'Her' was also Samantha, whom he knew had been trying to underplay the importance of his performance. He appreciated her trying, but he wasn't stupid. He knew that two of the English Football Association's employees coming all this way to watch was a big deal, the kind of chance that would perhaps never come round again in his lifetime. 'Her' was also Layla. He had sent her a pair of tickets. He still didn't know whether or not she would come.

Let me score a goal.

An hour before kick-off and the changing room was buzzing with energy. One of the defenders had rigged up a music system, which was pumping out aggressive dance music, the sort of thing he went out of his way to avoid but somehow seemed to suit the pre-match mood. They all knew what they had to do. They had to win. Although they could not see the crowd they could feel a palpable air of expectancy gathering as the minutes ticked by.

'*Where's the English?*' he heard one of them say, but he knew that they weren't talking about him – they were talking about Gabe. None of them thought of Joe as English – he was '*bachor*', the kid. The only person to make a fuss over his Englishness was Samantha, and for all the right reasons. He had dual nationality, he had never worn a national shirt for Poland, and so in theory he was perfectly eligible to play for England one day.

'Do you *want* to play for England?' she had asked, as if he might have some bizarre longing to wear the red and white of Poland instead of the Three Lions of England.

'Since the first day I understood who I was,' he'd said, 'that I was half English,' thereby throwing any ambiguity aside and making sure she knew just how much this meant to him.

Every footballer in the world would want to play for England. It was the spiritual home of football, perhaps not of the richest players or the sexiest skills, but it was where football had passion, where every player gave everything they had, where they gave a damn, where they gave their heart. Where the fans lived and died with their team's success and failure. So they never won anything, not for years, so what? It didn't matter. They had belief. Misguided, thwarted belief but magnificent belief nonetheless.

Did he want to play for England?

He would sell his mother for that kind of chance.

'*Where's your buddy?*' someone asked.

Gabe wasn't late quite yet, but a few more minutes and he would be. He hadn't seen him since that night in Podgórze, and although they had spoken on the phone a couple of times neither one of them had referred to it.

What happens south of the river . . .

Just as he was thinking about him, Gabe appeared. He looked relaxed, far more relaxed than Joe, and Joe tried to tune in to whatever it was that enabled Gabe to saunter in with a minute to spare and not feel like he was about to risk everything he had on a ninety-minute game. But perhaps it was the same quality that allowed him to cheat on his wife, in which case he wasn't sure he wanted to be like Gabe at all.

'All right?' asked Joe.

Gabe nodded. 'Yeah, you all right?'

'Yeah.'

Something had changed.

Samantha's guests arrived and soon she was too busy playing hostess to pay any attention to Lubin. She extolled the talents of Josef Wandrowszcki. She knew that he was a better prospect than Gabe Muswell. Youth was a valuable commodity. The two men from the FA were politely interested. She hoped that Joe's performance would make them sit up and take notice.

The players took to the pitch for the warm-up about thirty minutes before kick-off. Joe shielded his eyes from the low winter sun and looked into the increasing crowd. He had memorized the seating plan and knew exactly where the tickets were that he had sent to Layla, but the sun was too bright, it was too far away and he could not see. He ran with the rest of the squad; he tucked and jumped and side-stepped his way across the pitch. The crowd was still growing.

He told himself no, that she would not be there – she would be with her new boyfriend back at home. Why would she get on a plane to watch a game of football when she had told him again and again since they were seven years old that she didn't even like football very much. He shouldn't hope, and yet still he did. He hoped that she was there and that she was on her own. Not with the boyfriend. Not with *Daniel*. In fact, he sincerely hoped that she had broken it off with Daniel. He couldn't bear the thought of someone else kissing those pink lips. He knew it wasn't cool to care this much, but he did. He tried not to.

'Looking for someone?' said Gabe.

'Layla,' he said, and her name pierced his nonchalance like a silver-plated bullet. Once more he looked into the sun, but it was impossible to tell if she was there.

He needed to put his head down, stop looking and concentrate on his game. After all, what was more important: whether or not Layla had come to see him play or the chance to impress the men from England?

England, he told himself firmly. The team not the country.

What would his dad say, he wondered, as he stretched out his hamstrings, if he had the chance to play for England?

He ran twenty yards twisting at the waist and imagined his dad's face when he told him.

Just as the players were about to go back in he heard someone screaming his name.

'*Joe!* Josef Wandrowszcki! Joe, *over here!*'

Magically the sun slipped behind a cloud and when he looked in the direction of the voice, of her seats, he saw her. Too far away to be distinct, but he knew it was her. He could feel her presence. He felt as if he could see every windswept strand of hair on her head, every gentle crease of her pink lips when she smiled. He could smell the sweet scent of her. She was wearing a red woollen scarf and unfurling some kind of banner. If he screwed his eyes up he could just make out the words – HI JOE! – his heart mushroomed with pride. God, he loved her. He loved her so. He loved her.

I will be playing for you.

He waved, and she waved back and he couldn't tell who she was with and he didn't even care. She was here. She had come. His stomach settled and he felt as if he could do anything.

They were pitted against a lesser Italian side that hadn't won any silverware since the seventies. On paper they were evenly matched and for the first twenty minutes it was that way on the pitch too. Each promising run on goal was swiftly closed down, a well-placed pass would be given away a touch or two later, each hard-won tackle came to nothing.

The crowd started to shift in their seats, thoughts drifting away from the action, and down on the pitch the players could sense it.

Stranded as a lone striker Joe was frustrated. He shouted constantly for the ball, especially when it fell to Gabe, but the defenders were playing so far up that twice he was (wrongly he felt) pulled back for offside.

How was he supposed to perform if he didn't even get the chance? He was morbidly aware of the minutes ticking by.

When the ball went out of play at the other end of the field he huddled with Gabe and suggested a change of tactic.

'Let's trade,' he said. 'You avoid their offside trap and I'll feed you the ball.'

'Don't be daft,' said Gabe, 'I haven't got your pace.'

'The only thing my pace is getting me is some bad refereeing decisions,' said Joe. 'Come on, just for the last few minutes of this half.'

'We'll discuss it at half-time.'

'Look,' said Joe, his frustration spilling out into his tone of voice. 'I'm dropping back. If you don't want to be on the end of my crosses someone else will.'

The ball was back in play and Joe ran out of position to wrest it from a member of the opposing team.

Gabe backed up, struggling to keep a defender between himself and the goal and avoid the offside.

Meanwhile Joe ran down the left wing in world-class time, needing nothing more than speed to keep the defenders at bay. They couldn't catch him. When the time came to pass the ball in to Gabe he found he was pulling it back slightly, which meant Gabe was able to shake off his defender and step forward for the cross.

Gabe collected the ball calmly and controlled it with one touch before firing it at the goal. The woodwork denied him. The goalpost trembled and he lurched for the rebound, but the rattled goalkeeper beat him to it, grasping the ball firmly in both hands and sending his players deep into the outfield before the goal-kick.

The crowd began to take notice.

And up in the executive box they were taking notice too.

She was not aware she had been holding her breath until Lubin pointed it out to her shortly after the half-time whistle.

'You can relax,' he said. 'They are both playing well.'

It was true that in the last fifteen minutes of the first half Joe and Gabe were dominating the game, but she was glad he had spoken within earshot of the delegates from the FA.

'You think?'

'You clearly have an eye for talent. Why don't you trust yourself a little more?'

'I've been known to make some bad decisions.'

'If I wasn't sure that I'm the best thing to happen to you for a long time I'd think you were talking about me,' he said quietly.

She wished that his arrogance was a turn-off, but she'd never been one of those women attracted to humility. As far as she was concerned unassuming men were only modest because they had little to boast about. The truth was that she liked how much he assumed.

'I have to see you again,' he said. 'Tonight.'

'It's a bad idea.'

'Impossible. I don't have bad ideas.'

She didn't want romantic entanglements, not now, not when her business was so close to being a reality. The transfer window was just round the corner. It was just sex. Fierce sex. But she should be able to resist nonetheless. She ignored the lusty signals that her body was sending to her brain.

Be cool. Be business.

'I was planning on taking our two visitors for dinner,' she said. 'Perhaps you would like to join us?'

It would be good to show off to the FA with her Russian billionaire friend. Ever since Abramovich and Gaydamak sank their millions into the game people saw pound signs in Russian eyes and were inevitably impressed.

'There is a late cocktail party at the Czartoryskich museum,' he said. 'Perhaps that is something that you and your friends would enjoy?'

A private cocktail party would be perfect. She just hoped there would be something to celebrate.

Joe started the second half with fire raging in his belly. His team mates could sense it and so could the opposition. He had been close enough to scent the tang of goal. He had a taste for it now. He allowed himself to think once more of Layla watching him in the stands, watching and waiting for him to impress, and then he closed his mind to everything but the game that he was playing, the pursuit of the ball and placing it in the back of the net.

Gabe watched him and found himself longing to be seventeen again and have that kind of talent. The boy was something special. The thought of what he might be like in ten years' time was almost overwhelming.

Up in the executive box the two delegates from the FA glanced at each other. They had seen enough football games to know what they were looking for. Talent came in different packages. Sometimes a player was flashy, demonstrating flair in every touch; sometimes he was dogged and hard-working, unlikely to make a mistake, a safe player who would be a rock for any team. And sometimes a player was instinctive, the ball becoming part of his body, bending to his will. This was the kind of talent they saw in Joe.

But not Gabe. Gabe was tired and it showed. He had played a great fifteen minutes but that wasn't enough. Not against Joe who looked as fresh as if he had just run out. Gabe felt old.

When the goal eventually, inevitably, came it was a good one. A solo effort from halfway up the field. Some pedants would argue that against better opposition, against a stronger defence, Joe's goal might not have made it. But it hardly seemed fair to pick holes in a performance that fans would be talking about for the rest of the season.

The world slowed down for Joe and he was able to watch the satisfying path of his forceful strike inch by inch as it flew past the desperate face of the experienced goalkeeper and into the back of the goal, where it bounced twice and then was still.

Joe didn't waste any time celebrating. He picked the ball out of the net and ran it back to the centre circle so that he might have the chance to score another.

And he did.

The crowd roared and somewhere someone set off a red flare so that half of the stadium was engulfed in choking crimson smoke. If anyone had known his name, this new kid – *bachor*, they might have been shouting it, but they did not and so they roared the name of their team until the cold night air shook with the sound of it.

When the full-time whistle blew Samantha turned and looked at her new friends from the FA and her face blazed with triumph.

'See anything you like?' she teased.

'We'll be wanting tape of the match,' said one.

She felt an overpowering sense of relief. The kind that makes you relax and want to go to bed knowing you will sleep well. She needed to sit down. But the night wasn't over yet.

'I'm sure you'd like to meet Joe,' she said. 'And Gabe.'

The mention of Gabe sounded like an afterthought, and briefly she felt bad. Gabe had played well enough but the game had only one star. That much was obvious to all of them. She made sure that the two men had fresh drinks and then sat down for five minutes to enjoy the atmosphere of the triumphant supporters around her.

The dressing room was thick with the stench of mud and sweat. Players gathered around Joe congratulating him in the language that Gabe still didn't understand, completely ignoring Gabe and ignoring his contribution to the game. It was as if Joe had done it all on his own when Gabe knew, *he knew*, that he had been there feeding Joe balls, two of which made it onto the scoreline.

It wasn't just the attention and adulation – it was the talent, the youth, the limitless possibility that he saw when he watched Joe play. At seventeen Gabe had been juggling football with girls and beer, prioritizing nothing, considering whether he should do a City and Guilds in plumbing or take up the offer of a full-time job at the supermarket where he worked every Saturday. Why hadn't he had the ambition to pursue football with the necessary single-mindedness, like Joe? This chance, this wonderful chance for which he had been so grateful, had come twenty years too late and only served as a constant reminder of a wasted life.

At least that's the way it felt.

He was choking on the bitter taste of regret and felt like he needed a beer to wash it down.

Joe's locker was next to his. They were friends, weren't they? And when Joe came over and said, 'Nice one, mate,' Gabe was able to grin and slap the kid on the back and congratulate him. Perhaps he should have been an actor. Because upstairs as people gathered around Joe, important people who could change his life, nobody would have guessed that Gabe was jealous at all.

Joe made his way back to the players' entrance, the only place he could think to wait for her. Why hadn't they made a better plan? Was it because he had never really dared to dream that she would show up? He was gripped by a sudden fear that he might have imagined her up there in the stands, like some kind of vision, an angel to inspire him. Was he going mad? Had love sent him that far into unreality? Samantha had been giddy with congratulatory praise and introduced him to the delegates from the FA with an unmistakable pride. So if Layla was a vision it had worked. But he realized, shockingly, he would give back both goals to see her here, to feel her arms around him, however briefly, however platonically, to spend a few hours here together, just the two of them, even if they were at the most crowded party in the city. To make some more memories to last him on those empty nights when she was thousands of miles away, when they were apart.

Please.

He closed his eyes and made a vow. If she was real, if his vision of her had not been a vision at all but the truth, then he would tell her how he felt. He would tell her everything. Tonight.

And when he opened his eyes she was there.

25

Samantha had been chatting away to a perfectly charming girl called Elizabeta for fifteen minutes before Aleksandr joined them, bowed deeply and addressed the girl as 'Your Highness'. She stuttered on her next sentence. Royalty. And her, just little Sammy Sharp, sharing small talk and a bowl of stuffed olives. Not to mention the Russian billionaire-to-be by their side.

She was still on a high from the match and couldn't stop smiling.

A short while later Elizabeta asked them both to excuse her as she had spotted an old friend. Aleksandr bowed again when she left and Samantha found herself instinctively bobbing a daft little curtsey to match. She may have been a meritocrat, but she was still a woman, and every woman had once been a little girl. And every little girl once wanted to be a princess.

'Your Highness?' said Samantha.

'A princess of Spain and Poland,' he confirmed.

'I didn't think Poland had a monarchy any more.'

'Technically they don't,' he said, lifting two glasses of champagne from a passing silver tray, and handing one to her, 'but lineage is as important as it has ever been. She's from Madrid, the king's second cousin. Married a Pole. Her husband can trace his ancestry back to the fifteenth century. He is still royal, even if they no longer rule.'

'Where is he?' she asked. 'Her husband?'

He nodded towards a dark-haired man with a moustache slamming back shots of vodka in a smoky corner by one of the open fireplaces. His loud voice carried all the way to them and though she couldn't understand a word she could tell he was drunk.

'Eurotrash,' he said dismissively.

The cocktail party was in the vaulted cellar of one of the finest museums in Europe. Aleksandr had insisted that they all detour to inspect the Leonardo Da Vinci on the second floor before descending to the party below. Samantha had pretended to be impressed, but really art left her cold. If she had eighty million US dollars, the conservative estimate of the painting's value, she could think of far better ways to spend it. Nevertheless, the cellar made an atmospheric venue for a party, lit as it was by candles in sconces that reflected on the marble floor and made the glasses and silverware glint with the refracted light of a hundred separate flames. There was some serious money in the room. How many people here could afford to buy a Leonardo of their very own? Knowing they were partying beneath eighty-million-dollar paintings made it even more glamorous.

His voice dragged her back to the room.

'Sorry?' she said. 'I was thinking about . . . art.'

'I said your guests look as though they're having a pleasant evening.'

The two men from the FA were each embroiled in private conversation with a pair of beautiful Polish women. Their ties were loosened, looks of slight bewilderment on their faces. In England she suspected such attractive women to be well out of their league.

'Being English makes you popular with women,' said Aleksandr.

'Even here?' She gestured around her, meaning the trays of champagne and caviar that circled endlessly, the designer clothes and ostentatious bling, the obvious wealth that lingered in the air like the heady perfume.

'Even here,' he said. 'This is new Europe. It will take a few more years yet before it occurs to these people that they are equal to old Europe in every sense. Until then, the girls still dream of marrying an Englishman to take them away.'

'I think both those men are already married,' she said.

'That matters less than you might think.'

How very different this all was to a night out with her old Legends colleagues in some painfully trendy London bar where more often than not she pretended not to feel old while she watched Richard and his sort chat up women only recently out of their teens who would really rather have a footballer but would be willing to take a millionaire agent as a substitute. Trying not to feel jealous if Jackson played the part of a single man as she often insisted that he did to maintain their cover. The women here seemed more sophisticated, dressed far more elegantly, not a flash of thigh in sight. The age range was wider and, most unusually, nobody seemed particularly drunk. If this was England people would be dancing badly by now, a girl with new boobs would be offering a feel and Samantha would be thinking about going home.

There was only one couple dancing here. A blonde woman draped over a handsome young man she recognized as a defender from the White Stars team. He had the sort of build that would have been playing rugby if he had been born British, big and bearlike, and was gently stroking the hair of his dancing partner as they whirled a slow dance, lost in a world of their own.

The blonde looked awfully familiar.

'Leanne?'

Leanne raised her head from the bear's shoulder and winked at her boss.

She wasn't quite sure how Leanne did it, but she never missed an opportunity to mingle with footballers. Here as in London, or so it seemed.

Aleksandr saw her looking. 'Someone you know?'

'A friend,' said Samantha.

She wondered if he could tell how turned on she was just by standing here talking to him. The thought of his tight young body under those sharp clothes was distracting. The memory of going to bed with him meant that every time she glanced at his face she remembered how it had looked that night, furious with desire, desire for her. Her body felt liquid at the recollection. She fought the impulse to drag him into one of the convenient dark spaces to satisfy the need turning her body hot and molten.

Calm down.

'Whose party is this anyway?' she asked.

'Mine.'

Her eyebrows shot up in surprise. He should have said. If this was her party she would be installed on a throne somewhere watching over her guests.

She surveyed the crowd. Where was Joe? He had the address; he could have caught a cab and been here by now. Meanwhile she had another client to try to sell. Gabe hadn't played the best game of his life, not like Joe, but he had still made a valuable contribution. It would be worth trying to make an impression. She saw him on the opposite side of the room with Christine.

'You should mingle,' she said to Lubin.

'Mingle?'

'Mix with your guests.'

'I know what it means. I was curious why you think I would want to when I am here with you.'

'I should spend some time with my clients,' she said. 'And I don't want to monopolize you.'

He held her eye for a long moment, then nodded slowly and took her hand in his. 'Of course,' he said, lifting her hand to his lips and kissing it like an old-fashioned lover. 'But also you should spend some time with me. I will look for you later, after I have . . . mingled.'

She made her way over to Gabe and Christine. She was too busy thinking about the charming billionaire to notice that they were in the middle of an argument. She was close enough to hear them before she knew, even though they were talking in whispers. It was too late to change her trajectory. Christine saw her and nudged Gabe sharply in the ribs. They stopped talking abruptly, requiring her to fill the tense silence that followed.

'Great game, Gabe,' she said. 'I hope you're both enjoying yourselves.'

'We are, aren't we?' said Christine.

'Whatever you say,' said Gabe, and it was impossible to miss the sarcasm in his voice.

'I want to bring the chaps from the FA over to meet

you properly,' she said, 'but they seem to be a little pre-occupied right now.'

'These Polish girls definitely have their charms.' Gabe drained his champagne swiftly and swapped his empty glass for a full one as a tray passed him, drinking half of it with his first sip.

'Gabe,' said Christine. 'Don't you think you ought to slow down?'

'No,' he said. 'But obviously you do.'

She was with Christine on this one. Gabe needed to slow down, preferably stop. She was hoping that Gabe's natural charm would add to a solid but unspectacular performance and give him a chance of making it onto some wildcard list somewhere, but only if he was able to demonstrate some of the maturity that could be his greatest selling point. She knew from experience that too much to drink made most men, and footballers in particular, act about fifteen years old.

Samantha made a risky decision.

'Come with me, Gabe,' she said. 'Let me introduce you to Alan Bull.'

It was now or never. His lucidity was on the wane. She had to get this little meet and greet over and done. She reintroduced the two men and stood beside them while they talked about the current standing in the English Premier League.

The Polish girls stood beside them and pretended to look interested. They gave her outfit the once over and from the looks of things found her lacking in some department. Dressed as they were in frilled pelmet hems over black leggings and with matching asymmetric fringes that made them look like rejects from an eighties girl band she didn't feel particularly slighted by their judgement, but the intense scrutiny made her contribution to the conversation stilted.

'Gabe's a Tottenham fan,' she said.

'Or at least I was until I put a hat-trick past their goalie,' crowed Gabe. 'Now I just feel sorry for them.'

'That must have been some day for you,' said Alan.

Gabe took this as an invitation to launch into his favourite story, dressing it up with exaggerated descriptions and generally taking far too long to describe a game that had taken place months ago. She could sense Alan losing interest, but Gabe was oblivious. He painted a picture of the match kick by kick. She tried to push him to the end.

'It was a fantastic game, Gabe, and look how far it's brought you.'

'My favourite goal will always be number three,' he said. 'The clock was ticking . . .'

And off he went again.

Alan smiled politely and waited for a natural pause and then asked, 'Where's the boy? Wandrowszcki, right? That's some name.'

'Joe?' she said. 'He's on his way.' Though privately she echoed Alan's sentiment. Where *was* he? Between Gabe's pomposity and Joe's tardiness it wouldn't matter if they both played like Pelé – attitude was important too.

'Hey, mate,' said Gabe. 'I'm in the middle of a sentence here.'

Alan turned back to him and grinned benignly. 'It sounds like a day you'll never forget.'

'You taking the piss?'

'I beg your pardon?'

Alan looked across at Samantha to smooth over the awkward moment. She started to make vague apologies, knowing in her gut that if Gabe's undistinguished performance hadn't stamped out any glimmer of an international career then being rude to somebody this influential certainly would put an absolute end to it.

Gabe moved to swap his empty champagne glass for yet another one, but his hands were clumsy and missed their target. He tried to correct himself, but it was too late. What might have been a simple dropped glass became an entire tray of upset drinks crashing to the marble floor, drawing the attention of everyone in the room who saw Gabe swaying and swearing, almost slipping on the wet floor, ungainly and inebriated.

She looked across the room and saw Aleksandr – unexpected eye contact – and he was wearing what could only be described as a sneer and for a disconcerting second she thought it was directed at her. But no, he was looking at Gabe. When he noticed her looking he corrected himself and turned away. She took a step towards Gabe, but he backed off, stumbling further in the process, holding up his arms to say 'I'm fine' when it was obvious to everyone that he was not.

'Gabe!' Christine came running across the room, hurrying back to his side, holding him up, whispering something in his ear that nobody could hear but Samantha. '*Calm down*,' she whispered in gentle tones. '*Calm down. Come on, let's go, okay?*'

He shook off her arm and stood up stiff and rigid, making a point of his ability to stand on his own two feet.

'He's really not much of a champagne drinker,' said Christine, knowing that she was making a weak excuse to try and save a little face. 'I told you to take it easy,' she said, and forced out a little laugh. Gabe scowled but stayed quiet.

Alan just looked relieved that the incident was over.

'I think we ought to go,' said Christine, stating the obvious. 'Will you thank Mr Lubin for inviting us, Sam?'

'You'll be all right getting home?' she asked.

'We'll get a cab. *Prosze na Hotel Copernicus*,' said Christine shyly. 'I'm taking Polish lessons.'

It had started snowing again. They clambered into one of the many taxis lining up outside the venue. Gabe slumped into the corner, opened the window a fraction and breathed in the frosty air. He was sobering up quickly, too quickly, and willed her not to launch into a lecture, telling him all the things he already knew.

It wasn't just the champagne. The champagne was merely a symptom, something he was drinking to try to blot out a painful, inconvenient truth. That even when he played as hard as he could he was still not good enough, and it was too late in his life to get any better.

'You okay?' asked his wife, and slipped her hand into his.

But he was too ashamed to answer her. He'd embarrassed Sam. Sam, who only ever wanted to make his life better, and she had. He had no idea how he would ever make it up to her.

Christine was thinking of the trip she had made to a private fertility clinic that day, where she had sat and talked to a specialist who in perfect English told her that a cycle of IVF treatment would cost a fraction of what it cost them in England, that she and Gabe could begin by making a few lifestyle changes: a healthy diet, minimal stress and no alcohol. Christine wanted a baby. But she had no idea how to make Gabe want one too.

He could sense an aching gulf between them on the way home that night. She was slipping away from him, and he was mortified to find himself momentarily wishing he had never scored the hat-trick against Tottenham that day at all.

'Isn't that Joe?' said Christine, pointing out onto the street where Joe and Layla walked along hand in hand.

Kids like Joe, they were the future, and he was just Gabe Muswell, part-time player who'd had one lucky day against Tottenham that he would try to trade on for the rest of his life. Despite what he might have thought, that day hadn't been the beginning of anything; it had been the summit of his achievement, the pinnacle of his footballing career.

It had been the end.

Layla's thumb was resting on the back of his hand where she had clasped it casually. He fancied that he could feel the warmth of her fingers, even through the leather gloves that she wore. Black leather gloves. Sexy. His hand where she was touching him was an inferno, keeping the rest of his body toasty warm. And Layla was far too excited to feel the cold. She kept raving about the city, about the match, about him and all Joe could do was stare at her and grin like an imbecile.

How could she not know? To Joe it was so obvious that

he might as well have her name tattooed across his heart. The Eric Clapton song she had been named for ran in an endless loop in his head whenever he was close to her, the soundtrack to every conversation they had ever had. For Joe it was the ultimate love song, rich in unrequited desire, and it played loudly in his mind tonight, tuned into the pulse of the blood rushing through his veins.

Lay. La.

Maybe he should stop, look into her eyes and lean in to kiss her. He didn't have to use words; he could kiss her and she could kiss him back and they would always remember their first kiss in this place, on this night, the first kiss of so many kisses to come. Clumsy words would spoil it. A kiss could say it all.

But it was too late; they were there.

And Joe let another opportunity to tell his love that he loved her pass him by.

After Gabe left the party Samantha quickly drafted in Leanne to help with charming Alan, and she did an admirable job pretending that everything he said was fascinating, doing her best to make him forget that there had ever been an embarrassing moment – 'Really? British Airways? I came with easyJet. Would you like to dance?' – proving that she was perfectly capable of flirting with someone who was not a footballer. Samantha sat in the corner and fretted that she had lost any credibility she had managed to claw back since London.

Then finally Joe arrived.

And everything was okay again. More than okay.

They liked him.

26

For the next few days she worked hard on a whispering campaign about this boy wonder playing out in the back of beyond. She waited patiently for the phone to ring and for some third party to ask her to find out about him. Only then would she know that her subtle PR operation had worked and that the backrooms and boardrooms of English clubs had added a new name to their lists. It would be a pleasure to take such a call, to be able to say, why yes, I know him, he's mine.

But before that could happen she received a different kind of call. One she dropped everything to answer. Liam had been granted parole and was due to be released.

'It's all down to you,' he said. 'You know that, right?'

'Don't be stupid,' she said.

Tears of joy were spilling soundlessly down her cheeks and she forced her fingernails into the palm of her hand to keep control of her singing emotions.

'I mean it. That lawyer you got? He knew all the right things to do. Got my case referred to the Home Secretary right away. He requested all the reports on me, told me exactly what resettlement courses would look good and wrote the most amazing representation on my behalf. You should read it, Sam. You wouldn't recognize me. The guy makes me out to be some kind of hero.'

'You've always been my hero, Liam,' she said. And it was partly true.

'Until I killed people?'

'You didn't kill anyone, Liam. It was an accident.'

'A little dark humour, Sam, that's all.'

She heard him pull hard on a cigarette, his breath whistling down the line, and she realized that her big brother was scared. After all those years behind bars he no longer knew his place in the world. Except that he had a place with her.

'So you'll be here?' he said.

'Of course I will.'

She was nervous too. They had gone from being as close as brother and sister could be, to seeing each other at most once a week and talking of nothing important. Now their relationship was entering a new phase, the first really as adults, for she had only been a child when he was put away; she knew that now. Without drugs and drink to bond over, and with unlimited time to try, nobody telling them that visiting hours were over, she was fearful of what shape their new relationship would take.

She didn't tell Leanne the real reason she was heading back to England. 'Just for a few days,' she said, avoiding any further questions.

Leanne did not press her for details of her trip. Good. Leanne had been working with her for years. It was far too late in their relationship to say, by the way I've a brother I never mentioned. He's in prison – didn't I tell you?

She was waiting for him outside when, at a few minutes past seven on a Monday morning, he stepped through the gates of the prison and into the real world. They embraced each other, as close as lovers, and she thought she heard a sob catch in his throat but she couldn't be sure. He climbed inside her car and asked if he could smoke. She hadn't the heart to say no.

'Here,' she said, pushing over a small cardboard box. 'I got you a present.'

He pretended he wasn't excited, but the way he ripped the box open made her remember Christmases gone by. 'A mobile phone?' he said. 'Excellent.'

'It's just my old one,' she said. 'But it's ready to go. I put some credit on, charged the battery.' She grinned. 'You have anyone you want to call?'

'Nope,' he said. 'You're already here.'

He tucked it in his pocket. A phone represented freedom. It felt good.

They spent the first couple of days treading carefully around each other. Liam seemed to want to do little more than eat, sleep and shower, alternating between these three activities in a continual loop. She didn't push him. They had the rest of their lives.

London was much as she had left it. Her house was safe and clean, and she fell back into the familiar space gratefully, working in her study and taking an enormous amount of contentment from the occasional sound of her brother padding around above.

On the third day she decided it was time for his surprise. She couldn't wait any longer.

Announcing that she was taking him out for lunch she jollied him into the car and they set off for the short drive to his future. They headed for Kentish Town. He was confused, of course, when they pulled up in front of the small Victorian terrace, identical to its neighbours, but if he was uncomfortable she was too excited to notice. She tipped a set of keys into his hand.

'It's yours,' she said. 'I bought it for you.'

'What?'

'Years ago,' she said. 'Before it was expensive. You've done well out of the property boom. Congratulations.'

He turned the keys over in his hands, as if he didn't know what to do with them. 'Sammy,' he said, 'you can't buy me a house.'

'I did,' she said. 'It's yours.'

He didn't look as happy as she hoped he would. It wasn't as flash as hers – she hadn't wanted to overwhelm him and, besides, he had always had more modest taste. She had thought it was perfect. But something was wrong. He looked ill at ease.

'It's okay,' she said. 'It's really okay. The paperwork is all in your name. You can do what you like with it. If you don't want to live here you can rent it or sell it or whatever, I won't be offended.'

'Yeah,' he said. 'I'd hate to offend you.'

'What's wrong?'

'You bought me a house?'

She nodded. 'Don't worry, I can afford it. Come on, don't you want to see?' She was practically skipping up the path and so didn't see the look of horror on his face.

Inside she was oblivious as she showed him everything. The furniture she had bought, the bed in the master bedroom made up with fresh white linen. A few clothes in the wardrobe, a good pair of shoes and two pairs of trainers. A comfortable sofa in the spacious front room and a decent television and stereo system. In the kitchen the cupboards were full of plates and dishes, there were cleaning materials under the sink and the fridge was full of food. There were towels in the bathroom and soap on the side of the sink. She had thought of everything.

'I don't know what to say.'

'Why don't you try your new kettle and make us both a cup of coffee?'

'What? No cappuccino machine?'

Her face fell.

'It was a joke,' he said. 'This is all too much, Sammy.'

'It was a pleasure,' she said. 'It makes me happy.'

'I'm serious. I can't accept any of this.'

'Don't be silly, of course you can.'

His face soured. 'Don't you get it? How am I supposed to find my place in the real world when you've so pains-takingly made my place for me? You think you can just buy me a house, fill it up with crap, buy me a *life*? It doesn't work like that.'

'But . . .'

'I have to find my own way, Sam. And it won't help to constantly be reminded of how *fabulous* you are.'

'I'm not . . . I was trying to make things easy for you.'

'Why? Because I'm useless? Compared to you, Sam, everyone is useless, but maybe I'd like to try to be my own man. Or do you think it's too late? Is that it? I'm thirty-eight years old – you think I missed my chance of a life?'

She clenched her hands into little fists. This was not how she'd imagined it. Not at all. This perfect house that she had laboured over, cleaning it from top to bottom, filling the fridge with his favourite things so that he might have a place that he could call home. She had imagined his smile, his happiness and, yes, his gratitude, but not this. Not this look of total disgust, the rejection of everything she was trying to do. He looked as if he hated her.

'You have no idea,' he said. 'What do you think it's been like for me seeing you climb higher and higher, and all the while I was stuck in there, with nobody to remember me but you, a constant reminder of what a mess I'd made. You loved it, didn't you? You must have. You loved having a brother who was a failure so that you could feel even better about yourself. Well, when you looked down on me like that and thought "there but for the grace of God", just try to imagine what I was thinking.'

'I didn't think that,' she said.

But wasn't that a lie?

Hadn't Liam's awful predicament pushed her to succeed? Without him there to remind her of the moment that their lives had split in two, where might she be?

He didn't mean it. He couldn't.

She had been warned to expect irrational moods. His confidence was shattered; he would need patience and love if he was to regain a sense of self-esteem. She shouldn't, she mustn't, take it personally. It was just a house.

She started to cry.

'Oh for fuck's sake,' said Liam. He walked out of the front door, leaving her there wondering how this day, which she had been looking forward to for so long, had gone so terribly wrong.

When she got back to her house in Belsize Park she hoped that she would find him there. She hoped that he would be waiting for her and telling her sorry, that he didn't mean it, that he loved the house and had just been overwhelmed. But he was nowhere to be found. She had no idea where he might have gone. All she could do was wait.

Eventually at around three o'clock in the morning she stopped trying to sleep, got out of bed, dressed and walked out into the streets to look for him.

Going to Camden in the middle of the night was like visiting the past, but with a fresh coat of paint. She saw dusty old bars the two of them used to frequent, but many of them had been transformed into wine bars or gastro-pubs. She walked into those that were still open, hoping to see him propped up on a bar stool, slagging off his sister to a sympathetic barmaid. She paid to go into a handful of clubs where nothing had changed, where the clientele still dressed exclusively in black from the tips of their Doc Marten boots to the wings of their black eyeliner. In her biker jacket and grey skinny jeans she fitted right in. But she couldn't find Liam. She walked past the tattoo parlour where she had branded herself and the patch of flesh on her shoulder itched in recognition. Liam wasn't there. Nor was he in the all-night cafés that catered to the post-club crowd.

Then she remembered. And with a deep sense of certainty she started to walk towards Primrose Hill.

He sat on the same cold wooden bench that had accommodated them many years ago when they had been little more than lost children, searching for a fix, any kind of fix, to mend them. She had found her way, his sister, and he had stayed rooted in the past.

Prison was like limbo. The first few years were unbelievably hard, but gradually something changed and as
your memories of the person you once were began to
subside you forgot you had ever been anything other than
this. The life outside no longer exists. He had heard of
people becoming institutionalized, and would have sworn
that it would never happen to him. He relished the thought
of freedom. Except when his freedom finally came he
found that his heart was in his throat the moment he
walked out of the gates and it had stayed there ever since.
The life he once had had gone, and he had no idea what
was supposed to take its place. He had too many years of
being told what to do and when to do it, something he
had not expected to miss. But he did miss it. And he knew
that if he let Samantha take over his life, tell him what to
do, then things would be easier. But the fighter in him that
had longed to be free was struggling to make his own
choices.

He was conflicted, and so he had lashed out at the only
constant in his life. And that made him feel worse than
ever.

She was only trying to help, he knew that, but he felt
pushed into a corner. Sure, it was a spacious two-bedroom
corner in a nice part of town, but it was more than he
could cope with. And so he had run.

Because running away works.

His feet had taken him here and now his head was
bombarding him with memories. At first he'd thought
they were happy ones, his sister and him, enjoying all that
the city had to offer, but with so many years of perspec-
tive he could see how miserable she had been. He was her

big brother, he was supposed to look after her, but there could be no denying that Samantha's life had improved exponentially as soon as he was out of her existence.

He looked down on the view. It was an enormous slice of night sky and cityscape. He had forgotten how wide a sky could be. And this more than any decision he could make told him he was finally free.

'Liam?'

She had found him. Perhaps he had known that she would. Why else would he have come back to this place?

She sat down next to him and said nothing. She was scared of saying the wrong thing.

'Just like old times,' he said.

'I don't miss them, those times,' said Samantha. 'I'm glad they're gone.'

'They were the only times I've ever had.'

'I suppose.'

There was a cold breeze up here and she wrapped her jacket tighter around her. Were there too many years between them now? Had she lost the last family that she had? She still wasn't sure what she had done wrong and she was mad at him. She could stay calm and quiet on the outside but inside she was raging. The house was the biggest gesture she had ever made. Getting it thrown back in her face like that, it was impossible not to take it personally. But she stifled her disappointment.

'If you don't want the house,' she said, 'you don't have to have it. I was trying to help.'

'I know.'

'I've been waiting almost ten years to give it to you. Maybe I got carried away.'

'It's a beautiful house,' he said.

'But you don't want it?'

'Of course I do, it's just . . .'

'What?' she said. 'Tell me. I'm trying really hard to understand.'

He couldn't look her in the eye. 'Me too. If you figure it out you'll have to let me know.'

She looked out at the city, trying to imagine what it must be like for him to be here, but it was futile. How could she possibly know?

'I've always been jealous of you,' he said.

'Except when we were young,' she added.

'No, especially then. You always had drive. Sometimes I felt like I was just taking a free ride in your slipstream.'

'That's not true,' she said. 'Everything changed for me when you went into prison. You made me, Liam.'

'You're wrong. Maybe that's the way you remember it, but you're wrong. You were pulling away from me long before the accident.'

Was that right? And what difference did it make? They were brother and sister, family. But she knew that didn't count for much. Their mother certainly hadn't thought so. Nor their father before her.

'And then you pulled so far away,' he said, 'that I could hardly see you any more. Your name in the papers, millions in the bank, one success after another. In prison, you were the most interesting thing about me. And I hated that. I hate it. I know that makes me a total bastard – you don't have to tell me. I try to be happy for you, Sammy, but, God, sometimes I just wish that you would fail occasionally, you know?'

Tears stabbed at her eyes and she wiped them away with the back of her hand, telling herself to be patient. He didn't know what he was saying. If he needed to hurt her, well then she would let him. In the dark he wouldn't be able to see her cry.

'And then even when you fail,' he said, '– big scandal, national news – you just start over and it's all sunshine again. How is it possible that whole thing didn't knock you down?'

He said it like he had wanted it to.

'I didn't let it,' she said. 'That's all.'

'You make it look too easy, and life's not like that. Not for everyone, not for me.'

'It could be,' she whispered.

'Why? Because you buy me a house, an easy fix? Here you go, Liam. Everything is going to be okay. You think that will fix me, having somewhere to live?'

'It would be a start.'

'Whatever I do, it's a start. But you can't do it for me.'

They sat in silence for a while, both feeling wretched, each wondering why he couldn't just accept her gift of a new life graciously with the gratitude it deserved.

'I think I'd better leave,' he said eventually.

'And go where?'

'Away for a bit. I have a friend, sort of, he offered me a couch.'

'You have my couch,' she blurted. 'You have a spare room with me. Liam, you have a house.'

'I just can't, Sammy. You're my little sister. You're not responsible for me. I don't want you to be. I have to be more than that.'

'We take care of each other,' she said.

'Maybe I need to start taking care of myself.'

She looked down on this city that she had once loved, that she still loved, but it had disappointed her, and here she was again, being disillusioned by another subject of her misplaced adoration.

'You know what, Liam? I'm not going to apologize for being the most interesting thing about you. We both made our choices. And if you think I got here all on my own then you're just wrong. People helped me – people are still helping me – and I'm glad of that, I'm thankful. If I turned down help I might be where you are now. Is that really what you want for me?'

He didn't say anything.

'Is it? Is it what you want for yourself?'

She stood up. He didn't even look at her. She walked away down the hill, hoping with every footfall that he would chase her and say the words that would make everything all right between them again. But she didn't know if the right words existed.

She turned just once and saw him sitting there on the wooden bench as cold and immovable as a bronze statue. If that's where he wanted to be then she couldn't drag him away into a new and more hopeful life. She finally had her brother back, but she had lost him all over again.

27

Joe overslept on the day that the England Under-21 football squad was announced for their final World Cup qualifying match. He couldn't believe it. He awoke in the spare room in West Sussex and looked at his football alarm clock, the same clock he'd had for as long as he'd been able to tell the time, and thought he was reading it wrong. He stuck his head out from under his Arsenal 1998 Champions duvet and picked up the clock, his brain refusing to process what his eyes could see.

Huh?

'Nan?' It was light outside, so it wasn't the middle of the night. But how could he have overslept on today of all days, the day that had been red-ringed in his head for the last four weeks? The day that would change his life. 'Nan?'

His bedroom door opened and there was Nan with a cup of tea making tut-tut noises about how late he'd slept and pulling the curtains open as if today was any other Saturday.

'What time is it?' he said.

She looked at him oddly and then at his clock. 'If the little hand's on the eleven and the big hand's on the two . . .' she said with a twinkle in her eye. 'Do you want a cooked breakfast?'

'Please,' he said. 'But . . . crikey, Nan, have you been listening?'

'Listening?'

'To the news? Have they announced the squad? The Under-21s?'

'Oh, is that today?' she said. 'I'm surprised you slept in so late. I thought you'd be up at the crack at dawn with one ear glued to the radio.'

He was already up out of bed and pulling on his jeans.

Layla knocked on the back door as he was mopping up the last of his fried egg. She walked into the kitchen without being invited. She always did that. On the one hand he loved it, but on the other it felt a bit familiar, sisterly. Sometimes he wished that she was a little bit nervous around him, at least then he might be able to convince himself that she had feelings for him.

'Have you heard?' she said.

He shook his head, no.

'What time do they usually announce it?'

'I dunno,' he said. 'Usually I don't care this much. I mean I care, it's interesting and that, but I'm not, like, waiting for it. Not like now.'

'It's exciting,' she said, gripping his knee.

He gulped down the last of his egg and hoped that her hand on his leg didn't give him an erection. Of course, as soon as he thought about it he could feel the familiar stirring and so he was relieved when his nan came into the kitchen.

'Hello, Layla dear. Cup of tea?'

They both sipped cups of steaming tea while listening to golf on the radio. Golf! Was she as bored as he was?

'This is stupid,' he said.

'You want to come over to mine and we can check on the internet? They might tell you what time it'll be announced.'

'Okay.'

He had never been in Layla's bedroom before. It was warm and smelt like all kinds of soft things, perfume, sun-tan lotion, that orange shampoo that she used. It was grown up, decorated in shades of plum and grey with a double bed (made), and it made him think poorly of his own bedroom next door – pretty much unchanged since he was seven years old albeit with a poster of Jennifer Biel added to the football heroes on the wall. Layla had a black-and-white print of New York City on her wall, and a cork board filled with photographs of her and her friends. He wandered over to it as she fiddled with the Apple Mac on the big white desk. His eye was drawn masochistically to Layla and a boy he could only assume was Daniel. Their arms were wrapped around each other and he was laughing and looking at the camera while she gazed up at him with the kind of adoring expression that she directed at Joe in his dreams.

'Is this him?' he said. 'Is this Daniel?'

'Mm-hmm,' she confirmed.

He was in a couple of other photos too. He had a skin problem and bad taste in baseball caps, but other than that he looked like a nice enough guy. Joe hated him on sight.

At the corner of the notice board was her ticket to the UEFA Cup match. She had kept it. She had pinned it up with these special things. That had to mean something, right?

'I'm on the BBC website,' she said. 'But it doesn't say. Here, have a look.'

She moved over just a bit, perching on the edge of the broad chair so that he could squeeze in next to her, his sharp bony hip pressed into the soft yielding flesh of her perfect figure. He concentrated on the computer screen even though at first what was written there could have been in Japanese. Just as her proximity was becoming unbearable she leapt up and went over to the little speaker set she had for her iPod and some American hip-hop he didn't recognize filled the room.

'We'll check again later,' she said, and fell back onto her bed. He noticed a canary yellow bra peeking out from underneath it.

How much longer was it going to last, this stupid crush on the girl next door? He didn't know how much more he could take. It was starting to get so he could hardly even look at her any more. The twist in his gut was no longer recognizable as pleasure or pain. He would avoid her if he thought he was strong enough, but the idea of never seeing her again was frightening.

Just tell her.

'Come on,' she said, patting the bed next to her, 'tell me how many goals you're going to score on your England debut.'

Reluctantly, yet at the same time as quick as he could, he lay down next to her on her bed. His entire body was tense. He was on a bed with Layla. Holy shit. She gave off a hot energy like some kind of force field. What was it she just said? Goals. Football. Right.

Focus, Joe.

'I think probably just one,' he said. 'But I'll make sure it's a good one.'

'How good?' she said.

'Proper dead good,' he said, enjoying the game because it took his mind off the way her breasts fell together when she turned to face him and how easy it would be for his lips to travel the short (yet impassable) distance to her lips. 'It'd be so good they'd show it especially on *Match of the Day* and Alan Hansen would say "world class" and Ian Wright would nod like a maniac and get all excited and insist that they showed it again.'

'Then what?'

'Then every time I walked down the street there'd be people pointing and saying, there's that kid that scored that amazing goal against Paraguay.'

'Is that who you're playing?'

'Yeah.'

'Over there? In Paraguay?'

'No, here, at Wembley.'

'Oh good,' she said, 'I'll be able to come.'

'Will you?'

'Course,' she said. 'I wouldn't want to miss that amazing world-class goal, would I?' She rolled onto her back and stared up at the ceiling. 'Are you nervous?'

Funnily enough he wasn't. He was relaxed now. More relaxed than he could remember being for a long time. The warm energy from her body had infiltrated his willing flesh and unwound him. It felt so good lying here with her; it felt so right. He stared at her bedroom ceiling and thought about how many nights she would have lain here, the dreams she might have had.

'Not really.'

'Good.'

Her hand reached across the bed and found his.

Oh God. He was going to tell her. A shard of clarity cut through his fear. This was it, this was the moment. 'Layla?'

'Hmmm?'

Out with it, like a splinter. Now it was really here it wasn't as hard as he'd always thought it would be. 'I love you, you know.'

'I love you too, babe.'

Huh? What did *that* mean? He sat upright. 'But . . . no . . .'

A shout from downstairs. Next door. His nan. 'Joe? Joe! It's on. It's on the radio.'

Layla pinged up from the bed. Layla who had finally told him exactly what he wanted to hear, that she loved him too, though he seemed as far away from being with her as ever. She refreshed the page on the internet and there they were. 'Here!' she said. The sixteen names that would face Paraguay next month in the Under-21s World Cup qualifier.

Sixteen names.

None of them Joe's.

Samantha stared at Sky Sports News in disbelief, her silly little espresso frozen halfway to her mouth, which fell open in shock. Joe was a better player than at least three of the five forwards that had been selected. No question. They had made an enormous mistake. But there was nothing she could do about it.

Bugger. Her strategy for Joe's career relied heavily on some sort of international recognition. Without that nobody would care about some teenage striker playing in Poland's second city for a team that were struggling to stay in the top half of the domestic league. She had been so sure that he would be selected. She had delayed her return to Poland so that she'd be around for all the press an England Under-21s call-up would attract. Now she was stuck in England with nothing to do. The chaps from the FA had made all the right noises, the tapes she had sent had been well received from what little feedback she'd been able to gather and she had been confidently waiting for the nod. And now what? Now nothing.

It was a serious setback. For both of them.

Later the senior England squad would be announced and there was an infinitesimal glimmer that Gabe might be named in the team, but it was no more than that. Unlike the youngsters', the senior squad's match was a must-win fixture thanks to some lacklustre performances up to this point, and so it was not the time to be trying out new faces to see how they fitted. No, Gabe had next to no chance, which meant that Samantha Sharp's client list wouldn't contain a single well-known name, merely a few players from Eastern and Central Europe, the best kid nobody had ever heard of and a guy that once scored a hat-trick in an FA Cup tie. It was not the stuff of legends.

The transfer window loomed large in front of her. Trying to kick down doors she had hoped would be opened wide. She wasn't even sure she had the energy to try.

But no matter how bad she felt she knew there would be one person who would be worse. What a kick in the gut.

Poor Joe. He would be feeling dreadful.

*

Gabe didn't even notice that his good friend Joe had failed to make the squad. It was Christine who pointed it out to him. Gabe hardly ever watched the news from back home any more, but his wife was addicted to the satellite television in their hotel suite. So much so that he was prepared to use it as a bargaining chip if she started going on about buying a house again.

'Have you spoken to him?' she said, standing in the doorway of the bathroom and watching Gabe apply gel to his hair in an effort to drag it forward over his thinning temples. 'He must be gutted.'

'I think he's back in the UK,' said Gabe. 'He'll be fine. Come on, I'm starving.'

Downstairs, in the less formal of the two hotel restaurants Christine was greeted by name. 'Ms Muswell,' said a young waiter, 'lovely to see you again. Come with me, the window table is free.'

Gabe stopped and stared.

'What?' said Christine. 'You're out all day. I come here a lot, get coffee or whatever, read a newspaper, a book.'

'In Polish?'

'There's a shop on the square that sells plenty of English papers, books too.'

'And what's this "Ms" crap? It's Mrs Muswell, Mrs. Why didn't you correct him?'

'I think it's just the way he pronounces it, Gabe.'

'Yeah, well . . .' Gabe grumbled. The waiter was far too good-looking to be chatting up his wife. Under his crisp white shirt his arms bulged with muscles and he could see the faint shadow of a tattoo. Funny, he'd never really noticed that the waiters in this place were as good-looking as the waitresses.

They settled at their table, a fine table with views onto the pretty courtyard garden, shaded and still dusty with frost. When the waiter came back to take their order Christine made a point of introducing her husband. And the bastard sneered at him. At him! Gabe Muswell, White Stars star. Then he turned his back on Gabe to talk to Christine and started asking her about some Japanese museum he'd recommended, and she wittered on about the art like Gabe wasn't even there.

He took her out for lunch and this was the thanks he got?

'I'll have the hamburger,' interrupted Gabe.

Christine broke off mid-sentence, darted a look at her husband and glanced down at her menu. 'The *pierogi*,' she said, '*w boleta*.'

Great, now not only was his wife talking to another man, she was talking in a language he couldn't even understand. He was relieved when the waiter left them alone.

'You two seem pretty pally,' he said.

'I told you, I come here a lot.'

'Well, I wanted a special lunch, just the two of us, so lay off the locals for a while, okay?'

'If you wanted it to be special,' she said, 'you should have brought me somewhere else.'

'How was I supposed to know this was your local?'

'We live upstairs, Gabe! This is the hotel restaurant. How much more local can you get?'

'Point taken.' He grinned. He didn't want them to bicker. Apart from Joe he hadn't made a single friend, and while Christine was discovering the museums and the city of Krakow he was stuck out at the stadium either training

328

or winding down in the bar. He had a day off today and so he wanted this lunch to be special. Even if she did know the waiting staff by name.

His hamburger came, and her anaemic-looking dumplings in a thick grey sauce.

'Can I try one?' he said, and made a crap joke about Polish delicacies being grey and leaden.

She didn't laugh.

He had a couple of drinks with lunch and so when she wanted to take a walk around the city park he cried off. He'd much rather wait in their hotel room and watch the news for a while.

'When do they announce the senior England squad?' she asked.

'A few hours,' he said. 'But I'm not getting called up, no way. Don't get your hopes up, will you?'

He couldn't possibly be that lucky. More to the point, he didn't deserve it. He'd had a chance, just a tiny one, but somehow he'd blown it. Again.

Gabe had long been proud of his easy-going nature. Only now, as he approached middle age like a runaway bus, did he realize that his lassitude might be his downfall.

Later, lying there listening to the voice of BBC News as it bounced around the hotel room that they had never quite managed to move out of, a last flicker of hope teased him . . . *One big surprise in the squad . . .*

His heart raced as he thought maybe, just maybe . . .

The one they'll all be talking about . . .

Gabe Muswell?

Was the inclusion of little-known newcomer . . .

Say it.

Seventeen-year-old Josef Wandrowszcki . . .

A barrage of emotions assaulted him. Disappointment, regret and a modicum of pride, all of them swiftly burnt away by searing and overwhelming jealousy.

Joe was living the life that should have been his.

Samantha was stunned, utterly stunned, when she heard Joe's name on the news. Not for a moment had she contemplated that Joe might leapfrog his way into the senior England squad.

She froze, and yelped aloud.

Joe?

She had been listening for a miracle, for a call-up for Gabe, a call-up that many would say was unwise.

But *Joe*?

It happened sometimes. Young players were too good for the Under-21 squad and ready for the enormous challenge of the bigger stage. Players, it would seem, like Joe. It was an affirmation of what she'd thought the very first moment that she saw him. That one day he would play in front of the entire world.

Everything changed starting now. She braced herself for the phone to ring. This was exactly what she needed to claw her way back to the big boys' table. She would be Sam Sharp: Superagent once again because she had the hottest name in the game. She, and she alone, was representing the player that would be on every football fan's lips, on every back page and on every manager's wish list. Joe who?

. . . *Seventeen-year-old Josef Wandrowszcki has been enjoying a superb season as one of the top goalscorers in the Polish domestic league and scored both goals for the Krakow White Stars in last month's UEFA Cup group stage. Eligible for England duty by virtue of his English father . . .*

The newscast cascaded over her groundswell of professional pride.

'Ohmigoodness, ohmigoodness, ohmigoodness!' Layla barrelled through the back of the house next door like a wild thing.

'Layla, dear, whatever's the matter?'

'Jooooooooe?!'

He came thundering down the stairs and for once didn't give a moment's thought to what it meant if he held her. He threw himself at Layla, lifted her clean off her feet and spun her round in the middle of his nan's kitchen.

'Ohmigoodness!' she said.

'I know!'

'Will someone tell me what in heaven's name is going on?' said his nan, impatient and excluded.

'En-ger-land!' sang Joe. 'En-ger-land! En-ger-land, la la!'

'Oh, Joe,' said Layla, and she kissed him, full on the mouth, a smacker. Closed mouth, not at all sexy.

Their first kiss.

He would have preferred that it wasn't in front of his nan.

He hoped that the way he stopped mid-twirl and froze like an imbecile wasn't too obvious. He avoided her eyes and lowered her to the floor and twirled his nan rather more sedately. 'I made the England squad, Nan, not the Under-21s, the proper one.'

'With David Beckham?'

He laughed. 'With David Beckham, yeah.'

'I knew there must have been some kind of mistake yesterday,' she said, nodding with understated satisfaction. 'Well done, love.'

'Joe!' said Layla, who was now jumping from foot to foot and clapping her hands like a seal. 'Ohmigoodness, Joe!' She was incapable of saying much more.

He stood in the middle of the room and threw his arms in the air, flung his head back and let this marvellous moment wash over him, breathing the deep soulful breaths of the truly happy.

He thought of his mum back in Poland, and he thought of his dad. 'That's my son,' he could say now, and would too. The thought of making his dad proud brought the first tears to his eyes and they filled up as he stared at the ceiling above him.

Ohmigoodness seemed about the right word for it.

Headfuck would be another.

'I want to call Dad,' he said.

Samantha's fingers flew happily over a hasty press release like a pianist in the throes of exaltation. She knew enough about Joe to draft something to keep the press at bay for the time being. What was the name of that pretty blonde girl that he had brought to the party? Layla. That's right. Should she mention Layla? No, best not, these teenage romances had a tendency to flare and fade. Who knows? Joe might want to keep his options open. As of now he was officially a stud.

Word was already out that she was the point person for the new boy. She fielded calls as she worked, loving every minute of the matchless high that being this busy gave her. For the first time in several days she forgot about the look on Liam's face the last time she'd seen him.

'Yes, there's a press release on the way to you. No, no interviews. He's in Poland right now . . . well, because that's where he lives.'

She knew she was misdirecting them, but it didn't really matter and she hadn't yet been able to speak to Joe. He was in England as far as she knew, but the number she had for him in West Sussex was engaged every time she tried to call. Hardly surprising – he would probably be inundated with congratulations. This was the first of many great days to come. Why ruin it with a press siege? The last thing anyone needed was a gaggle of reporters descending on the kid out there. Because he was a kid. He might be about to play for England, but he was a kid nonetheless.

Over in Poland she made sure that Leanne was toeing the party line. 'Just send them the release and tell them he's not doing any press for the time being.'

'You think that will stall them?' asked Leanne. 'What if they all jump on the next easyJet?'

'Tell them he'll be doing a press conference back in England, back home.'

'Back home, like it.'

'Thanks. Other than that you'll just have to say no comment, I'm afraid.'

'I'll pretend my English is a bit ropey,' said Leanne. 'That'll stop them asking too many questions. *Ja, ja, mi scusi,* that kind of thing.' It was half German, half Italian, not at all Polish and it would probably work quite well.

*

She sent off her press release to everyone that had called her and tried not to think of the one person that hadn't. She thought maybe Liam would have heard the news and contacted her, if only to get the inside track on a headline sports story, as a fan if nothing else. Wishing that he might call to congratulate her was maybe too much to hope for. She hadn't heard from him since the day he'd left. He had gone to his friend's and, apart from a quick call to say that he was safe and not to worry, they hadn't spoken.

Would she ever have it all good together? Work and family? Or was that asking too much?

The phone rang yet again. 'Sam? It's Joe.'

'Man of the hour,' she said. 'Congratulations, everything okay?'

'What do you think?' he said, and she could almost hear the face-splitting grin across the telephone line.

Joe was about to be a superstar.

28

She drove down to West Sussex that night, checking into a roadside hotel and heading round to Joe's with her arms full of newspapers at seven o'clock the following morning.

He looked as if he hadn't slept at all, but he seemed well on it, rumpled and boyish, and when she looked at him she saw advertising and endorsements, torso of the week in *Heat* magazine, and perhaps if he played well even a calendar for next year. Lots of easy profit in a calendar.

'Does anyone know where you are?' she said.

'Only friends and family.'

'Good. No press calls?'

'No,' he said, his eyes dancing with excitement. 'I've stayed inside like you said. Please can I have a look at the papers?'

She passed them over and there he was. A lot of them had used the same library picture, a shot of him in mid-field, his left foot poised on the edge of a volley, taken sometime during the UEFA Cup match. You could just make out his face, but it didn't look that much like him.

Her mobile rang. 'Yes? . . . That's right . . . No interviews at this time . . . It would have to be at his convenience . . . I see . . . I can put that to him.'

Joe listened to the one-sided conversation while he read about himself in the newspapers. 'Was that about me?' he asked when Samantha had finished.

'Every call is about you,' she said.

'Cool.'

Over breakfast of perfectly fried eggs on toast prepared by his nan (and what a dream picture of quaint domesticity she was), Samantha outlined the need for a press strategy. 'We need to feed them,' she said, 'otherwise they'll get hungry and become restless. After we've taken care of that we can start thinking seriously about next season. You'll have options, I guarantee it.'

'I'm signed to White Stars for two more years,' he said.

She waved away his concerns. 'Let me worry about that.' The transfer window would be too soon. She would sell him in the summer. She would make White Stars millions. She would make Joe rich.

'Sam? I wanted to say . . .' He paused and rubbed his nose.

'What's wrong?' Blood rushed to her head and stopped her heart. Was he about to leave her too? It wasn't possible. Nothing could be allowed to spoil this; there was too much at stake. She was on the brink of success again, despite everything.

'Nothing,' he said, 'I just wanted to say . . . well, thanks, that's all. None of this would be happening if it wasn't for you.'

Instant relief flooded her, comforting her like a chiffon breeze on a sweltering day.

She turned his attention back to the coming weeks. 'You're going back to Poland day after tomorrow?' He nodded. 'Okay,' she said, 'and you've one more match before you're released for international duty. *Don't* get injured.'

'I'll try not to,' he said.

'Then you've Christmas, then the UEFA Cup third-round match with White Stars, then a weekend training with the squad, then . . .'

'Showtime,' he said. That grin again. That grin could make him a fortune one day.

'You might not play,' said Samantha. 'You realize that, don't you? You'll undoubtedly start on the bench, and then whether or not you play will really depend on how the match is going.'

'I know,' he said.

He was a dream to work with. She hoped that success and stardom wouldn't change him. She looked at his open face, awash with excitement and savoured the moment in case it did.

There was the crunch of car tyres on the gravel drive-way, the sound of a car door slamming and then a loud voice shouting Joe's name.

'Where is he then? Where's my boy?'

'Dad!' said Joe, and jumped up from the table, his face lit up like a ten-year-old on his birthday morning.

He ran helter-skelter outside and Samantha followed in time to see him getting a huge bear hug from a man who had Joe's eyes, and his cheeky smile. She was warmed by the picture of family love although she could only guess what it felt like and how much it meant to Joe to be the subject of the all-singing, all-dancing moment in which his absent father was currently engaged.

She was about to slip back inside so as not to intrude on the raucous father–son bonding session when she saw that Joe's dad, Simon, was not the only visitor. In the driver's seat of the car, a rather flash Audi come to think of it, was a man she knew.

She recognized him, but she couldn't think what he was doing here and so for a frozen second her brain refused to compute.

It was Richard Tavistock.

Behind him Simon and Joe were singing more football songs and punching the air.

'Hello, Sam,' said Richard, as if he had seen her only yesterday and on good terms, rather than watching with a sneer as she packed up her desk on the day she resigned from Legends.

'Richard,' she said, confused.

Joe stopped dancing, breathless. 'Dad?' he said. 'Who's your friend?'

'I'm Richard,' he said. 'And we're all friends here, isn't that right, Samantha?'

It was impossible to get a moment alone with Richard, especially since he didn't seem to want one. And she refused to tackle him about business in front of her client. He allowed himself to be charmed by Joe's nan, accepting her birdlike offers of tea and cake. Simon introduced him as an expert and Joe was too dazzled by his dad's all-consuming pride to pay much attention to anything other than recounting the story of how he'd felt when he heard the news, and listening to his dad wax lyrical about what a little star he was going to be.

'You'll be a millionaire before me at this rate, kiddo,' he said.

'Maybe,' said Joe.

Undoubtedly, thought Samantha.

'How's Layla?' said Simon. 'Gorgeous girl that one. Perfect for you.'

'She's all right,' said Joe. 'She's at college today. She'll be back later.'

'That's Arundel Technical College, isn't it? She's still doing that textiles course?'

'She wants to work in fashion.'

Simon and Richard exchanged a look that went unnoticed by Joe, but that Sam saw immediately. 'That's great,' said Simon. 'Good stuff. You two still . . . you know?' He made a movement with his fist. Samantha winced at the lewd gesture.

'Yeah, well, not exactly,' said Joe.

'Just wait. She'll be all over you now, mate,' said Simon. He stuffed a slice of cake into his mouth, sprinkling crumbs all over the white tablecloth and talking with his mouth full. 'Just you wait. She'll let you do anything you like.' He laughed, stamping his foot on the floor like a show pony.

'Whatever,' said Joe. 'Maybe.'

Samantha hadn't seen Joe act like this before, trying to be cool. She wasn't sure if she liked this version of him. He was trying to contain his usually easy smile as if smiling made him weak somehow. Instead he kept pulling this mean and moody look, which didn't suit him at all. Not at all.

She hated Richard being here. What the hell was going on with that? If only he would respond to one of her many sideways glances and allow her the courtesy of a two-minute conversation in the hallway, but when he did catch her eye he smiled blandly and sipped his milky tea. This day that had started so perfectly was gradually getting away from her. She didn't like to have this conversation in front of Joe, but she couldn't wait any longer.

'So, Richard,' she started, 'what brings you out here?'

'I was invited,' he said, nodding at Simon.

'You two know each other?'

'Like I said, we're all friends here.'

Joe's mobile rang – the jaunty *Match of the Day* theme tune was his ringtone, which made Simon laugh.

'You're a nutter, you know that?' he said, punching his son on the shoulder.

Joe checked the caller ID. 'It's Layla,' he said.

'You see?' said Simon. 'What did I tell you?'

Joe picked up the phone and his smile was replaced by a frown for the first time that morning. 'Slow down,' he said. 'Where are you?' Then, 'Stay there.'

'What's wrong?' said Samantha.

'She's at college,' he said. 'And about thirty reporters are waiting for her outside.' He looked at Samantha with bewildered blue eyes. 'Because of me.'

It was decided that Simon should take Richard's Audi and go to collect Samantha from a little-used entrance at the back of Arundel Technical College and hope to give the reporters the slip. Richard had offered, but Samantha had swiftly objected, saying that it was probably better if it was somebody that Layla knew. She had offered to go herself, but Richard had pointed out (rather too quickly she thought) that thanks to her scandal she was a known tabloid entity and if she was spotted it might add fuel to the fire. Joe wanted to go, of course, but everyone was against that idea.

'There might be a riot,' said Simon.

'That's stupid,' said Joe.

'But true,' said Samantha.

'I'll go get her.'

'All right,' said Joe, 'but, Dad, she sounded pretty freaked out. You'll be able to find her and everything, right?'

'Leave it to me,' he said. 'But I don't know what she's complaining about really. I thought all women loved attention?'

Richard was the only one to laugh.

After his dad left and his nan had taken herself off to the shops for more milk Joe said, almost to himself, 'I just can't figure out how they found her, or why really. It doesn't make sense.'

'She'll be okay, Joe,' said Samantha.

'But how come there's reporters following Layla at college but nobody here to see me?'

'Jealous?' asked Richard, joking, not knowing Joe well enough to sense that this was not the time to joke.

'Of course not.'

'The wives and girlfriends make the front half of the paper,' said Richard. 'Players only make the back. Don't ask me why.'

'But she's not my wife, or my girlfriend.'

'That's not what your dad says,' said Richard.

Samantha looked up sharply. It was obvious to her then that the press knew where to find Layla because Simon or Richard or both of them had told the press exactly where she'd be. Joe missed it. He was explaining why he might have exaggerated his relationship with Layla to his father.

'Dad wants me to be just like him,' he said. 'He wouldn't be very impressed with the truth.'

'And what do you think he is exactly?' asked Samantha softly.

'He's dead popular,' said Joe. 'With blokes as well as girls. Everyone gets on with him. He's a quick thinker, he's a good comedian, he's . . . Dad. Why?'

Because that wasn't the way she saw his dad at all. She saw a man who had seen his child grow up in fits and starts, who stashed him down here with his grandmother instead of getting his life sorted so that he might be able to accommodate his own son on his own turf before he was grown and gone for ever. When Joe was in town Simon was a forty-year-old man who still lived with his mother. She saw a man like too many footballing fathers she had seen before him, more interested in their son the soccer star than their son the boy. What's more, she saw a man who had sold out his son's friend to reporters and who, for reasons that scared her, had hooked up with Richard Tavistock, who treated players as cash cows and moved them around from club to club to turn a profit without enough thought to their long-term careers. There were good footballing fathers, great ones, like the Welstead boys' father, and then there were fathers like Simon.

'Sam's already thinking about your biography,' said Richard. 'Six figures from Hodder, right, Sam?'

'Something like that.' She couldn't be bothered to argue, not in front of Joe, but she hadn't made a single call about a book deal. Unlike Richard, Samantha preferred her clients to be footballers first, everything else could come later. Much later. She was interested in knowing Joe's story because she was interested in knowing Joe, as fully as she could. Richard wouldn't understand. 'How're Monty and Ferris?' she asked impulsively.

Richard grimaced. 'Opinionated,' he said. 'There's a soft drink, a big one, and they won't take the endorsement because they think the product is bad for kids.'

'Imagine that,' she said.

He didn't notice the sarcasm. 'Seventeen and nineteen and they think they know best,' he said.

She'd had enough. 'Joe? You mind giving Richard and me a moment to talk?'

'Will you be talking about me?'

She nodded.

'Okay,' he said. 'I'll be in my room.'

As soon as she heard the tread of his feet on the stairs she turned to Richard. He sat with an expression on his face that said he didn't give a shit, in his tacky designer polo shirt and too-blue jeans, his weekend get-up, probably a variation on the exact same weekend outfit he'd been wearing since his mother first dressed him in it. She hadn't liked him when they'd worked together at Legends and she liked him even less now that he was intruding on her turf.

'What are you doing here?' she said. 'In case you hadn't noticed, Joe has an agent.'

'I'm friends with his dad.'

'Bullshit. Since when?'

'Since his son scored two goals in the UEFA Cup. He called me, Sam. He wanted my advice. What would you have done?'

'So you're just going to poach him from under my nose? It won't happen. I won't let it.'

'You might not have a choice.'

'You're wasting your time,' she said.

Richard leant back in his chair, his arms up behind his head, a power play she had seen him throw before and one she loathed. She was almost certain that he'd been taught passive-aggressive body language at some weekend management seminar. 'I wouldn't be so sure,' he said. 'For one thing Simon has serious concerns about your track record. Your – shall we say? – past indiscretions.'

'And for another?'

'The kid deserves an agent that can deal in this country. He deserves the Premiership; it's what he wants, it's certainly what his father wants.'

'So?'

'You can't make deals in this country, Sam, not for three more domestic seasons.'

'What the hell are you talking about?'

'Your contract with Legends had some pretty stringent termination clauses. Didn't you check them the day you resigned?'

'The no-compete clause doesn't apply; I was forced to resign,' she said. 'That's tantamount to being fired.'

'Yeah? Potato, po-tar-toe, my friend,' said Richard. 'By the time you get through arguing that one in a court of law the kid's best days will be past him. Is that fair? Really? Think of the kid. And of course there's the unresolved matter of the mystery off-shore funds you acquired.'

'I didn't acquire them,' she said through gritted teeth. 'They were just *there*.'

'Nobody believes that, Sam. What did you think? That you'd set up in the hinterlands of international football and come back – all within the same year? – and everyone would forget that you're corrupt? Simon understands that his son needs a clean agent. He deserves it, a good man like me, not a woman with a scandal hanging round her like a cheap necklace. Now, I'm sorry, but pretty soon the kid will understand that too.'

'The kid has a name,' she said. 'Josef Wandrowszcki. And I'll bet you can't even spell it.'

'Your career's over,' said Richard with a smug smile that made her want to reach for a kitchen knife and do something awful. 'Why can't you be a good girl and accept that?'

Because she had never been a good girl, and she was hardly likely to start just because somebody like Richard was telling her to be. She wasn't over, she was only just beginning, and as soon as possible she would be paying a visit to Richard's boss, to Jackson Ramsay, to make sure that nothing would stand in her way.

Layla and Simon came home trailed by a pack of reporters. Simon parked the Audi badly across the end of the driveway and hurried up to the house and through the front door in a frenzy of exploding flashbulbs, his arm wrapped round Layla. He was shouting, 'No comment, no comment,' but laughing.

'I couldn't lose them,' he said, and she wondered exactly how hard he had tried.

Layla was half scared, but half excited too, and she cuddled up to Joe for reassurance.

345

'They think I'm your girlfriend!' she said.

If wishing made it so . . .

'You're all right though?'

She nodded. 'This must be how Posh feels all the time,' she said, her face shining. 'Imagine. Joe, you're famous.' She raised her eyebrows and giggled adorably.

'I think you should go out there, Joe,' said Samantha.

'What?' he spluttered. 'Why?'

'They won't leave until you do.'

'But what do I say?'

'Just be yourself. Tell them how happy and honoured you are, and that you're looking forward to scoring on your debut.'

'Then what?'

'Then nothing, then come back inside.'

Joe's eyes widened. He looked down to remind himself what he was wearing. Jeans and a black long-sleeved T-shirt, clean and vaguely trendy. 'Okay,' he said.

'You want me to go with you?' asked his father.

Samantha groaned a little inside when Joe said yes. Not only was Simon trying to oust her as Joe's agent, but it looked like he was hungry for the limelight too. She would have to keep a careful eye on him. He was the type who'd sell his story and not see how he was doing any harm by talking about family for money. Then he'd wait a month and do it again.

'Okay,' she said. 'Ready?'

'Now?' said Joe.

'Now.'

It was starting to get dark and the quiet residential street lit up like bonfire night when he stepped outside.

346

'Hello,' he said to the general inquisitive mass. 'All right?'

They launched at him, spitting a dozen questions all at once.

'What was your first reaction when you heard the news?'

'How did you feel?'

'Tell us what it was like, Josef . . .'

'It's Joe,' he said.

Sam watched from the doorway. He did pretty well she thought. His quotes would be bland, but bland was good when the alternative was inflammatory or arrogant. Right or wrong, nobody expected much from a footballer's intellect. He ducked awkward questions instinctively; when asked for his opinions about fellow squad members or the England manager he just repeated what he'd already said about being honoured and pleased and happy, and after five minutes when Samantha said, 'That's all, guys. He needs to get his rest – tomorrow's a school day,' she got a good-natured laugh.

The reporters all packed up their kit and were gone within fifteen minutes. They were on his side, for now.

The next day the back pages led with England's newest star. Most of them featured him before the fold too, as well as candid shots of Layla looking bewildered but very pretty. They said she was his girlfriend.

One newspaper christened him *JOE WONDER!* and Samantha hoped that it would stick. It was a great nickname.

But she knew what Joe perhaps did not. They might love him today, but they could turn in a heartbeat. A missed opportunity, a failed chance, and Joe Wonder would be nobody's hero. She liked Joe. She was involved. She was determined, no matter what his father thought, no matter what Richard did to tempt him away, to be there behind him should he fall.

29

She arranged to meet Jackson on neutral ground, a basement restaurant on Villiers Street. He'd suggested lunch. She'd lied and said that she was too busy, but she could meet him for dessert and coffee.

'Since when do you eat dessert?' he'd said.

'Just coffee then.'

So they met for coffee after her fictional lunch appointment.

She felt childish for wanting him to think she was rushed. She was trying to prove that he was an idiot for letting her go. He should have stood by her professional reputation rather than watch it slide into the mud, dragged down by a dirty tackle. What was the point of sleeping with the boss if it didn't even give you job security? Though of course that was never the point for her. She hadn't needed a reason to get involved with Jackson; she had needed a reason not to.

'How was your lunch?' he said, and the arch of his eyebrow made her suspect that her 'so busy' deceit may have been a big waste of time. He looked exactly the same and she couldn't meet his eye without having to acknowledge that neither time apart, nor his betrayal, had diminished their connection.

'Insubstantial,' she said, 'a salad.' Knowing full well he wasn't exactly asking what she'd had.

And then she ordered from the dessert menu because she didn't like the thought of being so predictable. Not even to him.

'Richard's got it into his head that I am bound by the non-compete clause in my contract,' she said. 'I know technically I resigned, but I need to work, Jackson. I know you don't want this to go fifteen rounds with the lawyers any more than I do.'

'How well you know me,' he said. She saw the twinkle in his eye and she found it simultaneously condescending and sexy. *Damn.* 'I won't be holding you hostage. Go ahead and rule the world.'

'I'd like you to put that in writing,' she said, staring firmly down at the cheesecake she didn't want so as to avoid being snared by his watchful gaze, 'to prevent any future misunderstanding.'

'That's sensible,' he said, nodding. 'Do you have something for me to sign?'

No, she didn't. Jackson could hardly sign a dinner bill without checking with his lawyer first. She hadn't anticipated that this would be so easy.

'I'll get something to you this afternoon,' she said. 'The transfer window is just round the corner and I need my business to be fully functioning by then. I don't want any speed bumps.'

'No,' said Jackson. 'You wouldn't want that.'

There was a playfulness to his tone that she found impossible to read. 'Is this amusing to you?' she said. 'Does my little business venture seem cute?'

'No, Sam, but you do.'

'*Cute?*'

'I heard a rumour about you and Aleksandr Lubin,' he said.

'I don't see how that's any of your business.'

'Be careful, Sam, that's all.'

'I stopped having to take your advice a few months ago,' she said. 'It's actually the best thing about not working for you any more.'

'And what's the worst?'

She stared at him, using all her pent-up disaffection to quash the desire that arose unbidden from within. 'I think you know,' she said, looking back down at the damn cheesecake and wondering why she felt like crying.

'Hey,' he said. 'I miss you too, you know. Every day.'

It was no good. She looked back at those eyes again and this time she let down her defences, knowing that he would see in her eyes how much it meant to her. How much he meant. The air between them crackled.

He pulled in a short sharp breath between his teeth and she felt a tug in her loins so hard she had to shuffle in her seat, which only intensified her desire, and she called on every ounce of her self-preservation instinct to stop herself reaching out for him.

He glanced at his watch. 'I have an hour. We could go to that place in Covent Garden, the one with the slate-grey sheets. See if it's still the same.'

'They were heather,' she said.

'They were grey,' he said. 'And I was kidding.'

'I know.'

'But you remember?'

Of course she did. It was the day she was awarded her FIFA licence, the small piece of paper that enabled her to play the game for real, to buy and sell the most talented footballers she could find. To make heroes out of school-boys.

She had danced on the street, literally danced, and Jackson watched her, knowing beyond any reasonable doubt that he was in love with this woman.

'How could I forget,' she said. 'I became an agent that day.'

Jackson didn't laugh very often but when he did he did so with his whole body and spirit, his shoulders shaking with guttural mirth that was instantly infectious. 'And that was the most important thing that happened that day? Becoming an agent?'

She had been truly happy then. She allowed the memory of it to infuse her muddled head with joy. Dancing in the street she had felt free.

'You're a good dancer,' he had said to her, and she had continued to boogie, wanting to jump up and click her heels together, the knowledge that she was the first woman in the country to be able to deal on his level making her more audacious than ever.

'Dance with me?' she'd said.

'I don't think so.'

'Come on, what is it you always say? Anything is possible?'

They stood in the middle of the indifferent London crowds and danced, laughing at first and then cheek to cheek. Their breath mingled and they knew, they both knew. Their movements became slower until they were just two people holding each other and she could feel his heart beating against her chest, the frantic pace of it making her realize that he was just as nervous as she was, just as excited. She was his equal now, almost, and so she allowed him to kiss her, their very first kiss, to surrender to the loaded glances and unspoken promises that had been between them for months, for years.

It was a good kiss, a great kiss, and she'd pulled away, scared.

'It won't work,' she'd said. 'Me and you together. You know that, don't you?' And she had been right.

'Relax, will you?' he'd replied. 'I didn't ask you to marry me.'

He knew a hotel and they practically ran to it. She didn't notice her surroundings at first, consumed with sensation, her body exploding with pent-up tension, erupting with suppressed desire from the very moment he was inside her.

That first time was frantic and afterwards she fell back on the bed and felt wonderful, and a short while later they had that inane argument about whether the sheets were grey or heather.

They spent two days in bed, trying to exhaust all the sexual attraction in a single bacchanalian frenzy. But it was hopeless, and without meaning to she had almost fallen in love.

Almost.

Now, a few hundred yards from where all that had taken place it felt like a hundred years. Opposite her Jackson's smile looked like a smirk.

'Yes,' she said resolutely. 'Getting my licence was the most important thing that happened that day.'

She pushed her plate aside, any pretence of appetite over and done with.

'We're finished here,' she said.

That night she called Lubin and told him that she was naked and horny. Only one of these was true.

'So what can we do about that?' Lubin said.

'I thought you might have some ideas?' she said. 'Use your imagination.'

Jackson had left her in a state of lustful hunger and she was afraid that if she didn't do something about it she could easily find herself at his door, yearning for release. Lubin was a distraction.

He worked.

The letter she sent to Jackson for him to sign was returned to her within an hour.

She arranged to fly back to Krakow on the same flight as Joe. She didn't want to let him out of her sight. Richard could be very persuasive – that's how he made his living. He was insidious. He was the kind of man who would travel a thousand miles and pretend that he was just passing. He wanted Joe and he was used to getting what he wanted. But she would cling on to Joe with everything she had. He was special. And he was hers.

'You know that things are about to change, don't you?' she said. 'Do you think you can handle it? You could be a few weeks away from being the most famous seventeen-year-old in England.'

'How do you know something like that?'

'Famous? Well, *if* you play, obviously, because you'll start on the bench,' said Samantha, 'then you need to play your best, but attitude is equally important and, I won't lie, you're a good-looking kid, which helps. It maybe be superficial, but it helps a great deal.'

'No,' said Joe, 'I meant how do I know if I can handle it?'

She saw the cabin crew whispering when they disembarked. Soon they wouldn't bother to whisper. With a little luck soon Joe wouldn't be able to take a step in public without being asked for his autograph.

And Samantha Sharp would be back on track for success.

Leanne had managed admirably in her absence. The deals were stacking up nicely. Nothing official of course, not until the window, but with a little luck there would be plenty to celebrate by the end of January.

'Can I have Christmas off?' said Leanne.

Christmas. She would most likely spend Christmas waiting for Liam to call. Watching festive television and resisting the urge to drink. What if that call never came? What if she never heard from him again? 'Sure,' she told Leanne. 'I don't see why not.'

'Fab,' she said. 'Thanks.'

'What are your plans?'

'Get back on the London scene,' said Leanne. 'Chinawhite, Volstead, Boutique 60. See who's available. Holidays are a stressful time you know, lots of break-ups, lots of footballers needing a little Christmas treat, if you know what I mean.'

'What is it with you and footballers?'

Leanne rolled her eyes. 'Let's see. Killer bodies, massive wages, long summer breaks, family values, VIP treatment . . . should I go on?'

'Don't you want more?'

'More than that? Are you kidding me? You're just bitter because you know I'll leave you as soon as I find the one for me.'

There was truth in that, but she also felt that Leanne's vision of success, to be a footballer's wife, was myopic. Leanne had great tits, but many other fine qualities too. 'Where will I find an assistant as good as you?' she said.

'You won't,' said Leanne, 'but we'll find you someone with potential.'

Samantha didn't doubt it. She was sure that Leanne would leave as neatly and efficiently as she did everything else. Unlike Sam, who had only ever had one real job and managed to leave it through an ugly conspiratorial back door.

I was shoved. By a man who said he loved me.

'Lubin asked for a meeting,' added Leanne. 'You'd think by now he'd call you directly.'

'He's being professional,' she said, but secretly she agreed. What kind of mixed messages was she getting when he took her call from London three days before for some filthy phone sex, but then called her assistant to set up their next date?

He asked her to meet him at the stadium during training. When she got there she found him down in the stands, close enough to the pitch to smell the damp grass. She saw Joe and Gabe, but they didn't see her. Her lover looked her up and down in a proprietary way that she wished she could find insulting rather than erotic. It looked as if he wanted to be somewhere else with her so that he could have her. And she would let him too.

'Congratulations,' he said. 'About Joe. It is very good for him, for you too.'

And White Stars, she added silently. They had never had so much international attention. First the UEFA Cup, now Joe – for a starfucker like Lubin it was the perfect end to the year. 'Thank you,' she said. 'He deserves it, and he's coping with the attention well.'

'And Muswell?'

They both watched Gabe running along the touchline. 'Disappointed,' she said. 'But it was a lot to hope for.'

'How many seasons do you think he has left in him?'

She decided to tell a half-lie. He was lucky to have had even one, but to say so would be a terrible betrayal. 'I don't know,' she said instead. 'He is fit, healthy. He needs to get his hunger back I think.'

'I have a proposition for you,' he said. 'For Gabe.'

He outlined the details of an approach from a team in Russia, explaining first why they had not contacted Samantha or White Stars directly. 'I am known to them,' he said. 'You are not. They know you only by reputation.' The team, a mid-table outfit with relatively little money, were looking to raise their international profile and needed a cheap striker with name recognition. 'There are not many around.'

She nodded, wondering why this all felt so peculiar. Her sixth sense was dubious. True, name strikers who came cheap were not common, but Gabe would be incredibly lucky at this point to play another year of professional football with any club. And yet Lubin seemed cautionary.

'It sounds like a remarkable opportunity,' she said.

'It is. And as such there would be certain . . . costs involved. There are a number of parties who would be interested in the opportunity.'

She looked him directly in the eye. This was not a language barrier, a mistranslation: he was asking her to consider something underhand.

Her sense of fair play told her to cut him down right now, have no further part in this conversation. And yet she sat and listened to what he had to say. Here it was, the shady side of football that she had avoided entirely ineffectively. Even with her many years of a tough moral stance, resisting temptation wherever she smelt it, she would for ever be connected with scandal anyway, thanks to the unexplained funds out there in the Cayman Islands.

So this time she listened.

It was a complex negotiation. The club needed to spend enough money on a striker to make a story out of it, but they didn't have the money themselves, which is where Lubin would come in. He would essentially be paying the club to sign Gabe Muswell, and recouping the money out of the subsequent transfer fee and signing bonus once the deal was approved by the club board. It was utterly fraudulent and discovery of such would surely mean the end of her career.

'I don't understand,' she said. 'What's in it for you?'

'There is an overlap of interests,' he said. 'My father needs some of these people to support me in a trade dispute.'

'You told me that your father was the last honest billionaire in Russia.'

'He has me to tread the edges. To divert.'

Her mind was cartwheeling between what was right and what was possible. 'I could get into a lot of trouble,' she said.

'You are already in trouble, no? Back in England. Is that not why you left?'

'Yes, but . . .'

'I listen to people, Samantha. You must guess what they say about you.'

'What who says about me?'

'The people I talk to on your behalf. Owners, managers, even players. They think you left England because it is too strict. They think that you want to work out here because we are not so . . . precise. It is a playground for those with the right attitude. Surely you considered this? Why do you think doors have been opened to you?'

She moved her business out here because she wanted to sign Joe, the best young player she'd ever seen. That this region was renowned for being the underbelly of shady football deals had nothing to do with it. Was that really what people thought? It made sense. It had been tough, but not quite as tough as she had anticipated. How could she have been so naive?

'What?' he said. 'Were you just hoping that if you worked hard enough then one day everyone would forget who you once were, that your past would just go away?'

It was exactly what she had been hoping. It was the strategy she had been counting on her whole life long.

'So what do you say?' he said. 'Do you want to play?'

'I . . . don't know.'

She couldn't say yes, but how could she say no? If people had been dealing with her because she was an agent who might be open to the occasional under-the-table payment she would soon lose goodwill when they found out that she was beyond reproach.

There was a part of her, a tiny whispering part, which seemed to be reaching out from beneath her ethics and begging her to pay attention to his offer. She wouldn't be the first or only agent out there to bend the rules when it suited, as long as they weren't caught. Even Legends, whatever Jackson might hope, wasn't immune to a few subtly shaded manoeuvres. There were rules being bent at right-angles across the game. And with the Lubin family in her corner, would she ever be caught?

'Can I think about it?' she said.

'I am returning to Russia until the new year,' he said. 'We'll talk again then. Obviously you must give me your answer before the transfer window closes.'

'Obviously,' she echoed.

He turned away and then seemed to reconsider, turning back to look at her intently, the way he had the very first night they'd met. 'You should come with me,' he said.

'To Russia? For Christmas? I . . . no, I don't think so.'

'It is a wonderful time of year to see my country. We could have a lot of fun.'

His flashing eyes made it clear the sort of fun he had in mind.

'You told me Russia was a hole in the ground.'

'I did? When?'

'The night we met.'

'When you got drunk and refused to sleep with me.'

'Yes.'

'So people can change their minds. Think about my other invitation. About Gabe. Think very carefully. It is a big opportunity for you.'

He dropped a brief kiss on her lips and then he left.

Had he seen something in her, something left over from her past, that was open to danger? And after suppressing that part of herself for all these years while she played it safe, perhaps, just perhaps, it was time for her to let go.

She watched Gabe and Joe running themselves into the ground at the other end of the pitch. It could be a second chance for Gabe to shine, something nobody would have predicted. But she wouldn't jeopardize her career for his sake. No, if she was going to change tactics and play dirty she would be doing it for herself. Playing by the rules had only served to sully her reputation, not to mention missing the biggest round of bonuses to date. Honesty does not prevail. All this fuss over three hundred thousand dollars. What about the million-pound bonus she would not be getting this Christmas? Someone somewhere was a million pounds up on the year because she was a million pounds down.

A new version of herself started to form in her imagination. Her toy-boy lover – a billion-heir, being at the heart of the scurrilous deals of the eastern frontier, sinking deep into a world she had self-righteously ignored. A frisson of excitement carried her imagination. So what if it wasn't strictly ethical? It was only business. Perhaps that was who she had to be to succeed.

30

It was early afternoon on Christmas Eve and Samantha was lying on her sofa in London staring at the television screen, watching nothing. She cycled through the channels with the remote control three times before it occurred to her to switch it off. The instant silence was an oppressive reminder of her less than festive mood.

How had she ended up alone?

She was Sam Sharp: Superagent. This was her first day off in months. Shouldn't she be having a fabulous time?

It was already dark outside, dark and cold. She wondered if it might snow. It would be snowing in Russia, she bet. Somewhere over there Aleksandr Lubin would be at some party, probably hosting one, surrounded by beautiful rich people and merriment. She was beautiful and rich. That's where she belonged. Not here, trying to find the energy to get up from the sofa and fix herself something proper to eat instead of picking listlessly at the hunk of Stilton cheese in front of her.

She missed her brother. She thought this would be a Christmas for them both, the first for years. When she was a girl, back before they lost their mother, before they lost their home, Christmas had been the only day of the year that they spent together, the three of them, the whole day, without Mum running off to see her friends or shutting herself in the kitchen with the radio on and the chink of ice into a glass. On Christmas Day they wore their pyjamas all day long and were little enough to want love more than presents. They would squish onto the sofa together, watch a Disney film and eat chocolates from a box. It was enough. They remained her favourite Christmas memories.

This was a Christmas she would gladly forget as soon as possible.

And what about Jackson? What would he be doing? Last year they had flown to Venezuela and checked into a five-star hotel on one of the tiny islands off the coast. Nowhere obvious she had said, and they both knew that she meant too much chance of bumping into someone that they knew in Barbados. She had been so afraid of ruining her reputation. It was almost funny if you thought about how ruined she had been in the end. But not actually funny at all.

No doubt he would have a new lover by now, all those Christmas parties, finally free to catch one of the beauties who regularly threw themselves at him. She conjured an image of Jackson in a bar with someone like Richard, taking their pick from the women, girls really, who fluttered around rich men like butterflies, and she was surprised by how much it hurt.

It was only because she was feeling lonely. Jackson could sleep with whomever he chose. What business was it of hers? Why should she care?

Right?

She had hours until bedtime. And then she could look forward to waking up in this empty house on Christmas morning and rattling around like a lost button in a tin. This wasn't Christmas, it was agony. She should have gone to Russia and had an adventure. Anything would be better than this.

His business proposal haunted her. She was reluctant to get further involved with him than she already was. And yet . . . cash in brown envelopes, a loyal circle of contacts, a Mafia-esque lifestyle. She wasn't immune to the charms of such a life. She'd missed out on enough opportunities because she was a woman. Was she now going to miss out because she was too principled to play around the edges of what was right? She was the naive schoolkid who thought that being a nice person was enough to make you popular.

When everyone knew that the opposite was true.

There was a knock at the front door and a truly awful voice began carolling outside.

We wish you a merry Christmas . . .

She stayed quiet and still hoping that they would assume nobody was in and move on. After all, how many people in this part of town had nothing to do on Christmas Eve? She might possibly be the only lonely soul on this street.

God, Sam, pity yourself much?

The terrible singing continued. She would put the television on to drown it out, but that might draw attention to her presence. The doorbell rang again and the melody changed.

Give up and go away.

Tears prickled her eyes and she wondered why, then she listened to the singing that was filtering in despite her best efforts to block it out. She tuned in to the voice. A bloody awful voice. Solitary and far too old to be carol singing. Except it wasn't a carol.

If happy little bluebirds fly . . .

She threw open the curtains and there he was. All she wanted for Christmas. He was the reason she was in London. In case this happened. In case he came back.

Liam.

He waved. 'Please let me in,' he shouted. 'It's freezing out here!'

And she hustled him into her warm home with a flurry of excited hugs, shushing him when he started to apologize, offering wine, making tea, finding crackers for the Stilton and unearthing a box of chocolates, and suddenly it felt a little bit like Christmas after all.

It soon became clear that something wasn't right. He took off his coat at her insistence, but sat stiffly, as if he might leave any moment, sipping his tea politely, as though he was visiting an old aunt.

'Where have you been staying?' she asked.

'Vauxhall,' he said. 'An old friend.'

She didn't know that he had any friends, certainly none that ever visited him in prison, so what kind of friends could they be? Why would he rather be with them, than here with her? Her feelings were hurt, but she tried to be cool.

'Liam,' she said. 'Is everything, you know, okay? I mean, I can't imagine what it's like for you, but I thought, well, I thought you might be happy, happier. It's over; you're out. You can get on with your life.'

He sighed, like she patently didn't understand, and she felt awkward and inept.

'I need to talk to someone,' he said.

'You can talk to me.'

He shook his head. 'No, I mean I think I need to talk to someone, you know, professional.'

'Oh.'

He smiled at her, a discomfited half smile that made her feel uneasy. 'No offence.'

'Why would I be offended?'

'I dunno,' he said. 'Maybe because you want to be the one who fixes me?'

'You don't need –'

'I do, Sam. I'm a mess.'

He started talking and she listened without saying a word, swallowing down every question that rose in her throat. He told her about the guilt that had been his constant companion since the day he was released, about how he couldn't sleep at night without hearing the screams of people dying in the back of that car.

'It's like it happened yesterday,' he said. 'I just wasn't expecting to feel this way.'

His parole officer said it was a common reaction, survivor's guilt, and he suggested a counsellor, and even though he was scared he was going to give the guy a call and set something up.

'I can't live like this,' he said. 'It's too much for me to handle. I killed them. And now I'm out and they're still dead.'

She swallowed her tears. It wasn't over. They had waited all these years for it to be over, patiently looking towards the horizon, only now they were here they saw that they still had another mountain to climb.

'About the house in Kentish Town . . .' he said.

She wished she'd never bought him the damn house. She could see now that her largesse had caused so much trouble.

'I won't mention that house again, until you're ready. Liam, I just didn't think. And, well, I'm sorry.'

'You don't have to apologize,' he said. 'Don't be silly. I just . . . I can't live there; it's too much. I was thinking maybe I'd sell it?'

'You can do what you like with it. It's yours. It's all in your name. I don't want it.' The truth was that she never wanted to see it again.

'Maybe I'll sell it, quickly if I can, as quickly as possible, just move it, and get myself a little one-bedroom flat or something.'

'What's the rush?'

'No rush.'

'Come on, Liam. You think I'm stupid? You just said, as quickly as possible.'

'I only want us both to get past this.'

When they were little she used to be able to tell instantly if he was speaking the truth by the hesitation that crept into his voice, the small pauses he took to allow himself time to think. She couldn't hear that hesitation now, but perhaps prison had made him a better liar. 'Are you in trouble?'

'No,' he said.

'Are you . . . clean?' The notion that he might still be using drugs was repugnant.

'Yes,' he said. 'I'm clean, I swear. It's too much, Sam, that's all. I don't need life to be so easy. I don't *deserve* life to be so easy. I'll stash the rest of the money away. Maybe one day you'll have a family of your own and they might want it?'

'You're my family, Liam.'

'I know, but . . .'

'If that's what you want,' she said, 'then that's what you should do. I want what you want.'

Liam looked at her, smiled and shook his head in disbelief. 'You can't be this amazing, you just can't be.'

She gestured to the room around them. 'I'm sitting on my own feeling sorry for myself on Christmas Eve. That's hardly amazing.'

'You're not alone,' he said.

They curled up on the sofa and watched a Disney film eating chocolates out of a box and she pretended that she was five years old again.

Was it possible that life had ever been that simple?

31

Thank God for January. Thank God for work. It was time to put all her carefully organized preparation into practice. The deals were poised, the transfer window was open and even though the club owners would dither over the fine print until the very last minute it was finally time to do some serious business.

She was ready.

Saturday dawned a beautiful crisp morning and she walked to the stadium watching the city emerge from the iron-grey grip of winter if only for one day.

She was about to watch her star client play his last competitive game before he wore the shirt for England. It was exciting. And as for Lubin and his proposal she was still hoping for inspiration. Perhaps when she saw him she would know what to do.

She was tempted. And confronting the lure she felt towards the illicit made her deeply uneasy.

She was a good girl. Wasn't she?

But Lubin wasn't in the players' lounge and so she went searching for him and found Gabe instead. She spotted him just outside the dressing room. He looked awful, exhausted and ten years older. Still, she was glad to see him. She rushed over and wished him a happy new year.

'I very much doubt that,' he said tersely, and slipped through the door without explaining himself.

Samantha couldn't ever remember seeing him looking so sad.

When the match kicked off she was so focused on Joe that it took her a while to notice that Gabe was playing erratically. Chasing everything, making selfish runs on goal and thoughtless passes. It wasn't until a big groan came from the home crowd, as once again Gabe went for goal instead of passing the ball to Joe who was wide open, that she started to pay close attention.

What the hell was he doing? He was playing like a child.

The right back sent a long ball towards the forwards and they both jumped for it, a clash of heads sending the ball spinning aimlessly across the grass where it was picked up by their opponents. The crowd groaned again and tensed collectively as the action went straight back up the other end, and the opposing team scored the first goal.

Down on the grass Joe knew Gabe was pissed off about something. He only wished that he knew what, then he might have half a chance of talking him round, and half a chance at goal.

They weren't friends any more though they pretended that they were. They called each other 'mate' when they passed on the training pitch, but they were faking it. They hadn't been out for a drink since that night south of the river. He missed him a bit, but what with the England call-up and everything he hadn't given it too much thought.

Gabe was furious with Samantha, but without good reason. All she had done was wish him a happy new year. Was he going mad? But they were all the same these agent types, weren't they? The game, the game of football, had gone crazy since they'd got involved, all about the money.

He never should have listened to Samantha Sharp. Coming out here was the worst mistake he had ever made. The gulf in his marriage was now so wide that he found it too complex and hence too much effort to traverse.

That morning he had asked Christine if she was going to bother to come and watch him play and she'd burst into tears. Just burst into tears like that. About nothing.

It was almost as if she knew. But she couldn't know.

Gabe felt guilty. He felt guilty all the time. He felt guilty that he hadn't made enough of this incredible chance, guilty that he had started smoking again and mostly he felt guilty about a teenage prostitute with nipples the colour of bubblegum, who had given him a blowjob he'd enjoyed so much he could no longer look his wife in the eye in case she guessed.

Joe could have stopped him that night. He should have stopped him.

He lashed out wildly at the ball again and sent it directly to the feet of an opposing player. His concentration was shot.

Samantha watched him with growing panic. She found herself willing the manager to pull Gabe off and put on a substitute.

Joe was playing well, but unable to compensate for Gabe's frequent mistakes. He fired off a ball towards goal and it ricocheted off the post into the arms of the waiting goalkeeper.

An easy save.

It was the closest White Stars had come to equalizing and Joe groaned with the home supporters, his hands flying to his head in an instinctive gesture.

Gabe was happy that the kid had missed. *Not quite the wonder boy everybody thinks, eh?* Nobody seemed to remember that without him Samantha never would have found Joe out here in the middle of nowhere, might as well have wrapped a bow round Joe's head and called a gift a gift. But did he get any thanks for it? Did he *hell*. Joe had his life in front of him, a life to train and become an even stronger player. Joe wouldn't have to fit a career into the sunset years, to try to force the best form of his life out in what few years remained for him. Joe would play in many FA Cups, of that he was certain, not just one, and by the time Joe was Gabe's age – in two fucking decades – he would have a thousand footballing stories to tell.

Not just one.

Joe would be a true hero. And Gabe would be long forgotten.

Fucking Joe.

Maybe if he scored now, maybe if he scored, then everyone – Joe, Sam, the fans, his wife – might think he was worth something after all.

The opposition goalkeeper bounced the ball a few times in preparation for his goal kick. He walked out towards the edge of his area, shouting at his team mates to try to organize them.

Samantha watched closely. The goalkeeper wasn't paying attention, clearly he had been rattled by the closeness of Joe's attempt on goal. He was about to step out of his box where he would no longer be able to carry the ball. White Stars would get a free kick in an incredibly powerful position.

She tensed.

At the very last second the goalkeeper looked down, dropped the ball with inches to spare and in his haste to correct his near-mistake he totally miskicked, sending the ball spinning half-heartedly to nobody and nowhere.

Joe and Gabe both had their backs to the ball and spun round when they heard the reaction of the crowd.

They both ran for the stray ball.

One of them would have to give way otherwise there would be an almighty collision.

Neither of them stopped.

Joe felt his legs swiped from under him as Gabe used his superior body weight to gain control of the ball and shoot at goal.

He missed.

But Joe hardly noticed. His knee screamed in pain as his leg buckled beneath him and he sank to the cold, wet ground in agony.

Samantha jumped to her feet in panic.

No.

Not Joe, not now.

Around her everyone was bewildered. Who ever saw such a thing? Two players from the same team involved in a nasty tackle like that. It might be funny if the team was not a goal down. Then the crowd noticed that their most promising young player was still to get to his feet.

And, like Samantha, they were scared.

She ran down into the stadium, her feet gathering pace as she took the stairs down to the touchline. She stood beside the players' dugout, watching with mounting horror as a stretcher was run out to the middle of the pitch where Joe lay on his back, his hands covering his face.

He looked like a child.

The referee and Gabe hovered over him, the other players looked on at a distance. When the team physio reached him Joe pulled himself up to a sitting position with some difficulty and then tried to stand. But he fell against the physio and was swiftly persuaded onto the stretcher.

It did not look good; it looked awful and it made her feel sick.

She watched him being carried off the pitch, wishing that she could close her ears to the crowd's applause for the returning Moras when he was substituted for Joe.

This can't be happening; this can't be over.

The game continued. She couldn't get close enough to speak to Joe as he was carried down the tunnel and away from the pitch. But she was close enough to tell that he was crying.

Gabe knew exactly what he had done as soon as his foot connected with Joe's leg. Up until that point he had been in a kind of daze but when he saw the trauma pass across his friend's face and his legs fold underneath him, it shocked him back into reality and, like watching a slow motion replay, he watched Joe's knee bend the way a knee wasn't supposed to bend and then saw him fall to the floor.

He knew what he had done.

And he knew why.

He didn't go for the ball with the intention of hurting Joe – he was genuinely after the ball, but he hadn't wanted

Joe to have it. He wanted to take it from him, to take the goal from him and deprive him of the glory. He had years of glory ahead of him. So Gabe ran for the ball with every ounce of speed and strength that he had in him and a single-mindedness that possessed him. And in those final seconds when he still had time to pull up, to stop running, to let the better player take the ball, he wasn't thinking of Joe – he was hardly thinking at all. He wanted to score.

But he hadn't even managed to do that right.

And when he saw Joe fall and when he saw that he didn't get up and they brought out the stretcher for him all he could think, all he could think for hours after, was – *What have I done?*

He was not a man who prayed, but he prayed for Joe.

They took him to hospital for a series of X-rays. He had nineteen days before the England game.

'I'm his agent,' she insisted, when she got there. 'I should be with him.'

The hospital's busy casualty unit didn't care.

The smells and sounds of the medical environment were exactly the same as they were the world over and she flinched as she watched Joe being wheeled behind swinging plastic doors and out of sight. She thought of the gleaming private health care afforded to players in the UK, the medical facilities on hand at the stadiums, and she yearned to go home. They wouldn't tell her anything and instead pointed her towards a bleak waiting room where she sat with Joe's mother, Ana.

'I'm his mother,' said Ana, 'I should be with him.'

But they wouldn't listen to her either.

Sam was reminded again how very young Joe was. This wasn't his last chance, she told herself, preparing for the worst-case scenario: a torn ligament, a shattered kneecap, surgery and months of recuperation, a year or more on the sidelines.

'Was he in bad pain?' said Ana.

It was impossible to tell if Joe had been crying because of the injury, or because of what it meant, but she just said 'no' anyway, 'not too bad', and hoped that Ana wouldn't be able to tell that she was lying. One way or another Joe was hurting.

It wasn't his last chance. But perhaps he had been hers. Was it selfish to think of the jewel of her list being damaged?

Yes.

But she thought about it all the same.

An hour passed by before anyone came to tell them what was going on, and then it was only to say that Joe's knee was being scanned so that they could compare the results of the X-ray.

'The other player,' said Ana. 'Gabe? He is Joe's friend?'

'Yes,' said Samantha.

'So why did he do that?'

Finally they were allowed in to see Joe. A nurse led them through the plastic swinging doors to a ward of curtained bays. He was in a bed wearing a hospital gown looking grim.

His mum ran to him and muttered a few words in Polish as she fussed with his pillows and wiped his hair off his face. He still had mud from the football pitch on his cheek.

'Have they told you anything?' he asked.

The two women shook their heads and then stiffened as the doctor appeared behind the curtain.

They spoke in Polish, a three-way conversation between Joe, the doctor and his mum. Samantha waited as patiently as she could until Joe translated.

'They don't know,' he said. 'An hour of X-rays, half a dozen scans and they don't know. They won't know until the swelling goes down.'

'They must have some idea?' she said.

'They don't.'

'The English FA is sending over one of their doctors,' said Samantha.

'Seriously?' said Joe.

'Of course.'

'For me?'

'You see any other England players here?'

'Blimey.'

His mum and the doctor continued to talk in Polish and it became clear that they were making arrangements for Joe to go home. Forms were signed, a wheelchair was produced and Samantha walked with them out to the car park and watched while Joe gingerly hopped into the front seat of his mum's car, his bad knee bound in thick elastic bandages. She thought of all that bone and cartilage rubbing against itself and prayed that he wasn't doing any more damage as she waved him off.

She would have to ensure that a translator was available for the doctor from the FA. There was too much at stake for anything to be left to chance or ambiguity.

Not just for Joe, but for her too.

Damn it.

She finally allowed in the selfish thought that had been whispering around the back of her mind since she saw him being taken away on the stretcher. She would not be able to sell him while his long-term fitness was in question. Unless Joe was given a clean bill of health before the transfer window closed, all the hard work she was doing getting the big clubs talking about him and making speculative approaches would come to nothing.

Without a big deal for Joe all the medium deals on Slovenians and Ukrainians would not be enough.

Her business would in effect be over before it began.

And yet even as she thought this she didn't care. She just wanted him to be well. He was a kid. A kid with an amazing future. To her surprise she realized that she wanted to see him well, even if it took far longer than the time the transfer window allowed. She wanted to see him healed more than she wanted to sell him.

A voice reached her from the shadows. 'What's the prognosis?'

Gabe stepped out from behind an ambulance, his face ashen. At first she thought that his breath was misted from the cold and then she realized with a degree of dismay that he was smoking a cigarette.

'Is he going to be okay?' he said. 'Will he be able to play?'

'They don't know,' said Samantha. She paused. 'You're smoking now?'

He shrugged and looked down at the cigarette in his hand then dropped it to the floor and ground out the stub with his heel. 'It would seem so, yeah.'

'What happened out there, Gabe?' she said.

'I wish I could tell you.' Tears glittered in his eyes. 'I fucked up, Sam. What can I do? How can I make it right?'

'I don't think you can, Gabe.'

It was cold and getting dark. She wanted to get back and make arrangements for the England team doctor. She wanted to call Joe and make sure that he didn't put any weight on his knee, none at all, and tell him to apply an ice pack for the swelling. She wanted to take Gabe by the shoulders and shake him with every muscle in her body and demand to know why he had done what he did. But she knew that he wouldn't be able to answer her.

'I'm worried about you, Gabe,' she said.

He raised his face to the sky and took a deep breath. 'We drew the match,' he said. 'One all.'

'Is that right?'

'I scored.'

'Congratulations.'

He gave a bitter snort of laughter that caught in his throat. 'Yeah.'

'I'm going to go now, Gabe,' she said. 'I'll be at my hotel if you want to talk later . . .'

'Okay,' he said, 'maybe.' But he had absolutely no intention of calling her. He didn't even know why he had come. He had showered and changed in record time and been waiting outside the hospital for what felt like hours, long enough to buy this pack of cigarettes anyway.

'I know you didn't mean to hurt him,' she said. 'I'm pretty sure Joe knows that too.'

'I didn't,' he said.

A taxi rolled by and she waved it down. 'You want to share a cab back to town?'

'You're okay,' he said. 'I want to walk.'

'Go home,' she said. 'Go home and we'll talk later.'

He nodded and waited until she had driven around the corner out of sight before lighting another cigarette.

She fell into bed when she got back to her hotel, but sleep eluded her for several hours, and she didn't wake up until late the following morning, disorientated and still exhausted. There was a pile of messages growing for her at the front desk, a flurry of calls from the FA back in England, plenty from the British press.

She was about to go upstairs when the receptionist stopped her. 'Ms Sharp? Mr Lubin is waiting for you in the bar,' he said.

He was sitting with his back to her, watching English Premier League football highlights on one of the many televisions that were scattered around the popular sports bar at the Sheraton.

She glanced up. Chelsea was playing. Both the Welstead boys were on the team and she watched as they played with one mind, and scored a goal in West London that was conceived somewhere in Yorkshire many years ago with the kind of instinctive teamwork that perhaps only brothers could hope for.

He saw her. 'Those boys are incredible.'

'Monty and Ferris Welstead,' she said. 'I know. They used to be mine.'

'I hope you made them a good deal.'

'The tenth biggest in the world,' she said. 'Ever.'

Had life ever really been that easy? Picking a multi-million pound deal out of several that had been on offer.

'How is Joe?' he asked.

'It was too soon to say. I'll call the hospital in a little while.'

'You are worried about him.'

'You're going to tell me I shouldn't get personally involved,' she guessed. She beckoned the barmaid and ordered herself coffee and juice.

'If I told you that would it stop you?' he asked.

'No,' she said. 'I can't help it. Perhaps it's because I'm a woman. They're my boys, all of them.'

And something suddenly became clear.

She looked around to make sure that they weren't being overheard. 'I won't do it,' she said. 'The Russian deal, I can't.'

He took his eyes off the television and fixed her with a penetrating stare. 'No?'

'If I need to cheat to win then my victory will always feel hollow,' she said. 'If it comes to that then my career is balanced on lies. People need to trust you. That's what's important.'

The stress of the last twenty-four hours was hanging heavy on her. She longed to crawl back into bed and sleep, but also she could see a bright clarity to her life that had been lacking for months. 'So, thank you for the offer, Alek, but I won't play the game that way. I'd rather not play at all.'

'Good,' he said.

'What?'

'Good. There was never any offer, Samantha. I wanted to know your true character before I helped you.'

'I don't understand.'

'There was no Russian offer for Gabe. I lied to you. Everyone keeps telling me you are corrupt and I needed to know for sure.'

'You were testing me?'

He nodded.

'You know something,' she said. 'What is it? Tell me. Please, tell me.'

'You lied to me, Samantha. You told me you were never married.'

'I wasn't.'

'Then who is Liam Sharp?'

'Where did you find that name?'

'At the end of a very long money trail. The three hundred thousand? It led to Liam Sharp. Who is he and why is he trying to ruin your life?'

32

Funny the things you take for granted until they are gone. Joe had never fully appreciated his two functioning knees before. Now one of them had gone and he missed it more than he missed his own father or Layla Petherick. He would give just about anything to have it back again.

The fateful moment replayed in his mind relentlessly. Gabe bearing down on him, the certainty that he would stop because Joe was closer to the ball and would reach it first. But Gabe didn't stop and the look on his face when he mowed Joe down was what Joe remembered most. For in that moment he saw hate. Pure hate. And he didn't know what he had done.

Samantha had been to see him, bringing along the doctor from the FA who unhelpfully reiterated the Polish doctor's opinion that they would have a better idea how to proceed once the swelling in his knee had gone down. It should take about two days. And there were seventeen days left until the England match. Seventeen days and four hours, the doctor had said, with a precision which gave Joe the shivers.

After the doctor left he called his dad who told him with great excitement about all the positive press coverage he was getting, and how the English people (while not to the extent that they once prayed for David Beckham's broken metatarsal) were emphatically behind him.

'Everyone knows who you are now,' he said, as if that might make up for missing out on England duty. What he didn't mention was that the bizarre circumstances of the injury, a tackle from a team mate, had driven most of the headlines. Like a comic 'and finally' story on the news.

Joe had never hated the view from his bedroom window, he had hardly even noticed it, but he thought that if he had to look for much longer at the same square of the grey communist-built building opposite, and the straggly tree branch that did nothing to improve its looks, he might end up throwing himself from the third-floor window in frustration.

Except that would be a really stupid thing to do because then he'd end up with a fractured leg on top of his dodgy knee.

So he couldn't even do that.

'Joe?'

His mum again, bringing more food probably, like scrambled eggs and *zurek* that might make his swelling go down faster.

'You've got a visitor,' she said, stepping aside.

His heart quickened because he was both thrilled and dismayed, and oh so slightly panicked. Layla Petherick walked into his bedroom. She looked like an angel.

'What are you doing here?' he said, wishing that he wasn't wearing pyjamas in the middle of the afternoon, wishing that his mum hadn't brought her in here but instead had let him hop into the front room so that he mightn't look quite as pathetic as he did right now.

Layla, of course, looked sensational, dressed in some sort of trendy voluminous coat in a vibrant pink that picked out the sweetheart curve of her lips and swung from side to side when she walked.

She smiled softly, which gave him a pain in his gut to match the one in his leg.

'How's the knee?' she said. 'It's awful bad luck, Joe, but on the news they said you might be okay, so fingers crossed, right?'

'On the news?'

Layla Petherick was in his bedroom taking off her coat.

She nodded and grinned. 'I know! How mad is that?'

It was mad all right. He couldn't quite conceive of himself on the news, spoken about within the same space as prime ministers and world events. But it didn't really cheer him up. You don't want to be on telly for having a gammy knee, being a bloody invalid; you want to be on telly for scoring a goal and winning a match. That was supposed to be the next part of the Joe Wonder story.

'You okay?' she said. 'You look really miserable.'

'What do you think?'

'Yeah, sorry, that was a stupid thing to say.'

'Yeah.' He knew he was being a twat but somehow he just couldn't help it. Layla had come all this way and yet he couldn't stop being annoyed that she was seeing him like this, vulnerable and sort of broken, annoyed with her, which was unfair but yet equally unstoppable. 'How's Daniel?' he said. *Daniel the Dick.*

She shrugged. 'I dunno.'

'You don't know?'

'We sort of split up.'

'You sort of did?'

'We did, yeah.'

'Why's that then? I thought you were crazy about him?'

She gave him an odd little sideways look, not quite sure why he was being so aggressive, but willing to give him leeway because of the circumstances. 'He couldn't really deal with all the newspaper stuff, you know, about me and you. Some of his mates were giving him grief.'

'And he split up with you because of that?' He felt guilty and delighted at the same time. When his thoughts strayed to Layla late at night as they inevitably did, he wouldn't have to picture her kissing someone else.

'Not quite,' she said. 'I thought he was being a bit stupid so we argued and, well, that was that.'

'That's a shame,' he said, and he didn't mean it and he didn't care if he sounded like he meant it either. She could tell.

She perched on the chair beside his bed, like she was visiting him in hospital. He was embarrassed, he couldn't think of anything to say, but she chattered on as if this wasn't awkward for her. Which went to show how stupid he was for having all kinds of romantic thoughts about her. His spirits sank deeper into the moody funk that just wanted her to leave.

'Guess what?' she said. 'An agent called me yesterday, asking if I had representation.'

'For what?'

'For, you know, celebrity stuff.'

'Huh?'

'They think we're together,' she said. 'You and me. I'm, like, a WAG or something. Isn't that stupid?'

'Did you tell them the truth?'

'I don't think they'd believe me. Besides, it all depends what happens, doesn't it?'

'What do you mean?'

'With your knee and that,' she said. 'It depends if you play or whatever.'

He stared out of his bedroom window again, at the shit-grey building opposite and the fucking ugly tree and thought how utterly incompatible this scenario was with his daydreams of seeing her again.

In his daydreams it was post-match, post-victory and she was all dressed up ready to celebrate and he was fresh from the shower and glowing with triumph. Instead he was sitting up in bed like an old man. 'Oh hey, I'm sorry,' he said, 'if my totally random injury is going to mess with your showbiz career. How inconsiderate of me.'

'Joe,' she said, her warm smile faltering and her eyes drifting down to the floor. 'Don't.'

'No, no,' he said wildly. 'Here was me just being selfish, didn't realize that my fake girlfriend would be inconvenienced by my pain.'

She shook her head and gave him the nearest thing to a dirty look a sweet girl like her could muster. 'You think it's been fun for me?' she said. 'Being followed around by reporters these last few weeks?'

'I do actually. I think you've probably loved every minute of it.'

'Then you don't know me as well as I thought you did,' she said.

'Obviously not.'

Her pink marshmallow cheeks were fast turning cherry red. Her eyes flashed with something and he couldn't tell if it was tears or rage. He was longing to sweep her up in his arms and apologize and cover her in kisses, but he couldn't even stand up, could he? And, besides, inside he was churning with all kinds of mixed-up emotions, feeling injured and injurious, proud and terribly angry. He wanted her to leave, but he wanted her to crawl under the covers and soothe his throbbing knee with her leather-gloved hands.

'You're acting like a knob, Joe. I came a long way because I care about you, but if you don't want me here then I should go.' She paused, waiting for him to say something but he didn't. A single hot tear plopped onto her lovely cheek. 'So yeah, I get it. I think I'll go. Good luck with the knee and everything.'

She stood up to leave. Her hands plunged into the small rucksack she was carrying and brought out a giant Toblerone.

'Here,' she said, 'I brought you a present.' She threw it at him and it landed squarely on his knee, his bad knee.

He screamed out in agony.

A red bubble of pain exploded, blocking out his peripheral vision and sending tremors from his battered knee to his toes and his thigh.

Layla's hand flew to her mouth, mortified. 'Oh shit, oh, Joe, I'm so sorry. I'm so stupid.'

He fought back the wave of nausea and the feeling like he was going to pass out. He closed his eyes tightly and didn't breathe for a few seconds.

'Joe? Are you okay?'

He nodded, not yet trusting himself to open his eyes or to speak. Gradually (and it felt like ages) the pain subsided until there was nothing left.

'Joe?'

He could smell oranges. He opened his eyes and her face was right in front of his.

He kissed her.

Her lips were warm and sugary and he forgot all about his knee, and the seventeen days and four hours, and the view from his bedroom window.

And then a miracle occurred.

Layla Petherick was kissing him back.

33

Samantha hadn't said anything for several seconds. Aleksandr Lubin was looking at her with an expression somewhere between curiosity and amusement.

Liam?

'Sam,' he said, 'is everything okay?'

'I need . . .' Her vision misted. 'I just need a minute, okay?' She grabbed the edge of the hotel bar. The waitress behind it sensed the private moment and moved swiftly away. Samantha could hear the blood coursing in her temples and wondered why. Of course it could not possibly be Liam.

Liam?

It was ludicrous. Liam was the only person she would trust with her life. It had been that way for as long as she could remember: the Sharp siblings against the world. Even from behind bars Liam had been there for her. It made no sense, no sense at all. What did he stand to gain from her downfall? Unless perhaps the downfall itself was enough.

'There's no way,' she said. 'There's just absolutely no way it could be Liam.'

'Who is he?'

'Liam? He's my brother.'

'You have a brother? You never mentioned him. You are not close?'

She laughed, almost hysterically. 'I love him,' she said. 'He loves me. We're close.'

Lubin took her hand. The gesture felt horribly intimate. Stupid considering what they had done together these last few months, but still she snatched her hand away.

'Then I'm sorry,' he said. 'This must be very painful.'

'You don't understand,' she said. 'You've made a mistake. I would stake my entire reputation on it.'

What little reputation she had managed to claw back, that is. She was still a long way from where she once had been.

'There is no mistake,' he said. 'The man I asked for the information does deals for my family risking hundreds of millions. When he tells you something you can be assured of his accuracy. He does not make errors.'

'This time he has. He must have.'

She had been at the very edge of ruin. It was impossible to conceive that Liam would take her there. He only ever wanted good things for her. He was proud of her. But . . .

But nothing.

Wasn't he jealous of her too? Hadn't he admitted as much one cold Primrose Hill night? He had said that he would like to see her fail. Just once. Hadn't he? And the look on his face that night. It chilled her soul to remember it. He looked as if he hated her. He had looked at her once like that before, years ago, when she had continually refused to get him an interview at the hotel in Seven Dials, condemning him to remain in the job that would ultimately ruin his life.

Was it possible that he blamed her? Anything is possible.

'No,' she said firmly. 'This is absurd. For one thing, he has no money, and I mean *no* money. He couldn't get his hands on three hundred pounds let alone three hundred thousand dollars.'

Lubin nodded. 'My associate tells me that the money was funnelled through a bonds and securities company.'

Wasn't that the same thing that the private detective had told her? Slowly but surely painful pinpricks of logic and doubt began to creep into her staunch defence. 'I know,' she whispered.

'So it is possible that he borrowed the money?'

'He would never be stupid enough to borrow such an amount without any way of paying it back. Besides which . . .'

'Besides which?'

She took a deep breath. 'He's been in prison,' she said. 'For a long time. That's why I didn't tell you about him. I didn't tell anyone.'

Lubin nodded. 'You are ashamed.'

'That sounds terrible, putting it like that, but yes, I suppose I was. We came from nothing; I didn't want to be known for anything other than where I was going. It's been hard enough for me, being a woman, I didn't need another handicap.' She stopped and rubbed her face, tired and overwhelmed. 'Wait, that's not what I meant . . .' She had been loyal to him, hadn't she? She had been a devoted sister.

'It's okay, Samantha, really it's okay. I understand. Families can be very complicated.'

'So how could he set up a loan like that from behind bars?'

'This kind of company, it is not – how can I describe it? – it is not particularly honourable. I would think that would be relatively straightforward.'

'Nobody would lend 300K to a criminal.'

'True perhaps, but has anyone actually seen this money? Is it real, or is it just paper money? Paper money can be bought very cheaply. You are paying for an illusion, for nothing. A criminal could find the means, or find a dishonourable company willing to extend credit.'

She could run away. Running away works. If she ran back up to her hotel room and never spoke to Aleksandr Lubin again, perhaps then he would stop talking. Every word that he said was beginning to sound more plausible, more convincing, and she could no longer refute his scenario out of hand. But she remained fixed to her seat as the case against Liam grew.

'He is out of prison now?' said Lubin. 'He has been released?'

'Just a few weeks ago.' There had been some brief days of awkward happiness and then their big falling out. That was the big reunion she had been waiting for all these years?

'The paper money debt would need to be settled. There would have been a fee, with interest. He would want to repay it very quickly. Has he asked you for any money?'

'No,' she said, grasping at the hole in the argument like a tear in a net, 'not a penny.' Then her eyes clouded with a memory.

'What?' said Lubin. 'What is it?'

She put her hand to her mouth. 'I bought him a house,' she said. 'I bought him this stupid house and we fought, and then at Christmas he told me that he wanted to put it on the market.'

'He wants to sell it?'

She pressed her lips together and nodded. 'As quickly as possible.'

Liam.

She threw her scalding coffee down her throat and pushed her seat back from the bar. 'I have to go,' she said.

There was only one way to find out the truth.

'Where?'

'I have to go to London. I have to see my brother.'

'Samantha, don't be stupid. What about the transfer window?'

'Nothing gets signed until the window's about to close. That's three days away. I'll be back in twenty-four hours. Leanne can handle the exasperating delaying tactics until then.'

'What about Joe?'

'You think Joe's knee will heal more quickly if I stay in town? Do I have magical powers? Alek, I have to go, don't you understand? I have to look my brother in the eye and ask him if he did this thing. I'll know. As soon as he opens his mouth, I'll know for sure.'

Lubin grabbed her arm to stop her running. 'Slow down,' he said. 'Let me come with you. He could be dangerous.'

'He's my *brother*!'

'It doesn't matter. Sam, please. We can take the jet.'

The airfield at Farnborough was overcrowded. High winds, rain and dreadful visibility meant that they could not land for forty-five minutes, but to Samantha every minute was too long.

'This is crazy,' she snapped. 'I would have got there quicker by easyJet.'

'Try to stay calm,' said Lubin. 'In a few hours your name could be clear, your reputation restored.'

He was right. But there was no comfort in knowing that her brother's guilt would confirm her own innocence. For months she had pictured the look on Jackson's face when she confronted him with vindicating proof. But not like this. The cost was far too high. If she lost Liam then she had lost everything that ever mattered. To learn that she had lost him months ago, years ago, hurt her more than any boardroom decision ever could.

Oddly, piercing her panic was a deep longing for Jackson's steadying influence. He would know what to do. She could sense that she was rushing headlong towards a confrontation with Liam, but was powerless to slow down.

'Let me come to the house with you,' said Lubin.

He wasn't Jackson. It wasn't his hand she wanted to hold. Lubin was exciting, excitable. And he didn't know her well enough to be a part of this. In a moment of crisis some matters become clear. And it was clear to her that things with Lubin would soon be over.

'I'm grateful for everything you've done,' she said. 'But I have to do this alone. If I need you I'll call.'

'Please, you must call me anyway. I will worry.'

'You?' she said. 'I thought you never worried.'

'Promise me?' His voice was soft and serious. 'Promise me you'll call?'

She reached out for him and drew him to her for a kiss, feeling nothing, wanting Jackson even more.

'I promise,' she said.

*

It was raining hard and the London traffic was crawling, so after leaving a message for Liam to call her she abandoned her cab, dashed through the rain, the puddles spraying water up her ankles, and jumped on the tube, wet and troubled.

She thought of all those times she had visited Liam in prison, not too far from here. Behind their light-hearted chat had he been thinking forward to wreaking his retribution? Had he perhaps been picturing her on the other side of the table, relishing the prospect? To make her pay for all those years of freedom that she had enjoyed? His imprisonment had altered his perception of reality.

He blamed her. And perhaps she was to blame. She didn't know any more. This morning seemed like weeks ago and the confrontation awaiting her was too immense to contemplate so she sat on the tube stubbornly fixed in the present as she whipped beneath the city streets, begging her mind to be still.

Her house was dark when she finally arrived, the low angry clouds were smothering the daylight and all the lights were turned off. She knew he wasn't there, but she called out for him anyway.

Silence. The drone of a nearby helicopter and a flash of lightning, immediately followed by a roll of thunder. She shivered. There was nothing to do but wait.

She searched her memory for some indisputable fact, some flaw in the case against him, that would prove that Lubin's source was mistaken. But how had he even known Liam's name? And if it was true – then what? Would she honestly be able to hand her brother over to the police?

She found herself in the basement office, so often her safe place in troubling times. Work had always been there for her, the most constant thing she had. She didn't know what she was looking for exactly, but the paperwork of her life was there. Perhaps there would be some clue, some diary page or forgotten document that would disprove the case against him.

Or, worse, condemn him.

If it had been her in there, in prison, paying for a moment of madness with the best years of her life, might she have gone a little crazy too? Perhaps it was enough to unbalance him. To unbalance anyone.

She would forgive him.

No matter what.

Had there ever really been any doubt? They could talk this through; they could work it out. It would take a long time, perhaps the rest of their lives, but she would try.

She thought she heard footsteps upstairs, coming her way.

'Liam?' But there was nobody there.

An enormous roll of thunder seemed loud enough to shake the entire house and the lights in the office flickered. She looked up apprehensively and instinctively tried the phone line. It was dead.

Then she heard the unmistakable creak of the basement door closing.

'Liam? Wait.'

And the sound of a key turning in the lock.

She ran up the stairs, two at a time, losing her footing in her haste to get there, but she was too late.

She was trapped.

34

Layla was right by his side, *holding his hand*, when the doctor told Joe the good news. Just a sprain, and a mild one too. A little bruising. By the time the swelling receded the damage was almost imperceptible.

'Your body overcompensated to protect the muscle,' he said. 'It sometimes happens to professional sportsmen.'

That's me, I'm a professional sportsman.

'So what now?' he asked.

'I think the best thing to do would be to rest for a couple more days and then get you to training.'

'At the White Stars stadium?'

'No, I meant England training. We can monitor your progress more easily in Hertfordshire. There's no pain?'

Joe shook his head. 'None. You're telling me I'll play?' It was more than he had dared to hope for, but then so was the affection of the girl sitting beside him and so far that seemed to be going well.

'That rather depends on the manager's tactics,' said the doctor pedantically, 'but if you mean will you be fit to play, then, yes, within a few days I see no reason why you shouldn't be fully recovered.'

After the doctor left Joe grabbed Layla and danced her around his bedroom.

'Be careful,' she warned, still wary of his knee no matter what the doctor had said.

'It's okay,' said Joe. 'You healed me.' He hesitated for only a second before he kissed her. Forty-eight hours since their first kiss and he still couldn't get used to being allowed to do it whenever he liked.

When they stepped off the easyJet flight at Luton airport the resident airport paparazzi sprang into action. It was the first photograph of the two of them together. Their fellow passengers craned their necks to see who was attracting all the attention, and even though most of them weren't sure who he was, a few took photographs with their mobile phones anyway.

'How did they know what flight we were on?' said Joe, but he didn't really mind. It was good to feel a bit like a star.

Those that did recognize him shouted out his name. 'Hey, it's that Joe Wonder!' 'All right, Joe?' 'Nice one, mate!'

Joe's remarkable recovery had made the nation optimistic about the football match the following week and the frenzied build-up was already starting. England expected a result.

A young girl approached them with a notepad and pen. His first autograph request, how exciting. He was frantically considering whether to sign Joe Wonder or Josef Wandrowszcki or what, when the little girl pushed the notebook at Layla and asked for her autograph instead.

She signed while Joe stood to the side, agape.

'What can I say?' laughed Layla. 'It's all about the WAGs these days.'

A voice penetrated a wonderful dream that Layla was his girlfriend and that he had been picked for the England team. *Wait a minute, I'm not dreaming . . .* Life was sweet.

'Joe dear? Wake up.'

His nan was standing over him. Something was wrong. For one thing it was the first time she had ever woken him up without a cup of tea in her hand. For another it was too early, still half dark outside and freezing cold.

'I'm sure it's nothing,' she said. 'There's a few people outside who want to talk to you, that's all.'

'What?'

'Outside,' she repeated. 'But I'm sure it's probably nothing.'

He staggered from his bed and rubbed the crusty bits from his eyelids. Who would be outside at this hour? He walked to the window.

'Be careful,' she warned as he pulled back the curtain and stared in amazement at the street below.

There were reporters and photographers for as far as he could see.

Their cars were blocking the narrow street; they had stepladders and folding chairs; there was a catering van, a small one that sold coffee, doing a brisk trade. They were surrounding his house, and Layla's house next door too.

He dropped the curtain as if it was hot.

The doorbell chimed.

'Don't answer it,' said Joe, trying to sound in control. 'What time is it?'

'Just before seven.'

'Call Samantha,' he said. 'She'll know what to do.'

Satisfied with that plan his nan left the room and Joe dressed, calling Layla's mobile as he did so, but it was switched off. He wanted her to check the internet, see if something had happened, because there was no connection here at his nan's. Maybe, and he hated to even think such a thing, but maybe he had been dropped from the squad? Did that ever happen? What if some player who was unavailable was now available again? What if the doctor had made a mistake and his knee was actually fucked? He experienced a psychosomatic twinge in his perfectly healthy knee.

His mobile phone rang and he leapt on it in an instant. 'Layla?'

'Nah, mate, it's your dad. In a spot of bother with the missus are you?'

'Something's going on, Dad, there's, like, a hundred reporters outside. Nan's a bit scared.' He wasn't about to admit that at this point he was a bit scared too.

'Haven't you seen the papers today?'

'No.'

'Oh dear,' said Simon, chuckling. 'Whatever happens remember this. I'm proud of you, son. You got that?'

'Is it bad? What's happened?'

'I'll be there in ten or fifteen minutes. I've got the paper. Try and keep your dick in your pants until then.'

What was that supposed to mean?

JOE WONDER SCORES FOR ENGLAND!

Hooker Tells All of Night with England Teen – *world exclusive*

England new boy Josef Wandrowszcki could be about to receive the red card from sexy girlfriend Layla Petherick after news of his Eastern European exploits were leaked by the prostitute at the centre of the latest sex scandal to rock the sport. Lithuanian grandmother and mother of four Agatha Lobieski, 46, revealed to reporters that 17-year-old super striker Joe paid the equivalent of one thousand pounds for a night of passion in a Polish brothel. 'Joe is a sweet boy,' said Agatha from an undisclosed location last night. 'And he will always be welcome here.'

'You should call Richard,' suggested Simon when he arrived.

'Why?'

'I'm just not sure that Sam Sharp's the best person for you. Where is she now, eh? In your hour of need? She should be out there reading a statement or something. She's probably dodging your call because she knows she fucked up.'

'No, Dad, she didn't fuck up – I did.'

But he had a point. Where was she?

'Call Richard, he'll make the most of this.'

'Make the most of it?' said Joe. 'I don't want to make the most of it; I want the opposite.'

'I don't just mean the money.'

'What money? What are you talking about?'

'The money you'll get for telling your side of things. Richard's great at that.'

'How do you know all this?'

Was his dad taking money for tip-offs? Was that normal?

'Was she worth the money, son? This Agatha bird? She looks filthy in her photograph. Filthy in a good way, I mean. Bet she was a freak in the sack, am I right?'

'Shut up, Dad, just shut up a minute, okay?'

Simon shrank back, scolded.

He kept trying Layla's mobile phone, but there was still no answer.

He had to speak to her, he had to explain. He couldn't begin to contemplate that the relationship he had waited ten years to begin might be over in a matter of days. He ran into the back garden in his bare feet, ignoring the cold earth, and he pounded on the wall between their houses. 'Layla? Are you there?'

Nothing.

'Layla, do you hear me?'

Still nothing.

'Layla, please.'

He knew she could hear him. He knew she was sitting in the kitchen pretending not to be there, but listening to him. He wasn't sure quite how he knew, but he knew all the same. He could picture her sitting there in one of her Juicy Couture rip-offs, clutching a cup of coffee with two sugars that she would let go stone cold before she drank it, an unfinished bowl of cereal somewhere near by. He knew that her hair would be in a ponytail because it was Wednesday and her hair always needed washing by Wednesday so that's how she wore it. The television would be on, but with the sound turned down, and she would have a pair of men's hiking socks on her feet instead of slippers. And the only thing that would be different was that instead of wearing that gorgeous sunny smile that he had been in love with for all this time she would be sad. She would have seen the photographers, she would have checked the internet and she would feel stupid and embarrassed.

You don't spend ten years crazy about someone without learning a little something about their habits.

'I think you can hear me,' he said, leaning up against her back door and talking as if she was on the other side.

'It's not true you know. Of course it isn't true. You know me, Lay, can you really see me paying for sex? Especially when' – *deep breath* – 'when I haven't even had sex. Ever.'

If he was going to be honest he might as well be honest about everything.

'It was Gabe's idea. You know – Gabe Muswell? And we thought we were going to a lap-dancing club, but the taxi driver took us to this place and, well, Gabe liked this one girl and he went off with her and the blokes were looking at me and making me feel pressured and this woman, this Agatha, not that I knew her name even, said we could just go and talk, to make it look like . . . you know, to make it look like what it looks like now. Cos I know what it looks like now, Layla, I know. I was stupid, but I didn't want Gabe to think . . .'

He stopped.

But there was only silence.

'Nothing happened. You have to trust me. If Gabe wants to sleep with hookers that's none of my business, I don't care. And if the papers want to say I did too then that's a bit harder to take, but so what? There's only one person I care about, and that's you. You're the only one I want to believe me. Because if you don't I don't know what I'll do. And I know it must be really embarrassing and you feel stupid and everything, and if I could change things I would, but I can't. So you'll just have to trust me. Please trust me. Because I love you, Layla. That's the truth. I love you something fierce.'

He pressed his lips firmly together because he felt like he was going to choke on tears. He was certain, absolutely certain, that she was there and listening to every word, but he had nothing left to say.

Then she opened the door he was leaning against and he fell inside.

She'd been crying, he could tell. But she was laughing now, at him scrabbling on the floor. And he thought that maybe everything was going to be okay.

'You all right?' she said as he clambered to his feet.

'Are you?'

She nodded. 'That Gabe Muswell is an idiot.'

'Yeah, I know. Do you believe me?'

'I do,' she said. She shuffled her thick hiking socks against the cold kitchen floor. 'And I love you too.'

The reporter crouching in the alleyway between the two houses clicked off his tape recorder and ran back to his car. The next day's headlines would be all about Gabe.

'What does Samantha say you should do?' asked Layla, after they had done a bit of kissing and making up.

'She hasn't called me back,' said Joe. 'Don't you think that's a bit weird?'

They waited all day for Samantha to call.

But she did not.

There were four telephone lines in the small Krakow office and they were all crying out for attention.

'So would you say that the recent revelations about Gabe Muswell have effectively terminated his White Stars contract?'

'Listen, prick,' said Leanne. 'What part of "no comment" don't you understand?'

She slammed down the phone and turned her back on the flashing lines. She needed five minutes. This was the worst day ever.

She intended to kill Samantha when she got hold of her. Well, not literally kill her, but she would at least scare her silly by pretending she was going to quit. What did she think she was doing? Running off to London with her toy boy was bad enough, but not answering her phones?

There was Joe. Poor little Joe Wonder dropped into the shit by a hooker. Didn't he know that every hooker had a price? He was telling anyone who would listen that he hadn't done anything, and personally Leanne was inclined to believe him, but she'd instructed him not to talk to the press until they'd had a chance to issue a statement on his behalf.

She'd expected Sam back yesterday. So now what?

Then there was Gabe. Silly old Gabe, sold out by the hooker's underage hooker mate. A few months ago Gabe was a national hero – now he was a national joke. It was a mess.

A mess Samantha wasn't here to clear up.

But these unfortunate scandals paled against the half a dozen or so signed contracts sitting on her boss's desk, each in its own pristine foolscap folder, the crisp paper stinking like cold hard cash. Those contracts Sam had slaved over needed to be sealed and delivered within the next thirty-six hours or the window would close.

Wherever she was Samantha was cutting it awfully fine.

To top it all off Leanne had a blinding hangover and was going to have to cancel dinner with an extremely sexy Wisła defender if things in the office didn't slow. And it didn't look as if they were about to.

She could handle the press. She'd been doing that for Sam's clients for years and, sordid though these latest revelations were, it wouldn't be the first time that a footballer had found himself on the end of some nasty truths or untruths. No comment got you a day, then a brisk statement if the story had legs enough for two, then a dignified silence would see you through the rest of the week.

But club managers were starting to call. They wanted to speak to Samantha, they wanted to know that she had instructed her players to sign their contracts, that they hadn't been outbid at the eleventh hour, that the window, when it closed, would close the way they wanted it to.

And she had no idea what to tell them.

She turned back to the flashing phone lines. Break over.

'Samantha Sharp?' she said. The business had no other name but that.

'Sam, is that you?'

'Hi, Joe, no, sorry, it's Leanne, she's out of the office. You're her first call when she gets in, okay?'

'I suppose,' he said. She heard muffled whispers and then Joe's father came on the line.

'Hello, sweetheart,' he said, making sure he got off to a bad start. 'Where the hell has she got to then, your boss? My Joe is in a right state and these fellas have been outside my mum's for two days and they aren't looking like they might leave any time soon. Now, look, I spoke to Richard Tavistock, you know him?'

'Richard Tavis-cock?' she said, using her old nickname for him just because she knew Joe's father wasn't really listening to her anyway. 'Sure, I know Richard.'

'Richard's a friend of mine,' said Simon.

I wonder why? He's not your friend, dickhead, he just wants to get in bed with your son. Metaphorically, of course, though she wouldn't put it past Richard to put out if that's what it took.

'Richard says we need to release a statement right now, nip this in the bud and let the vultures move on to this Muswell bloke.'

More muffled whispers.

'Joe tells me Muswell is a client of yours too? Is this a conflict-of-interest thing? I'm telling you, we're this close to taking our business across the street if you know what I mean. We've been very loyal to Sam, but . . .'

Loyal? They'd known her a matter of months. Even Leanne with her propensity for hard and fast had had relationships that lasted longer than that. Josef Wandrowszcki owed his place in the England squad to Sam Sharp. She had created Joe Wonder and Leanne was not about to let him go over a malicious bit of tabloid gossip.

Especially not to a cock like Richard.

'Sam's emailing me a draft statement in the next few minutes,' said Leanne. 'I want Joe to okay it and then I'll carpet bomb the media by the end of the day.'

'That's a start, I suppose,' said Simon reluctantly. 'But we're going to want to talk to her.'

'She's holding on the other line right now, as it happens,' said Leanne. 'Give me three secs and I'll patch you through.'

She crossed her fingers and hoped that she'd be able to pull off this little subterfuge.

One, two, three.

'Simon? Hi, it's Sam.' Leanne had been imitating her boss for years, and on asking herself 'what would Samantha do?' it was Samantha's very words that came to mind. *Do me*, Sam had said, *maybe I should put you on the phone more often.*

She smoothed out her West Country accent. 'I'm emailing a statement right now,' she said, with exactly the right tone of cool confidence. 'My assistant will text it to Joe and we'll go from there. Don't overreact, okay? It makes Joe look bad.'

'I don't want to do that,' said Simon.

'Of course you don't,' said Leanne, replicating Sam's brisk, bland efficiency, that Midlands accent long ago drubbed out until all that was left of her humble past was the chip on her shoulder.

'Where are you anyway?' he said.

'Bloody fog grounded my plane,' she said. 'But I'm working something out. I'll be back soon.'

Simon went away satisfied.

She banged out a two-line denial to release to the press on Joe's behalf, cleared it with Joe and sent it out.

When she eventually deigned to return, Samantha would congratulate her on showing initiative, right? She'd better.

Meanwhile, once she'd 'done' Sam once it was easy to do it again.

One contract at a time.

Leanne oversaw the busiest time of the year single-handedly. With what little spare time she had she thought about how big a pay rise she should ask for.

Much to her surprise she found she rather liked being rushed off her feet. It made the day go quicker for one thing and it gave her a sense of achievement, the likes of which she normally only got after a good first kiss with a top-flight player.

The following day a man called the office asking to speak to Samantha.

'And who might I say is calling?' said Leanne in a sing-song voice.

'I'm Liam.'

'Can I take your second name, Liam?'

'Liam Sharp. Her brother.'

'She's . . .' *Her brother? I thought Sam didn't have any family?* 'She's not available right now,' she said.

'Do you have a number where I can reach her?' he said. 'I've tried her mobile, but it's switched off. It's very important.'

Odd. Why would Sam lie about her family? Wasn't it more likely that this Liam bloke was lying to her now? It wouldn't be the first time that somebody had tried to sneak past Leanne, Sam's only line of defence, and get close to the real power. And yet . . . with every hour that went by Leanne grew more worried than she was pissed off.

She really should have been back by now.

'I'm really sorry about this,' she said. 'Liam, is it? It's just that Samantha never mentioned you and as you can imagine we get a lot of people claiming to be . . . well, claiming to be someone they're not. Sam relies on me to keep the crazies away, you know?'

'I understand,' he said. 'What would you like me to say?'

'Well, for starters, why *hasn't* she mentioned you?'

She doesn't want people to know she has a brother.

And who could blame her with a brother like him? All their lives he had been holding her back. He was a stain on her reputation, a drain on her resources. He was worse than useless.

'She gave me her old mobile phone,' said Liam. 'How long have you been her assistant?'

'Long enough,' said Leanne, immediately getting his point. 'I'll call you back.' She dialled the obsolete mobile number that her brain had stubbornly retained. It rang just once before he picked up.

She believed him. It was a quick way to prove his story, a smart idea, the kind that Samantha might have come up with. A brother. Who knew?

'You want more proof?' he said. 'She's left-handed, her middle name is Patricia and she's got a tattoo of a bluebird on her left shoulder.'

'Really? I would have thought she was far too uptight to get a tattoo.'

411

'She hasn't always been that way,' he said. 'Now can you tell me where she is? Please? I really have to speak to her as soon as possible.'

'I thought she was at her house in London. She's with, uh, with her boyfriend.'

'I tried her house,' said Liam. 'There was no reply at the front door. I, well, then I nipped over the back fence too but it doesn't look like she's there.'

Leanne shivered, a chill momentarily tickling her spine, and confided her growing sense of unease. 'They've been gone longer than she said and it's so totally not like her. Normally she calls in about a hundred times a day, but, well, I didn't know. I thought she'd be back by now.'

'You said she's with her boyfriend? She's with Jackson Ramsay?'

'I'm sorry?' said Leanne. 'Say that again?' Despite her apprehension she grinned. It was so unexpected and yet at the same time it made perfect sense. Samantha and Jackson? How long had that been going on? And how the hell had they managed to keep it under the radar? It was enough to make her wish she was back at Legends. That was the best bit of gossip she had heard in ages, in *for ever*. Jackson? *Really?*

'No,' she said, 'she's with Aleksandr Lubin. He's . . .'

'I know who he is. Listen, what's your name? Leanne? Listen, Leanne, I have to find her. There's something she has to know. What happened with her and Jackson? Maybe he would know where she is?'

'I'm behind on all of this,' said Leanne. 'I didn't know there was a brother and I don't think anyone knew about Jackson. Clearly she is a woman with a lot of secrets.'

Liam tugged at his hair with frustration. He could finally tell her the truth and now she was nowhere to be found. 'And you can't think where they might be? You don't have any ideas?'

'Wait!' said Leanne. 'There was this other house. I helped her furnish it, and she was always kind of mysterious about it. Nobody knew about it but me. It was in Kentish Town I think. I have the address somewhere.'

'No,' said Liam, 'I know that house. It's mine. She bought it for me.'

'So what now?'

'I don't know. I'll keep calling her.'

She couldn't help thinking that he sounded scared. 'Something is really wrong, isn't it?' she said. 'Something's happened? Is she in trouble?'

'Something happened a long time ago,' he said. 'And Samantha wasn't to blame for any of it.'

'What can I do?'

'I'll take care of it. I'll ask her to call you as soon as I find her.'

Leanne looked at the organized piles of paperwork awaiting Samantha's return. She couldn't think of a single reason big enough for Samantha to miss the transfer window, not after all the hard work she had put in. She didn't care how good the Russian was in bed.

Where was she?

She had a very bad feeling about all of this. And she could only think of one person that might be able to help.

36

Samantha awoke on the floor of her office, her throat raw with a raging thirst. She reached for the bottle of water that was by the desk and tipped it to her mouth although she knew that only pitifully few drops remained. One big gulp and it would all be gone. Then what?

What time was it? Down here in the windowless gloom she could not tell. Her computer said almost nine a.m. That would mean she had been asleep for almost four hours, which was more than the night before.

Should she scratch out the days on the wall to mark the passing of time?

She tried the phone again, but it was still dead of course. Not from the storm, she realized that now, but deliberately.

For the first time she contemplated the seriousness of her position. She was tired, hungry and thirsty, and though she may be able to sleep, there was no water and she had long ago drunk the dregs of a cup of coffee that was down here. The only food was half a packet of mints and a wizened apple that had rolled under her desk weeks ago.

She ate the remaining half of the apple to try to silence the insidious hunger that had been with her now for longer than she cared to guess.

Two days. She'd missed the transfer window, her business was dead. All that hard work, all that investment of time and money, gone to dust. But it didn't seem to matter any more. Right now she only had one concern. Finding a way out of here.

She had spent a lot of time trying in vain to connect to the internet or walking around the space with her mobile phone aloft searching for some hitherto unknown pocket of signal, all so that she could call someone for help.

She stood sentry at the basement door, pounding on it and yelling in case maybe her neighbours would hear her screams. She planned what she would do if her captor returned, how she would attack him, going for eyes and balls like you were supposed to, disabling him long enough to run up the stairs and be free.

But nothing. Nobody was coming. She was on her own.

Once, not that long ago, she had thought her home office marvellously spacious, another symbol of her blistering success. Now, not at all. It must be her imagination, but the walls felt closer today than yesterday.

Who would be missing her?

Alek. She had promised to call him and she had not. He had sent her roses once, he would know her address. Why hadn't he come?

Leanne. She was expected back in Krakow to sign off on a number of contracts, contracts she had spent the last few months negotiating and that were supposed to allow her business to launch. Deals totalling millions. Surely Leanne would be worried? The transfer window was closed now. Her dream of a new start was over. If this had been Liam's final desperate act of sabotage then it had worked. Was he really so determined to see her fail?

Another wander around her prison with mobile phone and laptop computer held high. No friendly neighbour's wireless signal to piggyback, no bars on her mobile phone.

She struck out at the wall in her frustration.

Surely soon somebody would come?

Liam would be back. She was his sister. Whatever he had done in the past, no matter how warped his perception had become, he wouldn't leave her here. Not indefinitely.

A few hours passed and she was on the chair clawing at the ceiling, hammering it with a broken piece of shelving, and wishing that she had paid more attention when the builders were renovating her cellar. She had no idea how thick the ceiling was, but she had made a small hole in the plasterboard and there was a space beyond it. On top of that, what? The kitchen floorboards, one of them was loose. Maybe if she could find that one . . .

The futility of her attempt was crushing. But she had to try, because what was the alternative? Shattered, and getting nowhere she sank back to the floor and closed her eyes.

How long was she expected to fight? Nobody could be expected to struggle for ever. It was too hard.

Congratulations. You win.

She woke up shaking, realizing that she might die here. A lonely London death.

She thought of her mother.

For the very first time she cried for her loss.

Her eyes fell on her Businesswoman of the Year award. The tacky gold-plated champagne bottle was mocking her, because champagne and gold, success, meant nothing.

Success was worthless when you started to dwell on life and death, on freedom. And so it finally occurred to her, as she slumped on the floor, hungry and afraid, that perhaps her entire life had been a waste of time.

He broke in carefully. Deadening the sound of shattering glass with his old leather jacket, wincing when the shards clattered on the kitchen floorboards and then stretching through the jagged hole to manipulate the back-door handle, reaching down to the first bolt and snapping it open, using the rake he had already stolen from the garden shed to pull up the floor bolt. The door finally swung wide and he stepped into the dark house as silent as a cat.

He studied the locked basement door carefully then twisted the key in the lock and crept down the stairs into the darkness.

Liam Sharp had never broken and entered before and couldn't help thinking that he seemed to be rather good at it.

Then out of nowhere something incredibly heavy struck him across the back of the head and he crashed to the floor before he even had time to cry out.

Samantha stood over him with a gold-plated champagne bottle, her heart racing, her breath coming in short, fearful bursts. Despite the ache in her wrist she held the bottle in mid-air as she looked down at her brother.

Liam.

He was out cold. She knelt down, overwhelmed by an unexpected rush of love for him. His face in repose looked so like it did when they were children. She stroked his hair, the exact same colour as her own.

And when she drew her hand back it was covered in blood.

'Don't panic,' said Lubin. 'Stay right where you are, I'm coming. You are sure he is breathing?'

'Yes,' whispered Samantha. She had held a mirror beneath her brother's nose to check and when she saw the mist on the glass she was so relieved she started to cry again. She was scared to feel herself drifting towards hysteria. She hadn't meant to hit him so hard, just enough to get past him. She wanted to call a doctor, an ambulance, but she was terrified of what would happen next. Would Liam be arrested? Would she? So she had run upstairs and called Lubin because Samantha Sharp couldn't do it on her own any more. She needed to be rescued.

'Can you secure him?' asked Lubin.

'What do you mean?'

'Can you put a locked door between you?'

'Yes,' she said. She would close the cellar door. 'Please hurry.'

'It's okay, Samantha. Calm down, okay? I will be there as soon as I can.'

She put her mobile phone in her back pocket, keeping it close by. Then she poured herself a glass of water and drank it down in one, feeling the lurch of her surprised stomach and almost throwing up. She poured herself another glass and sipped it more slowly this time, nibbling cautiously on a cracker too.

Then she splashed her face with water and went back downstairs.

418

There was nothing where he had been except a dull brown bloodstain on the tufted wool rug.

Liam was gone.

She instinctively reached out for the gold champagne bottle. 'Liam?'

There was nowhere in the room to hide. She knew every inch of it now. Upstairs she called his name, but there was no reply. He must have slipped by her upstairs and got away while she was making her phone call. Mostly she was relieved. Lubin would surely have insisted that she call the police and she didn't know if she was ready to do that. Her breath came more easily and she thought about calling him again to tell him this latest development.

She enjoyed the sensation of freedom.

Then she heard a flush from the bathroom and Liam stepped into the hallway rubbing the spot on his head where she had struck him.

'Sammy? What the hell?'

They stood in the stillness of the house and stared at each other, frozen, as if seeing each other for the first time in years. The seconds dragged on until Samantha broke the silence.

'All I ever wanted was to help you,' she said. 'How could you?'

She walked towards him, no longer afraid, feeling a remarkable sense of calm. He was her big brother, but she didn't have to try to look up to him any more and be confused and lost when she couldn't.

'First you frame me,' she said, 'then you make sly little calls to the press, telling them things I told you in confidence because I *trusted* you. God, I trusted you. I'm so stupid.'

He was her enemy. The one she never thought she had. She circled him, walking tall and proud, like she was wearing four-inch Louboutin heels.

'Sam, stop, you've got it all wrong.'

She stood behind him and leant close to his ear. She knew that she was scaring him and it felt good. 'Then you keep me prisoner in my own home to make sure that I miss the window and fail all over again. What's the matter, Liam, did I not fail enough for you the last time? Or did you just want me to know how it feels to be locked up?' She could see the matted patch of hair on the back of his head where he had bled.

He ventured a glance over his shoulder at her, and was shaken when he saw the tears tumbling down her face.

'*I trusted you*,' she whispered.

When they were little sometimes she would stay awake in front of the television waiting for their mother to come home and get so tired that she would start crying. He would try to make her go to sleep singing the songs that she liked and hoping that she would dream of bluebirds and not disappointment. The memory of it clawed at his heart.

'It wasn't me,' he said. 'I would never do that to you.'

'Why not? You have every reason to hate me.'

'I don't,' he said. 'I love you. And I don't need a reason for that.'

The guilt that Liam had been carrying with him had grown monstrous upon his release from prison. He had spent the last few weeks searching for a kind of absolution, an escape from the endless grinding remorse. But nothing had been able to help.

The answer came to him late one night in a sudden moment of inspiration. All this time he thought he needed Samantha to forgive him, or simply to forgive himself, but he had been looking for forgiveness in the wrong places.

He wanted to visit the graves of the people that he had killed.

Maybe then he could make peace with what he had done.

It didn't take him long to locate the final resting place of the man who had died that night. A few simple phone calls and within a couple of days he was able to lay flowers on a forgotten grave in south-east London.

When he wiped the polished granite headstone clear of debris he said a prayer and walked away feeling an unfamiliar lightness in his soul.

It was symbolic, nothing more; he knew that a few flowers and some unspoken words could never be enough, but it was all that was possible. He had done all that he could do.

But the woman who had died had been harder to find.

At first there was a veil of bureaucracy concealing her whereabouts, but eventually his search led him to a beautiful church in Knightsbridge, tucked back from the bustle of the high street. A noble kind of place set in its own pristine grounds. A sense of calm came over him almost immediately. He clutched his bouquet of white roses tightly, their sweet scent filling his senses as a thorn stabbed into the flesh of his thumb. Soon this would be over.

There was a sermon taking place and he slipped into a wooden pew at the back. He was struck by the simple elegance of the church, the stained-glass windows depicting scenes from Christ's life in clean lines and muted colours, the candlelight casting angled shadows across the warm golden stone of the walls and floor. It was the first church he had been in since the day they'd buried their mother and yet thinking of that day didn't make him feel bitter as it usually did, just sad.

It was a moment before he realized that the robed minister addressing the congregation was not speaking English. It was a language he had not heard before, except maybe once, that night, that awful night. The memory made him shudder and he went back out into the churchyard searching for the plot where she was buried.

It was a deceptively simple headstone, black like so many others, but not granite. Onyx. Discreetly but ludicrously extravagant.

He knelt before her grave, this woman that he had killed, and remembered her soft laughter in the back of his car that night, her red hair falling onto the shoulder of her lover, happy. He thought of the price that he had paid, the long lonely years in prison – was it enough? The ground was cold beneath his knees, and he knew that it would have to be. His punishment and his remorse were all that he could give her now. And finally he felt truly free.

He thought of his sister, of Samantha, and love flowed into his freshly open heart. He could face the future with hope.

He stood up and traced the name on the headstone. Natasha.

And then he froze. For he suddenly realized what language the minister had been speaking. And why the name on the headstone had seemed faintly familiar to him. And that his sister could be in terrible danger.

In the middle of his story Liam paused and reached out for Samantha's hand. She let him take it because with every word he spoke she knew that he was telling the truth. Just by listening.

'Sammy,' he said, 'the woman I killed that night was Natasha Lubin.'

Lubin.

'Say that again?'

'The woman in the back of the car, she was Natasha Lubin. Goran Lubin's wife. Aleksandr's mother.'

'I don't understand,' said Samantha.

'Everything bad that has happened. It's him,' he said. 'It's Lubin, it has to be. None of this is your fault. It was never about you; it was about me.' His head slumped under the weight of yet more guilt. 'The grave I found, it was at a Russian church; it was his mother's grave. I tried to tell you straight away, but I couldn't get hold of you. I called, I came round here a dozen times, I called Leanne in Krakow. Eventually I just broke in. Nobody knew where you were and I was worried. Thank God I did. I hate to think of you trapped down there while I was knocking on the front door.'

Samantha stood haunted by Lubin's words as they flooded back to her. *Killed in a car crash. Seeing another man. I was ten years old.*

'I'm so sorry,' said Liam. 'I know you were close.'

She shuddered at the memory of his kisses. Lubin held Liam responsible for the death of his mother. When he talked about family and reputation he had been mocking her. He had framed her, destroyed her and all because she shared blood with his enemy.

'And now I'm out of prison,' said Liam. 'We have to assume that he's going to come after me.'

She jumped up from her chair as if she'd been slapped. 'We have to get out of here,' she said, pulling him to his feet urgently. 'Are you feeling okay? How's your head? You think you can walk? I'll drive.'

'What is it? What's wrong?'

'I called him. Lubin. He's on his way here.'

They reached the house in Kentish Town in a few minutes and Liam led Samantha quickly up the path to the front door, opening it wide and pushing her inside. A dull pain thudded at the back of his head, but despite everything he felt good. He had saved her. And if anyone deserved to be saved it was Samantha. They would phone the police and he would tell them too. She was safe at last, his little baby sister. He had taken care of her just as he had promised his mother he would do.

They walked into the dark kitchen. Liam flicked on the light and Samantha screamed.

Aleksandr Lubin was sitting at the kitchen table and he was pointing the barrel of a dull silver handgun directly at them.

37

Lubin waved the gun at them to indicate that they should move out of the kitchen doorway and into the room, and though it was the very last thing that either of them wanted to do they had no choice.

'Come in,' he said. 'Come in.'

Silently the siblings talked.

What now?

I don't know.

His menacing smile was wide with triumph as he pointed the barrel of the gun into the corner where he wanted them to stand, the alcove furthest away from the door. 'I think we need to chat, Samantha. Don't you? I think it is time for us to break up. How nice of you to bring your brother to me as a parting gift.'

She closed her eyes and took a deep breath. This was for real.

Meanwhile Liam puffed out his chest and tried not to look like he felt inside. Inside he had crumbled to the floor. His bladder threatened to let go. His palms itched with sweat.

Of course he knew about the Kentish Town house, *of course.* He knew everything about Liam Sharp. He could have had him killed in prison with a single instruction, but he had waited. Because this way he got to see the look on his face.

'You wanted me,' said Liam. 'You have me. This has nothing to do with her.' Two bright red spots bloomed on his cheeks and a nervous blotch on his throat started to spread. He wasn't fooling anyone. His bravado was wafer thin. Knowing that he was responsible for Samantha's life falling apart was more than he thought he could bear, but now this, nothing between her and a man with a gun except six feet of air. And all because of him. There was a part of him that wanted to pull the trigger himself and make it stop.

'It has everything to do with Samantha,' said Lubin. 'You destroyed my family and I have enjoyed destroying yours. Tell me, how did it feel to watch your precious sister dragged through the mud?'

She could tell how scared her brother was. He was scared enough for both of them and so she tried to look at the situation objectively, as just another crisis that she needed to solve. Liam had been stupid – mindlessly, tragically stupid – but it was an accident and he had paid his debt to society, a long debt, the harshest sentence that the judge could pass. She had to keep everybody calm while she figured out how to get them out of there. When there's a gun in the room calm is paramount.

She appealed to Lubin's ego, stalling for time.

'I don't understand,' she said. 'Everything that happened to me, it has been you? How?'

He was proud to tell, as she guessed he would be. 'I've been waiting a long time to ruin you,' he said. 'Three hundred thousand, a few phone calls to the newspapers and to the father of your biggest clients. It was too easy.'

'But that wasn't enough?'

'Once I met you I saw that there was more than one way to screw you.' He laughed, and it chilled her, but she desperately tried to keep the dread from showing in her face while he addressed Liam. 'I've been screwing her, you know. She's a crazy fuck, your sister, you should really be proud of that.'

There was a drawer full of knives on the other side of the kitchen; there were heavy pans hanging from a rack there too, but they were out of reach. She knew everything in here – she had chosen it herself. There was a cast-iron griddle across the hob. She could do some damage with that.

Think, Sam, think.

Lubin was enjoying himself. 'You really thought that I would want your precious player, your Gabe,' he said, 'and then that I would want you? You are so self-important. It was a gift to me. I couldn't have achieved any of this without your unbelievable arrogance.'

She nodded, wanting him to keep talking, needing him to, so that the frantic mind behind her outward calm could seize upon a way out for her and Liam.

'Right from the start you pretended that you didn't know who I was. And then you told me it was Liam so that I would come running back to London, so that you could keep me away from the transfer window,' she said. 'How did you get to my house so fast?'

'Helicopter,' he said.

'Of course.'

'But then your stupid brother tried to be a hero, didn't you?' He turned to Liam. 'It makes me sick to think of you near my mother's grave. This is English justice: she lies for ever asleep while you walk free?'

'And now what?' she asked.

'Samantha, I would have thought the gun made that perfectly obvious.'

Liam started to panic. 'You want to kill me, then hurry up and kill me,' he whimpered. 'But, please, let Sammy go. She wasn't there that night; she hasn't done anything wrong.'

'You call her Sammy,' said Aleksandr. 'That's sweet. You love her very much, don't you? Of course you do, she is family.'

'We take care of each other,' said Liam, a sob catching in his vulnerable throat.

Samantha tore her eyes away from her brother. One of them had to stay in control. It was the only hope they had of both escaping with their lives. 'What happened to your mother was an accident,' she said. 'Are you planning to kill us both? In cold blood?'

'That's exactly what I'm going to do, yes.'

She glanced at the back door.

'Locked,' he said. 'You think I am stupid?'

'No,' she said. 'I don't think you are stupid at all. You suffered an enormous loss. I know how that feels – I do. We both do.'

He started to laugh. 'You think that will work? Appealing to my softer side? Your sister is a funny girl, hey?'

'You'll never get away with this,' she said.

'I am a Lubin. I can get away with anything. Money washes everything clean, a name, a reputation, even a murder.'

If this was really the end for them, then she didn't want to be weak, not for one moment. She would die as she had

428

lived, bravely and without fear. The blood thumping fero-
ciously through her body was laced with raw adrenalin.
But she wasn't scared. Perhaps she should be but she
wasn't. This was the biggest challenge of her life and she
hadn't backed away from a challenge yet.

'You really wanted to clear your name, didn't you, Samantha?' Lubin was giddy with the power he had over them
both, he was relishing every moment of the excruciating
tension. The wait to see what he would do next. 'The look
on your face when I told you I would help,' he said. 'It was
a special moment for me. But when they find you dead that
is the reputation the world will remember, not Samantha
Sharp: Superagent, but only that you were disgraced.'

'So?' she said.

Aleksandr looked surprised.

Good. Anything was better than his confident menace.

'Why on earth would I care?' she said. 'I'll be dead. I'd
rather be a dead disgrace than a cold-blooded killer.'

Liam looked at her with alarm and willed her to be cautious. What good could come from antagonizing him?

She saw the wrinkle between Lubin's eyes constrict.
She was getting under his skin. He was very young. And
he was deeply troubled. One mistake and she could jump
on it, make something of it. If he was distracted enough,
agitated enough, perhaps they would have a chance.

Liam was getting more upset with every passing minute.
'Please don't hurt her,' he said. 'She's my kid sister, man.
You know?'

'NO! I don't know! I never had a sister,' snarled Lubin.
'My mother was *killed* before she could have another
child.'

'Even a bastard half-sister would have been better than nothing, huh?' said Samantha. 'Do you think she was going to leave your father? Do you think they were in love, her and that guy, or just fucking?'

'Shut up,' he said.

And silently Liam agreed with him.

'My mother was not like you,' said Aleksandr. 'She was not a hard woman with a heart of iron. She was perfect.'

'The lovers died side by side,' she said. 'How romantic.'

'Shut up!' He slapped her across the face with his free hand and she stared at him defiantly, her eyes blazing.

The doorbell rang.

Two sets of eyes darted to the front door. There was a barrage of heavy rapping followed by a shout. But Samantha kept her eyes on the gun.

He let it fall a crucial inch, distracted for the briefest of moments.

In a flash she whirled to the hob and grabbed the griddle. She heaved it with all the strength she could muster, crying out with the effort, and swung it into his shocked face. She couldn't take a chance by hitting him with anything less than full force.

The blow might kill him.

They would be killers together then. Her and Liam both.

He fell to the floor with a grunt and the gun skittered out of his grasp. She kicked it into the corner of the room.

'Open up!' said the voice at the front door. The sound of somebody trying to break it down.

Blood poured from a deep gash on Aleksandr's forehead, but still he scrambled towards the gun.

'Shit, Sammy, what have you done?' said Liam, frozen with shock.

'Help!' she screamed. 'We're in here. Please help!'

Aleksandr groaned and his hand reached out for her ankle. '*Bitch!*'

She ground down his fingers with her stiletto heel, while Liam picked up the gun, pointing it at Lubin, trying not to let his hand tremble and betray his horror.

'Don't move,' he said. 'I'll shoot you, I swear to God I will, don't you dare move.'

The front door gave way and swung into the wall with an almighty crash, footsteps pounded towards them and Samantha watched in amazement as Jackson Ramsay appeared in the kitchen brandishing a cricket bat.

Jackson looked at the scene, bewildered: the girl, the guy, the gun.

Lubin seized the chance to make a run for it.

Liam's finger hesitated over the trigger.

'*Jackson!*' screamed Samantha. And he swung his cricket bat low, taking Lubin's feet from under him, then fell on top of him, answering a blow to his jaw by smashing the side of his hand into Lubin's nose. Lubin howled in pain. There was a lot of blood. Jackson dragged Lubin to his knees and jammed his fist into his stomach so that Lubin bent double. Then Jackson's left hook sent him sprawling backwards, landing on his hip with a painful thud. Clearly he had been bested.

Samantha's breathing was shallow and raw, her heart racing. She glanced at her brother and saw that he too was standing aghast, the forgotten gun hanging loosely by his side.

Jackson kicked Lubin so that he rolled onto his stomach and placed a foot squarely on his back, pinning his scrawny frame to the floor with ease. Lubin had surrendered or passed out – she really was unable to tell.

She couldn't believe that he was there. It was truly him. Saving her. Looking into his eyes she knew that he was the person she wanted to see because in his arms she would be safe.

'He was going to kill us both,' she said. 'What are you doing here? How did you know?'

'Leanne called me,' said Jackson. 'That girl was going mad with worry. Who's this guy?' He nodded his head towards Liam, who was fumbling in his pocket for his mobile phone, hastily wiping at the tears that had bled onto his cheeks.

'He's my brother,' she said. 'Jackson, this is Liam. I should have told you about him a long time ago. I just . . . it . . .' She sank into a chair and put her head in her hands, shaking with the fear she had not allowed to show.

'It's okay, Sam,' said Jackson. 'Everything will be okay. It's over.'

38

Gabe Muswell went out and got drunk in the morning so that he could watch the England game that afternoon with a solid beer buzz.

He needed it.

After all, if things had gone the way that they should have he might have been over there in Wembley Stadium right now warming up to play, instead of stuck here on his own in a hotel room, in a city he had grown to hate, working out the last few weeks of a contract with a team that hated him back. And, instead of the constant support of a good woman he'd never appreciated, he had a wife who was going to take one hell of a lot of convincing if their marriage was to survive everything that had happened.

Christine was out.

She went out a lot lately. Ever since the tabloids decided to exploit every mistake he had made. It was like she couldn't bear to look at him.

He would start trying to rescue his marriage tomorrow.

Today he just wanted to sink into a Zywiec-flavoured hole of self-pity and watch the luckiest kid in the world make his England debut.

Jammy little bugger.

Samantha looked down at the emerald pitch and felt the sharp tang of excitement she always did before an international game. Club-level football so often went to form; the internationals were left to provide the surprises. Her recent ordeal hadn't put her off surprises at all.

Aleksandr Lubin was using enormous chunks of his father's fortune to try to clear his name. She suspected that he might end up doing some time in prison. There was a rumour that Goran Lubin was about to cut him off. Then who would he be? Perhaps they had more in common than she had thought. They were both far less if they tried to stand alone.

The family-and-friends box at Wembley Stadium was crammed with people and optimism. She saw Liam, she saw Leanne, somewhere nearby would be Jackson, and so for the first time she didn't feel alone up here. She had family and friends of her own.

'Samantha?'

Toby Welstead was lingering by her side looking nervous. His son Monty would shortly be sitting on the substitutes' bench next to Joe, willing to get up and play his heart out if his country called on him to do so. In fact, Joe had told her that over the last couple of days he'd become friendly with Monty during training.

'Hey, Mr Welstead, how are you?' she said, shaking his hand. 'Congratulations.'

'Thanks,' he said. 'Do you think it's odd that I'm more nervous than he is?'

'It's always the fathers,' she said.

Joe's father was out there somewhere. He had refused to watch the game from the box, saying that he'd rather be with the real fans, but Samantha suspected he was scared of running into Richard Tavistock whose calls Joe had insisted went ignored. Whatever promises Simon had made to Richard were not his to make. Joe was happy with Samantha, and so he would stay.

There were parents like Simon and then there were parents like Toby Welstead. She knew which one she would strive to be. Lately the idea of having children had taken root and for once she hadn't weeded it out.

'I'm glad to bump into you,' said Toby. 'I was thinking maybe I could call you. We need some advice. Some of the endorsements the lads are coming across, well, they don't seem right. And now Richard's talking about a move next season . . .'

'Away from Chelsea?' she said. 'Already?' A good money-maker for Richard and for Legends, but they'd really only just arrived. They were young; they should settle some-where and learn for a few years.

'The thing is,' he said, 'I just didn't know, because of what happened with you and the boys. You never struck me as the type to hold a grudge, but . . .'

'I'm not,' she said. She'd had enough of grudges to last her a lifetime. 'I don't hold grudges, Mr Welstead,' she said.

'It's Toby,' he said. 'Jackson Ramsay said you might be going back to Legends. Now all the messy business has been cleaned up.'

'She turned me down!' Jackson appeared by their side and wrapped his arm round her shoulders. 'I offered her job back, with incentives, but she turned me down. Got a taste of freedom, right, Sam? She's the competition now.'

'There's room for everyone,' she said.

'Then stop trying to take over the world.'

435

'Why?' she said. 'When it's there for the taking?' The thing about the ladder of success was that there was always somebody above you, always, so she could climb all the way to the stars if she wanted to. And she did.

She turned back to Toby. 'Call me,' she said. 'Even if you just need to talk it out, I'll be impartial. I won't hold you to anything.'

'I'll do that,' he said, and walked off to find a stiff drink to feed to the butterflies in his stomach.

She looked up at Jackson and smiled. 'I suppose you're going to have a go at me for trying to poach your clients?'

'Would it have any impact?'

'Nope.'

'Then I won't bother,' he said. 'Sure you won't reconsider the job offer? Senior partner, seat on the board. I'll even give you my parking spot if that'll swing it. A raise for Leanne.'

They turned to look at her assistant schmoozing the VIPs. After years of flirting with footballers, hospitality came naturally to Leanne. So Samantha had put her in charge of corporate relations and told her to hire an assistant of her own. Leanne agreed; she was getting too old to trail around after footballers anyway. The company was growing. Samantha would always chase success, but with friends like Leanne and Jackson, and her brother close by and settled, she felt satisfied whatever happened.

'I can't come back to Legends,' she said. 'Not if something is happening between us personally – it just won't work. And if something's *not* happening then, well, that won't work either.'

'Oh, it's happening,' he said. 'And this time we do it my way.'

And right there, in the middle of the family-and-friends box at Wembley Stadium, where everyone could see, her lover kissed her long and hard.

No more secrets.

Joe had made his peace with the need to puke before every important match. It had practically become a ritual, as much a part of his superstitious preparation as his lucky pants or his pre-match pep talk.

Go for goal.

He hung over the toilet and was a bit disconcerted when nothing came up. Was it a sign? Perhaps he wasn't even going to play. Of course it was possible he would watch the entire game from the bench. Likely, some might say. Except he'd done well in training, he knew he had. And so he thought that maybe he would get a few minutes, at the end perhaps, and if he did, then he would play so well that Layla, the lovely Layla, his *girlfriend*, would be giddy with pride.

Goal.

One word. A new mantra.

Gabe looked up with a guilty expression when Christine came back to their hotel room shortly after kick-off.

'Are you planning on staying drunk all day?' she asked coolly.

'I'm not drunk,' said Gabe. He'd thrown the cans out of the window into the hotel grounds; she couldn't prove a thing.

'We've been together for fourteen years – you think I can't tell when you're plastered?'

'I should be playing,' he said mournfully.

'For England? Gabe, the truth is you had one lucky game. You could have made the most of it, but you didn't.' She sniffed the air. 'Have you been smoking in here?'

'Give it a rest, will ya?'

'Give it a rest?' She shook her head. 'I don't believe you. Listen to me. Gabe, stop watching the television for one minute and listen to me. Look at me.'

He did as he was told.

She was still beautiful. He had put her through far too much these last few months. The embarrassment of his infidelity being splashed across the papers back home. But he would make it up to her.

Just not right now. Not while England were playing.

'I'm leaving you,' she said.

'What?'

That got his attention.

'I'm leaving you. Right now.'

'Babe, come on.' Shit, he wished he wasn't drunk right now. If he wasn't drunk perhaps he could think of something better to say, because all he could think of was, 'Babe, don't be like this.'

'I'll be however I want to be, Gabe. I've had enough.'

He rallied. A bolt of sober thought smacked him into sense. He was really losing her, this was really happening.

'Let's go back to England,' he said. 'Our house, our home, our life. Our life together.'

'No,' she said. 'Neither of us was happy, not really.'